'. . . You know I was branded the Enemy, that Jenn was labelled the Ally, and another person was described as the Angel of Darkness. He tried to kill my brother twice and we discovered his real name was Carlan. This Angel was present at Elita when I used the Word of Destruction – but it didn't kill him. I ask you, how many of you have even heard of Carlan since that day? The most we've heard is the occasional rumour that something bad has happened somewhere, but nobody has actually seen anything at all. And why?'

Robert took a breath before going on, 'Because the Word hurt him badly. Put him out of commission for a long time. It has, in fact, taken him almost all the last five years to recover. There is even the suggestion that the recovery hasn't actually been as complete as he would like.'

Finnlay found himself standing, his heart pounding even harder. Memories of torture and pain, blood and darkness fringed the edge of his awareness. 'But you know who he is?'

Robert met his gaze steadily, almost sympathetically, 'Yes.'

BLACK EAGLE RISING

RISING

Third Book of Elita

KATE JACOBY

This edition published in Great Britain in 2001 by

Gollancz
An imprint of the Orion Publishing Group
Orion House, 5 Upper St Martin's Lane, London WC2H 9EA

A CIP catalogue record for this book is available
from the British Library

ISBN 1 85798 750 0

Printed in Great Britain by
Clays Ltd, St Ives plc

Acknowledgements

Thanks once again to my family and friends for the endless support and encouragement. Thank you to Karen for reading and answering so many questions. Thank you to Muther and Dad for providing the venues. To Jo Fletcher – thank you again for pushing; please continue to do so. A huge thank you to Jeffrey; I loved this poem the first time I read it and still love it as much now. Thank you for letting me borrow it. Lastly, thank you to Charles because your eyes are open and you know.

. . . and so it was that in the spring of 1361 everything changed forever. No howling wolves nor mystic seers foretold the shift in Lusara's fortunes. Rather, it was the rolling consequence of events reaching back many years. To most, the change appeared swift and sudden. To others, it was too long in coming.

But to understand that fateful spring, those years before must also be understood, along with those most closely involved.

In 1341, Selar of Mayenne conquered Lusara with a final battle on Seluth Common, his victory aided by a mysterious old man called Carlan. Immediately after that battle, Carlan disappeared. Selar married the daughter of Duke MacKenna, the beautiful Rosalind, and founded his own royal line with first a girl and then a son to succeed him. He then proceeded to crush any opposition to his rule and punished the whole country for daring to stand against him.

Of the old major Houses, only a few survived with any power. One of these was led by the young Earl of Dunlorn, Robert Douglas. His father had died a hero fighting Selar. Scion of the oldest House and heir to a long tradition of serving Lusara, Robert was forced to hide the secret part of his nature. He was a sorcerer – in a land where such a thing was almost forgotten but eternally reviled, and most certainly outlawed. Robert carried the hopes of his conquered people, but, seeing no other way, he agreed to work alongside Selar. In return for his oath of allegiance, Selar gave Robert the power to help his people. The two men became friends and for some years, a quiet peace lay over a relieved land.

However, this peace was not to last. Jealous of Robert's influence, the powerful Guilde moved against him. Robert found no support with the King for his defiance and, shattered, he left the court for his home. He arrived to find his young wife, Berenice, pregnant with their first child, horribly sick with a fever. Seeking to ease her pain, Robert applied his powers, but no sooner had he touched her than the power was twisted out of him, beyond his control. Both Berenice and the child died almost instantly. Devastated, Robert left the country, planning never to return.

The first volume of this secret history begins three years later when Robert did return, his most trusted friend, Micah Maclean, at his side.

1

Robert intended only to go home to Dunlorn, but his brother Finnlay demanded Robert act: he should take up the leadership of the secret sorcerers' Enclave – or, failing that, make a stand against Selar and free their people from tyranny. Robert had his own reasons for refusing, but before he could go much further, he was forced to rescue a young girl being chased by Guilde soldiers. In the excitement, Robert discovered that she was the only girl of the children abducted during the House feuds thirteen years before. Her name was Jennifer Ross, daughter of the Earl of Ross. And she was a sorcerer with very different powers. Against the advice of the Enclave, Robert took Jennifer back to her father's lands at Elita and continued home.

During Robert's absence, the Guilde had grown more powerful. When Selar discovered Robert had returned to Lusara, he grew fearful and imprisoned the newly elected Bishop Aiden McCauly in order to gain a firm hold on the wavering support of the Church, placing his own man, Brome, in the top position. The King also had a new friend: the Guildesman Samdon Nash.

Then tragedy struck. Robert's maternal uncle, the rebel Duke of Haddon, was killed by Selar. Stunned, and tortured by guilt, even now Robert couldn't break his oath. In an effort to distract himself, Robert agreed to help Finnlay find the fabled Calyx, an artefact of great power, but both were caught in an accident in the hills above Nanmoor. Robert was injured and temporarily lost his memory. Finnlay used his Seeking powers to try finding his brother, but was captured and charged with the heinous crime of sorcery – and word flew across the land. A real sorcerer had been caught at last.

With Jenn's help, Robert mounted a rescue and returned Finnlay to the safety of the Enclave. During her trip to Marsay, Jenn had sensed another sorcerer present at the capital and the Enclave wanted to send someone to investigate. Robert argued against it. The leader, Jaibir Wilf, demanded Robert go before the powerful talisman, the Key – the very thing Robert had avoided for most of his life. The Key took possession of Robert and told all who were witness part of a prophecy which Robert had known since he was a child: that Robert was Bonded to Jenn and that they shared the lost gift of Mindspeech. They were called the Enemy and the Ally – and against them would come a creature of evil known only as The Angel of Darkness.

Robert was banished from the Enclave for keeping even this shred of prophecy a secret. He was forbidden by his oath to Selar to help his country, but while his honour cried out for action, he was held back, paralysed by something he'd kept concealed all his life. It lay at the heart of the prophecy: the key had told him he could never avoid his destiny. Robert called it: the demon.

*

So who was this Angel of Darkness? For most of his life he was known by the name of Carlan of Bayazit, the old man who had helped Selar conquer Lusara. But Carlan had learned how to use the forbidden sorcerers' arts and prolonged his life with infusions of blood from vanquished sorcerers. He returned to Lusara a young man, befriended Selar and joined the Guilde, taking on the name Samdon Nash.

To some, his ambition appeared pale, but his goal was something they could never have imagined, and he was prepared to stop at nothing to achieve it. It was he who abducted the children during the Troubles, hoping to find among them the Enemy. He had deliberately taken Jenn from her home, knowing she was the Ally. And there were many other things he had done to secure his plans, including involving the Malachi, evil cousins of the sorcerers of the Enclave.

In 1356 the Guilde sent an investigator south to discover the truth behind the allegations of sorcery levelled at Finnlay Douglas. Governor Osbert met with Robert, but left convinced young Finnlay was dead. He was not to know the body he saw was an illusion Robert had created to hide the truth. Osbert returned to the capital sceptical that sorcery even existed, giving a complete report to his colleague, Nash.

In reality, Finnlay was safely tucked away at the Enclave. He worked to develop a new kind of tandem Seeking, and in the process, he had a vision of Jenn coming towards the Enclave, her teacher Fiona at her side. Jenn had returned to gain insight into Robert's recent banishment, but Wilf would only accept her presence if she made a vow to Stand the Circle once he was dead, to place herself before the Key as a candidate for Jaibir. Then Finnlay received another vision – of Fiona's mother, in grave danger; Ayn had gone to the capital, looking for the sorcerer Jenn had sensed. If this strange sorcerer was in fact the Angel of Darkness, only Robert would be able to help.

With news of Ayn's capture, Robert immediately set out for Marsay. Entering the capital in disguise, he rescued Ayn, but her wounds were great. With neither a name nor face to give to the evil man who had tortured her, she begged Robert to end her life using the ancient sorcerers' ritual of Convocation. If he did not, the evil one would find them both. Hating himself, Robert did as he was asked and left Marsay to return home.

His sleep plagued by a recurring nightmare of sorcery, King Selar sank closer into madness, taking out his rage and frustration on his wife, the beautiful Queen Rosalind. In an effort to contain Selar's madness, Nash revealed that he was a sorcerer, only to have Selar banish him from the city.

Concerned for her mother, Fiona insisted Finnlay use his new tandem Seeking to try and find Ayn. Unwisely, they left the safety of the Enclave, but while Fiona moved closer to the capital, Finnlay was captured by

3

Carlan. Through countless days of torture, Finnlay never saw the face of his adversary, but he discovered many important things. Carlan believed Finnlay was the Enemy – and voiced his lust for the Key. To prolong his life, Carlan began to take Finnlay's blood, but before the process was completed, Carlan was recalled to Selar. Finally alone, Finnlay escaped and wandered, dying, only to be rescued by Fiona and taken back to the Enclave.

Queen Rosalind, beaten, terrified and desperate to help her country, absconded with her children. The moment he heard, Selar ordered out the guard for an immediate hunt for his heir. At home at Elita, Jenn was surprised to find the Queen begging her help. Bad weather, sickness and injury forced her in turn to ask for help. She turned to Dunlorn.

Robert was horrified to find the Queen in such straits but concealed them in a secret chamber at Dunlorn Castle before organising a plan to get them all out of the country to safety in neighbouring Flan'har. Robert sent Jenn home under the care of Micah, with a veiled warning of the danger buried within the heart of the prophecy. Even as he pushed her away, he knew that he was in love with her.

Jenn returned home to find her father Jacob had discovered her absence. He threatened to disown her until she told him of Selar's plan to invade Mayenne, and of the Queen's escape. A descendant of ancient Kings himself, Jacob forgave her, though greatly wounded at her secrecy. He then told her that the King had arranged a marriage for her to take place in two weeks to the King's brutal cousin Teige Eachern, Duke of Ayr. Heartbroken and frustrated, Jenn was powerless to do anything to stop it. Jacob hoped to halt the war by sending a wedding invitation to Robert Douglas: he and Selar had once been friends and Jacob prayed the influence of Robert might work for the good.

Selar had his army out looking for the Queen and it was to this that Carlan returned, once again in the guise of Nash. Using a hideous perversion of the ancient Bonding technique, Nash tied the King to him. From that moment onwards, Selar's nightmares vanished – but he would never be able to deny any order Nash gave. Content with his work, Nash returned home to discover Finnlay had escaped. But not forever. With Finnlay's aura imprinted on his mind, Nash could Seek him anywhere in the country the moment he left the protection of the fabled Key.

Robert could not bring himself to refuse the wedding invitation, but he was unprepared to face Selar's public humiliation of him. With the demon flaring inside him, Robert left the hall. He was desperate to protect Jenn, desperate to avoid the Bonding. In his heart, he believed he had to avoid all parts of the prophecy in order to prevent the conclusion that haunted him.

4

Later that night Jenn, restless and alone, sensed Robert's distress and found him outside the castle walls. Robert admitted his love for her, but insisted it was merely the prophecy at work, and he must fight it. Jenn told him she needed him and, beaten by pain and anguish, he was unable to resist. He kissed her and saw their bodies surrounded by a blue light. He knew what this was. This was the Bonding as foretold in the prophecy.

Later, Micah, guessing what had happened, agreed to stay with Jenn, and watched as Robert rode away from Elita. Heartbroken but unable to do anything else, Jenn married Eachern the following day and went to live at his castle at Clonnet.

Eight months later Nash was entrenched at court, with Selar now under his complete control. Visiting Jenn at Ayr, careful to make sure she had no idea who he really was, he found her heavily pregnant. Meanwhile his aide, DeMassey, had finally found Rosalind and rescued Prince Kenrick. In the process, the Queen was killed, but the Princess had escaped. Nash rushed off to meet up with DeMassey and bring the Prince back to his father.

After mindspeaking with Jenn, Finnlay discovered the truth – that Robert was her child's father – though Jenn swore him to secrecy. Once more he foolishly left the safety of the Enclave, but before he could get too far, he was discovered by Nash. He fought off capture but, seriously wounded, Finnlay rode to Jenn at Elita for safety – with five hundred evil Malachi sorcerers at his heels, disguised as Guilde soldiers. He arrived at Elita safely, but collapsed before he could voice a warning.

Lords loyal to Lusara had rescued Bishop McCauly from prison, hiding him in a remote abbey in the Goleth mountains. His attention there was caught by a young man who worked silently, furiously in the garden, in sun or snow. When a fire threatened the abbey, this man risked his life to retrieve Abbey records. McCauly stopped him, calling him Robert.

Over the ensuing weeks, McCauly grew closer to Robert, until he explained the prophecy. At the age of nine Robert was given the Word of Destruction and told he was Bonded to this girl – and that, in the act of salvation, he would destroy that which he loved most. He had believed he was strong enough to withstand this destiny, but he had given into the Bonding, betraying Jenn with his desire. Now he had no choice but to absent himself from life, or he would become the very thing he had fought all his life to avoid.

Then word arrived that Archdeacon Hilderic would be executed if McCauly didn't give himself up. Robert agreed to go with McCauly, determined to rescue Hilderic, but they reached the town to find news of Finnlay's escape, the army chasing him – and the direction in which they were headed. Desperate to save his brother, Robert took McCauly to Elita, arriving in time to prepare the castle before the siege.

There Robert saw Jenn – and wondered if the child was his. Before he could ask, the castle was attacked, with the Angel of Darkness outside, driving the soldiers on. Earl Jacob defied them and was killed for his efforts. The shock drove Jenn into labour.

But Jenn was also in danger from Carlan, causing her pain that could kill her. Finnlay begged Robert to help – but there was a problem. If the child was Robert's, then he would kill Jenn just as his power had killed his young wife. Unable to explain with the truth, Finnlay insisted, believing that Robert's power had killed Berenice only because they weren't Bonded. Jenn would be safe because she and Robert *were* Bonded. Hating himself, but knowing he had no option, Robert reached out with his power and eased Jenn's pain, cutting Carlan's power over her. She and the baby survived, but in the process, convinced Robert the child couldn't be his.

Carlan attacked the castle in earnest, forcing Robert to withdraw everyone inside the main keep. Battered openly by sorcery, Robert found the demon inside him drowning him, driving him to desperate actions. Then Jenn's son was born and the last piece of damnation fell into place. Blind and deaf to everything around him, Robert reached the top of the keep. Unable to control the demon any longer, he raised his hands and uttered the Word of Destruction.

It was not until the following day that Robert was able to see the effects of his power. The castle walls had crumbled and only the keep still stood. For half a league in every direction, the meadow was blackened, trees felled and scorched. The Malachi Guilde had disappeared; everyone inside the keep survived, but all but the most faithful had scurried away in fear of the sorcerer. As Robert and his friends prepared to leave the ruins of Elita, he knew nothing would be the same again. He also knew he had failed to kill the Angel of Darkness.

Carlan, alone and sorely wounded, slipped away from the ruins, knowing at last who his Enemy really was. It would take him time to recover, but his plans had only been halted, not stopped. Armed with more knowledge than his adversary, Carlan escaped knowing it would be only a matter of time before he would finally be in possession of the Key – and Jenn, the Ally.

Robert left Lusara that day, along with McCauly and Micah. He went into his future, leaving Jenn to return to her husband with her son Andrew.

For five years Robert lived with his failure to defeat a prophecy already half-fulfilled. The demon inside him reminded him every day that his

The sky is full of eagles, hawks, and I feel as if I'm one
I must climb high into the bitter cold air.
Higher, higher yet
As the world slips by, silent and deadly,
I see all
Higher, higher yet
My lungs bursting, I scream my defiant rage
And fall, fall to that silent earth
I have failed
But oh, oh, what a glorious failure.

Jeffry A. McNair

Prologue

The night was dark, but nowhere near as dark as it could be. Before the folds of the forest, moonlight drenched a snowy field with winter blue. Long black shadows marked the path of a road leading to the village of Lagganfors and the gate of its Guildehall. Only the yellow oil lamps suspended above the stone walls brought any colour to the scene, but their glow was sickly as the hour grew late.

From within the depths of the wood, the hooting of an owl beckoned the night, and in response rose the cry of wolves to the north. Closer was the murmur of movement within the village, tiny things now as folk climbed into their beds for warmth and sleep. It was a quiet wrapped in winter toil and close companionship, but it brought no peace to the man who paused by his window within the Guildehall, gazing into the night.

Vaughn, Proctor of the Guilde, stood tall and lean, his long face devoid of humour. He had removed the clothes soiled from his journey and now wore vestments of pristine yellow, the colour of the sun, the colour of the Guilde. Manicured fingers held an elegant silver cup of mulled wine, but the Proctor ignored the warmth. Instead, his gaze remained on the fields beyond.

Behind him, close to the fire, stood Ulbert, Master of this Hall. His round face was flushed in the overheated room, his hands nervously picking at threads on his robe. He'd known the Proctor was to come to Lagganfors, but having to be in the same room, having to listen to his words – and, worse still, his silences – was a harsh task at this time of night. Only Vaughn would choose to go on a progress of his Halls in the middle of winter.

'Tomorrow,' Vaughn said, without turning from his window, 'I will view your accounts.'

'Yes, my lord.'

'You will therefore have all night to ensure they are an accurate representation and not the comely picture I'm sure you have prepared.'

Ulbert gritted his teeth. 'Of course, my lord.'

Vaughn remained silent for a few moments longer. Then he took a sip of his wine, swallowed and spoke again. 'What reports have you heard of raiders in this area? Or of the Outlaw?'

'Robert Douglas? Why, none, my lord! As for the raiders, we are remote here and being so close to the village . . . '

'None of which is germane to the danger, Ulbert! We are all at risk – except perhaps at Marsay. No blaggard would dare enter my Hall in the capital. And who knows where the Outlaw might raise his evil head?'

'Indeed, my lord.' Ulbert caught his fingers together and tried to present a semblance of calm, of confidence. Vaughn's obsession with the Douglas and his sorcery was well known – even though the man hadn't been seen for over five years. 'Even so, we have guards enough here, and the full support of the villagers.'

'That's not what I've heard.'

Ulbert swallowed as Vaughn turned a slate gaze on him. 'But, my lord, that was only a small misunderstanding.'

'Refusing to pay the tithe? Failing to make the required contributions to the upkeep of this Hall? Hiding rebel healers who do not hold the Guilde warrant?' Vaughn released him and turned back to the window. 'I expect discipline, Master Ulbert. The people of Lagganfors hold a duty to this Hall. It is your duty to exact it from them. I will not condone negligence. Do I make myself clear?'

'Yes, my lord.'

'Take what they will not give willingly. The gods demand their obedience. Remind them of that.'

'Yes, my lord,' Ulbert replied with a sigh.

Vaughn once more swept his gaze across the fields where a mist grew out of the depths of the forest. Few people travelled at this time of the year. Instead, they remained at home, obedient to the cold, doing their work, staying within the watchful eye of the Guilde.

'These raiders, my lord?'

'Yes,' Vaughn replied idly, already knowing what the question would be.

'Have none of them been caught? Is there no trace of who is behind it? And why only Guilde Halls?'

'Serin only knows, Master Ulbert,' Vaughn replied, barely moving. 'And those behind the raids are obviously slaves of the evil god Broleoch. Who else would do such a thing?'

'But what do they hope to achieve? Simple menace? They kill no one and that one hall which burnt down was as much due to accident as anything else.'

'Are you making excuses for them?'

'Of course not, my lord. It's just that I don't understand . . . '

The mist beyond the fields gathered the darkness, rolling forward like waves on a sea. Vaughn watched, entranced as the snow disappeared beneath the onslaught. Cold ventured forth with the mist, fingers reaching out to him, safe within his warm room. But he wasn't safe. The icy tendrils stole through the glass and into his heart and he gasped at their touch.

Now he could hear the waves crashing against the field, an ocean of pain and melancholy, salty and sharp. The mist enfolded his entire view and the room was lost to him.

He smelt fear on the air and it clutched at his innards, pounding blood through his body. He was powerless to move, to speak, even to think. Something came out of the gloom towards him. Not a man, but a bird, black and thick with feathers dark as treacle. Its cry pierced the silence, drowning his blood-filled ears with fury and revenge. He turned to run from it, but his terror held him frozen. The bird swooped, but shied away from his stance. In that moment, the feeling came to him, triumphant, sure – so very sure. This bird could not defeat him, could not sway him from his path . . .

'My lord?'

The mists faded even as the voice broke in upon him.

'My lord Proctor?'

A message. From the gods. A vision of a black eagle and of triumph.

'Please, my lord!'

Vaughn blinked as the field returned to its snow-blue serenity. Ulbert was calling him and he had to respond. But tell him about this vision? No. It was for his eyes alone. But what was he to do exactly?

A crash from below ripped him away from the window. Ulbert was already approaching when another crash rumbled through the building and made him stumble. Now he could hear cries of rage and fear coming from beyond the door. The Guildehall was under attack!

The door was kicked open before them. Two sturdy soldiers waited, swords held ready.

Vaughn stormed forward. 'I demand to know the meaning of this!'

One soldier grinned and shook his head. 'Come, Guildesman!'

Before Vaughn could voice further protest, the soldier took his arm, dragged him from the room and through the building. As they moved, the place grew quieter, with only the occasional shout, quickly silenced.

'Who are you?' Vaughn demanded of his captor. 'How dare you attack a Guildehall in this manner! Do you know who I am?'

'I don't care,' the man replied. 'Come quietly and you'll not be harmed.'

Vaughn had no choice. The man had a good grip on his arm and the sword was a reflex away from his throat.

Another raid – but this time he was here to witness it personally! If only Selar had taken his requests for help more seriously . . . but perhaps Nash had stopped him. Yes, perhaps Nash was behind this outrage. And Nash was in league with the Outlaw!

Vaughn emerged into the cloister to find his brethren gathered in a frightened clump in the centre, surrounded by a dozen soldiers. Ulbert followed behind. Swords were brandished but none were immediately threatening. The Guildesmen were being contained, not murdered.

Vaughn pulled his robes about him and turned towards the nearest guard. 'I demand you desist at once! To attack a Guildehall like this is treason! What do you want?'

'Your silence,' the man replied. 'And your obedience. Just stay quiet, Guildesman, and you'll live through this night with your throat uncut.'

Vaughn hissed in a breath, but there was nothing he could do. He turned to the man to his left and whispered, 'How did they get in?'

'Two men approached the gate, my lord, claiming to have been attacked in the forest. The moment the gates opened, twenty of them invaded. Our guards were overpowered almost instantly.'

'But who are they?'

'Rogues, the lot of them. Thieves, no doubt, and probably murderers, too.'

A movement from the corridor made Vaughn turn. More soldiers emerged from the darkness carrying torches. Behind them stood two men. One had his cloak hood pulled back to reveal curly red hair, a short cropped beard of the same colour. In his arms was a bundle of books. But the other . . . tall and powerful, strong lean lines and eyes an ocean of green . . .

'Serin's blood!' Vaughn murmured, suddenly unsteady on his feet as a shiver ran down his spine. That face was one he hadn't seen for a decade, and yet he would know it anywhere. A face that had not been sighted within the borders of Lusara for five long years.

The Duke of Haddon. Robert Douglas. The Great Outlaw.

The sorcerer!

No sooner was the thought complete when the man in question paused and turned slowly to look at the group in the cloister – and straight into Vaughn's eyes. Vaughn was frozen to the spot, unable to look away, unable even to move as the gaze held him, trapped, imprisoned.

Without taking his eyes from Vaughn, the Outlaw murmured something to the man beside him, took the books, then turned and disappeared into the darkness, breaking the moment.

His companion came into the cloister and stood before Vaughn and his brethren. Tall demonic shadows danced on the wall behind him, eerie against the glowing torchlight.

'Thank you for your hospitality, gentlemen,' he said, displaying no shame at his actions. 'We'll be leaving now, but please, don't make the mistake of trying to stop us. Your horses have been scattered and we'll leave the gate barred behind us. Goodnight.'

In one swift movement, the guards drew back into the corridor, heading for the gate. Vaughn watched them disappear, unable to move a muscle. There were noises of men mounting up and an echo as the riders vanished into the night. Then abrupt bedlam as all his brethren seemed to wake from a dream.

Vaughn remained apart from it, despite urges for him to do

something. Instead, he stood staring at the corridor, seeing again that familiar face and the glint of green in the Outlaw's evil eyes.

So, the Douglas had been behind those raids all along. But why?

The books! By all that was holy – the *library*! A collection of books from the time when sorcerers wandered freely through the land and worked alongside the Guilde in harmony. The time before sorcerers had betrayed the Empire. There would be many secrets in that library – and the Outlaw wanted them. How was he to know they were now hidden in a place where nobody would ever find them, that Vaughn was the only person alive who knew where they were? He'd gone to great lengths to protect the library from exactly this kind of incursion.

Abruptly, Vaughn started. *The vision!* That must be . . .

Turning swiftly, Vaughn barked orders for the gates to be burned down and the horses to be rounded up. He had to get to Marsay – and he had to leave tonight.

On a hill overlooking the village, Robert Douglas sat on his horse as the rest of his men gathered around him. He waited in stillness, his gaze never wavering from the Guildehall below, surrounded by the town and the snow-white fields. Only the animal beneath him moved at all, shaking its head lazily and stamping one foot, as if impatient to complete the escape.

A slip of moonlight caught his face, revealing lines of thought. The level eyebrows were drawn together more in surprise than displeasure. An icy breeze caught his dark hair, tossing waves around his cheeks. He paid no attention. Instead, his thoughts were entirely on the memory of Vaughn, his taut lean features, eyes full of fear and hatred. It was not the first time Vaughn had looked at him like that.

And all because Robert was a sorcerer.

He lifted his chin and breathed deeply of the midnight air. The smell of salt had gone back to wherever it had come from. No more could he hear the cry of birds, the crash of waves. He concentrated hard, but already the threads of the vision were leaving him bereft, the memory quickly fading to nothing.

'My lord?'

Turning his head, he glanced at Micah, waiting on his horse with perfect patience. In the moonlight, his red hair almost glowed, while his blue eyes seemed devoid of colour. But in this moment, it was his patience that spoke most about him. Patience and loyalty – above all, loyalty. Neither Micah – nor indeed any of these men – cared a whit that he was a sorcerer.

'We should move on, my lord,' Micah added quietly. 'I'm sure Vaughn won't wait until dawn to be on your trail.'

An involuntary smile lit Robert's face. 'No, indeed, and I can't resist the temptation to disappoint him once again.'

'It's a pity he was here, however.'

'Oh, I don't know, my friend.' Robert murmured, glancing once more at the village and the Guildhall on its edge. Even now new lights were glowing in the windows and he could almost imagine the activity within, driven by the frantic Proctor. 'Perhaps it's time they knew I was back. All of them.' Especially Jenn.

'Even the Angel of Darkness?' Micah whispered, a little horrified.

A small smile drifted across Robert's face and he nodded slowly. 'Yes, even him. Come, Micah, let's be over the border. The Angel of Darkness can wait until another day. These books, however, cannot.'

With a laugh, he turned his horse away and led his men into the night, leaving only the winter to wrap any comfort around the town.

1

A puff of flame bellowed out above the crowd, then quickly disappeared, leaving sighs of amazement in its wake. The onlookers offered applause and an expectant silence, waiting for the next feat. Balancing on top of his pedestal, the fire-eater somersaulted into the air and caught two batons of burning flames before he landed. Instinctively, the audience pressed back, both afraid and fascinated at the same time. The fire-eater spun around in front of them, waving the torches, then, with great ceremony, raised one above his mouth, lowered it – and extinguished the fire completely. The crowd roared with approval.

Archdeacon Godfrey, priest and Guilde Chaplain, stood on the fringes of the group, watching the crowd almost as much as the performers. They were entranced; Godfrey envied them. They really believed the man was eating that fire – they wanted the illusion.

Godfrey turned to another corner, on the opposite side of the castle courtyard, where more cheers split the midwinter night. He pressed his way towards it, glimpsing little more of the tumblers than the occasional figure flying through the air.

It seemed all of Marsay had squashed itself into the enclosure for these Caslemas celebrations – far more than had attended the church services earlier in the day. The King had appeared for mass in the Basilica, but he'd left quickly afterwards and immediately buried himself in these more secular activities. The festival of Caslemas was to honour the goddess Mineah, but any worship of the gods on this most sacred day of the religious calendar appeared little more than perfunctory. Even the winter-green decorations hanging from the castle walls had a pagan touch to them. The people – led by their King – were more interested in the vats of wine and ale which lined the walls, the smell of beef roasting and the tasty sweetcakes sold by bakers near the gate.

A flash of light illuminated the darkness near the tumblers and

Godfrey tried to get closer. Only occasionally would anyone notice his priest's robes and make space for him. He came to a halt behind a group of children who squealed and laughed at the performers. There were a dozen grown men, juggling now. Bottles of green glass and flaming torches were tossed between them, looping and spinning: a display of delicate balance and coordination amidst a flurry of dangers.

'Good evening, Father.'

Godfrey barely turned at the sound to his right. He would know Murdoch's voice anywhere, regardless of the crowd noise. 'You came after all.'

'There seemed no point staying away. Besides, I love a good show – even if the cost of all this comes directly out of our taxes. Perhaps I could interest you in a cup of ale?'

Godfrey said nothing. Instead, he glanced around to see if anybody at all was paying attention to him. By the time he stepped back from the tumblers, Murdoch was already gone. Godfrey found him again in a quiet spot beside the castle gate, two cups of frothy ale in his hands. Behind him, the shadow of the Basilica and beyond that, the city, stretched down the island hill to stop before the waters of the Vitala River. Murdoch had chosen a good spot, out of view of the royal pavilion to the left and conveniently hidden from the prying eyes of any guards close by – and nobody could get close enough to listen.

'As cautious as ever,' Godfrey murmured, taking a swallow of ale.

'We've had a good run, you and I, over the past few years. If anybody has ever seen us talking, they've thought nothing of it, and we both know how important it is to keep it that way.'

'Indeed,' Godfrey added quietly. He kept his gaze on the crowd before him, but the bulky presence of Murdoch was impossible to ignore. 'I don't suppose you have anything new to tell me?'

'Of Robert? No, I've not seen him for six months.'

'But do you have any idea where he is? What he's doing?'

'What? Impatience from you, Father?'

Godfrey glanced aside. Murdoch was watching him from under thick brows. 'It's been five years, Murdoch, going on for six. How many times has he been to see you? Perhaps ten? Am I – or your people – any the wiser as to what he plans?'

'No.'

'Are the lives of our people any better?'

'No.'

'Is there any immediate hope that that will change?'

'Not that I can see.'

'Then I think I'm allowed a little impatience.'

'As are we all.' Murdoch shrugged and took a good long pull at his ale. 'His brother and mother especially. They haven't seen Robert at all.'

Godfrey bit his tongue and looked away. He'd deserved that.

'I know how it is for you,' Murdoch continued, softer but no gentler. 'You live a precarious life, balanced between what you believe in and those you would fight. You know as well as I do that every time Robert comes in secret to Marsay, he risks his life. How much hope would we have if he was caught and executed? Ever since that night at Elita, the whole world has known he is a sorcerer.'

Godfrey flinched and glanced around once more to check no one could overhear them.

' . . . and anyone associating with him would die the same terrible death. You've done good work here, passing on information to me, so I can tell my people. It makes a difference, I promise you – especially in light of the fact that you're a priest. Even if Robert never comes back, you have made things better.'

'But he has to come back,' Godfrey murmured, gripping his ale-mug. 'He has to. Nobody else has the following or the ability to do anything. Even if he is one of you. Even if that's why he hasn't done anything so far.'

Murdoch grunted. 'You place a lot of hope in Robert.'

'Don't you?' Godfrey replied, turning his gaze on the other man.

For a moment, Murdoch said nothing. Then he smiled. 'And how is the King?'

'How do you think? If he does much more than spend his days entertaining himself and the prince, I see no evidence of it. He shamelessly spends most nights with his whore, Valena de Cerianne. His council takes on the work of governing the country – and that they do poorly.'

Murdoch was silent for a while as the crowd roared and cheered the tumblers again. In other corners of the courtyard, other activities were going on and the flow of people in and out of the gate seemed unending.

'I don't suppose you can tell me,' Murdoch said finally, 'anything new about Duke Eachern?'

Godfrey took his eyes from the crowd for a moment, but Murdoch wasn't looking at him. 'I still don't understand why you're interested in him above anybody else at court. I know he's Selar's maternal cousin and he does have some power – but he's a brainless idiot, useful only when he's got a sword in his hand.'

'It's not the Duke I'm interested in,' Murdoch replied levelly. 'It's his wife.'

'Jennifer Ross? But why . . . ' Godfrey paused. 'Is she one of you? A . . . '

Murdoch frowned. 'I'm sorry, Father. I know you've been Sealed and that protects you from revealing what you know of my people, even under torture – but even so, there are some things it's safer for you not to know.'

'So that's why Father John went to such great lengths to obtain his position at Clonnet? To be near the Duchess?'

Raising his eyebrows, Murdoch almost smiled. 'Can you tell me anything about Eachern?'

'No more than you already know. He spends most of his time either here or riding north. I can't find out why. It's some big secret I'm not sure even the council knows about. I think Governor Nash could be involved, because he disappears for weeks at a time. He's due back tonight, I believe. If I tried to find out what was really going on, somebody would notice my curiosity – and that's an unhealthy trait to have these days.'

Murdoch drained his ale. 'Then I think we should be going our separate ways, Father. We've been standing together too long as it is. I'll be in for confession as usual next week. Keep your ears open and be careful. If anything happens to you, I'll have to answer to Robert – and I can't tell you how that prospect chills me. Goodnight.'

Godfrey shook his head and smiled. 'Goodnight.' As Murdoch disappeared into the crowd, he finished his ale slowly. Even now, after so long, he found it difficult to believe he had actually volunteered to work alongside men such as Murdoch.

Sorcerers. Reviled, hated, feared. It was death to be discovered as one. A painful death, burning at the stake, after hands had been cut off and torture inflicted. To be found working with them was perhaps even worse – especially for a priest.

Every aspect of Church doctrine spoke of the evil of sorcery. Many laws and punishments Godfrey had memorised as a young novice. The Guilde itself had vowed to remove every sorcerer from the face of Lusara. The people, with a kind of morbid greed for stories of sorcerers, still shrank away from the reality.

So why did Godfrey find this work so easy? Why did his conscience never bother him? Why had crossing that line been such a simple thing for him?

Because it wasn't sorcery he was fighting for. Instead, it was something far more important: a release from bondage and tyranny for Lusara. He couldn't see the end of this fight, couldn't even begin to imagine it. All he knew was that men like Murdoch and Robert Douglas were all fighting on the same side. Light against the darkness.

Doctrine or no, that was, after all, why Godfrey had become a priest in the first place.

Vaughn didn't wait for his luggage to be brought up to his rooms in the Guildehall. Instead, he followed Godet along the corridor and up the stairs to where a hasty fire was being lit in his study. Serving Guildesmen rushed here and there, anxious to set things straight after his unscheduled return. Vaughn hardly noticed them. He dropped his cloak, ignored the wine poured out and ordered a pot of brew. Then he collapsed into the chair behind his desk and waited for the room to empty.

He sat staring at the wall, at the cool grey stone, the sharp edges and fine gaps between. As Godet closed the door behind the last man, Vaughn turned. Godet handed him the cup of brew and he sipped carefully. Eventually, after a long silence, the young man spoke.

'Is something wrong, my lord?'

'Yes.' Vaughn nodded without looking at him. 'Very wrong.'

He took another sip but Godet didn't fidget – one quality amongst others that had earned him his place here. 'I want you to do something for me.'

'Of course, my lord.'

'How long until sunrise?'

'Six or seven hours.'

Vaughn looked up. 'Wait until dawn and select a few of our brethren you can trust. Tell them to go out into the town, out of Guilde uniform, and spread the word.'

'What word is that, my lord?'

'The Outlaw has returned to Lusara.' Vaughn was gratified to see the young man's face go pale. 'Yes, Robert Douglas is back – not only that, but it seems he has been responsible for the raids on my Guildehalls across the country.'

'But . . . how do you know?'

'I saw him with my own eyes. Now go. Bring me some food, but other than that, I'm not to be disturbed. Wait outside in case I need anything further.' As Godet bowed and made for the door, Vaughn added, 'And I know you'll be discreet.'

Godet paused and threw a smile at him. 'Of course, Uncle.'

Alone again, Vaughn turned back to the wall, steepling his hands together in contemplation. Then he stood and pressed two fingers against the corner of one stone. He felt something click and he pushed hard. The secret door groaned against the uncommon movement and a rush of rancid air hit his face. Beyond lay a pit of darkness as deep and cold as that in his belly.

Slowly now, he collected a candle from the desk and stepped through the door. For a moment, his eyes struggled against the dimness, his skin crawling at the very thought of what he had to do.

The secret room before him was empty, just as he'd left it. Six years ago, he'd taken the library the Outlaw was searching for and hidden it in a place where no eyes would look for it. Now all that was left in this rancid space was the ghost of what those books contained.

He'd looked once, himself, long ago, when his predecessor had passed the secret on to him. He'd glanced through pages written hundreds of years before, gleaned enough of their content to understand, with horror, what they contained. Instructions for sorcerers. Rules by which they could master their evil art. Arcane tutorials for those who sought to enslave those without power.

These were the very books the Outlaw wanted to possess.

The same books Vaughn would now have to read in order to find what he wanted, what he needed.

A solution.

He knew there was one in there, buried beneath the rhetoric. Such a thing had been hinted at by his superiors when he'd first joined the Guilde as a boy. This library had been put together by both Guilde and sorcerers over the centuries, when each had worked alongside the other, when secrets had not existed between them, long before the Empire had crushed the evil.

Yes, he would find what he was looking for and he would find it tonight – for it was certain that if the Douglas was hunting for these tomes, so too would his minion, Nash. Indeed, in all likelihood Nash too was a sorcerer. If Vaughn was to safely extract the information he needed to begin his war, then he would have to do it before Nash returned to court, before he could find a way to interfere.

Grim and determined now, he left the empty room, pushing the ancient door shut behind him. His journey had tired him, but the taste of victory against evil was fresh in his mouth. He had to move and move quickly. If his actions called down damnation on his immortal soul, then he would make the sacrifice willingly.

With a satisfied ruthlessness, he crushed his natural fear of what he was about to do – for the vision had warned him: the Outlaw was back – and Vaughn had to find something that would rid him of sorcerers once and for all.

The slap of water against the stone steps was the only thing Nash could hear above the raucous noise of the city. From his boat, he could see clearly the glow in the sky above the castle, a bland swipe of gold across a black landscape. He'd been able to hear the celebrations all the way down the river, and had been tempted, that whole time, to turn around and head north again.

The oarsman swung and dipped his paddles into the water once more to bring the small boat alongside the stone jetty. Half a dozen men waited for him, all but one in Guilde uniform. Gilbert Dusan held a torch and reached out a hand to help Nash from the boat.

'Welcome back.'

'Where's DeMassey?'

'Keeping an eye on the Prince, as you ordered. Why?'

'Has Valena been near him?'

'Of course not.'

'Good.' Nash strode past his men and through the gate in the castle wall. He began to climb the steps, but had to slow as the old pain in his hip and leg began to play the whore with him. By Broeloch's breath, why couldn't he rid himself of this last vestige of failure? Would it haunt him to the end?

'Anything else to report?' Nash snapped at Gilbert as he strode alongside.

'Just that Vaughn has come back a month early from his annual progress. He only arrived an hour ago, so there's been no word of a reason. I guess the peace and quiet is over already.'

'Typical! Just as I thought he might be gone long enough for me to search the Guildehall. I know that library is in there somewhere. Now Vaughn's back, I don't have a hope of finding it before next winter!'

'But you said Osbert showed you the empty room, the ashes to prove the books had been burned. Are you saying he lied?'

Nash glanced at him, but there was no irony in his face. 'Oh, those were real ashes, from real books – I'm just not convinced a man of even Vaughn's limited intelligence would be so stupid as to burn the only weapon he will ever have against our kind. Knowledge is power, Gilbert, and Vaughn knows that as well as I do. No, Osbert may have convinced himself the books have been burned, but I'm afraid I don't really believe it. That's why I was hoping to have the run of the Hall this winter, to give me a chance to find them. Now I'll just have to push Osbert a little, get him to nose around for me.'

'And if he won't?'

Nash glanced aside at the tall man. 'If I push him any more there's a good chance he might turn and run – and if I'm not around to stop him, he could cause us all a lot of trouble. And before you ask, no, I can't afford to kill him yet; he's still too useful.'

He paused and took the travel-stained cloak from his shoulders. A pair of torches lit the gloom, their crackling fire drowned out by the festivities beyond the east wall. Gilbert handed him another cloak, a fur-lined garment of grey, more suitable for a court appearance. With a sigh, Nash ran his fingers through his hair, drew himself up and mentally prepared himself to step back into the public world. Once more he would become the actor.

Leaving Gilbert behind and taking only two guards with him, Nash strode out of the small courtyard into the larger, crowded one. Half the fools of Marsay had squeezed themselves into the main square of the castle and even with the help of his guards, Nash had difficulty making his way to the dais where Selar and his council sat. As usual, Selar greeted him laconically, waving him to his usual seat, to the right. Of Prince Kenrick there was no immediate sign and Nash had to stop himself from asking. The less Selar knew about the activities of his fourteen-year-old son, the better.

Instead, Nash accepted a cup of sweet spicy wine and relaxed back, carefully stripping the lines of fatigue from his face. His position was never so secure that he could afford anyone thinking he had a weakness to be exploited. Besides, who could tell whether the Enemy might one day decide to strike?

He smiled into his wine at the thought. As if the Douglas even knew the identity of his adversary! Ah, prophecy was such a delight to play with.

Conversation wafted around him, muffled by the roars of the crowd. A space had been cleared before the dais where a huge black bear thumped around at the end of a long chain. Two dogs snarled, darting forward to sink their teeth into the bear's legs. A mighty swipe of its hand sent one of them flying. The dog landed at the feet of its trainer, bleeding profusely and not moving. The other, more wary and much more canny, continued dancing around the bear as it rose to its feet. The crowd applauded and gasped in awe at the size of the animal.

Trinkets thrown to please the moronic mob. Every year they went through this pointless ritual. The mass said in the morning, the prayers sent up to the ears of deaf gods, all the while assuming their lives would go on unbroken by destruction, as if this superficial stability were the only possibility they need consider. As if they had any idea of what lay ahead.

Nash settled back, lacing his hands around his cup, willing the warmth to penetrate his bones. He had spent so much time, so many years, gaining this position here. He had won an important part in all this only to further his own ambitions and yet, these people here thought of him as nothing more than a faithful Guilde Governor. Not one of them knew of the prophecy – or what he really was.

He sipped his wine in silent comfort. He would have to spend an hour or more sitting here, wasting time when there was so much else to do. He glanced around, counting the familiar faces. Bishop Brome was in attendance as usual. His fat face oozed sweat, as if merely sitting was too great an exertion for him. His intellect was at best thin, and having to be spread about so great a girth, only diminished its power more. Other councillors were there, of course, with their ladies. Except for Eachern. He stood alone on the end of the platform. His lady was never allowed this kind of pleasure. Never even allowed to come to court.

And never allowed to know why.

The crowd to his left parted and Kenrick appeared, taking a great leap onto the dais. Selar instantly straightened, his eyes glowing at the sight of his son. Despite his youth, the Prince was already tall and would soon gain the height of his father. But the resemblance did not end there. Kenrick had Selar's good looks and fair hair, but his eyes were hazel, as his mother's had been. But while Selar's ambition and avarice had consumed his life, something else entirely played the same part with Kenrick. Something he kept well hidden, even from Nash's spies.

'I see you've come back, Governor.' Kenrick displayed no pleasure as Nash rose to his feet and bowed. 'Your sport in the north became a little dull, did it?'

Nash portrayed every aspect of the obedient servant. 'My task was completed, Highness. I return according to your royal father's wishes.'

'Then perhaps,' Kenrick sneered, in open contempt, 'my royal father's wishes need to be expanded beyond the sewer.'

With that he turned away, leaving Nash to regain his seat. He drained his wine in one mouthful, burning his tongue. A few minutes more and then he'd be able to leave and get some rest after his long journey. Even so, his gaze remained on the boy-Prince. The child destined, one day, to rule Lusara in his father's place.

No, it didn't do to display a weakness in public – especially when danger was as close as the heir to the throne.

Godfrey tilted his head back to take a proper look at the incredible ceiling above him, bathed in cool winter sunlight. Only once before had he had an opportunity to see it, and that, briefly. The Guildehall in Marsay was considered sacred ground and only those who had sworn the oath could look upon its glories. However, the Guilde Proctor was permitted to exercise discretion and invite those necessary for a specific purpose, and it was under that aegis that Godfrey now admired the famous vaulting.

The entire hall was dominated by a single stone pillar in the centre, the base for every pointed arch in the ceiling. A maze of arcs and joists, yet somehow, the roof made architectural sense, with this solitary stone brace holding it all in place. On every surface, in the darkest corners even, could be seen figures painted right onto the stone: masons, shipwrights, blacksmiths, weavers and many more, representing the myriad trades which made up the Guilde. The background was a midnight blue and decorated by tiny stars painted with real gold. Other colours could be seen, reds and greens, light blue and white. The overall effect was one of mystery and intrigue, of spaces within spaces, inviting discovery. A lifetime of study would not reveal all the secrets of this ceiling. There was nothing else like it in the world.

Godfrey dropped his gaze and rubbed his aching neck to find Vaughn watching him.

'Would you have all of Marsay trouping in here to gawp at such a sight?' Vaughn asked with precision.

No matter which way he looked at it, Godfrey still found his skin crawled whenever his work forced him into contact with this man. He'd long since learned to swallow his distaste, while trying his hardest not to show it. Not an easy task at the best of times.

Now Godfrey folded his hands beneath his surplice and bowed his head in apology. 'Forgive me, my lord Proctor. I was unaware that I was . . . gawping.'

If Vaughn detected the ironic edge to Godfrey's tone, he made no sign. Instead, he turned and wandered a few steps away. 'As you can see, we have more than enough room for the new season of initiates in here. I understand you would rather witness the oaths in the chapel . . . '

'On hallowed ground,' Godfrey couldn't help adding.

'But our numbers have more than doubled on last year and those were double the year before. The chapel is no longer able to support such numbers.' Vaughn finished this with a sniff of pride; the Church could certainly not boast such an increase in interest. Godfrey couldn't even blame it on the fact that the Church was led by an empty-headed buffoon – for was not the Guilde afflicted in the same manner?

Godfrey had to suppress a smile at his silent joke. Vaughn had no sense of humour. 'I would need access to this room the day before the initiation, to set up a temporary altar, consecrate it and have it ready for dawn the next day.'

Vaughn nodded, watching Godfrey carefully, as though his mind was not fully on the arrangements. He paused for several long moments, then asked quietly, 'How long have you been Guilde Chaplain?'

'Eight years, my lord.'

Vaughn nodded again and turned to glance at the ceiling. Godfrey could only wait, as Vaughn had not dismissed him yet. But what was this about? The summer initiation was still almost five months away, and who knew what changes those months could bring? Why, anything could happen. The earth could tremble and shake and bring this magnificent building to the ground. Selar could die and Kenrick could commandeer the place as a new dwelling – or a rebel army could overrun the capital and crush the entire Guilde in its path.

Oh well, one could only hope.

'What,' Vaughn asked without looking at him, 'do you know about sorcery?'

Godfrey's heart leapt into his throat, but he managed an answer without too great a pause. 'No more than most men, my lord.'

'I dare say you've had plenty of time to think about it. It is, after all, some five years and perhaps a couple of months. You were, at one time, good friends. How do you stand now on the subject of Robert Douglas, the sorcerer?'

Godfrey swallowed and kept his voice restrained, voicing the lie he'd practised a hundred times. 'I've not seen him since he left Lusara ten years ago. Yes, we shared some friendship during the few years he was at court – but as for supporting him now that he's . . . ' Godfrey refrained from actually saying the word. The less he said on this subject, the fewer lies he would do penance for at his next confession. 'I'm surprised you even ask me the question, my lord. Have you any reason to doubt my loyalty?'

'Have you ever looked into the eyes of sorcery?' Vaughn continued, turning slowly. 'I have.'

As Vaughn came back across the empty hall, Godfrey folded his hands together, calmed his thumping heart. 'My lord, I . . . '

But Vaughn had moved on already. 'What would you say to a man who had a waking dream of a black eagle attacking the Proctor?'

Was Vaughn becoming unhinged? 'I . . . I'm not sure, my lord.'

'Would you not feel it was a vision sent from the gods? Does not the presence of the bird suggest to you the involvement of Robert Douglas? The black eagle is the sign of his House, is it not?'

'Yes, my lord, but . . . '

'I've seen him.' Vaughn's voice returned to its usual grating tone. 'The Douglas. He raided the Hall at Lagganfors while I was in residence. I saw his face with my own eyes.'

Robert? Raiding Guildehalls? What was going on?

'I wish to show you something.' Vaughn gestured towards a desk set by the door. Godfrey hadn't noticed it before, but now he couldn't look away. In the centre of the table was a small object covered by a single white cloth. He approached it warily. Vaughn came to his side, but didn't touch it to begin with.

'Five hundred years ago, when sorcerers betrayed the old Empire, the Guilde severed its ancient bonds with the evil ones and swore a sacred oath to their total annihilation. I have dedicated my whole life to that purpose and now, at last, thanks to the foresight of my predecessors, I have the means to begin that work. All along, the great task has been to identify the sorcerers hidden among our number – so that we may execute them for their crimes. This talisman here will give us what we've always wanted.'

With no flourish, Vaughn removed the cloth to reveal a round glass bowl, almost perfect in shape. It was filled with a greenish fluid and what appeared to be a small stone rested at the bottom.

'It's called a Bresail,' Vaughn began carefully. 'The bowl is nothing special, the oil costly and imported from the southern continent. The stone, however, is very special. It's called an *ayarn*. It once belonged to a sorcerer and it can find any of its like. When it does, it will glow, alerting us to his presence. As you can see, you have tested well. The stone remains dormant.'

Godfrey took in a long slow breath and let it out noisily. He could hardly begin to absorb what Vaughn was telling him – and he would have to warn Murdoch immediately. Nevertheless, his stomach was full of lead as he took his eyes from the Bresail to find Vaughn watching him again.

'I know what you're thinking,' the Proctor added. 'Is this talisman not sorcery itself? Am I not endangering my immortal soul by using it? Very probably – but I tell you this, I am prepared to do anything to rid this land of the evil I have seen at its very heart. This is the real reason I brought you here. I need your help.'

'My help?' Godfrey was suddenly breathless.

'Yes.' Vaughn nodded with the hint of a rare smile. 'Our war against sorcerers begins this very day – and our first martyr will be Governor Samdon Nash.'

2

The winter night bit into Godfrey's face as he hurried through the city. It was all he could do not to actually run, but he was at risk of falling flat on his face on the icy cobbled road. The streets were busy with folk trying to keep warm, but he pushed past them urgently. He had less than an hour to reach Murdoch's little tailor shop, warn him, and then return to the Guildehall before he was missed.

He turned off the main thoroughfare at the bottom of the hill and followed the alley which lined the inside of the city walls. Dirty snow was heaped up against shops and taverns while yellow lamp-light glowed through windows to warm his path. Soon he came upon the door and knocked hard. He could hear footsteps coming from inside and then the door was wrenched open.

'Godfrey!' Murdoch glanced up and down the street. 'What in the name of . . . Quickly, come inside before you're seen.'

Godfrey stepped out of the cold and into the shop where a single candle cast strange shadows on the walls. The heavy smell of oily wool made him giddy as he caught his breath.

'What are you doing here?' Murdoch demanded, his heavy eyebrows drawn close. 'You know how dangerous it is for you.'

Godfrey gulped. 'You have to leave Marsay at once.'

'What?'

Calming himself a little, Godfrey leaned back on the solid counter for support. 'I only have a few moments, so you'll have to listen carefully. This morning Vaughn called me to the Guildehall and showed me some sort of talisman. He called it a Bresail and insisted it was capable of indicating if a sorcerer was present. At first, I thought he was losing his mind, but then he decreed the entire Guilde membership within Marsay at this moment should come before him and renew their vows. He wanted me to witness them as Guilde Chaplain.'

Murdoch drew Godfrey further into the shop. 'Go on.'

'More than two hundred of them were in the Hall at the same time. He didn't say what was really going on but, Murdoch . . . I saw it with my own eyes. This stone in the bowl – it glowed! There were sorcerers in that Hall!'

'Sweet Mineah!' Murdoch shook his head. 'What happened?'

'That's the surprising thing. Nothing. The stone glowed for the first few moments, but then, as soon as the first man was brought forward, it stopped, and didn't glow again. Not once. You know these bad sorcerers you told me about? The ones Robert caught in Guilde uniform?'

'Malachi.'

'Yes, them. Could they have broken this Bresail in some way, so it wouldn't catch them?'

'Not without touching it, I wouldn't think – but I'm not an expert. What happened then?'

'Each Guildesman made his vow, but the stone remained dormant. Vaughn was furious, but what could he do?'

Murdoch nodded and turned away, scratching his chin. 'Well, he certainly won't let it rest there, I'll bet. You're right, I'll have to leave at first light – if only to warn my people not to approach the city.'

'And what about Robert? What if he comes back here?'

'Let's hope he doesn't. I should think word of this will fly around the country pretty fast. With any luck, he'll hear about it before he comes.'

'There's something else.' Godfrey moved back to the door, put his hand on the latch. 'For some reason, Vaughn seemed convinced he would get a positive reaction from one Guildesman in particular.'

'Who?'

'Nash.'

'And did he?'

'Of course not. He was the first to be tested. I can't say I really know Nash, but he was furious that he was there in the first place – *and* he noticed the Bresail on the table behind Vaughn. Personally, I just think Vaughn is jealous of the position Nash has with Selar. There could be trouble in that quarter in the future.'

Murdoch studied the alley through the window. 'Look, for all we know, the Bresail might be faulty. Either way, when I leave tomorrow, you'll be completely on your own. As soon as I hear the Bresail has moved out into the countryside – as I'm sure it will – I'll try to come back and see you.' Murdoch paused and put a hand on Godfrey's arm. 'I want you to promise me that if you're in any kind of danger, you'll leave the city immediately. Go directly to St Germanus Abbey. You'll be safe there.'

Godfrey nodded slowly, drawing the sign of the trium in the air before Murdoch's face. 'And you be careful, my friend.' With that, he opened the door and dashed back out into the cold.

'I don't give a damn what you think, DeMassey,' Nash snapped, climbing the stairs two at a time. 'I want every Malachi in the city out of Guilde robes within the hour! Even those who weren't first called to the Guildehall. Vaughn won't stop until he's had every man in uniform in there for his pathetic vow renewal ceremony.'

He reached the door and kicked it open. He pulled off his gloves and tossed them away, making straight for the desk by the window. DeMassey followed him in, his stance as elegant as usual. Nash had never seen a man wear his good looks as though they were a suit of armour the way DeMassey did. Some days just looking at the Malachi made Nash want to throw up.

'And where's Gilbert?' Nash demanded, not bothering to contain his fury. 'Why is he never around when I want him?'

'He doesn't wear Guilde robes. Never has. He is in no danger of being tested,' DeMassey insisted.

'What has that to do with it? He was supposed to be watching Vaughn. I want him to explain to me how Vaughn got hold of this . . . thing . . . without his knowledge. Tell me, is everyone around here incompetent?'

DeMassey took a step forward, spreading his hands wide, rings glittering on almost every finger. 'Look, is this really such a disaster? Once Vaughn has played his little game and lost, he'll put his toy away, assuming it doesn't work, and that will be that. Is there any real need to act so precipitously?'

Nash came around the table slowly, his gaze never wavering from DeMassey. 'Are you a complete idiot? Do you really think that now Vaughn has the scent of blood in his nostrils he'll be happy until he catches someone to burn? We both know why he's got this thing in the first place. He hopes to catch Robert Douglas with it. He'll fail, of course – but how many others will he take instead? All along, I've worked with Selar to prevent his supporting an all-out pogrom against sorcerers because it would make moving around the country very hard for us. It doesn't matter that our Malachi aren't actual members of the Guilde – if they're in uniform, they will be expected to attend this farce. Now – you think about this very carefully – today I was able to shield you and all our other men in the Hall. What happens when I go to sleep? Or have to leave the city? Are you really willing to risk your own neck on a chance?'

DeMassey raised an eyebrow, but didn't respond.

'In only a matter of days, word of this thing will spread throughout the country – and the one man we wanted to catch out in the open will also be the first to go into hiding.'

'Then you believe that rumour? That the Douglas is behind the Guildehall raids?'

'Of course he is!' Nash snapped. Shaking his head in frustration, he turned and poured out some wine. He took two long swallows before facing DeMassey again. 'Vaughn's intervention is going to cause us a lot of problems – and you can thank the power of my shielding that the first one wasn't your immediate execution. All hope of us catching the Enemy by surprise has gone. We'll have to pursue our alternative plan with haste. Now you make sure our men are out of Guilde uniform.'

Nash drained his wine, but refrained from slamming the cup down. 'And when you've done that, find Gilbert and bring him here – before midday. After that, I'm off to Clonnet to see our lady. I need to be sure about her.'

DeMassey took his dismissal without a word, closing the door quietly behind him. With a sigh, Nash came back around the desk and sat on the edge of his chair. Some days . . .

Why did he always have to do the thinking for these people? Were they not all after the same thing?

Actually no – but most of them didn't know that. Not even DeMassey, though he thought he did. All any Malachi could think about was wresting the Key from the clutches of the Salti Pazar, wherever they might be. It didn't occur to them that there might be greater goals to aim for.

Grunting, he leaned back and stretched his bad leg out before him, easing crampy pain from his muscles, but he couldn't do so without being reminded of the man who had inflicted the wound in the first place.

The Enemy. Robert Douglas.

His leg was mostly healed, yes, but there was still the persistent limp displaying his failure to all he knew.

By the blood of Broleoch, the pain – the *humiliation* – of that night at Elita. He'd been lucky to survive . . . but . . . Since when had luck been a major part of *his* plans? Two whole years it had taken him before he'd been well enough even to step outdoors. Even now, these last few pains lingered on, hampering him in so many subtle ways. His only means of repairing the damage lay forever beyond his reach. So far, all he'd done was fix the external bits, shore up the signs of creeping age, mend the superficial wounds. The rest was . . . The rest would have to wait. He would get it in the end. By the Blood, he *would* have it and never again feel a rotting ancient body hampering his actions.

'Where are you, my friend?' Nash whispered into the empty room. 'Why are you hiding? Are you afraid of your destiny?'

And that was the crunch, really, wasn't it? If Douglas didn't know about the prophecy, why didn't he just come out into the open? But he must know – or else why would he raid the libraries of a dozen Guildehalls in search of books to expand his knowledge? He must know – and he would be looking for another answer.

No. There was little chance he'd been to see her. Nash would have known. The spies would have noticed something, or there would have been some change in her. No, Douglas hadn't been to Clonnet – yet. But he might go soon, especially in the light of this damned talisman Vaughn had created.

A knock at the door made him look up. Gilbert stood in the frame, a cloak falling from his shoulders like a raven's wings. For a Malachi, he had no great display of powers and yet had achieved high honours amongst his people. He was exceptionally ugly, even as his childhood friend DeMassey was exceptionally handsome.

'Where have you been?' Nash sat up straight. 'I expected to see you long before now.'

'I've been busy. I hear you've had some trouble.'

Nash winced at the lack of concern displayed. He came to his feet. 'What do you know of it?'

'Enough to tell you that Vaughn's little toy is called a Bresail. There are books about such things in the library at home in Karakham. You would have known, if you'd bothered to look. Still, I suppose you were too focused on finding mention of the Key, weren't you? Is that why you want Vaughn's supposed library? Because you think it will point you to where the Key is hidden?'

Nash ignored the question. 'So how does this Bresail work?'

Gilbert shrugged. 'Very simply. From the sound of it, the stone inside once belonged to the young Finnlay Douglas, taken when he was arrested in Kilphedir, six or more years ago. That's the key – especially if he's a strong Seeker himself. Once the stone is placed into the Saili oil, no further action of sorcery is needed. Our people once used them regularly for Seeking, but they were discarded as being too cumbersome and awkward to travel with – and our Seekers developed equal if not better skills themselves. I've never actually seen one myself.'

'Then Vaughn does have a library of books hidden away somewhere.'

'Obviously.'

'And that little room Osbert showed me was a ruse, probably set up by Vaughn to throw me off the scent – however unwittingly. Damn it! I don't have time to go looking for it now – and if I try, Vaughn will pounce. No, I'll just have to leave it for the moment.'

Gilbert nodded but made no move to leave. 'You have to come with me.'

With a frown, Nash said, 'What? Why?'

'I have a horse waiting. It's almost dawn so the city gates will be open by the time we get there. I have someone who wants to speak to you and I'm afraid you have no choice.'

'No choice? There's no such thing . . . '

But Gilbert merely turned and headed down the stairs.

'This had better be worth it.' Nash hissed, grabbing his cloak.

In winter, the hills surrounding Marsay and the river Vitala were not known for their beauty. Riders in search of snow found only mud and slush, driven brown by the heavy traffic.

Gilbert didn't take Nash far from the city, just far enough that he couldn't call for help, should he need to. They rode to the top of a small rise where three scraggly trees clung tenaciously to the rocky ground. It wasn't until he actually came to a halt that he realised why this had been kept so secret.

The man waiting for him did so with great patience. It was written into every line of his weathered features. Spiky white hair was held back from his face by a headband of copper. The eyes, almost colourless, regarded Nash as if he were not there. The square jaw, rigid mouth and flattened nose were all tanned from decades of exposure. The clothes were white, down to the boots. Even his horse was a mottled grey. With very little effort he could have vanished into a snowing landscape.

Nash took a deep breath and threw Gilbert a sharp glance.

Turning back to the old man, he began, 'Well, well, well. I never thought I'd see the Blood of the Chabanar this far into enemy territory. And in winter, too. I am impressed.'

'A liar as well as a thief,' the old man said quietly, untouched by Nash's sarcasm.

'What do you expect, Aamin? Do you want me to organise a feast to honour your arrival?' Nash snapped. Then he turned to Gilbert. 'What is this about? I don't have time to waste . . . '

'You will return to me what is mine,' Aamin interrupted with that same quiet voice. 'You will return it today.'

'What are you talking about?'

'Malachi belong at Karakham,' Aamin replied. 'They will return with me today.'

'They can't! They're busy!' Nash snapped.

'They will return to Karakham and have nothing more to do with your plans. The Baron DeMassey has affairs and responsibilities he is neglecting as Master of the D'Azzir while my grandson . . . '

Gilbert's horse whickered and sidestepped until he calmed it down.

'My grandson knows where his place is,' Aamin continued. 'As for Valena de Cerianne, she has chosen to follow your path. She may return with the others if she so desires. If not, she may stay with you.'

'You can't do this . . . ' Nash protested, looking to Gilbert for help, but getting none.

'I can do this, Carlan, and you cannot stop me. You came before me ten years ago and asked for my help then. I refused. Now you seek to gain my aid via subterfuge. We have already lost too many of our number at the hands of the Enemy. Need I remind you of our sacrifice at Elita? The Chabanar has never blessed your scheme and at this rate, never will. I have tolerated the involvement of my people in the hope that it would soon reveal the whereabouts of the Key. But—' Aamin paused. For all that he had not once raised his voice, there was still an incredible power behind the man. He had not been supreme ruler of his people for nearly thirty years for nothing. '—but, in view of this Bresail in the hands of the hated Guilde and the reported presence of the Douglas back in this country, I cannot allow my people to be endangered any longer.'

'I won't let you . . . '

'You cannot stop me, Carlan. It is already done. Be grateful I offered you the courtesy of informing you in person. Certainly more than you gave me. Gilbert?'

The old man turned his horse and disappeared over the hill. After a moment, Gilbert moved to follow him. He glanced over his shoulder at Nash. 'I'm sorry. I have no choice but to obey my grandfather.'

In a moment, Nash was alone.

Godfrey packed slowly and with great care, using the movements as an exercise to calm, drawing peace from the bare walls of his monastery cell. Vaughn had finally finished with him, but that did nothing to ease the disquiet within his soul. This trip had been planned for a long time, but with things as they were, the risk was almost too great. But what could he do? Sit around here, aching with frustration at being able to do nothing?

And they would be worried if he failed to appear without explanation. Duke McGlashen and Earl Payne already walked a dangerous tightrope and Godfrey could only struggle to match their courage.

Perhaps he should have told Murdoch about the meeting. But no, these men would have nothing to do with an unknown sorcerer – and they would begin to question Godfrey's reliability. No, he would have to go, and alone at that.

He'd made the arrangements carefully so that a messenger would come, supposedly from his home village in the west, with word that his brother was ill. He could be gone two or three weeks and nobody would question.

Another lie. Another penance. These days he was stacking them up with a phenomenal speed. Was he wrong to be placing his trust in this manner? Would the outcome be worth the sacrifice?

Questions only the gods could answer – and they remained blithely silent. With a glance at the small wooden trium on the wall above his bed, Godfrey lifted the saddlebag and headed out.

He could Sense her draw near, like the approach of dawn upon a virginal morn. Her feet made no sound on the fresh snow, her form cast no shadow on this moonless night. It was as if she existed in this world, only for him.

Luc DeMassey stepped from the darkness of the arch and into the torchlight so she could see where he was waiting. Valena wore a cloak of the finest blue velvet. The hood was cast back and her eyes glowed amber and gold as she smiled up at him. As always, her beauty snatched his breath away. He took her hand and drew her into the shadow. Even as he moved, his Senses stretched wide to encompass the steps to his right, the alley behind. For the moment, at least, they were alone.

Her lips brushed his cheek as she whispered, 'I heard the news. How long do you have?'

DeMassey shook his head. 'Minutes only, my love. If I delay longer, I'll miss the gate and who knows what might happen if I spend another night in this city.'

Valena stepped back a little until he could see her face. None of the untamed seductress for him, no. She used no Malachi power on him as she did with the King. Had never needed to. 'Luc, I'm afraid.'

'Of the Bresail?'

'No. You know my shielding is strong enough to avoid detection. It's this . . . preparation. What if he's wrong?'

DeMassey reached up to brush the hair from her face. 'I think you're more afraid of Nash being right.'

'It's all the same. If this works then . . . if he Bonds with her I'm as good as . . . '

'Hush, my love. I've promised you I'll never let him harm you.'

Valena nodded, but her gaze was troubled. 'He doesn't talk to me as he used to. Once, he would share every plan with me. Now, since Elita, there is a distance between us.'

'You know he's jealous of the time you spend with Selar.'

'At his behest! If Nash wants me for himself, why doesn't he find a replacement for me in Selar's bed?'

DeMassey pulled her close, wrapping his arms about her waist. 'Because there is no other he could trust as he does you. You are not tainted with that perversion of the Bonding he insists on using with his other minions. You can still think for yourself. Even though Selar is completely Bonded to Nash, he does have an awful lot of power. Nash needs you at Selar's side.'

'But for how long?'

DeMassey could only shrug. He could hear the call of the city gate closing for the night. He had to move. 'I beg you, come back with me. Get away from Nash once and for all. He'll not dare touch you if you're surrounded by the might of the Malachi.'

'I can't go, Luc. If I leave now, he'll have nobody to help him – and what chance of success will we have then? No, you must go.'

'But I'll return as soon as I can. You'll have some peace for a few days at least. Nash has just left for Clonnet.'

As her face clouded over, he pulled her closer, urging faith. In response, she kissed him, holding him tight for one brief moment.

'I won't let him hurt you, Valena,' DeMassey murmured firmly. 'Trust me. I'll be back very soon.'

He kissed her once more, then left her alone in the archway. He didn't look back.

'Godet!' Vaughn bellowed. 'Where's that hot water?'

'Coming, my lord.'

Vaughn sank into the bath as Godet returned with another pail and emptied it around Vaughn's feet.

'I'll have your supper taken to your bedroom, Uncle.'

'Why?'

'Aren't you going to get some sleep? You've been working without rest since you got back.'

'I don't care.' Vaughn closed his eyes and enjoyed the searing heat for a moment. 'Nash may have found a way to slip past the Bresail – but I know I'm on the right track. I'm not going to stop now, so you can take my supper and put it into my study.'

Godet's voice was disappointed. 'Yes, my lord.'

Nash rode at the head of the squad and tilted his head to catch as much of the pale sun as he could. The warmth was fragile, but the best he could do. Carefully, he stretched each part of his body, easing out the kinks caused by the tavern bed last night.

Eachern rode behind, but, as usual, the man said hardly a word. He didn't have the intellect for a real conversation about anything other than horses or swordsmanship – and Nash could hardly have cared less for either of those subjects. Besides, now he could smell the salt on the air and, as always, his blood quickened as he drew closer to her.

It was almost midday before he saw the first red stone peak above the sandy hills, with the glistening sea in the distance behind. Clonnet Castle was not the most beautiful house in the country, but it held a thing more precious than anyone could imagine. Encased within walls of rock, towers ungainly in proportion and squat flat walls, was the one he travelled to see.

She must have had word of their approach because she awaited them in the narrow courtyard. For a moment, Nash forgot he needed to dismount. He couldn't take his eyes from her.

Jennifer Ross, Duchess of Ayr. The Ally. Small and still young, her thick dark hair trailed down her back in a braid laced with ribbon. Her gown was deep blood-red; her eyes the most glorious blue he'd ever seen. She gave a perfunctory greeting to her husband, but couldn't hide the genuine smile of welcome for Nash.

'I had not thought to see you back here so soon, my lord Governor. You are well?'

Nash slid down from his horse and took her hand to kiss it. 'All the better for seeing you, Your Grace.'

Even her laughter was beautiful, full of the sea air and the endless sand dunes.

'There are refreshments laid out in the hall,' Jennifer added, glancing at Eachern. He merely grunted and headed inside. Visibly relieved, Jennifer turned back to Nash. 'Perhaps you would prefer to walk off your ride in the garden? It is a lovely day, if a bit windy.'

'I would indeed.'

She led him through the gate and into the one area she'd been allowed some influence over. A low stone wall enclosed a garden added onto the castle a century before. The layout was simple, but the garden nevertheless glowed with colour, even at this time of the year.

'How are things at court?' she began easily.

'Dull as always. The Caslemas celebrations were quite a show, though.'

'We had a simple day here, as usual. Nonetheless, Andrew still managed to get considerably over-excited.'

Nash laughed. 'I wonder how you control that boy. He is terribly headstrong.'

'Believe it or not,' Jennifer replied, 'I use reason.'

'Reason? But he's only, what five or so?'

'Almost six – and yes, it does work – mostly.' She stopped beside a thorny bush, bare of leaf or bud. 'How long do you stay this time?'

Nash took in a deep breath. 'Just tonight.' Unfortunately. It was always same. Come for a night, leave, suffer the emptiness, the frustration. Come back again for another night and leave again. But soon, yes, very soon, he would come back here and make her his own. She would welcome it, he was sure. Three years of hard work would make it so.

'Perhaps,' she murmured, barely glancing at him, 'we could persuade you to stay tomorrow. My husband usually goes hawking when he returns to Clonnet. We have some very fine birds. I'm sure you would enjoy it.'

Nash glanced over his shoulder, but they were alone. Carefully, he reached out to touch her hand with his fingers. 'And I'm sure you must know I don't come here to go hawking with your husband.'

Startled, her hand moved beyond his reach while her eyes searched his face.

'I'm sorry,' he added, softly, 'I didn't mean to imply . . . It's just that your friendship has come to mean a great deal to me. You have no idea the boors I must endure at court. Interesting conversation is something both of us find in short supply.'

'Yes,' she murmured, still a little unsure.

'You know I have tried to convince your husband to allow you more freedom,' Nash lied, 'but he is adamant you have no place at court. I'm just glad he tolerates my visits.'

'Yours are the only ones he does allow,' Jennifer added a little bitterly, turning away.

Nash took a step back. It was only a small mistake and she had already forgiven him. Nevertheless— 'I'm sure I could manage another day away from the King – if the invitation for hawking still stands?'

Jennifer turned with a smile. 'Of course. I'm sorry. It's just that . . . '

'Don't apologise. Will I see you at supper?'

'I'm going to the market in town this afternoon. I'll be back before dark.'

'Till then.' Nash sketched a brief bow and walked back through the garden. Perhaps it would be better if he did stay a little longer. The next time he touched her, he must be able to set off the Bonding – and the only way to do that was to make her want him as much as he wanted her. Yes, there was still a little work to be done.

Jenn pulled her cloak out of the way and mounted the horse. Addie and the half-dozen guards were already waiting for her and turned for the gate. With a sigh, she followed behind, unable to avoid glancing back over her shoulder to the window where she'd seen Nash's face.

What was it about him? Why could she talk to him so easily? He never made any demands on her, never forced her to do or say anything she was not comfortable with – and yet, the moment he'd touched her, she'd shrunk away.

But – damn it – he was a Guildesman! She was a sorcerer. If he knew, he would turn her in and she would be burned at the stake while he stood by and applauded. How could she honestly keep up a friendship with a man like that? Especially when he seemed to . . . feel . . .

Suddenly impatient, Jenn kicked her horse and rode to the head of the guard. They would have walked their way into town, but she forced them to canter behind her.

She was married. Why would he think she would give her affection to him simply because he'd offered her the only friendship she was allowed outside Clonnet? Of course, he knew she was lonely but her life wasn't *that* bad.

Was it?

She had the faithful Addie, the only person from Elita she'd been permitted to keep with her. And she had Father John: as good a friend as anyone could hope for. Not only that, but he was a sorcerer as well, and understood the danger they both lived with each day.

So why did Nash's visits always brighten her life? Was he in love with her?

Did she want him to be?

Would she mind if he was?

It wasn't as if she didn't feel anything for him.

The road led down a hill towards the grey town walls. Everything about this part of the country was grey, except for the sea which stretched far and wide beyond the port. In the harbour, a dozen ships scattered the water with colour. Jenn was unable to help galloping down towards them, enjoying the brief moment of freedom.

Perhaps that was it. When she was with Nash, she could exercise some measure of freedom. She could talk about almost anything. And he did make her laugh.

Hell, her days were so drab and empty she'd find almost anything interesting. If it hadn't been for Andrew, she would have gone mad over the last five years. But it was worth abiding in this prison of sorts, if only to make sure he was safe.

As the road flattened out, she drew her horse back to a walk, catching her breath with a sigh. No. There was no freedom anywhere in this life. Circumstance had trapped her within a web of deceit and lies. Nash didn't know she was a sorcerer. John didn't know that Andrew wasn't Eachern's son. No matter which way she turned, there was always at least one lie she had to keep.

There were some days, however, when it seemed that John betrayed his own hopes. He kept in contact with the Enclave even if she didn't. Although Finnlay no longer tried to mindspeak her, almost every time John received a letter or a visit from someone he would pass on the same message from Finnlay: when was she going to run away and live at the Enclave?

Swap one prison for another? Leave her son without a future?

Robert's son?

She frowned as they entered the town gates. They stopped before a hostelry and left the horses. With only two guards, Jenn led Addie through the streets and out into the market square beside the dock. The whole space was crowded with stalls and buyers, colours and noises, seagulls squawking overhead, swooping to pick up unattended scraps. Almost unconsciously, she began to relax.

Five years, and in all that time, she hadn't seen or heard from Robert once. She only knew he was still alive because Father John received messages from Murdoch. And even though she tried so hard not to, she awaited each new message with a barely contained urgency.

He'd told her he loved her. Would always love her. But if that was true – why did he stay away so long?

Because he had to. Because he had his reasons. Because it wasn't safe for him to be anywhere near her and he'd sworn to protect her. Because she was married and there was no future for them. Because . . .

Because he *did* love her.

She'd held on to that. Held on to it through every long, dark night alone. Through every trial since that day at Elita when they'd said goodbye. Held on, though it gave her no hope. She'd needed to. That's why he'd told her to remember his love, why he'd made so sure she knew.

She'd needed to remember, almost as much as she'd needed him. The memory of his love had kept her resolve firm all this time, despite the pain, despite the emptiness. She'd chosen this path herself, to give her son the life he needed. Nobody had pushed her into it. She'd told Robert she wouldn't go with him, even if he'd asked. This was hardly the time to be regretting it, no matter how much she wanted to be by his side.

Jenn immersed herself in the market, picking up some cloth for Andrew and some as a birthday gift for Addie. She also bought a beautiful blue glass bottle for Bella, though the gods only knew when she'd be able to visit Maitland and give it to her.

She tarried, ignoring the guards. Almost content now, she wandered through the lanes of stalls, taking her time, feeling the wind in her hair and making the most of the afternoon. But it couldn't last forever. As the sun began to edge towards the western hills, she passed her purchases to Addie and climbed the stairs to the church door. For more years than she'd been alive, this tradition had been kept up; the Duchess resident at Clonnet would always pay her respects to Mineah in Jardye's small, neat chapel.

It was cooler inside, but at least the guards remained behind. There were a few people already scattered across the seats, mostly on their knees, probably praying for release from Selar's tyranny. The gods knew Jenn prayed for the same thing.

The priest greeted her as usual, then left her to find her seat one row from the altar. She sank to her knees, clasping her hands together and lifting her eyes to the trium suspended on the eastern wall. Dim candlelight and incense wafted towards her, making smoke for the threads of sunlight breathing through the stained glass window. All sounds of the market died away and she allowed the peace of the chapel to seep into her flesh.

Yes, she had chosen this life and although she may have made a mistake, it was too late to change it now. She had once lived a life roaming the country, a homeless child free of all bonds. Now she was a mother and a wife. She'd once dreamed of helping her country free itself from Selar, but she was almost as much a prisoner now as Lusara. It might have been the wrong choice, but at least she could see the worth of it. Andrew grew every day, filling the drab hours with a joy she could never have imagined possible. As long as she had him, what need had she for men such as Nash – or even Robert? Andrew was her life now, and it was wonderful because of him.

She signed the trium from her forehead to her shoulders then sat back on the seat. She had a few moments still, to enjoy the peace. A few moments before she would have to go back and deal with . . .

Jenn?

The blood drained from her face. Involuntarily, her heart began to thump hard in her breast.

Jenn? You can hear me, can't you?

She swallowed loudly, frozen to her seat. Who could be mind-speaking her? Could she even remember how to respond?

Please, say something, Jenn.

She clasped her hands together and formed the thought, a single word. *Finnlay?*

Sorry, no. His worthless older brother.

Her heart stopped completely. *Robert?*

3

Robert?

Yes, it's me, but don't make any sign, he added quickly.

Yes, it was him. She knew that silent voice – had known at the first call of her name. But . . . this was impossible! He couldn't be . . . *But how . . . Where are you?*

Sitting four rows behind you.

Behind me? Jenn flinched, but managed to stop herself from turning around. *But what if somebody sees you?*

I'm in disguise. Nobody will recognise me.

She paused and took in a deep breath, scrambling to catch hold of this. She had to think straight, had to still the sudden thumping in her chest.

He'd come back. At last. Relief and something like fear flooded through her too quickly to examine. Desperately she wanted to turn, to face him, to see once again the love in his gaze.

He was safe. Alive and well. Sitting right behind her. She could have laughed. *What are you doing here?*

I thought you might like to know that Micah is well. And Bishop McCauly. He's with me now.

In the church?

No.

Why have you brought him back to Lusara? So many questions, so great a desire to keep him, hold him here for a few minutes when for so long he had been no more than a memory. It was reckless, she knew, but she couldn't help it.

He had some things he needed to do.

Why are you here?

A pause before the reply. *I need your help.*

His reply was steady, no tremor in his mental voice, as if this sudden meeting was something they'd done every week. His perpetual cool, calm exterior pervaded his tone – and nothing else. It was easy to imagine him sitting behind her, hands folded casually as though this were horribly normal.

He needed her help?

I don't want to do this to you, but nobody else will do.

Jenn blinked, keeping her gaze on the trium above, forcing herself to obey the rigid strictures she'd adhered to for six years. He needed her help. That was all. *What do you want me to do?*

Get me back into the Enclave.

Why?

For a few seconds, she could almost hear him thinking, considering his reply, but when it came, some sinking part of her wasn't surprised at all.

How could she have been so . . . naïve?

I can't explain. I just need to get back into the Enclave as soon as possible.

Jenn took in a deep breath. He wouldn't tell her. He would expect her to take the risk but he wouldn't explain why. So typical of him.

From out of nowhere, her anger flared. *Are you mad?* Take him back to the Enclave? Did he have any idea how closely she was watched? If Robert was discovered anywhere near Clonnet, she would be immediately implicated. Her marriage to Eachern would not protect her a second time – and Andrew . . . by the gods, Andrew would be the one to suffer. She couldn't afford this cause any more. She simply couldn't. *You have to get away from here. Now!*

Get away and leave her with the memory. The reality was much too . . .

Please, just listen for a moment. I know you're angry but this is important.

I sincerely hope it is, because if you've risked my life and my son for something trivial, I'll turn you in to the Guilde myself!

There was a moment of silence but then his voice came back, strong and determined. *I can't get into the Enclave without you. If you can just get away from Clonnet for a couple of weeks, I can get you to the Enclave and back without anyone noticing. The risk would be minimal.*

I don't care. I can't do it! Jenn snapped back. Did he think she was a fool to be duped twice? Oh, but she was, she was such a fool. *I have a son to think of . . .* she pushed straight through the hesitation . . . *and I'm not about to risk everything I've worked so hard for simply because you need me for this – especially when you won't even explain why. You'll have to find another solution, Robert because I can't help you and I won't.*

I understand. There was disappointment in his voice, but no real surprise. If anything, that only made it worse.

No, you don't. How could he? He'd been the one to give her the lifeline and now, uncaringly, he had taken it away. He didn't love her – he just needed her to help without even explaining why. *Leave me alone, Robert. Don't come back here again.*

She stood then, absently made the sign of the trium and turned for the door. She tried not to, but she had no power over her eyes. They had a will of their own and found Robert sitting where he'd said, four rows behind her, heavily disguised as an old man. He was watching her steadily and, for a moment, she caught a glimpse of that sea-green gaze before her feet took her away.

Nothing. Nothing but regret in his eyes.

The church door banged shut with a finality which rang around the stone walls and clattered against the windows, dull and solid. A murmur, a rustle from the locals quietly praying gave Robert a few moments to compose himself, huddle down in his robes and bury everything raw inside his disguise. He didn't get up and leave, didn't even send his Senses out of the building to follow her, trace her journey back to Clonnet.

All in all, it would have been best if he'd never fallen in love with her. She might have been spared all this, and the ache that filled him now might have been abated. And though every part of him had wanted so much to just reach out and touch her, he had, as he'd done through every year since they'd parted, kept his soul hidden. It would do neither of them any good.

Could he trust her, afford to tell her the reasons for his trip to the Enclave?

No. Not yet. Not until he could be sure; too many lives depended on it.

As silence prevailed once more, he lifted his gaze to the rows of candles before the altar. Tiny flickering globes of yellow against a grey backdrop, voices of faith surrounded by impenetrable stone. So much faith and so little hope. How could one co-exist so innocently with the other?

And what if you had only hope, but no faith? Would lighting a candle awaken the gods then?

A shadow passed over the window, enhancing the gloom within the poor chapel. It would be dark soon – and it would rain. He had to move or McCauly would start to worry, pace up and down in the forest clearing, jumping at every little noise in the darkness. The Bishop was a brave man, but he wore his courage uneasily, as though afraid it would desert him at the first sign of real trouble.

Robert let out a deep breath, easing the tightness in his shoulders. He came to his feet, his eyes on the trium above the altar. Slowly and precisely, he moved his hand from shoulder to forehead and back to his other shoulder. Then, his shuffled gait carefully in tune with his mood, he turned into the aisle and headed for the door.

Rolls of thunder bellowed from the east to crash against the copse without mercy. Rain splattered on the leafy ground, forming puddles and rivulets running towards the fern-choked stream. If Aiden McCauly could have peered further into the gloom, he would have seen only more of the same. But he didn't try. Instead, he kept to a corner of his little shelter, as far from the wind as possible, attempting to shrink his body inside his clothes. Even so, the rain got him, pelting his legs, forcing his boots to sink deep into fresh mud. Behind him, tied to the oak tree, the horses stood in the downpour, their heads hung as if in shame.

Aiden was deaf to the movement in the copse until he saw the shape come towards him out of the darkness. The disguise was gone now as Robert strode forward, cloak slapping wet against his thighs, hair drenched and matted against his head. He stopped before the shelter without actually coming inside. Even in the darkness, Aiden could see the smile on his face.

'I'm back.'

'So I see,' Aiden replied, keeping staunchly to his corner. 'How did it go?'

'Fine, fine. A bit damp but otherwise, fine.'

'She said yes?'

'No.' Robert frowned a little, raising a hand towards the collection of branches and twigs Aiden had constructed when he'd seen the clouds forming beyond the town. 'What's this?'

Aiden drew himself up. 'I made a shelter.'

'Under a tree? In a thunderstorm?'

'What's wrong with that?'

With a chuckle, Robert ducked inside and clapped a hand to Aiden's shoulder. 'Lightning has a bad habit of seeking out nice tall things sticking up from the ground. Believe me, if this lovely oak gets hit, you don't want to be standing underneath. Come on, there're better places we can shelter in tonight.'

Aiden looked around, but the night had come full down and the woods gave no sign of what he was seeking. 'But we can't leave just yet.'

'Why?'

'Because . . . '

'It's all right, Father,' came a voice from behind the tree. 'I'm here.'

Robert turned. 'Grant? What, in Serin's name are you doing here?'

The horses stamped their feet as Grant Kavanagh, Duke of Flan'har, rode up to the shelter and swung down with a splash of mud. He was a big man, both tall and wide, with a hearty laugh to match, not to mention a rather ribald sense of humour. His voice was deep and rich, emerging from a thatch of red beard falling to his chest. He pushed his cloak hood back, glanced warily at the shelter roof and stepped under.

'I thought you were on your way back to Bleakstone,' Grant began, pulling his gloves off, finger by finger. 'Was it wise to leave the poor Bishop here alone while you were off gallivanting in town?'

'And you said you were spending the entire winter in Flan'har. If you keep running off like this, your subjects are going to start missing you.'

'I know,' Grant grinned, his teeth flashing in the almost-invisible moonlight. 'But we all have our burdens to bear.'

'So, what are you doing here – apart from getting wet, that is?'

The Duke chuckled and opened his cloak. He reached inside and drew out a slim leather pouch. He handed it to Robert. 'I was on my way back from the west. I stopped in to see Micah in Dromna. He's well settled in. He asked me to give you this. He said he would meet you as arranged.'

Aiden stared at the pouch as Robert made no move to take it. 'A message? From Micah?'

'That's right,' Grant nodded. 'Here, do you want it?'

'No! I . . . ' Aiden glanced quickly at Robert. The calm easy humour had vanished completely. Instead, his eyes glittered with an inner light. Slowly, he reached out and took the pouch, opening it with a short gesture.

With his mouth set in a line, he took out the paper. It crackled dry in his hand as he unfolded it and began to read. Aiden held his breath, all thoughts of his wet feet abruptly drying up.

After a moment, Robert hissed, crunched the paper in his hand. He tossed it into the air – and it suddenly burst into flame. It was little more than a blackened remnant by the time it landed in the mud. Without a word, Robert turned away.

Another groan of thunder echoed around the copse as Aiden waited. He couldn't ask – but he didn't need to.

'It appears that, despite all your prayers, Bishop,' Robert said slowly, his voice low under the rain, 'I was right after all.'

'Sweet Mineah!'

Grant frowned. 'What? You mean that's it? I was carrying *that* and Micah never said a word?'

'Of course he wouldn't,' Aiden murmured, his attention staying on Robert. 'What are you going to do?'

'What do you mean, what is he going to do?' Grant demanded. 'It's obvious, isn't it? Serin's balls, haven't we just spent the last year planning, just in case? He doesn't have a choice any more.'

'There are always choices.'

'I'm sorry, Father, but that's pig's swill! Robert knows I'm right. Just look at him. Do you think he'd be standing there like one of those black storm clouds if this was just any old day?'

Robert turned at that, his gaze steady, but warmed with a gentle humour around his eyes. 'Will you stop the night with us? The Bishop makes a fine lamb stew.'

'Here in the forest? Are you joking?' Grant switched from one mood to another without pause. 'I'm a wealthy Duke with a fine independent nation to my name – not an outlaw with a price on my head, like some people I could mention. I'm not accustomed to skulking around in muddy woods for the fun of it.'

At that, Robert smiled. 'So you're on your way back to town.'

'Damned right I am!' Grant laughed heartily, swinging the reins in his hand. 'I'm off to find myself a hot meal, a warm bed – and perhaps someone warm to share it with.'

'Your Grace!' Aiden gasped. 'You're a married man!'

Grant backed out of the shelter, his hands raised in apology. 'Sorry, Father, just a little joke. Robert will explain it to you after I'm gone. I'll see you in Flan'har when you get there. Try to keep out of trouble, will you?'

He was on his horse and riding away before Aiden could say another word.

'He's hard to resist, isn't he?' Robert murmured at Aiden's side.

'Perhaps, but I just hope the ladies of Jardye don't think the same.'

Robert chuckled and picked up the saddle bags. He swung them over his shoulder, untied the horses and led Aiden out into the rain.

'So, what are you going to do?'

Robert strode ahead, aiming for a dark patch within a thicket of bush, barely tall enough for him to stand under. He stopped and dumped the bags, tying the horses under the natural shelter. Without glancing at Aiden, he dragged together dead logs lying on the ground, ready for a fire. 'We've talked about this, you and I, over the last five years. Preparations, couriers – all to one purpose. And now you ask me what I'm going to do. What do you think I'm going to do?'

'I don't want to say it.'

Robert came to a halt with a saddlebag in his hand. He laughed softly. 'I've always said we're as bad as one another. I still wonder what would have happened to us if Selar hadn't thrown you in prison the moment you were elected Bishop.'

'Well,' Aiden murmured, unable to look away, 'if McGlashen and Payne hadn't rescued me, I'd probably be dead by now. I don't know where that would have left you.'

Now Robert smiled properly and knelt to light the fire with a wave of one hand. 'A screaming lunatic – or long in my grave. Take your pick. Come on, let's eat. I'm hungry.'

Aiden crouched down before the fire and took the cooking things as Robert handed them to him. Somehow, now the moment had passed, it didn't seem quite so bad to think about. 'So – we go to Elita tomorrow after all?'

'I don't see that we have much choice. My letters to Tirone have gone unheeded, your attempts to find some dialogue with Brome have failed. We've spent the last three years trying to avoid this, but now we just have to take the plunge – and Elita is the first, necessary step. After that? Well, I'll just have to find some other way into the Enclave without blowing the gate up. I can't see that would win me too many friends, can you?'

Aiden glanced up, but there was more to Robert's humour than he was giving away. He knew he shouldn't, but he just had to ask. 'Was she angry?'

Robert's façade was unchanged. 'I've told you before, Bishop. I will not talk about Jenn – not even to you.' With that, he turned away and busied himself unsaddling the horses.

Aiden turned his attention to preparing a meal. As he balanced a pot on the fire, he sighed and said, 'I tell you one thing.'

'What's that?'

'I'd be more impressed with this sorcery of yours if you could do something about the damned weather!'

Robert clapped a hand on his shoulder and chuckled. 'You and me both, Bishop. You and me both.'

The fire crackled and spat, but Jenn paid no attention. She just kept pacing up and down on the soft carpet in her room, unable to keep still for even a moment. She should have been getting dressed for dinner, but she couldn't even begin to think about it yet. All she could see was that glimpse of Robert, the face buried beneath the beard, the alert eyes above. The presence of regret, the absence of anything else.

He'd expected her to refuse – so why had he asked in the first place? Why did he need to get back into the Enclave? Why wouldn't he tell her? And she was supposed to help because . . . because he asked? Because the damned Key had told him it would not let him through the gate unless she was there.

Gritting her teeth, she shut her eyes, tried to shut out the questions going around and around in her mind. There'd been too much of that in the early days, after her arrest.

No. She was being both childish and unfair. Even if Robert wouldn't tell her his reasons, he was sure to have some – and, no doubt, powerful reasons at that. But . . . she was no longer free to help him and he should know that. She had a duty to protect their son – no, *her* son. Robert had other people who could help him – Andrew had only her.

No, her anger and disappointment aside, she'd made the right decision. She was sure of it.

Wasn't she?

The door behind her opened, but her Senses had already warned her it was only Father John.

'Are you not going down for supper?'

'No.' Jenn opened her eyes and resumed her pacing. 'I mean, yes. In a moment.'

John stood close, reached out a hand to her arm. 'Is anything wrong?'

She paused, glanced at him, then turned away. Inside, everything was breaking apart and she didn't know how to stop it.

'Jenn?'

'I . . . ' the words stuck in her throat but she had to continue. John deserved to know the truth. 'I saw Robert in town.'

She turned around then, but John showed no shock, just a subtle paleness around his eyes. 'He spoke to me in the church – silently, of course. He wanted me to help him get back into the Enclave.'

'Oh.' The gentlest of men, John made no further response.

'Of course I refused,' Jenn continued quickly. 'What else could I say?'

'What else indeed? Was he alone?'

Jenn turned away, fidgeting with the embroidery she'd left on the table. 'He said McCauly was with him.'

'Are you going to mindspeak Finnlay?'

'I don't think I can. It's too far. You can send one of your messages, can't you?'

'Of course I can send a message. It's a pity only the three of you have the gift of mindspeech – and that Robert can't contact Finnlay directly.'

There was a knock at the door, but before Jenn could respond, it banged open and a small, black-haired creature flew across the room to dive at her skirts.

'Mother, Mother save me! The monster is after me!'

Jenn knelt down to put her arms around the boy. Andrew lifted his head to look at her with eyes of mischievous blue. There was no monster. This was merely Andrew's favourite ploy to get her attention when he was tired of waiting to see her. She was gradually weaning him out of it, but at this moment, it became a convenient escape for her as well.

She kissed him and lifted him off the ground. He was already too heavy for her to do this easily, but she persisted. 'Have you finished your lessons?'

Andrew's expressive eyes grew serious and he glanced at John warily. 'Not yet.'

'Well, you know your Uncle Lawrence will be here in a few days. You know how he loves to talk about history. What will you do if you don't have the right answers?'

Andrew raised his eyebrows – in exactly the same way Robert did – making her heart sink. 'I'll make something up.'

'No, you won't!'

Andrew squirmed and began to giggle and Jenn couldn't help smiling. She put him down, but kept hold of his hand. She turned her attention back to John. Without prompting she said, 'You think I was wrong to refuse?'

John shook his head, but his face gave nothing away. 'It's your decision, your risk. I understand.'

'But you still think it was wrong.'

John turned for the door. 'Send Andrew to me before you go down for supper and we'll get those lessons finished.'

Nash helped himself to more wine, filling the silver goblet to the brim before leaning forward to take a sip. The table was laid out ready for the meal. Eachern was already seated and complaining about something or other. Over the years, Nash had grown practised at appearing to listen without ever actually having to.

How was it that he could manage to be in the same building as her and still keep this carefully detached distance from her, when the knot of anticipation ground against his insides every moment she was near? Even now, as he waited for her to appear, he did so with exquisite patience, savouring each moment as it passed.

The door opened and the object of his adoration entered the room, dressed in a gown of exquisite crimson which made her cheeks glow, her hair shine and her eyes sparkle. She smiled at him and his stomach did a somersault.

Blood and fire – how much longer was he to moon over her like some farm boy?

'Good evening, gentlemen,' Jennifer took her seat between them at the small table. The dining room was kept heated throughout the winter and used for just these occasions. Fine hangings kept out the draft while a tidy fire crackled in a hearth between the diamond-paned windows. As the first course was brought out, Jennifer continued, 'Are you to stay tomorrow and go hawking after all, Governor?'

'He can't,' Eachern grunted. 'The birds are sick. Damned hawker hasn't kept them out of the cold so he'll have to wait till next time.'

Jennifer raised her eyebrows but refrained from expressing any disappointment. Instead, she changed the subject. 'When I was at the market today, I saw a ship in the port of a type I'd not seen before.'

'Do you know where it was from?'

'I had to ask. It was a galley from Esteria.'

Nash nodded and picked up his cup. 'They don't come through here very often. I understand they have a mortal fear of pirates.'

'I don't blame them,' Eachern growled, keeping the majority of his attention on his food. 'We've lost six ships in the last year alone.'

'A galley from Esteria,' Nash observed, 'would be carrying carpets, I should imagine. I swear that country does little else but breed sheep and weave rugs. They don't have much else to export – nor to show for so many years as a civilised nation.'

'Have you ever been there?' Jennifer asked, steering the conversation skilfully away from her husband.

'Several times, mostly on Guilde business. We don't have many Halls in Esteria, though we've tried hard over the centuries to develop our interests there.'

'You mean, you've tried hard to take over the carpet industry,' Jennifer replied without hesitation.

Nash smiled in defeat. 'I was trying to be diplomatic. However, as usual, you see right through me. Yes, we would like a greater control over the carpet industry, but you might be comforted to know that there seems no likelihood of that happening in the next few decades.'

'Why is that?'

'Because almost every man in the country knows how to make a carpet of some sort. The whole skill is so ingrained within their culture I doubt we'd ever be able to formalise the training regime, nor ever be able to document the process properly. You know their religion forbids such a thing?'

'Really? I thought they had the same religion as Lusara. Don't they worship the same three gods?'

Nash shook his head as the next course was placed before him. 'You could almost say they don't actually worship any gods at all. They practise the Nasforantel religion, which is more a worship of the land itself. It's one of the most ancient religions in the world. They have their followers here in Lusara, as well as just about every other country both north and south of the Gulf. Every century or so our Tria Church tries to stamp it out, claiming it borders on the worship of magic idols and such, but to be honest, it's basically harmless. It has little formal structure, but many festivals throughout the year. Nobody really takes it seriously because one of its main tenets is to preach peace and harmony. No real threat, you see?'

'That's a very pragmatic attitude.'

'Life has taught me to be pragmatic – especially over the last few years. The older I get, the easier I find it to be tolerant.' Nash smiled at the end of this. Sometimes, the rubbish he found himself saying almost made him gag. Pragmatic? Tolerant? Hah!

But Jennifer was intrigued – even if Eachern was so bored he was gazing into the distance, chewing meat like a cow.

'Do you know any more about this Nasforantel? I mean, if the religion has so little structure, how can it be forbidden to document the process of cloth and carpet making?'

'I don't claim to understand it,' Nash replied with a shrug. 'I've really only read about it – and seen a little with my own eyes. Don't be fooled, though. There are stranger religions in our world. There's Safailanlani, whose followers worship no less than one hundred and twenty-seven gods. Each receives three days of worship every year. At the other end of the scale, I once read about a people who believed in only one god.'

'One? Was it good or evil?'

Nash burst out laughing. 'I've no idea. The culture was one of the most ancient on record, but it's probably extinct by now. They used to live on the Alusian peninsula, but there's been no record of them for over five hundred years. I've no doubt they were probably annihilated during the battle between the Empire and the sorcerers.'

'And good riddance to them,' Eachern added, probably to prove he was actually paying attention. 'I've heard,' he leaned forward abruptly, spreading his wine-drenched breath across the table, 'that the Empire kept a spy in every major household. How would you like that, Governor? Having someone reporting your every move to the King?'

Nash did smile then, though the poor man would never know why. Nash couldn't have cared less if Selar did know what he was up to – but what would Eachern say if he knew Nash's spies had been in this castle for the last five years? Still, a little prodding could be fun. 'How do you know Selar doesn't already practice such a thing?'

Eachern screwed up his face in disdain. 'My men are loyal to me and me only!'

Jennifer raised her eyebrows at this and threw Nash an apologetic glance. She then changed the subject artfully, with her usual grace. She had matured since the birth of her son. She was still only twenty-five, but there was, around her eyes, a shadow of something. What was it? Did she still mourn the loss of her father? Her freedom?

Yes, there was still a lot of independence in those deep blue eyes. An independence he couldn't afford to let her keep.

Three weeks.

That's when he would do it. He'd waited all this time because of the injuries the damned Enemy had left him with. He couldn't attempt Bonding with her until he was at full strength, full fitness. Only that way could he ensure it was complete and permanent.

But some time in the next three weeks, he would get hold of some fine innocent sorcerer and finally heal the last of his wounds. He could find some excuse to get Eachern away, and then he would have her all to himself.

He would finally Bond with her – and then there would be nothing left to stop him.

When the meal ended, Nash rose and excused himself, pleading fatigue. He brushed past Eachern's shoulder, leaving a silent message as he passed.

You will push her until she turns to me and me alone.

This Bonding *will* work – he would make sure of it.

Once Nash left the table, Jenn knew she would have to wait some time before she could get to her own bed. Eachern never seemed to want to be alone with her, yet there were times when he insisted she not leave his sight. Unfortunately, she could never tell which was which until she got up to go. This night however, he gave her a clue.

'You have been very sweet to our Governor Nash, my lady.'

Jenn swallowed. There was something in the tone which made her very nervous. Did he suspect Nash's feelings for her? 'Of course, my lord. He is an honoured guest in this house, is he not?'

Eachern drained his wine cup and immediately refilled it. He turned his gaze on her, a mixture of contempt and fear . . . and something else.

Jenn began to push her chair back, ready to leave the table, but his hand reached out and held hers down on the table edge.

'You move too hastily, wife. I have matters to discuss with you. Matters to do with my son.'

At this, Jenn paused. For some reason, an image of Robert flashed before her eyes, not as she had seen him that day in the church, but as he'd said goodbye at Elita.

'He's five years old now and will be six this summer,' Eachern continued, letting go her hand, but keeping his eyes firmly fixed on her. 'I think it's time the boy left us to begin his real schooling.'

A blush of panic pushed Jenn's heart into her mouth. 'Left us?'

'Why not? It's customary. This is how all boys receive their education. Your priest has taught him to read and write, some of our history – but he has much more to learn than these womanish things. I have arranged for him to go to Meir. He'll leave at the end of next month. I expect you to have him prepared.'

'But so soon? Couldn't it wait until after his birthday?' She knew she was whining, but to use stronger language would sound like a challenge – and Eachern hated her to challenge him.

'He will go when I say, wife!' Eachern stood and leaned over the table. 'Are you arguing with me?'

Jenn had come to her feet as well. She knew she should stay quiet, but this was Andrew's future . . . and Meir was so far away . . . She would never see him again. And when . . . and when he developed his powers, he would be helpless and completely alone.

'I beg you, my lord, don't send our son so far from here.' Unthinking, Jenn reached out for Eachern's hand. Immediately he grabbed hold of her so hard that she thought he would snap her wrist in two.

'How dare you!' Eachern pulled her close, bending her over backwards. His breath burned her face and too late she cursed her rashness. Words came to her to soothe him, to protect herself, but it was useless. His hand held hers like a vice and she couldn't break free of him. He pushed her away and with his free hand swung wide, belting the side of her face with such force her legs buckled beneath her. She crumpled to the ground and didn't move.

He wasn't fooled. He dragged her up and hit her again in the same place. This time she staggered back and fell hard on a chair by the wall.

'Get up!' Eachern bellowed.

When she didn't move immediately, he kicked her. Then he grabbed both her wrists and hauled her out of the dining room and into the hall. Jenn could hardly breathe; her legs didn't work properly. She struggled to walk, but she kept stumbling on her dress as Eachern dragged her behind him. She feared what would happen next.

Gaining some stability, Jenn tried to pull back on her hand, tried to get free. If she could get some help . . . Perhaps if she cried out, Nash would come . . .

Eachern whipped around and his fist impacted in her stomach, completely winding her. For long moments she was dragged along behind him, unable to draw any air at all. When she could breathe again, he was hauling her up the stairs, muttering senseless words.

'Teach a lesson. My wife, must obey me . . . No more defiance, wife. No more.'

Defiance? By the gods, if only she could dare to defy him, if she could risk it and use her powers to stop him – but he would kill her for it. He hated and feared sorcery and if he ever found out . . .

But she did have one more breath of defiance in her body. As she reached the top of the stairs, she grabbed hold of the rail and didn't let go. Eachern stopped and gazed at her with amazement, his eyes wild like a madman. Jenn held back a wave of nausea and kept her grip.

In response, Eachern dug his fingers into her wrist, laughed at her, then pushed. The sudden change in momentum caught her off guard. Her hand slipped from the railing and she tumbled backwards, down and down, until she came to a stop at the bottom.

Strangely, all the pain had gone away.

And then so did the light . . .

John held the door open as Addie slipped through with the last bowl of water. Like the others, it was covered with a cloth. There was no one in the gallery and Addie reached the other end without being seen. John closed the door and went back across the room, pausing to stir up the fire and put another log on. After that, he went to the window and pulled the curtain aside, allowing sharp sunlight to pool along the floor. Then he pushed the window open and a slice of morning air sparkled in the sunshine before invading the rest of the room.

He turned and watched the figure lying unconscious in bed. Jenn hadn't woken once and now he was beginning to worry. Apart from the two marks on her face, she had a very nasty cut on her head, beneath her hair, and a host of other bruises. If only he had Healer's Sight, he could tell how bad they were. How long would it be before the Duke asked after his wife? What would John say? Come and see for yourself, Your Grace, how you almost killed her . . .

By the gods, she was a mess – though, he supposed, not as bad as she could have been. Even so, he'd tried to avert his eyes as Addie had cleaned her up, but he'd seen enough; the faint scars from at least one other beating.

How had this happened without his knowing?

He heard a moan and moved forward to the edge of the bed.

'Jenn?'

'What . . . ' Hoarse and indistinct, Jenn's voice faded into nothing. Then abruptly, she sat up, her eyes wide open. 'Andrew!'

John held her shoulders, forced her to look at him. 'Andrew is with his nurse. He's fine. I just checked on him.'

For a moment, her eyes still held a glaze of panic, then gradually her breathing steadied, her shoulders relaxed and she slumped back onto the bed. She reached up a hand to rub over her face, then gasped in agony.

'Do you remember what happened?' John asked quietly.

'No.'

John shook his head. 'I can make your apologies to Governor Nash when he asks why you're not around to bid him farewell. He leaves in less than an hour.'

'Thank you.'

'Is that all you can say?' John snapped, then sucked in a breath. It was not his place to go losing his temper. He began again, 'How many times has he beaten you?'

She said nothing.

'Jenn? Answer me. How many times has this happened? Why have you been hiding this from me?'

Jenn finally opened her eyes and pushed herself up in bed again, pulling the covers together. 'I remember tripping on my gown. I must have fallen down the stairs. I was lucky . . . '

'Tell me the truth,' John whispered.

For a moment, she said nothing, but then a huge sigh escaped her and her voice emerged, roughened by reality. 'What would you have me do, Father? Yes, he's beaten me before, twice. How am I to stop him? I am his wife. There is no law that says he can't—'

'There is the law of the gods!'

'And he's *such* a pious man, John!' Jenn closed her mouth abruptly, eased air back into her and shook her head in apology. 'He . . . I . . . can't Seal him without his consent and he'd never give it. If I use my powers to stop his violence, he'd kill me at the first opportunity. If he thought the mother of his son was a sorcerer . . . '

John closed his eyes and nodded. She was right, she had no

choice. All he could do was to stand by her and hope there were enough pieces to patch together after the next beating.

'Why did you call for Andrew?'

'Did I?' A frown washed across her face, then cleared. She grabbed John's hand. 'Eachern. He's sending Andrew away. In a month. To Meir. It's on the other side of the country! I'll never see him again.'

'Jenn, you knew this was going to come one day,' John began gently. 'Of course you'll see him . . . '

'No!' Jenn snapped, gripping his hands tight. 'You don't understand! That can't happen to Andrew. He's not . . . He can't . . . '

'What?'

Jenn's mouth moved, but no sound came out. Slowly she calmed. 'Andrew will be a sorcerer.'

'But I've Sensed no power in him. He's five; it should be detectable by now – if there is any ability at all. He's too young to be able to shield.'

Jenn shook her head. 'He can shield. I can Sense it.'

'Because you're his mother?'

'Yes, because I'm his mother.'

'But this goes against every principle we know about sorcery.'

Jenn took his hands and held them up before his eyes. 'And haven't I? When I first went to the Enclave, Henry told me I was unique, unusual. They'd never seen a power like mine before. Doesn't it stand to reason then that my child might also be different?'

John let go her hands. He got off the bed and silently pulled the window closed. Another raking of the fire and some warmth began to edge around the room again. Addie returned with a tray of food for Jenn, then disappeared to get some for John. As the door closed behind her, John finally turned his gaze back on Jenn.

'You know what you have to do, then?'

Her eyes glistened with what could have been tears, but the steely determination in the rest of her face told the real story. 'Will you watch the door while I call him? I was never good at holding a Warning while mindspeaking.'

Robert was saddling his horse when he heard her voice out of the still forest. Not soft and gentle as he remembered it, but short and curt.

Are you still close by?

Jenn? Why, how far do you think you can call?

I don't have time for this, Robert.

How close do you want me to be?

Close enough to meet me at Maitland in a week. Can you manage that?

I suppose so – but why would I want to?

Because I've changed my mind. I'll meet you in the woods south of the house an hour after sunset.

And then she was gone, as quickly as she'd come.

4

The wetlands of eastern Lusara lay enfolded in late winter snow like a down mattress, all lumpy and soft. The cold did its worst just before dawn, making Aiden vent forth an unending stream of complaints about how he was too old to be playing this game and wasn't there somebody else who would do just as well. He tried not to – but it seemed to be the only way to keep warm. Of course, Robert's response was nothing more than laughter.

Robert had kept up a brisk pace, insisting they rise every morning before the sun made its first bleak appearance, stopping only when it was well dark and the horses were ready to drop from exhaustion. As usual, Robert chose roads which wound around the many small lakes, staying away from towns and villages. Aiden knew Robert was more concerned about a rebel Bishop being recognised than an outlaw. Truth was, if either of them were captured, mercy would be left far behind them. Not that mercy was exactly a common feature in Lusara these days.

They passed many people on the road, too many of them beggars, shifting from one part of the country to the other, searching for work or food or simply a place to shelter from the snow. Past them rode the wealthy merchants, lords and ladies, deliberately blinding themselves to the pain their profit was inflicting on those weaker than themselves. For a long time, the division between Lusarans and the immigrants from Mayenne had appeared almost invisible. Now the riches of the latter, the destitution of the former could be seen as plain as day. If ever a people looked conquered, it was these.

As they turned off the road towards Elita, Aiden began looking about at the land. He'd only seen this area once – and that was in summer, under the worst conditions possible.

Five years. It didn't seem that long. So much had happened and he'd been so busy he'd not noticed the time flying past. Five years ago he'd been in prison, wondering if his bones would lie in that damp hole for ever. Never for one moment, in two years' incarceration, had he thought his freedom would be tied to the man who rode beside him. A sorcerer.

Oblivious to his thoughts, Robert travelled in silence. As usual, his garments were black and with his cloak hood down, the shoulder-length hair fluttered around in the breeze, dark enough to almost blend into the cloth. Robert watched the horizon with eyes of deep forest green, his level eyebrows raised in gentle humour, his wide mouth set easily. Taller than most men, Robert could dominate a room simply with his broad-shouldered presence, the underlying hint of strength – and possibly danger – that graced his easy manner and confident smile.

If they'd never elected Aiden Bishop in the first place, would he still be a priest, living and working in Marsay, hoping this outlaw might come and strike down the usurper King? Or would his fear and horror of sorcery make him hate Robert Douglas, as so many others did?

'You look worried, Bishop,' Robert said evenly.

'No,' Aiden replied. 'More contemplative.'

'Oh dear.'

Aiden sniffed at the laughter in Robert's voice. 'Do you not wonder where the last five years have gone?'

'Almost six. And no, I don't. What's wrong? Missing Bleakstone?'

'A little.'

Robert glanced aside at him, an eyebrow raised in mock horror. 'I don't know, you priests are never satisfied. It's times like these I really miss having Micah as a travelling companion.'

'Ah,' Aiden raised a finger, 'but would he argue with you as I do?'

'Only when it suits him. He's got far more sense than to raise his hackles every time I open my mouth.' Robert grinned. 'He's been around me since he was six years old, Bishop. He knows what a contrary creature I am. You, I fear, need a little more practice.'

'May the gods forgive me,' Aiden added, keeping a straight face.

'And besides,' Robert added, 'what makes you think I enjoy listening to your arguments?'

Caught, Aiden opened his mouth to reply – then found Robert laughing at him. 'I hate you.'

'We all have our weaknesses. Mine is seeing that look on your face. Come on, the sun is almost set. We need to get a move on.'

Night came quickly as they moved into the mountains, bringing with it a cold that drenched Aiden right to his bones. Robert made no ceremonious pause on the ridge above Elita. Instead, they continued on into the crisp night, passing the wide flat lake encrusted with ice and snow. At one time, the beautiful castle of Elita had stood on the further shore, jutting out into the water. Now only an empty tower remained, the walls and everything else banished by the fire of Robert's power.

'This is the right night, isn't it?' Aiden asked quietly as his horse picked its way between shards of stone buried beneath the snow.

'Yes.'

Aiden glanced at him. There was enough moonlight to see Robert's face clearly as he made his way through ruins he had made himself. His eyebrows were drawn together in concentration as his gaze seemed to drift elsewhere, beyond the grey night. Was he thinking about the last time he'd been here? About Jenn?

'What is it?' Aiden asked as he brought his horse to a stop before the tower.

'They're here – though they've done a damn fine job keeping their tracks hidden.' Robert dismounted and stood for a moment on the step, his gaze lifting across the scattered rubble towards the lake.

Was he Seeking for any possible danger? It was impossible to guess. Very little of Robert's feelings ever surfaced in his expressions.

Yet still – even at this remove – there was something almost feral about Robert Douglas. Something untamed that five years living the life of an outlaw had done nothing to erase.

'It's clear. Nobody within a dozen leagues.' Robert nodded to Aiden. 'Let's go in.'

Aiden winced as the horses clattered into the empty hall. There were no signs of life. Aiden remembered this hall well. Earl Jacob had died here and Jenn's child had been born.

They left the horses and Robert led him down a passage and into darkness. There was a corner and some stairs, then another door. More stairs, deep underground, then Robert came to a halt before a door. Aiden held his breath and waited, straining to hear the soft sounds of voices beyond the stone wall.

After a moment, Robert pushed the door open, flooding them with light. Cries of shock, the slice of steel being drawn – and then a pause. Aiden squinted into the room. Bare walls shone slimy with damp, untouched by the ancient straw scattered on the floor. A table, some chairs and a brazier glowing red in the candlelight. There was Donal McGlashen, Duke of Ballochford, Everard Payne, Earl of Cannockburke, Godfrey and a dozen others, all turned towards the door, their faces ashen with surprise.

In the silence, Robert stepped inside. 'Well? Isn't anybody going to say hello?'

Godfrey was the first to move. He stepped forward, giving Robert a brief hug. Only then did he turn to Aiden, his long, lean face betraying a deep amazement that touched Aiden and made him smile. Godfrey went down on his knee to kiss the Bishop's ring Aiden should have been wearing, but Robert stopped him.

'I wouldn't do that if I were you.' He helped Godfrey to his feet, dropping his voice lower. 'And whatever you do, don't call him Bishop. He gets a little testy about it.'

'Oh, leave the poor man alone, Robert.' McCauly steered Godfrey away and turned to face the rest of the room. Nobody else had moved, but Payne's face gave away his delight.

'Of all the sights I thought I'd see here,' he murmured, failing to suppress a laugh, 'you two were not even in the counting!'

Robert bowed his head slightly. 'So pleased I can still offer some entertainment in my old age.'

The room became still again and Aiden glanced at each of the others, desperately trying to read their expressions. The other two priests appeared in a quandary – with both their rightful Bishop and a sorcerer in the same room together. He wanted to say something to warm the chill in the air, but he had to go carefully and gently. The thought did nothing to calm his nerves.

'Please, gentlemen, take your seats. We've come to talk, nothing more.'

It was enough. One by one the others sat until only McGlashen and Robert remained on their feet. There was a long history between these two. Years ago, when Robert had tried to work with Selar, both McGlashen and Payne had held seats on the council. Now both men had lost those seats, left behind because Selar no longer needed any of the old Lusaran Houses represented in his court. Fifteen years of toil had left Payne and McGlashen bereft of any real power to help their people and had brought them here, to this place, in secret – and now in fear of their lives.

McGlashen gazed across the empty cellar at Robert, the scowl on his face barely hiding the expectation in his eyes. With a lazy hand, he scratched his fingers through his black beard. 'What are you doing here?'

Robert moved towards the table. He took all of the others in his glance. 'Actually, I think the question you should be asking is what *you* are all doing here.'

He stopped before Father Chester. The priest watched Robert with undisguised wariness – and why not? Six years ago, Robert had buried himself in work at the man's abbey, under the name of Martin, never once letting on who he was, what he was doing there. He'd hardly spoken to anyone in the eight months he'd stayed, until Aiden had arrived and changed everything. Even then, Chester had remained ignorant of Martin's true identity.

'How are you, Father?' Robert continued warmly. 'Does St Germanus still flourish? How are Brother Damien and Archdeacon Hilderic?'

Chester swallowed, uncomfortable and suddenly angry. 'Why do you ask?'

'Because I remember your kindness,' Robert replied, 'even though you had no idea who I was, why I was there, why I kept

71

myself apart. You accepted me unquestioningly and gave shelter to a rebel Bishop, fully understanding the dangers.'

'I didn't understand I was harbouring a sorcerer.'

'But you weren't.'

Chester lifted his chin and frowned.

Robert continued, 'You took in a man in need of solitude, nothing more.' He held Chester's gaze until the priest looked away.

'St Germanus survives. Both Damien and Hilderic are well.'

'I'm glad,' Robert replied with sincerity.

McGlashen grunted, 'How did you find us? Did Godfrey tell you?'

'No. How I found you doesn't matter.' Robert paused and folded his hands together. His artless calm had more influence in that moment than any words he could have spoken. 'You are all rebels, meeting in secret in the hope of finding some way to crush Selar's hold on our beloved country. It heartens me to see there are still some of you prepared to take such a risk.'

When nobody responded, Robert continued, 'I know what you're all thinking. You're all asking yourselves: is it true? Is he really a sorcerer? Did he live a lie all those years we trusted him?'

There was a moment's pause, ended by Payne. 'Well, you can hardly blame us.'

'I don't. I'd feel betrayed if I were you.'

'But you're not answering the question,' McGlashen added.

'Are you sure you want me to?'

At that, Chester slammed his hand on the arm of his chair. 'But you still won't say why you're here!'

Robert turned slowly to face him. 'I have come to ask you for your help – and any others who would join you. To ask you to join me in a venture that could quite possibly endanger more than your lives. You've seen the evil in our land, of ignorance, apathy and abandonment, where our people are left to starve. But there is also another evil at its heart – far greater than you could possibly imagine. I can and will fight it alone if I must – but alone, I will lose. I need your help.'

'For what?' McGlashen murmured, immobile.

Robert's voice dropped to a whisper. 'To go to war.'

*

The questions were endless, but Robert was prepared. Ways and means of getting men over the border without Selar noticing. Supply lines and arms. Stores, fuel and ships, horses and carts. On and on it went, until his head was ready to spin off. Every now and then he would glance across at Aiden to find him deep in discussion with the other priests – and none too happy about it either. Oh well, that was his job, after all.

Aiden had thrived on the years spent as a rebel. His light brown hair showed little of his fifty-two years. Lines about his grey eyes were white with tanning and were often creased in a gentle smile. His priestly tonsure was gone and apart from the small trium peeking out from his jacket, there was little to mark him as a man of the gods. But that had never been on the outside. That had always come from within: a patience and wisdom seemingly born to him, an insight and feeling for the human soul, its many struggles and pains, an empathy so quiet as to be almost hushed. An extra-ordinary man living in extraordinary times – exactly what this cause needed.

Finally, after hours of argument and negotiation, Robert sat back and pushed the last sheet of paper towards McGlashen. He took the ale Payne handed him as some of the men prepared to leave.

'You know,' McGlashen began, his rough voice quiet, 'It's been so long, I never thought you'd actually do this.'

'Nor did I,' Robert agreed, sipping his ale.

'But with what you've told us,' Payne added, taking a seat beside him, 'I'm not exactly surprised. And I'll bet there's a whole lot more you're keeping to yourself.'

Robert looked up at both of them. 'I won't lie and say there isn't – but for the moment, it's safer that you don't know the whole story. Until you and your men are safely across the border and encamped at Bleakstone, you and this whole venture are at risk every day.'

'That's all right.' McGlashen raised a hand. 'I'm not sure I want to know – but I have to tell you, Robert,' he leaned forward, dropping his voice, 'I don't give a damn if you are a sorcerer. I'm sick of seeing my countrymen trodden underfoot as though they were nothing more than dirt – and sick of not being able to do anything about it. If you mean to carry this through, then I'd fight alongside you if you called down the fires of Broleoch on our heads!'

Robert met his gaze for a long moment. In the background, the voices of the priests intruded, soft words, urgent insistence. 'I wish there were more who thought like you, Donal, but the truth is, we can't ignore what I am. Trust me, if it was so easy to separate my . . . abilities from my actions, I would have done this long ago. But it's not just me. There is a whole country out there, terrified of something they know nothing about. And don't be fooled – sorcery *will* be brought to bear against us. For centuries, sorcery has been seen as the ultimate evil. I can't help thinking this war will only support that idea.'

McGlashen snorted and sat back again, lacing his fingers together. 'Then I say you know nothing of how the people view you. You know you've always been a hero, from the moment you took a seat on Selar's council, the wars you fought against the Sadlani in the north – and everything you did for them while you could.'

'But I left.'

'For the best of reasons.'

'And what good are my reasons when people are forced out of their homes, left to starve through one cold winter after another, while those responsible for their welfare are silent in their greed? How can I remain a hero when I, more than anyone else, understand the gravity of what I've done, what I haven't done?'

McGlashen shifted and glanced at Payne. The younger man shrugged and offered a smile. 'They sing songs about you, you know. Of course, they don't use your name. I don't know if anybody else would have got away with it – but you, you'd already proved yourself to them. If you were really going to do something evil, you had plenty of opportunity to do so at Selar's side.'

'If that's the case – then why are those priests so deep in conversation? I promise you, they're not discussing the weather. No, my friend, it doesn't matter which way you look at it: sorcery is anathema in Lusara. Just as I cannot separate myself from it, neither can our future be decided without it. I wish that were not the case, but I've had five years to count the cost of one single action and I know it's not a simple question that can be addressed by my leading this army.'

'Perhaps not.' McGlashen rose to his feet, gesturing at Payne to join him. 'On the other hand, you should never underestimate the power of legend. Farewell, Robert. I'm damned pleased to see you again. With any luck, by the time I get to Bleakstone, I'll have ten thousand men at my back.'

Robert chuckled and stood himself. 'I'd rather they were at your side.'

Payne laughed, but McGlashen looked puzzled for a moment – then raised an eyebrow to acknowledge the dig. 'Three months.'

'Three months. And you be careful.' Robert nodded and then they were gone.

It was long past midnight when McGlashen and Payne gained the ridge above Elita. They paused on the edge looking back at the view. The sky had cleared, leaving half a moon to shine down on the white land. Only now could the true level of devastation be seen.

'I came by here once, last summer,' Payne murmured. 'You know there's a local superstition about this place.'

'What's that?'

'That Earl Jacob's figure walks the tower every year on the anniversary of his death. He achieves in death the very thing he couldn't manage in life. It's quite sad, really.'

McGlashen said nothing to begin with. Then he reached forward and patted the neck of his horse. 'Is Robert serious?'

Payne didn't dare look at his companion. 'I believe so.'

'Can you do as he asks and still be ready to meet him in Flan'har? On time, with all your tasks accomplished?'

'I'll make sure of it.'

McGlashen frowned. 'And what about the sorcery? Did he do all this we see below us?'

'I think so.'

'Then why keep dancing around the truth? Does he not trust us?'

'Of course he trusts us. The evasion was for the benefit of the priests. Until they can reconcile the doctrinal conflict, he can't afford to admit the truth. I mean, how can they promise to follow him if they believe for certain that his path will lead them into the arms of Broleoch? That's why he risked bringing Bishop McCauly with him.'

'Doctrinal conflict be damned! McCauly has the right of it. Save the body in this life before you go worrying about the soul in the next.' McGlashen gathered his reins together and glanced once at the moon. 'It doesn't matter anyway.'

'Oh, why is that?'

'I'll still see Robert on the throne, sorcerer or not.'

Robert held Godfrey's horse as he mounted up. All the rest had gone now, leaving only the three of them standing before the keep. The snow was trampled, but Robert would cover it over before they left. No need to worry the village of Fenlock about strange goings-on at the ruin.

'And where are you off to next?' Godfrey settled himself, gathering his reins together. 'Back to Flan'har?'

'For the Bishop only,' Robert said. 'I have other things I must do before I return to Bleakstone. Listen, are you certain about this Bresail? That it works?'

'Positive.'

'But you have no idea how he knew how to make one?'

'I can't imagine anybody telling him – so I suppose he must have found it written down somewhere.'

'I suppose so.'

Godfrey tilted his head. 'Promise me you'll be careful.'

'Oh, I'm always careful,' Robert laughed. 'And you're comfortable with the courier arrangements? This is going to be far more dangerous for you than me. I wish we didn't need you so much. McCauly would love you to keep him company at Bleakstone. He hates the place.'

'I do not!' McCauly asserted from the door. 'I tell you, Godfrey, that man does nothing but spread malicious gossip about me whenever he can!'

Robert glanced up to find a twinkle in Godfrey's eyes. He reached up and slapped the horse's neck. 'You be careful at court, my friend. You're all alone now. Stay out of trouble.'

Godfrey nodded a mock bow. 'As you wish – but only because I want to hear more of this gossip one day.'

With that, he turned his horse and vanished around the corner of the keep.

Robert glanced at McCauly. 'Would you mind waiting here?'

'Why?'

'There's something I have to do.'

McCauly settled back onto his stone seat and waved him permission. Robert turned inside the keep and headed for the stairs, bounding up without pausing. He only slowed when he reached the last flight, the steps that took him out onto the roof. There he stopped, bathed in glowing blue from the winter's half-moon above.

It was done. The army was called, long-laid plans now put in motion. Now . . . now he could remember.

Five years ago. Midsummer. The castle surrounded by Malachi in Guilde uniform, the pounding on the gate, breaking it down, Jacob's death, the lives at stake, Jenn . . . having the son that wasn't his . . . the demon and the power building up in his body, the burning desire to use it, the inability to even think about controlling it . . .

It wouldn't work. Sure, he could see himself doing it, using the Word of Destruction – but to vividly re-live how it *felt* was completely beyond him.

Well, perhaps it was best not to remember that part of it. Stay right away from all thoughts of the demon inside working away at his frustration, failure and feeding on buried anger. The Word had once given the demon power, but these days it took what it could, whenever it suited. Every day he remained in control was another victory.

No. Stay away from that indeed.

But if not to think about that, then why come up here? Alone, in the silence?

Ah, this feigned innocence was so charming and so seductive. How many hours had he spent deliberately refusing to understand?

Of course, there was always an excuse. A perfectly good one. Valid in all its complexities. The Key and the prophecy it had given to him alone.

By your very means, Enemy, that born unto your hands alone, you will be the instrument of ruin. In the act of salvation, you will become desolation itself, destroying that which you love most.

What was life like for those who were not born with such a curse? Could they live their lives without the canker of rot pervading everything they did? Could they work, sleep, fight and love as they chose?

Five long years – no, more than that. Twenty years. And still, finally, he had no other option but to go to war. All the efforts of the past to avoid tearing this country apart had been in vain. Would the prophecy, in the end, come true – simply because he had failed to find another way?

He should have done something before.

'I really wish you'd talk about it.'

Robert whirled around to find Aiden standing behind him, his face half in shadow, his hands clasped together. Robert hadn't even Sensed him coming up the stairs.

'I mean,' the priest continued quietly, gently, 'you need to be certain about this. It's not too late to stop it – but in a day or so there'll be no going back. Those men will be committing themselves. I don't want you to assure *me* – I want you to be sure for *yourself*. You have to believe in it, or none of us will.'

With a sigh, Robert sat on the low stone wall encircling the roof. 'Even I have my doubts sometimes. I'm not perfect, Aiden.'

'Then why do you keep thinking you should be?'

'Because I must be, or this whole thing will fail.'

'It won't fail as long as you believe.'

'Your optimism is entirely unfounded.' Robert gave a dry chuckle. 'You have no evidence to prove such a preposterous statement.'

'And still – I believe it to be true.'

'Which is why you became a priest and I didn't.'

Aiden was silent as he moved a little closer. 'I know you can't help the way you feel, Robert, but really, things might not be as bad as you assume. Jenn might not hate you after all.'

Robert came quickly to his feet. 'I told you . . . '

'You've never treated me like an idiot, Robert, so don't start now. I'm not blind.'

For a long moment, Robert held his gaze, then slowly turned to look out over the still lake, a flat sheen of grey in the night. Trees lined the western bank, white ghosts standing guard. He sat slowly and when he spoke, his voice grated against his calm, awakening memories he wished he could forget. 'Five years ago, when I left

Elita, she had a new-born baby and a husband to return to. She wouldn't have come with me.'

'You didn't ask her to.'

Robert didn't move. 'I couldn't. You know why.'

'But still you wanted to.'

'Did I?' Robert whispered, peering into the night, trying to conjure up the image of her face as he'd seen her that night, in the mill. The night when he'd given in to the Bonding and taken the first step of the prophecy. Everything he'd done since had been born in that moment. And all because he couldn't convince himself that his feelings were not entirely the product of the Bonding alone. She'd trusted him – and he'd betrayed her. Was that how all people expressed their love?

'It's been five years, my boy,' Aiden continued softly. 'You know it was the right choice to leave her behind, no matter what's happened since. Jenn never blamed you for the Bonding. I just wish that you could forgive yourself.'

Too many mistakes. Too many assumptions. Whichever way he turned, he would still have to face the Angel of Darkness, unprepared, with the demon biting at his heals to be let loose.

And never once had she told him she loved him.

'She was angry.'

'Of course,' Aiden took a seat beside him.

'She warned me she'd turn me into the Guilde if I ever went back to Clonnet.'

'She'd never do such a thing!'

'Are you sure?' Robert turned to face him. 'I mean, if you've got any doubts, speak them now. Once I leave here, there'll be no turning back.'

Aiden blew out air noisily, then composed himself once more. Carefully, he put a hand on Robert's shoulder. 'You haven't talked to her yet. You don't know what's really been going on. Although I can't fault your logic, you might still be wrong about all this. You must trust her, at least until you have an answer.'

'And by then,' Robert sighed, 'it could be too late. I warned her a long time ago that we were on opposite sides.'

With a snort, Aiden stood. 'Might be – could be. Robert, the truth is, you don't know anything for sure. For all you know, this whole prophecy might be just one almighty joke, handed down through the centuries.'

Robert was unable to suppress a smile. 'Pardon me, but are you about to suggest *I* stop worrying?'

Aiden rolled his eyes as Robert came to his feet. He took in a refreshing breath, stretching his arms up to loosen his shoulders. 'Well, I can see why you became a priest. You do have such faith in miracles. Come on, we can't stand up here all night. You have to get over the border safely and get stuck into all that work waiting for you at Bleakstone.'

When Aiden didn't move immediately, Robert took his elbow and steered him towards the stairs. 'I really wish you'd stop worrying about me, Bishop. You know I'll survive. You can't get rid of me that easily – though you keep trying.'

'And one of these days,' Aiden replied dryly, 'I'll succeed – about the only way I'll stop you calling me Bishop!'

As the sun drifted below the horizon, Maitland Manor was bathed in a glow of blood-red. The eastern sky was almost black and only the most enthusiastic stars could be seen. Jenn stayed by the window for as long as she could, feeling, for reasons she could not name, the deepest, strangest calm.

Her sister Bella, however, could not be accused of the same. She paced back and forth in front of Jenn, throwing up every argument she could to get Jenn to change her mind.

'I just don't believe you're doing this. To willingly go with that man, across the country? Your husband could return home any day and ask where you are.'

'And he'll be told I'm here visiting you. You aren't well and I'm here to nurse you back to health.' Jenn's gaze remained fixed on the darkening sky. He would be out there now, waiting for her. She could have sent her Senses out to find him, but she didn't need to. She knew he was there.

'But you didn't ask Eachern's permission!' Bella insisted. 'He'll come straight here looking for you!'

Jenn shook her head slightly. 'No he won't.' And how did she know this? Because Eachern was a coward and a bully and there was something about Bella that scared him. No, he would not come here. He would leave things alone for the moment and busy himself with his work.

And Eachern wasn't to know Bella knew nothing of the beatings.

Bella stamped her foot and grabbed Jenn's arm, forcing her around to meet her eyes. 'I'm not going to let you go, Jenn. Not with Robert. You forget I know what he is, I know what he did. Every day I still count the cost of his actions. I only have to look at my poor Lawrence to know that Robert Douglas means trouble. You're not going to get involved with him again, I won't have it!'

Jenn took her hands and held them between her own. 'If something happens to me, you'll have to act quickly. I want you to have Andrew. You must not, ever, leave him to the devices of Eachern. Keep Father John with you, also. Promise me you'll do all this?'

Bella rolled her eyes to the ceiling. 'You just won't listen to reason, will you?'

Jenn let go and started for the door. 'I should be back in no more than three weeks. I've already written letters for Eachern that you can send each week I'm gone. There's another there in case something happens and I don't come back. It says you knew nothing of what I planned to do.'

'But I *don't* know!'

'I'm going to get changed. I'll see you before I set out.'

Robert waited at the edge of the wood, just south and a little west of the house. He could see it clearly from his position, in the shadow of an enormous fir tree. Lights shone clear from a dozen different rooms, there were four steady torches by the gate. Would she come out that way, or was there some other exit?

He sat quite still on a log with his back to the trunk, one knee up in front of him. The time for pacing up and down was gone, along with the hours he'd spent wondering why she'd suddenly changed her mind. A cool breeze rattled through the bare branches above and his horse nuzzled at his elbow, anxious to be out of this inhospitable weather.

She would be here soon and soon, he would once again have to hide how he felt about her. It seemed such a betrayal after what he'd said to her, and yet, what choice did he have? What good would it do to constantly remind her of what they could never have?

He did still love her – and always would – but things had changed and he no longer had the right to depend on her loyalty. If he ever had.

Would she Seek him to find exactly where he waited? Probably not; her Seeking abilities had always been poor. He couldn't bring himself to try Seeking her. He would see her in the night if it were a thousand times darker than this.

And so he did. She came not from the gate, but from the opposite side of the building. She led her horse silently, lifting her skirts with her free hand. It wasn't until she was hidden by the oak's shadow that she actually stopped and looked at him.

'You came,' he murmured.

'Yes.'

There seemed nothing more to say so he gathered up his reins and mounted his horse. 'This won't take too long, it's not far.'

It had been so very long since she'd ridden through a forest in darkness. And it was so cold! She'd put on an extra jacket over her dress, and worn the heaviest lined cloak she could find and still she shivered. She kept flexing her fingers to keep them warm, pointing her toes and trying to move her legs, but it made little difference. In an hour or so, she'd be fainting with the cold.

Such a great way to begin a journey with *him*!

He didn't speak. He just rode a little ahead of her, not even glancing in her direction. He looked different now, of course, without a disguise. It was strange, but there was, about these first few moments, a feeling that time had not passed at all, that this was simply another leg on some long journey they'd undertaken and never quite finished. But it was winter now and snow drifted in waves along the forest floor, breath gathered in clouds about the animals' faces and the cold had penetrated her whole body right into her soul.

No, time *had* passed. Nothing would ever change that.

The ride didn't last for ever, though for a while, Jenn thought it might. Eventually she began to hear noises ahead; nice, friendly noises. Robert still said nothing, so she was forced to wait until light appeared between the trees ahead. Two, no, three fires, and some lamps.

They stopped on the edge of a small clearing where two brightly coloured carts stood at angles to each other. There were horses hobbled to one side and some kind of tent erected to the right. The fires sat in a triangle and a myriad pots were suspended above them. Around the fires appeared to be about fifty people, all talking at once, laughing and some even singing. As Robert dismounted, a man waved a greeting at him, urging him closer to the fire.

Jenn held back, not dismounting immediately. 'What is this?'

'Convenience,' Robert replied in a whisper. 'These gypsies are going the same way we are. We'll travel a little slower, but it will be a lot more comfortable and a lot safer with these people.'

'How much longer?'

'Two days, no more. Really, it is safer.' He held her horse as she got down, but still she couldn't move towards the light, the warmth. 'What's wrong?'

'I could ask the same thing.' Jenn smoothed down her gown and straightened her cloak. Suddenly all the peace, all the quiet had gone and she couldn't bring herself to look at him.

'It's not too late to change your mind,' Robert said levelly. 'I can take you back if you're not sure.'

Jenn kept her gaze on the promising campfires, trying to regather herself, to find something to hold onto, something she could trust. Something that time wouldn't betray. 'Why do you need to get back into the Enclave?'

'I . . . I can't tell you that.'

'Why not?'

'It's safer this way.'

'Safer for whom?' When he didn't answer, she turned and looked up at him. She'd forgotten how tall he was, how . . . strong he appeared. Still she could see nothing in his gaze, nothing that she needed to see.

At one time, he would have told her, would have shared his thoughts, his reasoning, his plans.

Time had indeed passed.

Jenn swallowed heavily. 'You don't trust me, do you?'

With a sigh, Robert stepped closer, 'It's got nothing to do with trust, I promise you—'

'Don't promise.'

He blinked at that, then nodded. 'I will tell you when we get to the Enclave. Not before.'

He *didn't* trust her. Why? Simply because he didn't love her any more? Was that sufficient reason to . . . Or . . . had he found out about her friendship with a Guildesman? Had John told Murdoch and Murdoch told . . . Robert?

By the gods!

John had betrayed her friendship simply because Nash was . . .

Jenn banked her fury and turned away from Robert, unable to think clearly enough to risk broaching the subject again. 'Fine. Don't tell me. I don't really care. I'm not doing this for you but for my own reasons. I don't know how long this journey will take, but I want to have as little to do with you in that time as possible. Do you understand?'

Robert stood there for a moment, breathing heavily. Eventually, he replied, the one word short and clipped, 'Perfectly.'

'Good.' With that, she turned and walked towards the fire.

5

Finnlay shivered and rubbed his hands together, then pulled his thick woollen jacket further up around the back of his neck. Nevertheless, the draught still wormed its way into his bones and he gritted his teeth to stop them from chattering. With an inaudible sigh, he hunched forward in his chair and gazed once more at the chequered board before him, his pieces artfully arranged in a tactical masterpiece of cunning genius. Patric would never get out of this one – not this time.

'Well?' Finnlay said. 'Are you going to move or are you finally going to concede?'

Patric didn't respond at first. Then he shook his head, his eyes fixed on the game. Absently, he reached up and brushed the long hair out of his eyes, tapped his index finger against his chin, then slowly reached forward until his hand hovered above one of his pieces.

A single hissed breath made him pause. A rustle of movement from the man seated to his left encouraged Patric to choose a different piece. He picked it up, moved it and sat back with a grin just for Finnlay.

'Oh, stop looking so smug,' Finnlay grunted, forcing his attention back to the board. He would ignore the presence of Deverin and Owen beside them if it killed him. And anyway, his masterplan would still work. Everything was in place. Patric hadn't seen the trap waiting for him, and wouldn't until it was too late – no matter how much interference he had to put up with!

All the same, Finnlay waited a good long while before making his next move. He already knew what it would be, but if he didn't wait, they would accuse him of impatience. So he sat, drumming his fingers lightly on the tabletop.

'My lord, you might want to . . . '

'What?' Finnlay snapped, sending a glare of dire proportions in Owen's direction. The older man was obviously trying to hide his amusement. He shrugged and leaned back against the cave wall, lacing his fingers together in a gesture of withdrawal. For good measure, Finnlay shot a warning glance at Deverin, seated opposite, then turned his attention back to the game. Some days he really wished he'd never suggested they come and live at the Enclave.

Deliberately now, he chose his piece and moved it – and immediately both older men sighed loudly and shook their heads.

'Will you stop that!'

'I'm sorry, my lord,' Deverin's deep voice barely contained his laughter, 'I didn't say a word.'

Finnlay pressed both hands against the hard edge of the table, willing patience. 'If you can't keep quiet – both of you – then you'll have to find somewhere else to sit. Look, you've got the whole great cavern to play in. Do you have to sit at this table and annoy us?'

'Oh?' Owen murmured, 'we were not aware Master Patric was annoyed.'

Finnlay leaned forward. 'That's because you're helping him – and you know that's not fair.'

'But Master Patric did not learn this game from your father, as you did. He does not,' Owen paused to frame his words, 'have the advantages of your education.'

'It's all right, Finn,' Patric added with an easy smile. 'They're not annoying me, really. Look, there's my next move – and they didn't say a word. See? Happy now?'

Swearing under his breath, Finnlay turned back to the game, studied the board and shifted the next piece of the trap. Instantly he glanced at the two older men, but both sat there with innocent expressions. Frowning, Finnlay said, 'Haven't you two got something else to do? Drills to take the cadets through or something?'

'Finn,' Patric murmured, 'sunset was four hours ago.'

'Was it?'

'Yes.'

'Then why don't they speak for themselves?'

'Because you just told them to shut up.' There was a twinkle in Patric's eyes Finnlay really hated, but he was too tired now to say anything. Instead, he got to his feet and wandered away from the table.

His boots made empty sounds against the stone floor of the cavern, which echoed against the walls to the ceiling high above. Slowly he strode the length of the cave to the tunnel door then turned and paced back. He paused before the alcove set into the wall where two low steps led to a wooden platform upon which the Key sat, quiet and unheeding. The ironwork arms of the pyramid appeared overly decorated in this light and the innocuous bell suspended from the apex dull and lustreless. Like this, it was hard to believe the object before him was one of such enormous power and influence. Instead, it looked more like some refugee from an old sailing vessel, unwanted and disused. 'This is taking too long.'

'It's taking as long as it needs to,' Owen replied carefully from his seat.

'Well, I just wish Robert was here,' Finnlay murmured into the empty cavern.

'Why?' Patric laughed. 'So you could ask him to show you how to beat me?'

Finnlay turned an acerbic gaze on Patric. 'I don't need my brother to show me how to beat you. I promise you, I can do that all on my own.'

'Then come and sit back down and prove it.'

'That wasn't the kind of beating I was referring to.' Finnlay fought, but he couldn't help laughing at himself. 'Well, go on, move. I don't have all night to stand around here.'

'Finnlay?'

He turned around to find his mother at the tunnel entrance. She looked tired, but wore a smile – and that was enough for him. Without thinking, he moved towards her, as the others followed quickly behind. 'Well?'

'You can come now,' Margaret said with a smile. 'Fiona's asking for you.'

'She's all right?'

'Of course!' Margaret laughed and gave him a brief hug. 'And so is your new daughter.'

'Daughter?' Finnlay knew he was grinning like an idiot, but he didn't care. He glanced over his shoulder to his friends. 'Did you hear that? I have a new daughter!'

The tunnels of the Enclave were empty and cold as Finnlay hurried to his rooms. Still, he could hear voices and noise, some music in the distance, and that same integral warmth that had always been a part of this place, hidden high within a mountaintop as it was. Almost nobody ventured near the Goleth Mountains and at times like this, it was hard to remember there was a whole world in the valleys below, ignorant of this community of cave-dwellers.

He reached his door to find Martha waiting for him. She said nothing, simply waved him into the bedroom. The room was well lit and showed the shadows of exhaustion around Fiona's face. Nevertheless she smiled, both beautiful and tired. Finnlay came to the side of the bed and sat gingerly, leaning forward to kiss her.

'Are you all right?'

'Fine,' Fiona murmured, touching his face. 'Meet your daughter.'

She lifted her arms and turned the bundle around until he could see the small face almost obscured by swaddling. The baby's eyes were closed; her face folded up in what looked to be a frown of deep contemplation. Holding his breath, Finnlay reached out and brushed a finger over her cheek and was rewarded with a tiny hiccough. With a grin, he turned back to Fiona.

'I was getting worried. It took much longer than last time. Are you sure you're all right?'

'I'm fine, I promise you. Your mother and Martha were here to help and I even had Arlie waiting outside in case I needed a Healer. Really, sometimes these things take a while. I got the distinct impression your daughter wasn't exactly in a hurry to come into the world – unlike her father.'

Chuckling, Finnlay settled onto the bed next to her, putting his arm around Fiona's shoulders. He planted a kiss on her forehead and let his gaze drop to the baby. She looked so . . . so perfect. Too beautiful to be real. 'Where is Helen?'

'With Martha's aunt. She was fast asleep last time I asked. I think we may as well just leave her there until morning. There'll be time enough then for her to get all excited.' Fiona paused. 'I'm sorry, Finnlay.'

'Sorry?' Finnlay replied absently, relaxing for the first time that day. 'What on earth for?'

'I know you were hoping for a son.'

Finnlay frowned and shook his head, squeezing Fiona's shoulder to press his point. 'Don't be an idiot.'

'But . . . '

'No. I won't hear another word about it. Now you just rest. We both know that the worst is yet to come.'

He felt rather than heard Fiona's soft laughter as she buried her head against his chest. He continued with a contented smile. 'There'll be all those sleepless nights to look forward to when this poor child doesn't realise she should be fast asleep like her parents. Then there'll be the crawling when she turns our humble home into a ravaged battleground. Then we'll have to contend with her talking and the endless questions she'll ask – and when she starts walking – well!'

Fiona lifted her head to kiss his cheek. 'Always the bringer of good news, aren't you? And you haven't even mentioned when she gets old enough to be looking at boys.'

'Well,' Finnlay grinned, 'I hope by then I'll have had some practice with her sister's adventures and with any luck, I'll have worked out exactly how to scare them all off.'

Now Fiona was laughing aloud.

Finnlay reached across and again caressed the cheek of his daughter. 'Have you chosen a name? Will you be ready for the Presentation tomorrow morning?'

'The Presentation, yes – but I don't know how many of the festivities I'll stay around for afterwards. You men never understand how a woman suffers in childbirth.'

'Oh, dear,' Finnlay sighed, wrapping his arms around both of them, 'you're starting to sound like Martha. If you really insist, I'll stay with you next time and that way, I won't have to take your word for it.'

Fiona eyed him askance, humour twinkling at the edges of her feigned frown. 'And what, dear husband, makes you think there's going to be any more children?'

Finnlay opened his mouth to reply – but kissed her instead. There was always one way to get around logic and argument.

Margaret stifled a yawn and settled back into her chair. It was a pity the musicians had stopped playing, but it was late and most people had left the celebrations to go to bed, leaving the alcove almost empty. Half a dozen doors led off this communal area, and most of the families had young children of their own. Even Fiona had departed to get some rest. Older folk like the Jaibir, Wilf, and his friend Henry, had already gone.

Before she could say no, young Patric leaned forward across the table and refilled her cup with more mulled wine. He was a good lad, if a little over-enthusiastic at times. He generally worked – and thought – with a tiring speed. His fair hair was long and straight and never cut short enough around his face, so it fell over his dark eyes whenever he moved his head. Perhaps more than anyone else, he had played an integral part in her making a home in this strange place, surrounded by sorcerers and their families. He had always taken the time to explain things to her, to help her understand much of what this Enclave was. Even so, every day she couldn't stop herself wishing she could go home to Dunlorn.

'You know,' Finnlay said quietly, to avoid disturbing the baby sleeping in his arms, 'I'm not sure I'll ever get used to the idea of being a father.'

Margaret smiled. 'Your father used to say the same thing.'

'Really?' Finnlay glanced up. 'When?'

'Usually when you and your brother were embroiled in another fight.'

'Oh.' Finnlay grinned and hung his head.

'I only wish I could see Robert as happily settled as you,' Margaret continued. 'It would change his life to have a family of his own.'

Finnlay nodded, but didn't look up. 'There's still time, Mother. He's only thirty-five.'

'And I'm almost fifty-two, Finn,' Margaret laughed. 'I really would like to be around to see it. I don't suppose we've heard anything more since that last message from Murdoch?'

When Finnlay didn't answer, Patric put down his wine. 'No, nothing.'

'But it's been almost seven months. What can Robert be doing that he's not able even to send us word that he's alive? It's bad enough that he's been gone five years . . . '

'Just be grateful, Mother,' Finnlay interrupted, 'that we know Robert is still out there somewhere. If it wasn't for Murdoch, we'd have known nothing at all.'

'But we still have no idea what Robert is up to,' Patric said.

'Is he up to anything?' Finnlay murmured. His attention was entirely on his daughter.

'Over the last five years, Robert has been to Marsay in disguise a dozen or so times so he can give messages to Murdoch. Now I understand he can't come here to the Enclave on his own – but why would he risk so much going all the way to Marsay? The capital is the most dangerous place in the country for him. If he isn't up to something, why have Archdeacon Godfrey spy on the court for him?'

'Speculation will get us nowhere,' Finnlay said.

'But what about the prophecy?'

At this, Finnlay did look up. His dark hair was shorter than Patric's, shadowing his deep brown eyes. The old scar on his cheek was invisible in the candlelight. 'Look, there's been no word of the Angel of Darkness since Robert injured him at Elita. As long as he doesn't come back, Robert may as well ignore the prophecy. Why shouldn't he? Hasn't it ruined enough of his life already?'

'But . . . '

'If Robert's been moving around Lusara in secret, then he's better qualified than us to judge if there is any danger. You know as well as I do that if there was, Robert would come back here whether he'd been banished from the Enclave or not. Please, Patric, just enjoy the peace. We have no idea how long it will last.'

Patric sat back and took another mouthful of his wine. 'And it won't last.'

'No.' Finnlay shook his head and allowed his gaze to drop once more to the baby in his arms. As Margaret watched him, he frowned and for a moment, he appeared horribly vulnerable and alone. She moved to reach out to him, but he glanced up with a smile. 'Anyway, Mother, I told you before you shouldn't worry about Robert. He's a big boy and can more than look after himself.'

Margaret turned to Patric. 'You know, it's never ceased to amaze me that for years I told Finnlay what to do and he rarely, if ever, paid any attention to me – and now that he's a grown man, he seems to think I should give him complete obedience in return. Is it me – or is there something strange about that?'

Patric laughed and got to his feet. 'It's not you, Lady Margaret. Everything about Finnlay is strange. I'm off to bed. Goodnight.'

As Finnlay reached the doorway, he stumbled and banged into the wall. He stifled a groan and forced his sleepy eyes open a little more. He trudged into the living room, trying not to trip over Helen as she ran around his legs.

'I'm hungry, Papa. Hungry, hungry, hungry!'

'Yes, I know. Just keep still and let me at the fire.'

'Let me help, Papa!'

Helen almost bounced up and down with an energy Finnlay couldn't begin to emulate. His brain had turned to sludge and most of his limbs objected to any command to move. How many hours' sleep had he had? Two? Three, perhaps? It had been the same every night for the last two weeks. At least Bronwyn was asleep now – even if Fiona was exhausted.

He took out plates and handed them to Helen. Gravely now, she carried them to the table and tried to arrange them as she'd seen her mother do. He cut bread for her, cheese, and poured milk, then sat her down and told her to stay. With a tray in his hands, he went back to the bedroom.

Fiona was sitting up, her hand gently rocking the cradle beside the bed. She smiled as Finnlay placed the tray on her lap.

'Fun, isn't it?' he whispered. A loud knock on the outer door made him jump, then wince. But it was all right. Bronwyn was undisturbed. With a glance at Fiona, he dashed back into the other room and opened the door. Patric stood there, his hair wild, barely awake himself. 'What is it? You almost woke the baby.'

'Sorry.' Patric abruptly waved the objection aside. 'Have you heard? The council has been working since midnight.'

'Why? What's wrong?'

Patric grabbed his arm urgently. 'Murdoch returned from Marsay last night . . . '

Instantly Finnlay thought of Robert, but Patric didn't wait for questions.

'He had a message – a warning from Godfrey. Vaughn has made a Bresail!'

'By the gods,' Finnlay breathed, cold rushing from his head to his feet. 'But what . . . '

'The council has ordered messages to be sent out, recalling our people as quickly as possible. They're opening up some of the lower caves to house them. By now the Bresail will have moved out of Marsay and into the country. Everybody is at risk.'

'Including Robert – and Jenn! Serin's blood! What can we do?'

Patric ran a hand through his hair. 'I don't know. Perhaps Deverin can get to Clonnet and warn Jenn – but Eachern's men might recognise him. As for Robert . . . '

Finnlay stepped back into the room, rubbing his hands together, trying to get his mind to work properly. 'The Bresail can't detect an aura through really strong shielding, can it?'

'Not that I know of, but nor would I want to test it out.'

'Nor me – but Robert's shielding is adamantine. I know. I've tried for years to Seek through it. Jenn is also strong, so perhaps they'll be all right.'

'Perhaps?'

Finnlay turned around to face him, another thought striking him. Andrew.

Would he have shields? Would he be in danger?

'You're right – Deverin would be too much of a risk to send to Clonnet, but there must be someone else. There has to be!'

*

Wilf heaved himself out of his chair and tried to straighten his back. He'd been sitting far too long, but standing was equally uncomfortable. As Henry, Martha and the other councillors droned on with various different arrangements, Wilf's gaze turned to the walls of the chamber. The long room was entirely decorated with paintings put there by previous generations, a pictorial history of their people. Nowhere, however, was there a single hint of a threat like Vaughn's Bresail.

It was only at times like this that people genuinely understood how fragile the existence of the Enclave really was. Everyone knew the ever-present threat of the Malachi, but few ever encountered them and until now, the danger had always been a legend rather than a reality. The only other menace the Enclave dwellers had faced had come from the old Empire and a war that had almost wiped out sorcerers – and sent the few survivors fleeing north. Some had chosen to found this Enclave, the others had disappeared, later to become known as the Malachi.

All in all, those in the Enclave had so far lived a charmed life. In more than five hundred years since its founding, not once had its existence been discovered. With the protection of the Key, the Seal all Salti had placed on them, the test of the gate to pass through, and numerous fables of monsters and the like inhabiting this mountain range, no physical threat had ever encroached on their mountaintop peace.

As the voices behind him grew quiet, Wilf posed the question that had plagued him since Murdoch had first arrived. 'Can any of you tell me what would happen if the Malachi got hold of this Bresail?'

A slight cough and the scrape of a chair were his only answers. He turned around and faced them. 'I mean, assuming a Malachi could actually get his hands on it, do you think it's possible it could remove the protection of the Seal? Vaughn alone is a danger, I admit – but the Malachi are something else entirely. They know we Salti are somewhere around – they've just never been able to find us. What happens if they capture one of us using this Bresail and manage to break past the Seal? More to the point, what if this Angel of Darkness got a hold of it? I mean, the Key has said he's the greatest danger to us. Who of us could withstand torture to keep the secret of the Enclave?'

'It's impossible to guess,' Henry replied. 'The Seal has never been tested in that way – and I can't see anybody volunteering to do so now.'

Martha sat forward, placing to one side the papers she had before her. 'I don't want to speak out of turn, Wilf, but I think you're going too far, too fast. First, a Malachi would have to get close enough to steal the Bresail without actually being discovered himself. Secondly . . . '

'It only requires truly solid shielding to protect against a Bresail,' Wilf interrupted.

'Second, even if a Salti were captured, there's no reason to think a Seal is any more breakable than before. A Seal prevents any mention of the Enclave unless it's voluntary or in the presence of other people who are also Sealed. It's withstood the test of half a millennium, Wilf, I don't think this is the time to be doubting it now. We've got enough to worry about as it is.'

'Even so,' Wilf persisted, 'it is possible. As Henry says, it's never been tested.'

'No.'

Wilf turned back to his chair, but didn't sit. 'If Finnlay hadn't been so careless in the first place, Vaughn wouldn't have his *ayarn* to play with. If his cursed brother hadn't been so arrogant as to use the Word of Destruction for all to see, Vaughn wouldn't feel the necessity to react against the . . . *evil* of sorcery! By the gods, those two . . . '

Martha stood, gathering her things together with a gentle smile. 'I suppose you don't want me to remind you that Finnlay has been responsible for providing us with a ready combat force should any threat actually make it up the mountain – and his . . . cursed brother is the only man – according to the Key – who can stand between us and the Angel of Darkness.'

Wilf grunted. 'I don't know about that, but I want you all to remember what you promised. I allowed Finnlay to send that messenger off to Jenn because she could indeed be in danger, although with her husband, I think that's unlikely. However, I did want to remind her that we are still here and that she gave me her word.'

'I doubt she's forgotten, Wilf,' Martha said.

'All the same – she vowed to Stand the Circle when I am dead and unless I miss my guess, it could take all of you to convince her to come. I doubt Finnlay would mindspeak her of his own accord.'

'Nobody's arguing, Wilf.' Martha smiled. She was such a creature of gentleness, Wilf couldn't stay angry for long when she was around. One of his best decisions had been to ask her on to the council. Thank the gods she'd agreed. She'd been invaluable over the last twenty-four hours.

Martha turned for the door. 'I'm off to get the Dunlorn men sorted out. They've volunteered to head out into the valleys to get in more supplies. I want to send them out a few days apart in small groups, to reduce any suspicion. Try to get some rest, Wilf. Arlie has a wonderful tonic that would help your back. I'll ask him to bring some to your rooms. Good evening, gentlemen.'

She opened the door – but there was somebody standing there about to knock.

'What is it?' Wilf asked, moving forward.

'Forgive me, Jaibir, but you've been requested to go to the gate.'

'The gate? What on earth for? Don't you know it's dark outside?'

'Yes, Jaibir, but the sentries have seen someone on their way up.'

Wilf sighed. This day was going to have no end at this rate. 'Any idea who?'

The young man swallowed and nodded. 'It's Robert – and he's not alone.'

Travelling the Goleth range in winter was a fool's task at the best of times, but climbing the last treacherous paths under cover of darkness bordered on madness. Nevertheless, Robert kept on, keeping the horses to the trail, his Senses extended to the maximum. There was no other way to guess if the path would collapse beneath them, sending them sliding down into the valley in an avalanche of snow and ice.

Jenn travelled behind him. Only occasionally would she break the absolute silence she had kept for a week to voice a warning of some danger he hadn't seen. He didn't say anything to her, even though her silence made everything so much more difficult. She had every right to be angry. Every right to hate him.

And she wouldn't say why she had come in the first place.

It was fortunate his sight was so enhanced by his powers, or he would never have seen the huge snow-covered rock which hid the gate from idle eyes. Behind it stood a wall of mountain, white and grey, the embodiment of winter itself. As he approached it, he pulled his exhausted horse to a stop and dismounted. He waited for Jenn to join him as he took off his gloves. 'Can you remember how to do this?'

'Get through the gate? I think so. I can't make a light, though, can I?' Her voice was little more than a whisper.

'Not until we're actually through the gate, no.'

'Robert?'

'Yes?' He glanced across to find her staring at the dark cavern beyond the rock.

'Are you sure this is going to work? If the Key has altered the gate so you can't get through, how can I change that?'

'This is really not the time to be asking that particular question – especially since I don't know the answer. All I know is what the Key told me. *Come not again within these walls unless she is with you.* By she, it meant you. Well, we're both here, so it should work.'

'And if I wasn't here? What would happen if you tried it alone?'

That was a question he'd asked himself for the last six years – and still not come up with a very nice answer. 'Well, you are here.'

She nodded. 'Let's just get it over with.' She reached out in the blackness until she could touch him. 'You take the horses and give me your hand.'

Holding his hand firmly, Jenn moved forward, allowing Robert to nudge her in the right direction. They moved further into the black void, neither feeling nor Sensing anything different. One step after another until—

Robert lost the horses . . . and Jenn's hand . . . he could touch nothing at all. He floated Senseless, hearing nothing, seeing nothing. *Jenn?*

You came back.

Yes.

Why?

You're the Key!

Why come back?

If you're the Key, you should know.

Something snapped against his eyes and his sensation returned, along with his sight. Jenn was still holding his hand, but now she had a light going and she was watching him warily.

'What happened?'

Robert glanced about him. The horses were behind, the reins in his other hand, the cavern open and familiar. All was as it should be. 'The Key . . . let me in. What did you see?'

'I was moving forward and then I felt the same tingle I always feel coming through the gate. I took another step forward, but you were gone. I stopped – and you were back again. I know it sounds strange, but that's exactly what happened.'

Robert shook his head and smiled a little. 'No, it doesn't sound strange at all. Come on.'

They followed the tunnel down to the end where it opened out onto the mountaintop – but there was a reception waiting for them: a dozen armed men holding torches, with one old man standing between them.

'Hello, Wilf,' Robert said warily.

The Jaibir stood with his arms folded, his head shaking in disbelief. 'I thought there was something wrong. I really thought the Key had started to malfunction. I just couldn't believe it when I was told you were on your way up the mountain. And you brought Jenn with you. How practical.'

Jenn pushed her way around Robert to stand between them. 'The Key let him through the gate, Wilf. You can't throw him out. Not now.'

'The Key let him through?' Wilf repeated, with an ironic smile. 'How little you understand how it works. You've made it through the gate, Robert, but you won't make it any further unless you tell me right here and now what you want. Why have you come back?'

'That's something I wish to discuss with the full council.'

Wilf's smile widened, almost triumphant. 'So you haven't come back just to see your family?'

'Wilf,' Jenn insisted. 'Please. We've been climbing the damned mountains for almost twelve hours. Can't we discuss this inside?'

'You can go if you like, my dear – but Robert stays until he answers my question. I'll not have him poisoning the Enclave with his lies again.'

Jenn glanced at Robert, but she didn't leave.

'Well?' Wilf continued. 'Are you going to tell me what you're doing here – or are you going to start back for the foothills now?'

Robert looked at each of the men behind Wilf. He knew a few of them and could tell none of them were very happy with this situation, but that didn't make it easier on any of them. He shook his head wearily. He didn't have a choice. Quite ironic, really, considering why he was here.

'Very well. I'll tell you.' He shot a glance at Jenn before he continued, 'I'm here to see my family, yes. But I've also come for another reason. To ask your help and because . . . '

'Because?' Wilf enquired archly.

'I know who the Angel of Darkness is.'

6

The hush inside the caverns was unmistakable. A dozen times, Finnlay went out into the corridor, only to be told to go back inside his rooms. Fiona had more patience. She sat quietly by the fire with Margaret, talking about all sorts of things. Every now and then she would get up and make them a brew, but other than that she appeared to hardly notice Finnlay's increasing agitation.

'What's taking so long?' he said for the tenth time. He got up once more, but this time he heard a noise. He pulled the door wide and stepped into the corridor, Fiona and Margaret behind him. He could hear voices from around the corner, one voice he recognised in particular. Then Patric, Arlie and Martha appeared at the junction and Finnlay almost ran to meet them. He turned into the main passage in time to see Wilf come towards them and behind him was—

'Robert! Jenn!'

His brother looked up and a huge grin creased his face. Then they were caught up in hugs, greetings, and expressions of disbelief. Margaret was crying, but Wilf didn't let the mayhem continue for long.

'I'll call a council meeting for the morning, Robert. In the meantime, keep quiet about it all, will you? As a favour to me?'

The whole group moved off down towards Finnlay's rooms, but he paused to take Jenn's arm. Quickly he murmured, 'How are you?'

'Fine.'

'And how's Andrew?'

She looked sharply at him and nodded. 'He's . . . fine, Finnlay. Really.'

He couldn't work out why, but Jenn seemed a little subdued – but she would be tired after the journey. How in the name of the gods had Robert convinced her to come here? Well, he would find out later, no doubt. In the meantime, he took her along the corridor to his now-crowded rooms.

Fiona was waiting for them – and he suddenly remembered the other thing he had to do this night. With a grin already on his face, he opened the bedroom door and Helen flew into his arms. He picked her up and turned to Robert. 'Brother, I want you to meet your niece, Helen.'

Robert's face froze, then his eyes grew wide as he looked at the girl. A smile began to grow. 'My niece?'

'And this one too.' Fiona joined them carrying a bundle and held it up for Robert to see. 'This is Bronwyn. She's only two weeks old.'

Robert's mouth opened, but no words came out. Margaret took his arm, her eyes sparkling.

'Do you have any idea how we've longed for this moment?'

'Obviously some of you have been prepared to wait more than others.'

'Here,' Finnlay laughed, lifting Helen in Robert's direction. 'You'd better take her for a while. She can get a bit heavy. Now, Helen, what are you going to say?'

The little girl with the huge eyes turned to Robert and said, 'Hello, Uncle Robert. Papa told me about you, but all of it was very bad things.'

The entire room erupted with laughter.

'You coached her, Finn!' Robert howled with the injustice. 'That's not fair!'

Finnlay grinned smugly. 'That's what you get for going away, brother. It's your own fault.

Jenn moved to the outside edge of the room, away from all the noise and excitement, and glanced around for somewhere to sit. It would only be a matter of minutes before the questions would begin, before people would start asking why she hadn't kept in contact over the years, why she now sat on the fringes, and she didn't want to have to say that she didn't feel like she belonged to any of this.

It was all just too much, too far away from the harsh reality she had to live with each day. This humour, this warmth and camaraderie was an illusion she couldn't afford to indulge in.

'You look tired.' Martha came towards her. 'Would you rather leave all this and get to bed?'

'I have to confess . . . ' Jenn began but Martha didn't require further encouragement.

'We've moved to bigger rooms,' Martha began, taking Jenn's arm and steering her into the corridor. 'We also have another baby.'

'Really?'

'A boy. He's two now – so we had to have more space. We have a spare bedroom that's yours while you're here, if you want it.'

A turn past the junction and Martha stopped before another door. 'The children are asleep, but I'm sure you'll see them in the morning. This is your room.'

Martha opened a door painted with green leaves along the top and bottom. There was a bed, two chairs and a table with wash bowls already laid out. Jenn was speechless. She glanced at Martha, who merely smiled.

'I'll get the water from the fire while you undress.'

Jenn ventured into the pretty room to find Martha had even laid out a sleeping gown for her. It had a blue ribbon around the throat.

Absently, she began to undress, dropping her clothes onto the nearest chair. Weariness flooded through her body, dragging her further down with each moment. Martha brought the water in and helped her off with the rest of her clothes.

'My, you must have had a tough journey,' Martha murmured in sympathy. 'No wonder you're tired.'

Jenn frowned but said nothing as Martha held up the nightgown for her to put on. 'Those bruises look painful. Did you fall from your horse?'

Abruptly the haze cleared and Jenn pulled the gown down to cover her body. 'Yes, but before I came here. It was one day riding. Nothing serious.'

'Oh,' Martha said. 'Well, get some sleep. I'll try to keep the children out until you wake up, but I can't promise anything.'

She left then and Jenn climbed into bed. She lay there a long time before she finally went to sleep.

Robert stretched out with his feet on an empty stool, his back to the fire and another cup of mulled wine in his hand. The chair beneath him creaked as he moved, eliciting a warning glance from Finnlay. Patric helped himself to another piece of cheese and settled back onto the floor opposite Robert, cross-legged. Finnlay finished refilling his cup and put the flask on the floor between them.

The others had all gone to bed, reluctantly, leaving Robert to talk late into the night. Robert was tired, but it had been so long since he'd been able to do this, it was almost impossible to move. And there were a lot of questions to ask; a lot to answer.

'You can't begin to imagine the rumours we heard about you,' Patric said, warming his cup between his hands. 'I only wish half of them had been true.'

Robert chuckled, closing his eyes. 'Yes, well, I have heard some of them and I'm not sure how to take that.'

There was silence for a moment, then Finnlay cleared his throat. 'I guess I can understand Jenn not being too happy to bring you here in the middle of winter, but is there something else wrong with her?'

'Why?'

Another long silence made Robert open his eyes to find Patric and Finnlay sharing a look he couldn't account for. 'What's going on?'

It was Patric who answered. 'You know they put her in prison for two months after you left Elita?'

Robert nodded grimly. 'Yes. I couldn't do anything to stop it.'

'Well, Jenn hasn't really been in direct contact with us since they let her out.'

Robert frowned and swung his legs off the stool to sit up. 'But she can still mindspeak Finnlay, can't she?'

Finnlay shrugged. 'I assume so – but she's not done it for a long time. I try every now and then, but she doesn't respond and I'm just not strong enough to force the issue. As a result, the only news we have of her is what Father John passes on. He's managed to get himself assigned as chaplain to Clonnet.'

'Yes, I know.' Robert frowned again, sitting forward. 'Are you telling me she's been completely and utterly isolated from the Enclave – from all of you – for the last five years?'

'Don't get me wrong,' Patric began, holding his hands up, 'we tried. I went out there a dozen times. At first of course, it was impossible to get to see her, but even after that, John would pass on the message that she didn't want anything to do with any of us. The last time I went to Clonnet was at the end of this summer. Jenn wouldn't see me and warned what would happen if I ever went back.'

'Serin's breath!' Robert said. 'I thought it was just me.'

'Have you tried talking to her?' Patric asked.

Robert glanced sideways at him. 'Me? Are you joking?'

'Well, you just crossed half the country together. Are you going to tell me you didn't talk in that whole time?'

'As it happens.'

'Then,' Finnlay paused, 'if you've got no objection, I'll ask Mother to talk to her.'

'Would she mind?'

'Not at all. She's always been very fond of Jenn. I know she'll be happy to. Who knows how long it will be until we get another chance.'

Robert held out his cup again while Finnlay emptied the last of the wine into it.

'So,' Patric began quietly, 'are you going to tell us what this is all about?'

'Well, that depends on whether you're interested in doing a little job for me.'

'Me?'

'Yes,' Robert replied with a grin, 'Exactly your speciality.'

It was too cold in Robert's room for him to stay there long once the morning noises woke him up. He could have built up the fire, but restlessness drove him to dress and climb through the caves until he reached the outside. He walked clear into the centre of the field, ankle-deep in fresh snow, before he came to a stop.

Breathing in the clear mountain air, he tilted his head back and gazed up at the blue-grey winter's sky. Above him the spindle edge of the Goleth range ringed the open field with sharp stone towers only partially covered with white, like an enormous rocky crown. Before him, the field stretched out, softened by a blanket of new snow.

This was such an odd place, the Enclave. What had driven those sorcerers, five hundred and more years ago, to search through these mountains looking for a place like this? A perfect conical mountain with this rich and flat meadow at its heart? A lot of the tunnels and caves below were natural – the rest had been carved out of the living rock over the centuries – but even now, new caves were being discovered beneath. This mountain, the highest in the country, solid and intimidating from a distance, was in fact a honeycomb of hollows, housing a banned and reviled people. An odd place indeed.

And now he was back – even stranger.

He should have done something before this, made some move to stop Selar, to halt the tide of callous cruelty which had crept across this country over the last twenty years. Oh, it was all very well and good saying he'd made an oath – but it was more than six years since Selar had dissolved that oath, and yet Robert had waited until now. And what was he doing? Going to war, just as he'd always promised himself he wouldn't.

A war against his own people.

Would they follow him, fight alongside a sorcerer – against the King? Without doubt, his actions at Elita would be neither forgotten nor forgiven, but Robert prayed this pressing issue would be enough to make them take a stand.

For so many years, he'd been badgered to do just this: to lead his country back from the dead. And yet, while a part of him rejoiced at the action, another part questioned the wisdom; war was not a toy to be played with. Was the war he was offering them any better than the life they suffered under Selar?

The bitter taste of inaction had caused Robert too many sleepless nights, had fed the demon too much of what it wanted. Oh yes, they would ask him, why not just kill Selar? Surely he had the power to simply slip into Marsay and slit the usurper's throat. But civil wars were started that way, and the fight would last much longer than this one. The country would be a wasteland before it ended.

And what about the Angel of Darkness?

Robert wandered across the field, kicking up clumps of snow with his boots. The leather was well oiled but he could feel the cold through the soles.

The Angel of Darkness, the prophecy – and Jenn. All bound up together in one indecipherable knot no amount of picking could unravel; he was no closer to understanding any of it than he had been five years ago. The prophecy still stood there, waiting for him. The Angel was out there, playing his own game – and Jenn?

Jenn was lost to him.

Perhaps it was best that way: he would never be able to give her anything but pain; the past spoke that for him. And she was married, with a son by her husband. She hated Robert. Well, she wasn't the only one there. But she was in danger – even if she didn't realise it – and he had vowed to protect her at all costs.

All costs. No matter what.

He stooped and picked up a handful of snow. He rolled it together and swung back his arm. The snowball flew into the air in a perfect arc, landing against the nearest rock to be splattered into nothing. With an almost childish laugh, he pulled together another and sent it after the first. Perhaps if he pressed it firm enough, threw it hard enough, he might even reach the mountain peak itself.

Finnlay stood at the tunnel entrance for some moments, watching Robert wander across the field, kicking snow, and then make snowballs as they had done when they were children.

By the gods, it was so good to have him back – in one piece at that. And he looked well, not really any older, and about as fit as Finnlay had ever seen him. Standing out there in his black cloak, stark against the snow, he looked every inch the scion of the House Douglas, rebel and outlaw – though at the moment, throwing snowballs, he looked more like an overgrown ten-year-old.

With a sudden wicked grin, Finnlay stepped onto the snow and scooped some up for himself. Wadding it together, he crept forward until the distance was just right. Then he let fly.

Robert let out a yelp as the snowball hit him on the back. Finnlay instantly stepped back into the tunnel, unable to stop laughing. Robert stormed after him, gathering snow as he went. Finnlay backed away, but Robert was determined and caught him, dragging him back outside again. Then, with forceful hands, Robert pulled open his collar and thrust a handful of snow beneath Finnlay's shirt.

With a gasp, Finnlay twisted away. He scrambled to get rid of the stuff. It was already melting and absolutely freezing. 'That's not fair,' he cried, laughing despite the discomfort. 'You're bigger than me!'

'There's no such thing as an unfair advantage, Brother,' Robert chuckled, keeping a safe distance should Finnlay opt for retaliation. 'Still, it's nice to see you haven't become stuffy now that you're an old married man with no less than two children to run around after.'

Finally getting the last of the snow out, Finnlay pulled his collar up higher. 'Well, don't laugh – uncles have to do a fair bit of running around as well, you know.'

'Oh, I'll be in my dotage before those two can get into too much trouble.' Robert paused, brushing the hair back from his face. 'You're very lucky. I hope you appreciate that.'

Robert had not intended it so, but Finnlay still felt a stab of uneasiness at the comment. But he'd promised Jenn he would never tell Robert about Andrew, and he couldn't go back on his word. Not without talking to her first. Instead, he gestured towards the tunnel. 'The council is waiting for you. I don't suppose you'd care to tell me what this is all about?'

Coming forward, Robert swung an arm around Finnlay's shoulders and together they went inside. 'But that would spoil the surprise. You're looking good, I have to say. So is Mother. I'm surprised so many of our people from Dunlorn are here, though. I would have thought I'd scared them all off after Elita.'

'So did Wilf,' Finnlay said. 'But that's loyalty for you. Still, it's been hard explaining to them why you couldn't just come back here on your own. Few of them understand what the Key is, let alone the fact that it banished you.'

'Yes, well,' Robert agreed with a laugh, 'I'm with them on that score. So, is the whole council ready?'

Finnlay was about to answer when they reached the great cavern. It was full! It appeared everyone in the Enclave had gathered for this. The council chamber had overflowed with interested people to the point where the table had been brought out into the great cavern. Even the balconies were crowded.

'I wanted a quiet meeting with just the council,' Robert muttered in Finnlay's ear as they squeezed through the crowds.

A gap opened up and they emerged into an open space before the table. The council was seated around it already and Wilf rose to quieten the cavern down. Finnlay found an empty chair saved for him and sat as the last of the audience settled. He looked around, but couldn't immediately spy Jenn.

'Very well,' Wilf spoke clearly, his voice carrying across the sea of heads. 'I'm sure you've all heard some reason why we're here. However, I will remind you that this is a proper council meeting and therefore none of you may speak without permission. Now, Robert,' he said, turning towards him, 'Would you care to explain what this is about?'

'I know,' Robert began, standing a little to one side of the table, 'that all of you are wondering where I've been all this time, but to be honest, it's a very dull story. However, I come back now to beg your help in a conflict that is about to engulf us all.'

There was a murmur of concern throughout the hall before Robert continued, 'It's now twenty years since Selar conquered Lusara. In the time I was with him, I discovered a secret Selar had kept hidden fairly successfully all this time. In his heart, Selar has always felt his brother was too weak to rule Mayenne. When Tirone came to the throne, Selar wanted to kill him. He always believed that it was his destiny to rule in his brother's place. Selar invaded and conquered Lusara solely so that one day he could, in turn, invade Mayenne and put himself onto the throne. Five years ago, Selar was on the verge of attempting to achieve this ambition, but the Queen thwarted him by abducting his children. Selar couldn't very well invade another country without an heir to follow him, so he called off his plans. I'm sure that he would have made plans for the following year he got Kenrick back, but another problem stood in his way.'

There was a small movement to Finnlay's left as Jenn squeezed through the crowd to take a seat next to him. She glanced at him, then turned her attention back to Robert, pausing only to take a sip from the mug she held.

At this point, Robert smiled a little and spread his arms wide. 'I'm sure you're wondering what all this has to do with you, but bear with me. You all know what happened when I was banished from the Enclave. You all know the prophecy the Key revealed to everyone that day. You know I was branded the Enemy, that Jenn was labelled the Ally, and another person was described as the Angel of Darkness. He tried to kill my brother twice and we discovered his real name was Carlan. This Angel was present at Elita when I used the Word of Destruction – but it didn't kill him. I ask you, how many of you have even heard of Carlan since that day? The most we've heard is the occasional rumour that something bad has happened somewhere, but nobody has actually seen anything at all. And why?'

Robert took a breath before going on, 'Because the Word hurt him badly. Put him out of commission for a long time. It has, in fact, taken him almost all the last five years to recover. There is even the suggestion that the recovery hasn't actually been as complete as he would like.'

'Are you saying you've seen him yourself?' Wilf asked.

'No, I've not seen him.'

Finnlay found himself standing, his heart pounding even harder. Memories of torture and pain, blood and darkness fringed the edge of his awareness. 'But you know who he is?'

Robert met his gaze steadily, almost sympathetically. 'Yes.'

Voices were instantly raised around the room, almost deafening. Wilf had to call several times to quieten them down. 'Robert, continue.'

'For the last five years, Selar's treatment of Lusara has deteriorated even further – and yet, he's done nothing about building up an army to further his ambition. And why? Because the man who would ensure its success has not been at his side for those five years. Selar has – probably without even knowing it – been under the influence of Carlan for a long time. But without Carlan around, Selar's ambition had to wait. But no more. There is at this moment, an army being prepared, equipped and armed, ready for a spring invasion of Mayenne . . . '

Voices rose at this and Robert's volume increased to be heard over them.

'In the ranks are thousands of ordinary Lusarans who are about to lose their lives fighting a war they cannot win. Hundreds of Sadlani mercenaries have been brought over the border to train with them. Selar is paying them money from taxes collected from the very people he would murder.'

The uproar was now deafening and it took Wilf some minutes to regain quiet. Eventually, Robert continued, 'Selar is willing to risk everything to gain the throne of Mayenne from his brother – but he is only able to do this because his friend and mentor, Carlan, has now returned to his side. A man the rest of the country knows as the Guildesman Samdon Nash.'

There was a gasp to Finnlay's left and the crash of a mug hitting the stone floor, which was drowned out by the gasp from the audience. Finnlay turned to find Jenn white as snow, her mouth open, staring at Robert. She stood, then sat down, then stood again.

'Are you all right?' he whispered.

'He can't be . . . right . . . '

He didn't hear any more as clear questions were now coming from the floor, questions Robert was forced to answer.

'But what possible use can the Angel of Darkness have for conquering Mayenne? Why help Selar do such a thing?'

Robert shrugged. 'I'm not sure. All I know is that five years ago, Nash was prepared to go to extreme lengths to give Selar what he wanted. We've always believed it was Malachi who killed the Queen and returned Kenrick to his father – Malachi in the pay of Carlan. I also believe Nash is the man who was responsible for abducting Ayn. Before she died, she told me what he wanted. He was looking for me, the Enemy – and he wants the Key. This invasion could be his first real attempt to find it.'

This time there was a silence which nobody appeared brave enough to fill. Robert let it settle for a moment before going on, 'This is why I've come to you. Lusara is faced with an evil she doesn't know how to defeat. The country will be ravaged by a war it will lose. But not only that, we are at risk. If the Enclave does nothing to resist the Angel of Darkness, it will be only a matter of time before he finds this place and by then, we will be powerless to stop him. There is no way a man powerful enough to survive the Word of Destruction should ever get his hands on the Key.'

Wilf asked, 'I'm curious – are you certain this Nash and Carlan are the same man?'

Robert glanced sideways at him, half a smile on his face, as if he'd been expecting someone to ask that question but was rather hoping they wouldn't. He shrugged. 'Not exactly, no.'

Wilf forestalled interruption by raising his hands again. 'Explain.'

Robert straightened up and took in the entire room with his glance. 'Samdon Nash is the one common factor in all the major events for a number of years. When Ayn was abducted, she was held in the house of a Malachi, Valena. Nash was seen very often in her company. Of the children who were abducted during the Troubles, of whom Jenn is the only known survivor, one was found to be inside that same house. When my brother was caught and captured by Carlan, Nash was absent from court. The force that attacked Elita was almost entirely Guilde, and deeply infiltrated by Malachi. All along there has been a close association between Selar's deterioration and his dependence on the Guilde – and his growing friendship with Nash. If a man such as Carlan wanted to rise and get close to Selar, he would assume the best way to do it would be via the Guilde.'

Robert paused to take breath. 'But perhaps the most damaging evidence comes from the last five years. For reasons nobody appears able to explain, immediately after my . . . actions at Elita, Governor Nash disappeared. He was not seen again until almost two years later. When he did reappear, he did so in public for only short periods at a time. He was also visibly injured, though again, no explanation has been given. No, I don't know for sure that Nash is Carlan – but give me enough time and I'll prove it to you.'

A general murmur of dissatisfaction rumbled around the room and Wilf rose to his feet. 'I think that's enough for one day. Thank you, Robert. The council will consider this request for aid and give you an answer tomorrow.'

With that, people began to move, scraping chairs and raising voices in conversation about the revelations. Finnlay couldn't take his eyes from Robert. That he should know that Nash was . . . that he was real and . . . Couldn't they just go and kill Nash? Couldn't they . . .

Jenn left his side and hurried over to Wilf. Without thinking, Finnlay followed her.

'Wilf, I . . . ' Jenn paused, glancing nervously to the other councillors.

'This isn't about your oath to Stand the Circle, is it?'

'No.' She shook her head with a cross frown. She took a deep breath and started again, 'This is something different. I want the council to consider helping me with something. I can't organise it myself for obvious reasons. But I assure you it is imperative something be done.'

Wilf softened a little. 'What is it you want?'

'My son, Andrew.'

As Jenn paused again and swallowed, Finnlay shot a glance at Robert. She ignored them both and continued, 'I want somebody to abduct him and bring him back here to live.'

7

'Are you mad?'

Finnlay started as Robert strode towards Jenn, looking like a thundercloud about to burst.

Jenn faced him. 'This has nothing to do with you, Robert. I don't have a choice . . . '

'After everything that you've heard, you want to bring him here?' Robert snapped, not letting her finish. 'And will you come with him?'

'No,' Jenn replied flatly. 'I'll stay at Clonnet.'

Wilf took this moment to intervene. 'Is your son in danger?'

'I . . . ' Jenn struggled, feeling Robert's gaze on her – and Finnlay's as well. 'Not danger, not at the moment. But his father plans to send him away, to Meir, and that would be dangerous. Andrew doesn't understand and I think . . . I think he has powers.'

'He's too young for you to be sure of that, but,' Wilf held up his hand to forestall her, 'even so, abducting him might not be the best course of action. However, the council will discuss the matter.'

Jenn nodded and almost ran out of the cavern. Finnlay turned back to Robert, who was staring at her back. He put out his hand and caught Robert's elbow. 'Come, let's go.'

Robert didn't speak as Finnlay drew him along the corridor and up the long sloping tunnel until they were caught in the draught of icy wind as it drew across the heavy doorway. Finnlay pushed the door open and Robert followed him. If there was going to be shouting, the best place was outside – the price of living in a cave community. The sun was still shining, but its warmth was an illusion against the cold.

'No matter how hard I try, or how many years I take, I'll never understand her!'

Finnlay glanced at Robert. There was a frown of incomprehension on his face. 'Why would she want her son to come here rather than somewhere else? She's not exactly a great supporter of the Enclave. Hasn't she just spent the last five years trying to sever all connections with it?'

'Haven't you?'

Robert turned at this and raised his eyebrows. There was the old familiar Robert, both surprised and vulnerable at the same time, still lightly self-mocking and yet entirely ignorant of the dichotomy. 'I suppose if I dare to say I have my reasons, you'll point out that Jenn probably has her reasons, too.'

Finnlay nodded and continued to walk. Robert paced alongside him, his hands behind his back.

'Still, I'm at a loss why it is that you understand her better than I do,' Robert went on, his voice level. 'You've seen no more of her in the last five years than I have . . . '

'But I'm not in love with her,' Finnlay replied carefully. Nor was he the father of the son in question – and perhaps it was because he knew that, that he did understand a lot more than Robert thought. Was that why Jenn wanted Andrew here? Did Jenn think that with Andrew living here he would at least see his real father a little, rather than never?

No matter which way he looked at it, he could see there was a logic to Jenn's request, but how to explain that to Robert without actually telling him the truth? Of course, that's exactly what Jenn should be doing – telling Robert the truth.

'Do you remember,' Finnlay began in a lighter tone, 'how I used to argue with you over every decision you made? You kept refusing to join the Enclave, but you would never say why, and the more you refused, the angrier I got. In the end, my anger prevented me from having the patience to work out why you refused.'

Robert nodded. 'But I'm not angry with Jenn. Just confused. She's the one who's angry with me.'

'That's not what I'm getting at. Whether it's anger or something else; unless you approach her with patience and kindness and actually ask her what's going on, you won't get any better a reply than I used to get from you.'

'It should be more than obvious to everyone that Jenn would rather throw herself from the top of this mountain than have a decent conversation with me. It's a nice idea, Finn, but it will never happen.'

'But doesn't it bother you that she seems to hate you so much?'

Robert's face hardened, but Finnlay couldn't look away. He stopped, lacing his fingers together in the same gesture of calm he'd seen Robert use many times. Perhaps it would have some mystical effect on him, make his next question that much easier.

'Well?' Robert grunted, aware of the hesitation.

'Does there have to be a war?' Finnlay swallowed. 'I mean, if this is all about Carlan – Nash – wouldn't it be . . . easier . . . or something if you . . . '

'Faced him on my own? Without dragging the whole country into it?' Muscles stood out on Robert's jawline, hard and inflexible. 'I thought you knew me better than that.'

Finnlay steadied himself. 'I thought I'd never see you go to war against Selar. I haven't seen you for five damned years, Robert. What am I to think?'

'Whatever you like. Work it out for yourself. You were, after all, the only one who worked out that I had the Word of Destruction. *Before* I used it. Of course, the whole world knows about it now, don't they?'

'Including Nash.' Finnlay was abruptly chastised and horrified at the same time. 'But surely if you used it against him again . . . '

'He survived it once, Brother,' Robert replied, easing out the tension in his voice with a sigh. 'I can't risk getting close enough to him to try it again – even if it might kill him. If it doesn't – what if he hears it? Learns how to use it?' He paused, running his hands through his hair. 'You know I can't even think the Word? I can only say it – and you've already seen the consequences. And you're too tactful to ask the other obvious question. What if I fail against him?'

'What?'

Robert raised his eyebrows, a self-mocking smile on his face. 'I'm not invincible, you know. Nash can kill me – and if I'm dead, how will Selar be stopped? Especially if Nash has the Word. No, my first priority is to stop this insane invasion of Mayenne, because if I don't, Tirone will retaliate with an invasion of his own and Lusara will burn. Nash is looking for the Key. When he doesn't find it in Mayenne, he'll look elsewhere. Perhaps here. But I tell you this, he won't stop until he has it. If I face him alone now, without some other weapon to bring against him, I can't assume I'll survive.'

Finnlay studied him for a long, silent moment. Quietly he added, 'And you won't be around to protect Jenn from him.'

'No.'

Without moving, Finnlay whispered, 'Are you afraid?'

Robert allowed his gaze to sweep over the rocky peaks before returning to Finnlay, steady and open. 'Yes.'

Then he smiled gently and reached out to touch the side of Finnlay's face. 'But don't tell anyone.'

Finnlay gave an involuntary laugh. 'And who would believe me?'

Robert dropped his hand and shook his head, a sly smile on his face. 'Believe it or not, I actually worried about you living here. I worried that things hadn't worked out with Fiona, that Mother had found the place unbearable, or that Deverin and the rest had found homes somewhere else. I never dreamed you'd really make a life here – or become a father, twice over. I confess, there's a part of me that's envious of what you have. I know you see it as being a curse, having to stay here so Nash can't Seek you – but look at what he has, unwittingly, given you. In some ways, I was so worried I couldn't

113

bring myself to find out the actual truth. It's often easier to go on wondering than risk knowing the worst.'

Just exactly who was Robert talking about, here? Finnlay couldn't help frowning. 'As to that . . . '

'What?'

'It's not just me, Robert, it's everyone. Nobody's asked because we're all afraid to know the answer – but I can't stand it any longer.'

Robert was about to speak when his gaze shifted slightly. Finnlay knew that look and didn't interrupt it. When the gaze returned to him, Finnlay continued, 'I'm sorry but I have to ask.'

'For the love of Mineah, Finn, get it out.'

'Micah?' Finnlay blurted. 'You've not said a word about him. Has something happened?'

Robert blinked a few times. Abruptly he grinned, and shook his head. 'By the gods, I'm sorry! Actually, until a moment ago, I couldn't honestly be sure myself – but Micah is fine. Absolutely fine.'

'How do you know?'

At that, Robert chuckled outright and turned around. 'Because he's just coming through the gate. Look!'

If it was possible to bring sunshine underground, then Micah Maclean was the one to do it. Margaret couldn't help noticing the difference in her family at the appearance of the young man – bushy brown beard and all. Finnlay was laughing, Deverin and Owen kept slapping Micah on the shoulder and saying how much he'd grown and filled out over the years – and Robert was visibly relieved. For the second time in two days, there was an impromptu party in Finnlay and Fiona's rooms. The poor children were overwhelmed.

It was so good to see Robert again – and Micah. So good to see them all together and happy, at least on the surface. Despite the atmosphere outside in the caves, here, around this fire, there was laughter and excitement, the promise of something. Everyone was involved and everyone responded. All except Jenn.

Certainly she was pleased to see Micah appear fit and well, but still she sat on the sidelines, closed and cold. It was as though she didn't want to belong and every attempt to include her was rejected. After a while, Margaret couldn't stand it any more. She collected two fresh cups of the lovely nutty ale the Enclave produced and moved towards Jenn's corner in a way that prevented Jenn from escaping. She took a seat and passed a cup to Jenn. 'You must miss your little boy, being away from him like this.'

Jenn nodded quickly. 'Yes, I do.'

'Is it the first time?'

'I do get to visit my sister every now and then. Eachern won't allow me to take Andrew.'

'But Bella and Lawrence visit Clonnet?'

'Yes.' Jenn held the cup in her hands as though it were some kind of lifeline.

'He'll be six in a few months, won't he?'

'Yes.'

'And who does he favour? You or his father?'

Jenn paused to take a long mouthful of the ale. 'I'm pleased to say he looks more like me than his father. He has blue eyes and lovely dark hair.'

Margaret watched her carefully. 'And is he mischievous?'

That question elicited an involuntary smile from Jenn – a rare occurrence these days. 'He certainly has his moments.'

'I had the same problem with both Finnlay and Robert,' Margaret replied. 'Even worse when they were old enough to fight each other. Fortunately, although Robert was six years older than Finnlay and could have used the size difference to his advantage, he never did. I'm not sure Finnlay even remembers that small fact. When Trevor died, all combats of that kind were forbidden and my boys were relegated to fighting with words only. I guess that's why they're both so good at it now.'

Jenn was silent for a moment, but the brooding gaze had gone. She glanced up with a gentle smile. 'And now you're a grand-mother.'

Margaret smiled herself, but before she could say another word, Jenn's expression changed as Martha came across the room to join them.

'It's getting quite crowded in here,' Martha murmured as Jenn came to her feet.

'Yes, I need some air. I have a headache pounding behind my eyes. If you'll excuse me, I'm going to lie down.'

Margaret could do nothing to stop her as she vanished from the room. She turned back to Martha, whose distracted gaze turned to Robert across the room.

'Are we going to lose her completely?'

Martha shook her head. 'Not if I can help it.' With that, she turned and moved up behind Robert, murmuring something in his ear. For a second, he looked confused – then his eyes glinted in a way Margaret had never seen. Abruptly he turned and left the room.

Robert made his way along the corridor to Martha and Arlie's rooms and knocked on the outer door. There was no answer, so he silently pushed the door open and slipped inside. Jenn's room was on the left, the door prettily decorated by the creative Martha. Robert stood before it, hesitating for a moment. This was not a moment to have a repeat of the last time they were alone.

He knocked. There was no response. Was she asleep? She'd left complaining of a headache. He knocked again. There was a movement inside and suddenly the door was wrenched open.

'What . . . ' Jenn stopped with her mouth open then began to close the door.

Robert put out his hand to stop her. 'I just want to talk. Let me in, Jenn. Please.'

She stiffened, but eventually stepped back. The room was dark, only one candle lit. The bed was unruffled.

'How is your headache?' he began quietly.

'Fine. What do you want, Robert? Have you come to berate me about Andrew? I think you're a little premature. Until Wilf gives me an answer, you've got nothing to argue against.'

Robert took in a deep breath. Be calm and reasonable. Nothing else. 'Are you certain your son will develop powers? Is that why you want him to come here?'

'It's none of your business, Robert.' Her face was the picture of icy calm, her voice steady and remote, even bitter. The wall she had thrown up around herself was no less adamantine than the one he tried to create around the demon.

Casually, Robert leaned back against the sideboard and folded his arms. 'I'm just curious, really. From what I've heard, you've done a good job separating yourself from the Enclave and everyone in it.

Now you want your son to come and live here – on his own? Don't you even want to be with him?'

'I told you it's none of your business, Robert!' Jenn snapped. 'Now if you don't mind, I would prefer to be alone.'

'And what about the bruises?'

She stopped cold at that, turning wide eyes on him. For a second he saw a flash of fear in them, which abruptly changed to betrayal. 'What bruises?'

'Martha told me, Jenn,' Robert replied briskly, taking a step towards her. 'Tell me the truth, did Eachern do that to you?'

'Why should I tell you . . . '

'Did he?' Robert thundered. He grabbed her arms and shook her a little. 'How long has he been beating you?'

Jenn shrank in his grasp, breathing heavily. Her eyes were wild for a moment, like a trapped animal, desperate for an escape. He couldn't hold onto her any longer, not when she looked like that – not now that he had his answer. Gently he let her go and stepped back, hating himself.

'Why do you put up with it?' Robert asked quietly, his stomach leaden. 'You have the power to stop him.'

Jenn straightened her dress with shaking hands, her voice tremulous. 'And how would I manage that without revealing what I was? I have neither the skill nor the training to put a thought into his mind and, to be honest, I doubt it would stick there more than a moment. He hates sorcerers, he hates you. If he found out what I was . . . '

'Have you tried Sealing him?'

'More times than you can imagine, but to gain the consent I need, I would have to tell him – and then he would never give it. So you tell me, Robert, how am I to . . . defend myself against him?'

She did not turn to face him and his hands moved, to touch her, to offer some kind of comfort – but he held back. What comfort could he offer? He should never have left her behind. He should have taken her with him six years ago and damned the consequences. He should have . . .

It was too late now. The damage had been done. But perhaps he could prevent further damage.

She stood with her back to him, her arms folded protectively across her chest. There had once been a time when he'd thought that fragility of hers was little more than an impression given out by her diminutive size. But five years had given it body and scope and now she was fragile in fact as well. How far dare he push her?

'You're not going back to him.'

About that far. Her head snapped up and once again that fiery temper flared. 'How dare you . . . '

'I won't let you go back to him,' Robert added, firmly, more confidently than he really felt. If he ever got his hands on Eachern . . .

'This has nothing to do with you, Robert!' Jenn took another step forward, menacing in every line of her body. 'I don't need your protection or your interference. I'll return to him whether you like it or not – and what's more, there is nothing you can do to stop me. Now get out!'

Perhaps he couldn't stop her, but maybe he could do something to Eachern, to make sure he never touched her again. Was he also beating the boy? Was that what this was all about? Unlikely. Knowing Jenn, she would have killed Eachern by now if that were the case. But still, he couldn't leave it there.

He caught her gaze, met her anger with his own calm. 'You are really incredible, you know that? If only I'd known you'd be so easy to control, I would have married you myself! You let a thug like Eachern beat you up and yet you can muster a solid fight against me when I only want to help you. Strange logic indeed. Very well, I'll take you back to him – but don't think for one moment that's the end of this subject.'

As he turned and made for the door, she chased after him. 'You leave him alone, Robert. I'm warning you . . . '

'Or you'll what?' Robert turned to face her, his heart pounding in his chest. 'Will you tell your good friend Nash about me?'

She stopped as though he'd slapped her. 'Get out!' she hissed, every ounce of venom she could produce instilled in those two words. 'Get out and don't ever come back!'

She physically pushed him out the door and slammed it shut behind him. He could almost feel the warning she placed upon it – but he had no intention of going back. He couldn't afford to. Not now. The demon rumbled and complained inside, darkening his already black mood. He had to get away, regain control, ease it back down into silence.

What an idiot! What a complete and utter, brainless idiot he was.

As soon as he'd finished breakfast, Micah headed outside to breathe the cool crisp air of a mountain morning. With any luck it might clear the gentle pounding against the back of his eyes. Too much ale last night, that was the problem. Self-inflicted wounds were always the worst to deal with.

The sky was a flat lead-grey, the air a little warm, hinting of more snow later on. There were plenty of people about: children playing in the snow, adults at work. The winter was long in the mountains; any chance to get outside was usually grasped with both hands – though how anybody could willingly live their entire lives inside a cave was beyond Micah. Pulling his cloak around him, he wandered around the rim of the bowl until he saw Jenn sitting on a rock cleared of snow.

'Good morning.'

She looked up in surprise and then smiled. 'Good morning yourself. I didn't think you'd be up for some time. Lady Margaret mentioned how you and the boys sat up into the wee hours. Have you drained the Enclave's supply of ale yet?'

'Oh, I hope not.' Micah grinned. 'Is there room on that rock for two?'

'Take a seat.' Jenn shifted a little and Micah sat beside her. 'I'm sure you've already had plenty of comments on it, but I think I like the beard. It suits you. Not sure about the brown hair, though; I miss your usual red curls.'

Micah glanced at her and tried to ignore the shadows around her eyes. 'Thanks. Finnlay says it makes me look older.'

'Well, you are older. I mean, you look at least five years older than the last time I saw you.' She tossed him a smile which, for a moment, made the shadows disappear. 'How have you been? For that matter, where have you been?'

Micah picked up a handful of snow and squeezed it together in his hands. 'In the north. Dromna. It's where Selar's army is gathering. I've been there off and on over the last year, ever since we first heard something was going on. I have a job in a tavern –

hence the beard and the hair dye as disguise. I can't wait to wash it out.'

'I didn't know a beard was required when working in a tavern.'

With a chuckle, Micah threw the snowball away. 'What about you? How is life at Clonnet?'

Abruptly, Jenn's voice dropped and bitterness framed her face. 'Is that your question – or did Robert send you out here?'

'Hey.' Micah turned to face her squarely. 'This is me – remember? For a while, the only honest friend you had in the world. I ask because I care and I want to know. Nobody sent me here, believe me.'

She met his gaze, searching for something, but her mood only softened a little. 'Life is . . . fine.'

'And Andrew?'

For a moment, she didn't answer, then her gaze dropped. 'I wish you could meet him. He'd really like you, I'm sure. But I don't suppose that's going to happen any time soon. Micah?'

'Yes?'

'There is going to be a war, isn't there? Robert is serious about all this?'

'I'm afraid so.' He sighed and folded his arms. 'I think you're the only person here who understands how he has fought against doing just this. In one way, there's a kind of positive effect on him because he's finally doing something, but on the other hand, he just keeps reminding himself how many Lusarans are going to die simply because he can't find another way of stopping Selar. Oh, he'll do all he can to minimise the damage – but war is war and no matter how it's fought, people will get killed.'

Jenn said nothing for a moment and simply leaned against his shoulder. Her silence drew out until she sighed. 'You will promise me to be careful, won't you? In Dromna – and afterwards? I really . . . don't want anything to happen to you.'

Micah took her hand and squeezed it. 'I promise. And when it's all over, I'll find some way to visit you at Clonnet and meet Andrew.' He swallowed, steeling his courage. 'Does he resemble Robert?'

She should have stiffened at that, but instead she shook her head. 'No – fortunately.'

Micah glanced aside at her, but the bitterness this time wasn't directed at Robert. She caught him watching her and lifted her chin, giving his shoulder a gentle push.

'And why haven't you found some nice girl to marry?'

Micah sighed loudly – why did everyone have to ask him the same question? 'Every year when I visit my family, I get asked the same thing. I go all the way to Flan'har, with lots of news to entertain them with, and all they want to know about are the girls I've met. Just because all my brothers and sisters have married and produced numerous children, everyone assumes I'll be following along behind.'

'Does that mean you don't want to get married?'

He took in a breath and held it for a few seconds. He could get away with telling her the truth. She at least would understand – unlike his family. 'No. It means that I can't afford to. Not yet.'

Jenn shifted around until she faced him. 'Because of Robert?'

He met her gaze without faltering. 'I won't leave him, Jenn. Not until this is over. Don't ask me to, don't expect me to explain why. I've met a couple of girls and well . . . yes, if it wasn't for Selar and Nash and the prophecy and if we'd been allowed to live normal lives, I probably would be married by now – but the point is, I want what Robert wants, what you want. I'm not going to just leave him to do it all alone while I go off and have a happy normal life, because it wouldn't be happy and it wouldn't be normal. I just can't do that.'

He finished, and found Jenn smiling at him.

'No, you haven't really changed at all, have you?'

'Well,' he replied, starting to laugh at himself, 'I grew a beard. Doesn't that count for something?'

'Oh, it counts for everything. Come on, we'd better get down to the council rooms. The big decision is due any moment.'

Finnlay kept to one side of the council chamber as everyone entered and took seats. The last to come in were Micah and Jenn, looking a little more relaxed than she had before. Not much, but a little.

Wilf didn't go for any great ceremony. The moment the door was closed, he got to his feet and addressed the room, and Robert in particular.

'For the first time in my life, I find I am in agreement with you, Robert – and so is the rest of the council. There is a very real threat to us if Selar goes through with this war, if this Carlan or Nash, or whatever his name is, is allowed to run amok with Selar's army. We will help in whatever way we can as long as we still have enough people left here to defend the Enclave.'

'Of course.'

'I just want you to be clear on one thing: our support is for this campaign and nothing else. We are doing this to stop Carlan finding and destroying us. Now, what kind of support do you want?'

Robert glanced around and cleared his throat. 'Forty Seekers with substantial combat training.'

'Only forty?'

'Any more will be a drain on your resources. I'll also take any Dunlorn people who are willing to fight.'

'When will you want them?'

'I can't answer that yet. Tomorrow, Micah heads back to Dromna. He'll stay there until he has word that Selar's army is marching. When I get that word, I'll come here, collect the force and take it to my army.'

'And you can make all your arrangements before you leave tomorrow?'

'With Finnlay's help, yes. My mother, Deverin, Owen and a few others will be going straight to my base at Flan'har. I, of course, have to take Jenn back home.'

Finnlay glanced at her. She stood by the door, leaning against the wall, her eyes on Wilf. The old man pursed his lips, but didn't look at her.

'I'm sorry, Jenn. I appreciate your difficulty, but I'm afraid we are unable to help you. To do so would be to risk your husband's efforts to find Andrew and get him back. With a Bresail at hand and on the eve of war, the hazard is too great. I couldn't guarantee his safety.'

In a flash, Jenn's expression altered completely. Her eyes hardened and, without a word, she turned and fled the room, slamming the door behind her. After a moment, everyone else began to move as well, but Finnlay stayed where he was until Robert gained his side.

'Please, Finn,' he murmured.

Finnlay didn't need a second request. He turned and pushed past the others out into the corridor – but she was already gone. Without pausing, he brought his *ayarn* into his left hand, sending his Senses through the Enclave.

Yes, she was on her way outside.

By the time he got there, she'd managed to walk almost halfway around the field, completely ignoring the snow creeping up her skirt. With a sigh of exasperation, Finnlay ran across to her.

'By the gods,' Jenn cried, stomping the ground, 'why won't anybody here just leave me alone!'

Finnlay caught her arm. 'Just wait a moment. I've just come to see if you're all right.'

'I'm fine. Now go.'

It would have been a simple thing to do, but he'd never taken the simple path in his whole life and he was too old to start now. 'Jenn, don't you see we're only doing this because we care about you?'

'Oh, yes,' she snapped, twisting out of his grasp. 'You all care so much you gave me absolutely no support against the council. I would have thought you above all people would want to see your nephew here, out of harm's way.'

A movement behind her caught his eye. He glanced up to find Robert had followed him, but had paused at the tunnel exit. Silently, Finnlay willed Robert to go back inside. He was the last person Jenn wanted to see right now.

As though he read Finnlay's intent, Robert hesitated a moment longer, then turned and disappeared into the darkness. Finnlay faced Jenn again.

'You're right,' he said. 'I would love to see Andrew living here – and you as well. But I'd also love my brother to know that he has a son. Are you going to keep him in ignorance forever? Do you really hate Robert that much?'

'Serin's blood, Finn!' Jenn yelled, spreading her arms in sheer frustration. 'Are you blind? Don't you see the position I'm in? What am I supposed to do with myself? I'm a married woman. I don't have your freedoms, your right to make decisions for yourself. I live in a tiny narrow prison and the only light in my window comes from Andrew. Of course I don't want him to go away – but I'd rather that than leave him under the influence of the monster I have to claim is his father. You've spoken to Murdoch – you know how Kenrick is growing up. I won't have that for my son!' She paused, gulping in air.

'But just abducting him . . . '

'Don't fool yourself, Finn. If I just ran off with Andrew, Eachern would tear the country apart looking for us. Hell, he's had a perfect example in Selar. And the people I left behind would suffer for my actions. And Bella and Lawrence. If we brought Andrew here, we could make it look like he'd died in an accident. Didn't Carlan manage to abduct me and have my family think I was dead for almost fifteen years? It can be done – if there is a will. But nobody believes me. They're all too concerned with what your damned brother has to say. Too busy trying to fight a war when I'm just trying to—'

She ran out of words as huge sobs racked her body. Finnlay reached out and held her, but she didn't give in. After a moment she pressed him back, wiping her eyes with irritation. 'And what do you think would happen if I told Robert the truth now? Would he just nod and smile and say that's nice? Would he be content to leave Andrew where he is? What would he say to you, Finn, when he found out both you and Micah have known all along and never told him? We both know he's never asked anything more from you both than your loyalty. You know how hopelessly important that is to him. Do you really want him to go into this war – to face the Angel of Darkness – doubting if he can trust the two men closest to him in the whole world? Is that what you want, Finn? Is it?'

Tears glittered in her eyes; gently, Finnlay reached out to brush them away. 'Of course not. But will you tell him? One day?'

Her voice was a leaden murmur. 'I'm not sure there will ever be a moment when Robert's whole life isn't dominated by the prophecy. Andrew was conceived because Robert and I were Bonded. I don't want to give him something else to regret, another reason to hate himself. He has enough with me already.' Jenn lifted her head and breathed deeply. 'I know your lives are all bound up with this prophecy, Finn, but I've never really been able to understand what my part in it is supposed to be. Maybe I will one day, I don't know –

but until then, my first and only concern has to be my son. Surely, as a father yourself, you must see that.'

Reluctantly, Finnlay nodded. 'Just don't expect me to like it. Come on. I'll take you back inside. It's way too cold out here and Robert's probably got some damned job for me to do.'

If only he hadn't given her his word.

It was an ugly morning to be getting up so early, but Micah didn't really have a choice. Robert was already having breakfast in the refectory by the time Micah joined him. No one else was about yet.

'Is Jenn awake?' Micah asked, tucking into his food with haste.

'Yes. I've seen her already. She'll meet us with the horses.'

Eating in silence, Micah couldn't help watching Robert. After a while, he ventured, 'You will be able to get her back on time, won't you?'

'I don't see why not.' Robert concentrated on his breakfast.

Micah studied him for a moment. 'She blames you for everything that's happened.'

Robert got to his feet and Micah joined him as they headed for the door. 'Yes.'

'But it isn't your fault. You know that – she knows it. So why does she blame you?'

Robert glanced across with half a smile. 'Why not? She's got to blame somebody. The events at Elita were always going to impact more on Jenn than anyone else. At the time we knew her marriage to Eachern would protect her from the worst, but even so, we knew it wasn't going to be easy.'

'But she thinks you just deserted her when you didn't. Why don't you tell her about—'

'Forget it, Micah. No matter what I say, the situation is never going to get any better. She hates me and that's all there is to it. Jenn might find it easier if you travel with us as far as possible. It seems she's still happy to talk to you. I would appreciate it if you could do your best to find out as much about her life at Clonnet as possible.'

There was an edge to Robert's tone that hadn't been there before and Micah glanced sharply at him as they approached outside. The sky was loaded with heavy clouds, boding ill for the journey down from the mountain. 'Is something wrong?'

'Yes,' Robert said. 'But don't worry, I'm determined to fix it before I leave her at Clonnet. Look on the bright side, it'll give her something else to hate me for.'

Micah frowned, but it was too late to pursue the subject. Finnlay met them at the tunnel mouth.

'I guess you can't wait another day?'

Robert shook his head and lifted his saddlebag over his shoulder. 'Don't worry, Finn, you can handle all the details. I trust you.'

Finnlay nodded. In that moment, Micah was struck by how closely they resembled their dead father. Both tall, broad-shouldered, lean and fit. Fighting men, in the true tradition of the Douglas House. Trevor would have been proud.

'Finn,' Robert began carefully, his gaze lighting on Jenn as she waited with the horses by the gate. 'I need you to make it clear to everyone that all this has but one purpose: to stop Selar invading Mayenne. It's no good just warning Tirone of what his brother plans. Tirone can't keep a fully equipped army sitting on the border until the day Selar dies. Not only that, we don't want Tirone to start thinking that the only way Selar can be stopped is for him to invade Lusara and be done with it. What we want is to stop Selar before his troops can reach the border, make him disband his army and make sure he never thinks of invading Mayenne again.'

'Oh?' Finnlay bit in his lip and Robert turned back. 'And what if that means you have to kill the King?'

For a moment there was no reaction, then a little shake of his head and the usual smile. 'I doubt it will come to that. Take care, Brother. I don't know when I'll be back. Look after my nieces while I'm gone.'

Finnlay nodded, obviously unhappy. 'And you be careful – both of you.'

'Oh,' Robert laughed, 'Micah's got the safest job of the lot up at Dromna. Nobody will recognise him with that damned beard.'

Micah looked up. 'What's wrong with my beard?'

'You really want me to answer that?'

8

The Thesium had an air of quiet, of contained study, underscored by the sounds of thirty Guildesmen as they bent their heads to their work. The scratch of pen on vellum, the pause to dip into black ink, the careful shift of a stool or elbow moved on a desk sang a gentle song to Vaughn, a hymn to the glories of the Guilde's sacred duty.

As tall as it was wide, this room was something of an oddity within the Guildehall. Constructed almost three centuries before, of imported rose sandstone, it formed a kind of bridge between the cloister and the Great Hall, and Vaughn never tired of walking its length. Windows began above his head and rose to the ceiling, tall and arched, allowing light to penetrate the room winter or summer. Vaulted sections in the roof joined in star-points, decorated with the badge of the Guilde carved out of complementary white stone, golden now with age. It was the least fussy of all the Hall's buildings, but it was more the work it sheltered than any love of architecture that drew Vaughn here.

He wandered the length of the room quietly, glancing aside at each man he passed, noting if any paused at his gaze. Laid out before every scribe was a copy of the same document, being copied faithfully. Vaughn breathed deeply of the air and paused only when he reached the door at the end, where Godet waited for him.

'Well?' Vaughn asked quietly, hoping not to disturb the important efforts of his brethren.

'I have collated the last few reports, my lord.'

'I sincerely hope you kept their arrival out of sight of our dear Governor Osbert?'

'Of course, my lord. He has been with the King all morning.'

'Good. And?'

'The results are surprising, to say the least.'

'In what way?' Vaughn kept his gaze on the room, deliberately watching, deliberately provoking. More than a few scribes squirmed under his scrutiny.

'The Bresail has had limited success out in the country. We have hunted down and executed nine sorcerers in all.'

'What's so surprising about that?'

'Only three of them had one of those small stones in their possession. The others were all young, little more than children.'

'Then we get them before they can do too much harm. I still don't see your problem.'

'My lord, the Bresail has been out for some weeks now. Surely we should have caught many more than this?'

'So, word has got out. They're all fleeing the country in fear of their lives. I don't really care. Of course, I would love to burn the lot of them, but having them gone is sufficient for the time being.'

'But is it not possible some might have escaped detection? If we—'

The room grew dark, but no cloud passed across the sun. Vaughn frowned. The patches of light drawn on the floor were just as sharp as before, but even so, his vision shrank away, dying before he could utter a word. An icy chill leaked into his bones . . . just like that night at Lagganfors . . .

He was engulfed in grey, the air scented with something familiar. Incense and salt, and something else warm and inviting, like a baker's oven. A glow formed in the distance, growing to highlight the edges of an arch, gilded with intricate patterns carved into the stone, more in the floor . . . and pools of something glistening against the distant light. Blood.

He knew this place.

A voice murmured in the emptiness, confusing his attempts to remember. Words came to him, but meaningless, a language he knew nothing of. Then, more ominous, the grating of steel upon stone. A cry of pain, curses languishing in the darkness.

A sword arced its way around one pillar, followed by a hand. A boy – a young man. Standing clear beneath the arch, lit from the glow behind, the light forming a corona around his head. The words were coming from him, but still meaningless. He was wounded, cursing his enemy – but who was it? Vaughn strained to move forward, his urgency building with each sound. He had to know . . . had to see who was standing . . .

'My lord?'

Like a slap of cold air, Vaughn returned to himself. The Thesium was as before, Godet still at his side. Quickly, Vaughn moved his mouth, forming a question. 'What?'

'Are you sure the Bresail is as powerful as you believe, my lord?'

Carefully Vaughn turned to look at his nephew. There was nothing on the young man's face to show he'd noticed anything unusual. Vaughn released a pent-up breath. 'Yes, I am. More so now than before.'

Especially in light of these . . . visions.

What had he seen? The future or the past? Was that boy . . . the Prince? Was he in danger, was the vision to warn him?

Vaughn glanced once more around the room, then ducked out the doorway into the cloister, keeping Godet at his side. Almost absently, he took the path back to his study, hiding his disquiet. 'When the hunters return to Marsay, I want you to gather the three stones they collected. We need more Bresails if we're to do this job properly.'

'As you wish, my lord.'

Governor Osbert watched as Kenrick pursed his lips, then reached forward to move his next piece. The board before him was already scattered with his father's pieces and now Kenrick was perilously close to an outright loss. Selar merely sat back in his chair opposite, his hand idly running through his close-cropped beard. His eyes never once left his son.

Osbert tensed as Kenrick picked up the wrong piece and moved it. Did the boy never listen? Hadn't they discussed this very strategy last night? Hopeless!

'I think,' the King murmured, moving his hand slowly across the board, 'that you've just given me another victory, my son.'

Kenrick watched as Selar lifted a piece, moved it and completely trapped his own pieces. He'd lost.

In one swift movement, Kenrick's arm swept up under the table, collected the board and sent it flying through the air. Pieces clattered across the tiled floor, coming up to rest against the open door where Nash had just appeared.

Inside, Osbert willed himself to be calm and serene, but that was becoming harder each day. Especially now.

'Good morning, Sire,' Nash said, stepping gingerly over the pieces as he approached the table.

'Did I send for you, Nash?' Selar enquired lazily.

'Of course you did, Sire.'

Selar raised his eyebrows in feigned surprise, but eventually smiled. 'Oh, yes, now I remember.'

Kenrick pushed his chair back from the table and barred Nash any further advance into the room. 'I heard a rumour, Governor.'

'Did you, my Prince? And what rumour would that be?'

If Kenrick was at all intimidated by the tone of Nash's voice, he certainly didn't show it. He was either a very brave or a very stupid Prince. 'I heard you're a sorcerer.'

Selar burst out laughing at this. 'Oh, son, we've all heard that one many times before. Hasn't everybody claimed they saw a sorcerer, or knew one at one time or another? With Vaughn's toy roaming the countryside, that gossip will soon die out.'

The Prince glared at his father, his teeth clenched together. 'It was a fair question, Sire, and not one which deserved laughter.'

'Really, Kenrick, I don't think this is something you need to get upset about.'

Kenrick planted his hands on the table and leaned forward, his face close to Selar's. 'If I brought you proof that your pet was a sorcerer, would you put him to the sword?'

'Don't be ridiculous!' Selar laughed.

'Would you?' the boy bellowed.

'Please, Kenrick,' Selar replied indulgently, 'you're being rude.'

With that, Kenrick straightened up, his eyes flaring. Without another word, he turned and stalked out of the room.

Osbert breathed a sigh of relief as Selar turned from his son to his favourite.

'Nash, what has Vaughn got stuck in his bonnet now? Some idea that you're mixed up with sorcery? What have you done to offend him? Come, tell me the truth.'

'Nothing, Sire,' Nash said, his gaze firmly on Osbert. 'Though you might think of having a word to him on the subject. I can't see his efforts will keep peace in the country for much longer.'

'If you think that's wise.'

'I do. If you will excuse us, Sire, Osbert and I have an appointment with the Proctor this morning.'

Osbert was out the door with Nash's hand at his elbow before he could say a word in protest. At the bottom of the stairs, however, Nash cornered him, his eyes fierce in the shadows.

'You've managed to avoid me quite well over the last few weeks, my friend. So tell me, where did Vaughn hide the books in his secret library?'

Osbert shook his head immediately. 'No, I showed you the room, showed you what he'd done with them. You know as well as I do he'd rather burn those things than have the likes of you get hold of them. I tell you, there is no secret library any more.'

'Then how has Vaughn suddenly gained the information to make his Bresail?'

Holding firm, Osbert replied, his voice only slightly trembling, 'Perhaps somebody told him, or a new book has come into his hands.' He paused, affecting haughty injustice. 'Why do you assume it's my fault? If Vaughn has had these books all along, why has he only just made this Bresail? It doesn't make sense since he's hated sorcerers all his life.'

For a moment, Nash held his gaze with dark eyes, a frown drawing his eyebrows together. Then slowly he said, 'You're either a better liar than I thought you were, or you're telling the truth. Either way, if you hear anything, see anything that might indicate where those books are now, I want to know. Do I make myself clear?'

Osbert could only nod his agreement as Nash turned and left him.

It was an enormous display of patience, almost – in Nash's mind – as great as the wait *he'd* been forced to endure. Not only over the last five years, but the eighty-odd since he'd first determined on his destiny. He kept his stance unmoving as the tailor shuffled around him, carefully, and perhaps a little nervously, pinning tucks of cloth this way and that. Considering the amount of time the man had taken on this one garment, it should rival the coronation robes of the greatest King in history!

What to do about Osbert? It was certain those books were long gone. Finding them now wouldn't be impossible, but did he have the time to go chasing after them? Surely only the most elongated torture would get the secret out of the damned Proctor, and there'd be questions and a mission he'd trust nobody else with to get the books back. How could he waste precious time on something that might not even get results when, in only nine days, he would be making his way to Clonnet?

And in the end, would the books give him what he wanted? Would there be any mention in them of where the Key was hidden?

'And when,' Nash said carefully, 'do you expect to have this jacket finished?'

The man swallowed. 'Er . . . another two weeks, my lord Governor. You see, we had that problem with the lining and I've had to wait for a new order to come in.'

Without moving a muscle, Nash dropped his tone. 'I can't wait two weeks. I need it in one.'

'Of course, my lord.' The tailor finished and helped Nash remove the jacket. With a gesture, Nash dismissed him, to find his servant Taymar standing in the doorway. He waited until the tailor had gone and then turned an easy smile on Nash.

'I have good news, Master.'

With a sigh, Nash stretched and sank onto the chair behind his desk. 'Has Vaughn's Bresail caught the Enemy?'

'No, Master.'

Nash collected his wine and glanced up. Taymar waited patiently for him to ask. Patience was something Taymar seemed to have in abundance. Despite the fact that he was completely and wholly Bonded to Nash, most of the time, Taymar displayed an independence of thought not often exercised by those still free. He obeyed every command Nash gave, no matter how odious, never questioned, never failed, unless circumstances prevented him. Until that night at Elita, his brother Lisson had served Nash in the same manner. Not once had Nash found occasion to fault either of them. But Lisson had been killed along with all the others, leaving Nash with only this one man he could trust completely without ever having to explain what or why.

'Very well,' Nash nodded, 'tell me your good news.'

'You requested I find you some means to complete your regeneration so that you may Bond with the Ally at last.'

Nash nodded again.

'I have done as you asked, Master. Someone who can give you all you need to finally regain full strength.'

The lazy mood abruptly dissipated and Nash came to his feet, hardly daring to hope.

'Yes, Master. I have captured one of the Salti Pazar.'

Godfrey sat at the end of the long table, doing his best to swallow one mouthful of food after another. This stuff was too rich for him, but Bishop Brome would notice if he didn't clear at least one full plate. For some reason, the obese prelate believed a man's soul could be fed on pepper cream sauces and roasted swan alone.

A lute player sat in the corner of the winter dining room, his fingers drawing a lilting tune out of his instrument. Normally, Godfrey would have enjoyed such an accompaniment to his meal, but since he'd returned from Elita with Robert's words of warning in his ears, simply relaxing in the company of Brome had become almost impossible.

Of course, relaxing around Brome had never been easy. His leadership of the Church had become almost a laughing matter among the younger, more liberal priests – and as for their brethren in other countries? Godfrey chose not to think about it.

One day – soon, with any luck – Brome would be removed from the position he'd never been entitled to and McCauly would take up the reins that had been denied him so long.

And then everything would be set right and they could all live in peace and never have to worry about a King who would presume to set himself above even the gods.

A secret smile grew at the corners of Godfrey's mouth. He hid it behind a piece of bread and munched contentedly for the first time. Life would be so dull without the occasional flight of fancy, even if he only had himself to amuse.

The others around the table continued their discussion. About hunting. Again. Not a word about the impact of sorcery on a Church already groaning under the strain of Brome. Nothing about the secret army preparing in the north. Nothing about the hideous consequences of Selar invading Mayenne.

Were they completely ignorant, or simply uncaring?

If Selar actually invaded Mayenne, tried to take his brother's crown, Lusara would be crushed in retribution. Twice the size of Lusara, Mayenne had a fine standing army, well-trained and armed, paid for by a King only too aware of the threats to his borders from the north and from his own brother. In his youth, Tirone had been a sickly child, but as a man, with no less than three heirs to follow him, he knew full well what was at stake. Only a fool would think himself strong enough to play those odds.

Godfrey struck his fork against the plate – it would serve Selar right when Robert brought an army against him!

'Are you keeping something from us, Archdeacon?'

Blanching, Godfrey glanced up to find every face at the table turned to him. 'Your Grace?'

'Did the plate do something to offend you?'

'Er . . . no, Your Grace. My apologies.'

Brome laughed and returned to his discussion, the others attending him fully.

Imbecile! If he wasn't careful, he'd end up incriminating himself without anybody else's help.

And Robert would simply kill him.

Taymar had done well and for once, Nash was happy to show it. The hut was sparse and run down, but perfect for the occasion. Thin roof straw hung about the mud walls, some bits touching the ground. The river ran by silently only feet from the door and there wasn't another dwelling for almost a league. Marsay was more than two hours' ride away. This stretch of the bank had always been plagued by flooding, the land boggy and stinking of rotting flesh. Tall spindly grasses stuck up into the air. It was an excellent place to come face to face with another Salti.

Taymar pushed the door open and led Nash inside. Two lamps lit the single room, both suspended from the creaky roof. A table, knee-high, sat by the left wall and beyond it, a cot on which lay a young man.

'His name is Ben,' Taymar announced quietly.

'Is he drugged?'

'He should be just about awake now. He's had neither food nor water since I brought him here last night.'

Nash wandered across to the table and sat on the edge, removing his gloves as he studied the young man. He would be about twenty or so, fair and fine, fit and healthy. Absolutely perfect. His hands were bound in front of him, his feet to the cot. A strip of cloth gagged his mouth and Nash gestured to Taymar to remove it. As he did so, the young man stirred, opening his eyes with horror. Almost immediately, he struggled to push himself further against the wall, away from Nash.

'Now don't you get all excited,' Nash said. 'You can't escape, so you may as well save your strength.'

Taymar straightened up. 'Shall I get the bag from your horse, Master?'

'Tell me how you found him.'

'I did as you suggested and followed the Guilde hunting party. They brought the Bresail out in a small village a few leagues from the Sadlan border. I stood back in the crowd and noticed this man making a hasty exit from the village. I followed him and over-powered him.'

'Marvellously simple, eh Ben? I would have thought you Salti would know better in these times than to trust a stranger. Yes, Taymar, go and get the bag. You can set things up while I chat to our young friend here.'

As Taymar vanished outside, Nash put his gloves down and removed his cloak. All the while, Ben watched him. Every now and then, his hands would strain against the ropes binding him, only to relax in futility. There was fear in his eyes, but he held it back, controlling the worst.

'You're Malachi?' Ben asked, breathless.

'No,' Nash replied. 'Though many of your people before you have made the same assumption – to their detriment.'

'You are Guilde, though.' The young man's voice shook with each question.

'In name only.' Nash folded his hands together and rested them on his lap. 'Now, before we go any further, I want to ask you a question. I don't have much time to spare, so I'd appreciate it if you could give me the truth straight up. Where do you keep the Key?'

Ben's face went blank. 'What key?'

Nash sighed. 'Oh dear. Tell me, are all Salti as stubborn as you? Very well, I'll try another. Where is Robert Douglas?'

At that, Ben frowned. 'How should I know?'

'Come, come,' Nash snapped. 'You're a sorcerer – so is he. You must have at least some idea where he is.'

'No, I don't.'

Taymar returned with the bag and Nash waited as he removed a heavy silk sack from inside. He let Ben watch as the orb was taken out, held up before his eyes, laid down on the floor beside the cot.

'Thank you, Taymar. You can wait outside.'

'Yes, Master.'

As the door closed, Nash settled in his seat and watched Ben for a moment. 'You're afraid of the Malachi, aren't you?'

'Who wouldn't be?'

'Well, your people won't give them the Key, so I suppose it's your own fault.' Nash smiled. 'What do you think of Taymar, eh? Oh, he has no talents, I assure you – at least, not as you and I do. Nonetheless, he's managed to do something neither you nor I have done.'

When Ben struggled again, Nash held up his hand. 'I wouldn't bother trying to appeal to his better side – his loyalty is to me alone. Really, you were doomed the moment you spoke your first word to him.'

Ben's eyes flickered to the door. 'He might change his mind – when he finds out what you are.'

'I own his mind. Only I can change it for him.' Nash laughed. 'Have you ever heard of Bonding?'

When Ben didn't answer, Nash continued, enjoying himself, 'Centuries ago it was a process whereby couples were joined together, to marry. A perfect Bonding would always last for life. Taymar is joined to me in a similar way – but infinitely more effectively. I have found a way to alter the Bonding technique, to use a man's blood to make him my slave. The process – and the result – is quite different to the original, and much less pleasurable. However, it is far more rewarding to me in the long run. Just ask Selar.'

Ben's eyes opened wide at that, then dropped to the orb sitting on the floor. 'You would do that . . . to me?'

'No.' Nash shook his head slowly. 'Unfortunately, the only real essence of the original process that survived my changes was the need for consent. You must want to become my slave – and I can't see that happening in a hurry.' Nash left his perch and came forward to the bed. He knelt beside the orb and slowly removed the dagger from his boot. 'Do you know what that is?'

Ben deliberately didn't look down, deliberately kept his gaze on the wall opposite. Muscles in his jaw clenched tight, his response was curt. 'No.'

'You should. If you Salti hadn't been so perverse and deserted your Malachi brethren, you would know about the important things. You carry a small stone about with you, using it to channel your powers. In the days of the Cabal, these orbs were common-place – and used much the same as you use your stones now. But they also had other purposes. You'll get a close look at one tonight. You may have heard of it? The Darriet D'Azzir once practised this art. It is called the *Folinet aro Shar* – the Feeding Blood.'

Ben sucked a breath as the meaning sank in. After a moment's hesitation, his mouth clamped shut.

'I see,' Nash said, unsurprised. Why was it that every time he got his hands on a Salti, the same thing happened? Not one, in over a century, had ever given him a single answer he wanted. No matter the torture, the pain he inflicted, the result was unchanged. It was as though they all shared the same mighty will never to betray their brethren. Although it was plainly obvious, even faced with this death, this young man had not even as much as admitted he was Salti.

It was a known fact that some degree of willpower could be drawn from the power inside a sorcerer – but this? It was impossible that they were all this strong . . .

Unless . . .

The Key protected them in some way?

In a rush, Nash closed his eyes and concentrated. He was only inches away from Ben and yet the aura he Sensed was faint, lacking focus, as though he were entirely human.

By the Blood! It had been there all along and he'd been too busy, too determined to see it! The Key *was* protecting them! It had to be. It had found some way to disguise a Salti aura so it would never be detected by a Malachi – or by anyone else bar the Bresail.

What a fool!

Nash opened his eyes, only just containing laughter. 'My dear boy, you don't know how much you've helped me.' With that, he reached out and cut through the bonds at Ben's wrists. Before the young man could even move, Nash raised his right hand and Ben froze, enmeshed by a power he could not begin to combat. Nash then grabbed Ben's right hand, stretched the arm out across the bed and, with one swift strike of the blade, he sliced a long wound in the soft under part of Ben's forearm, almost from elbow to wrist. Ben gasped as his blood began to flow, but Nash didn't waste a drop. He held the arm out and down and watched as the glorious red mess drained slowly into the orb.

'Normally,' Nash continued, matter of fact, 'I'd do this more slowly – it helps retain quality – but you see, it will take me about three days to absorb all this and complete my regeneration, and I'm in something of a hurry. I have an appointment with a lady – a beautiful lady with rich dark hair and sparkling blue eyes. Just to see her is enough to make a man's heart leap – but you would know. I'm sure you've met her at some time. Her name is Jennifer Ross – of course, most people these days know her as the Duchess of Ayr – but I won't let that get between us. You might also know her by her other, older name. The Ally?'

Ben's face was pale already, his eyes barely able to stay open. His mouth moved and Nash leaned forward a little to hear better.

'Monster . . . of Darkness.'

'Very good, if a little late.' Nash chuckled. 'And don't worry, I don't take the insult personally. It's just a matter of prophecy, you see. The Ally and I are meant to be together. I have only waited this long to Bond with her because I had to regain my full strength. And not the crass new Bonding like with Taymar, but the old, original form, in its truest, purest sense. She will not be my slave – unless for love. You see,' Nash paused, leaning forward to whisper, 'it must be a perfect Bond or it won't last more than a few weeks. She will give me more power than you could possibly imagine – and she will do it willingly. I don't know about you, but that's the part I always liked best. Such a sweet creature and good, right to her very heart, but in the end, she won't be able to help it. She is fated to love me just as I am to love her. She will take that good and twist it to help me. Didn't you people ever wonder why she was called the Ally?'

Nash glanced back at the young man, but there was no response. His eyes were closed, his face ashen. Only his lips showed signs of the life that was draining away. He would be unconscious in moments.

'No,' Nash whispered, glancing down at the orb as it absorbed the dying man's blood. 'I don't suppose you did. And it's too late now. Much too late.'

9

There was cold, and then there was cold, and Robert knew which of the two he preferred. As he stopped his horse beside Jenn's at the top of the last rise, the hills of eastern Lusara stretched out before him like a sea of undulating white, glowing with three-quarters of a moon. The icy air caught in his throat.

Such a beautiful place. Swept with snow, in the grip of an old winter, Lusara still inspired the hearts of poets. But even the most gifted could never capture moments like this.

He glanced over his shoulder, but Micah was long into the distance. He would be in Dromna within four days.

He'd certainly done his work well, keeping Jenn company from the Enclave to Maitland, even though Jenn had talked little – at least while Robert had been around. Quite deliberately, he'd ridden either behind them or some way in front. There was no need for him to make the journey east any worse for her than it needed to be. With a silent sigh, he led Jenn down into the valley and on into the wood.

He had to wait until it was completely dark, dark enough to hide any movement. Fortunately a layer of cloud soon obscured the moon, but his Sight still gave him a clear view of Maitland Manor between the trees, the grassy field before and Jenn's face beside him.

It appeared Aiden's faith in miracles was indeed unfounded this time. Jenn did hate him. Watching her, even from a distance, had been hard, knowing how she felt. His skin crawled at the way she looked at him sometimes, the chill in her blue eyes far worse than any winter could afford.

And yes, there was a part of him that knew she was right to hate him, to blame him, to curse him and everything he'd done. And yet, if only she wouldn't.

She couldn't stand still. She claimed she wasn't cold, but she kept moving from one foot to the other, pacing back and forth and he'd long since given up warning her that someone might see them if she didn't stop. It seemed she couldn't wait to get away from him.

One by one the lights of the manor went out, leaving only three pinpoints in the night.

'When will you go back to Clonnet?' he said, his voice soft against the padded forest.

'Dawn tomorrow.'

He should ask her about Nash. He needed to understand how much influence the man had gained over her – and he needed to know, to quell the constant rumble of irrational jealousy he'd suppressed over the last few years. But explaining that to her was impossible. He'd been a fool to think, even for a moment, that it wouldn't be this way – but he'd been so sure she loved him when he left Elita. Well, perhaps she had, for a time.

The thought left him hollow and empty. 'I've scanned the area; it's all clear.'

She didn't leave immediately. 'Are you sure?'

'Of course.'

'No, I mean about Carlan . . . Nash? Are you sure?'

He glanced at her, masking his surprise, and found she was watching him, her eyes dark. 'The moment his injuries had mended enough for him to move around again, he was visiting you at Clonnet. Keeping an eye on the Ally, gaining your trust, becoming your friend. Your only friend. What else would the Angel of Darkness do?'

'How do you know he's been at Clonnet?'

'That doesn't matter. But if you know anything that might help us . . . '

'Know anything? About Nash?' Her eyes widened, turning abruptly sharp. 'Oh, I see. You think I keep his secrets, the way I do yours? You think I would . . . ' She turned away again, shaking

140

her head a little. 'The man I know has nothing to do with the Angel of Darkness. I can't tell you anything.'

For a moment, Robert was again seized with the desire to put his arms around her, pull her close, whisper apologies and whatever words he needed to make everything right between them – but she would never allow it. Especially now that he'd as much as accused her of taking Nash's side. Instead, he held firm, clenching his fists together and breathing deeply. 'It's dark enough now. You'd better go while it's clear.'

She began to walk away, then paused, glancing back at him, her expression shuttered. She said nothing, however, and, after a moment, resumed her journey, pulling her horse along behind her. He followed her progress until she reached the house, disappeared inside it, and still he Sensed her. Then he drew back, moving deeper into the forest. But he didn't leave. Instead, he found a comfortable low branch of a tree, wrapped his cloak around him, looped the reins around the branch and settled down to sleep.

If the circumstances had been different, Robert might almost have enjoyed the journey north. The weather had inexplicably cleared, a blissful sun shining down on a weather-beaten land. The further he travelled, the more the snow melted and eventually disappeared altogether. At times he could even feel his face burning.

He kept a good distance from the road where Jenn travelled with her guard and luggage. She'd never been much of a Seeker, but Robert shielded as hard as he could, regardless. Besides, who knew when Vaughn would next bring his Bresail out into the country?

Then finally, just after dusk on the second day, the bleak visage of Clonnet appeared in the distance and Robert changed direction. With his Senses alone, he kept track of Jenn as she passed through the gate, heard it close behind her.

Then he moved.

He left his horse saddled in a sandy copse as near to the castle as he could get. Then he crept forward under cover of darkness until he stood with his back to the wall. He snuck along the wall, reaching the tiny old gate by feel alone. Opening it and slipping through took less power than he'd expected and he stopped on the other side, ready to raise a mask.

He was alone in a dark corner beside a building, before him, a maze of red stone, doorways and windows. People moved around in the distance, but he remained motionless and invisible.

Six years ago, Micah had come to Clonnet to serve Jenn after her marriage. It had taken him just a few weeks to get to know the castle like no one else. Now Robert conjured up in his mind the plan Micah had drawn, the path that would take him to the unused passage, up the stairs to the gallery where Jenn's rooms were.

He waited, watching the movements of the castle workers. The moment the timing was right, he took in a deep breath and held it, bullying up dusty powers from deep inside. But he was rested and alert and the effort caused little strain. With only the smallest of thoughts, he took a mental dimensional step sideways, causing his body to vanish from any eyes that might look his way. A mask would have been easier and less complicated, but a mask would hold only when kept stationery, and that would do him no good at all.

He'd never regretted not telling anybody of his proficiency with the forbidden side of his abilities. After all, it wouldn't do to go encouraging people to copy him. Not everyone could do so without risking their lives.

Ready now, he took a step forward, moved around the back of the old stable, along another wall to a staircase. He ducked under and pressed his hands against the shape of a wooden door, dirty with disuse. It didn't budge initially, then he realised he should be pulling the handle instead.

With a sigh of relief, he slipped inside, into darkness, and immediately released the shift. Quickly he put a foot out to find the first step. Micah had warned him not to make a light – cracks in the wall would show such a thing to anyone looking – so he had to continue with only his night-enhanced sight.

He forced himself to move slowly and carefully, but before he even reached the top of the stairs, he could already hear raised voices. By the time he found the door, the voices were clearer. He couldn't hear the words, but he knew who it was.

Jenn and Eachern.

A sudden crash made him jump. He quickly placed his hands against the wood, extending his Senses beyond. Jenn's voice had stopped, but Eachern continued, bellowing rage and violence.

Holding his breath, Robert pushed the narrow door open a crack. The gallery was empty, the noise coming from behind a door to his right. There was another crash, a scream, and the door banged open.

He froze, but it wasn't Eachern who ran out into the gallery. It had to be Andrew. The boy was halfway towards Robert before he stopped, his eyes wide, his breathing no more than a gasp.

'Come here, Andrew,' Robert murmured, holding out his hand. He took a step forward into the light and went down on one knee.

The boy glanced over his shoulder at the noise, then came closer, gulping in air.

'What's wrong?'

'Mother. She's hurt. I'm going to get Father John.'

Robert kept his voice low. 'Who's hurting her?'

'Papa,' Andrew whispered, sobbing now. 'He said she'd been bad. He's killing her.'

As the demon rumbled around inside him, Robert reached out and grasped the boy's shoulder. 'Don't worry, I'll help her. You go and get Father John. Tell him to hurry. If you see Addie, tell her to come as well.'

Andrew nodded, wide-eyed, then turned and ran, disappearing into the staircase to the left.

Robert didn't wait any longer. The demon wouldn't let him. Eachern's voice still echoed around the gallery as he took out his rage and frustration on Jenn. It appeared he hadn't believed the story of her absence after all. Damn!

He got to the doorway and drew his sword silently. Slowly he put his head around until he could see into the room. A table sat in the centre of the room with a dozen candles arranged along its length. Eachern stood at the near end, his gaze on something at his feet. Even as Robert watched, the monster swung his leg and kicked.

'Get back!' Robert ordered, moving into the room. He had his sword up at Eachern's throat instantly, forcing the man against the wall.

'Who are you? No, wait . . . ' Eachern was drunk, his speech slurring. 'I know you – Dunlorn!'

With one eye on Eachern, Robert crouched down beside Jenn, put his hand to her face. 'Jenn? Can you hear me?'

143

In that moment, Eachern pounced and Robert was powerless to stop the table crashing down on them both.

Jenn could hear Robert's voice . . . but it had to be a dream. She had left him outside Maitland two days ago . . .

No. He'd followed her.

She lifted her head in time to see the table crash down, knocking Robert sideways. Pain again, noise and heat. The candles! Fire, burning the rug, the hangings . . . smoke stifling and Eachern yelling out for the guard . . . more voices . . .

Robert moved beside her, pushing the table up, pulling her clear.

'Andrew? Where's Andrew?'

'It's all right. He's gone to get help. Quickly, can you stand?' He put his arms around her and lifted her up. She opened her eyes, but everything was smeared with red, her left eye already puffy and closing. The air was acrid now and she began to cough.

'We have to get out of here,' Robert hissed, grabbing his sword.

'No, Robert, you go. He'll kill you!'

He got hold of her wrist and pulled her towards the door. 'I'll kill him first for this!'

She continued to protest, but he paid no attention. By the time they got to the door, more voices reached her, guards coming towards them, swords raised. Eachern was somewhere, calling for more help against Robert.

. . . thank the gods Nash wasn't here as well . . .

'Come on, this way.' Robert half-dragged her away from the soldiers, towards the other stairs – just in time to meet more coming up. With swift thrusts, Robert dealt with the first two, pushing them back down on top of those following. 'We'll have to go up.'

She could hardly see anything. Stumbling and falling, she held onto Robert like a drowning child. She reached out to steady herself against the stone, but her other hand was bleeding and she slipped. Robert caught her and held her as he took the stairs two at a time. He put her down on the next landing and she turned in time to see Andrew running towards her, John and Addie close behind.

She swept the distraught child into her arms as Robert clashed swords with more guards. They came up the stairs, slowly but inexorably.

'Is there another way out of here?' he called.

Jenn couldn't think – but John could. 'Yes, this way.'

The priest took Andrew from Jenn. He led them to a narrow corridor she'd never seen before. After a moment, Robert joined them. Breathless, he hurried them along in the darkness. They stumbled down a few steps and John ushered them into one room, then on to another, the door of which he kicked open.

Jenn was lost by now, but all around her were the sounds of alarm: voices crying out in the night, panic and screams echoing throughout the castle, as though the entire place was under attack. Still she stumbled along behind John, Addie holding her arm. Every now and then she felt Robert's presence slip behind as he fought off their attackers – sensed the demon leaking out of him in lethal shards – then he would join them again, urging more speed.

Suddenly, after a maze of turns, steps, corridors and halls, they emerged into the night. The abrupt cold air cleared her thoughts, though darkness halved what she could see.

'Where are we?' Robert grunted, closing the last door behind them. He held his hand over the lock for a moment and Jenn saw it glow and fuse shut.

'West Keep,' John replied. 'If we can . . . by the gods!'

Jenn scrambled to the wall and gazed across at the gallery, bright in the night as flames tore through the building, bringing an orange day to this dark. 'No—'

A banging on the door came and Robert moved again, taking Jenn's arm as they hurried across the roof. Addie had already reached the other side and was about to pull the door open when it burst apart. She shrieked and fell back. Robert ran to her, dragging her to safety.

'There they are!' Soldiers flooded through and Robert was pressed back, his sword a flash of steel in the firelight. He fought hard, but there were too many. He couldn't hold them back alone, nor could he pause to summon the power to do it.

Suddenly John put Andrew down with Jenn and moved forward. He stood to Robert's left and raised his hands. A flash of light flew out, exploding into flames at the guards' feet. For a moment, they were stunned, then, eyes wide and the word *sorcery* on every lip, they turned and fled, pushing the others down behind them. Chaos reigned as they strove to get away from the evil sorcerers.

'Well done!' Robert ran forward to check the stairwell. 'Now how do we get down from here?'

He turned back to John but the priest only shrugged. 'That was it. We're too high up to jump and Clonnet doesn't have a moat – as I'm sure you've noticed.'

'Damn! If we had some rope . . . '

Smoke drifted towards them as the banging on the other door increased. Robert turned to face the new threat. Then the banging stopped and the door exploded, sending woodshards everywhere. Two figures darted onto the roof, only one of whom wielded a sword.

'Malachi!' Robert hissed, instantly stepping forward to face the first, but it was the second who threw the initial blast. A woman, her face was familiar to Jenn.

Two Malachi living at Clonnet? Nash – he must have . . .

'Now I have you!' Eachern bellowed, emerging from the stairwell.

Jenn reached for Andrew, but John already had him. In a terrified bunch, they backed away, knowing the wall and a great drop below were all that awaited them. Behind Eachern, Robert battled with the two Malachi, his sword glowing as bright as the fire, each blow strengthened by his powers

For the first time in her life, Jenn begged the demon inside Robert to strike out.

As Eachern closed in, Robert swung his sword once, cutting the Malachi across the chest. The man fell back, his sword falling with a clang. The woman stepped forward to pick it up, but she didn't live a second longer. Without pausing, Robert swung his sword again and blue flame cut into her. Her body was tossed backwards, as light as if it were driftwood.

Eachern rushed forward himself, raising his sword high above his head. Robert, turning to face him, only just brought his blade up in time to deflect the blow. Steel clashed on steel, the blades flashing with firelight. But Eachern was a big man, heavy and strong, and his rush pushed Robert back first one step, then another, closer to the edge. Robert's legs caught on the wall and he stumbled, his sword sheering off at an angle. Eachern saw his opportunity. He swung once more—

Jenn screamed. Without thought, she wrenched together a spear of scorching power. Pure and unhindered, it shot out of her hands, straining every fibre of her being to blast Eachern in the centre of his back. He arched, frozen in movement – then toppled forward. Slowly now, his body caught Robert, dragging him half over the wall. Then Eachern disappeared and, a moment later, Jenn heard the thud.

She dashed towards Robert but John was already there, holding on. Together they hauled him back onto the roof. Sucking in air, Robert scrambled for his sword. 'Come on. Let's get out of here!'

The night sky glowed gold, flooding the dunes with false dawn. Robert watched the distant conflagration in silence, the horse beneath him edgy and excitable. There would be nothing left of Clonnet in a few hours, just a blackened husk, empty and smouldering.

Robert glanced across at Father John. He had Jenn draped on the saddle before him, her head on his shoulder. Dazed and only semi-conscious, she said nothing, her face half-obscured by swelling and blood. On the other horse sat the faithful Addie, still terrified, but holding on. The boy Andrew sat behind her, his arms around her waist, his eyes wide.

With a nod, Robert kicked his horse and led them down into a gully and away from the castle. For a long time, the only noise was the soft sand beneath the animals and the gulls crying out above. Then, just as the first dawn light filtered across the heavens, Robert stopped outside a tiny inn.

Getting a room at this time of the day was easy. Avoiding explanations was considerably more difficult – especially with the blood, soot and grime. But Robert just made up one lie after another, creating a fabrication of robbers on the road, of sword fights, horses stolen. In pity, the innkeeper both gave them his best room – and quickly brought up hot water and ale, shortly followed by a whole pot of stew.

Robert carried Jenn to a bed and laid her down. He took the cup of ale from Addie and lifted Jenn's head so she could drink. Her lips took a single sip then she turned her head away.

'Is my mother dead?' Andrew squeezed between Robert and the bed, his hand tentatively reaching out to Jenn.

'No, of course not,' Robert replied, smoothing the boy's hair down. 'She's just got a few cuts we need to clean and dress. She'll be fine when she's had some rest.'

Addie brought the bowl of water over and handed Robert a cloth, but when he touched her face to wash the blood away, Jenn flinched from him, as though he would hit her.

He stood and handed the cloth back to Addie. 'You'd better do it. Come Andrew, let Addie help your mother.'

'And you'd better let me see your wounds,' John added. He steered Robert to a chair and sat him down. As he worked, he added, 'We can't stay here long, can we?'

'A couple of hours at most. I don't know how many people heard Eachern bellowing my name, but once the alarm is raised, they'll be after all of us.' He closed his eyes and winced as John applied pressure to a cut on his arm.

'Jenn needs to rest – and so do you. Some of these cuts are quite deep. Is there anywhere safe close by?'

An insistent tugging on Robert's sleeve forced him to open his eyes. He looked down to find Andrew watching him with a blue gaze so like Jenn's it was eerie.

'What's your name?'

Robert smiled, though it hurt, but it was John who answered for him. 'This is Duke Robert, my lord.'

Andrew frowned a little, as though some memory tugged at him. Then, his gaze on Robert perfectly steady, he said, 'You saved Mother.'

'I suppose so.'

'Thank you.'

Robert nodded, wincing again as John found another cut.

'Does that hurt?' Andrew asked, his eyes mirroring his wonder.

'Honestly?' Robert replied with a laugh. 'Yes it does. A lot.'

'I'm sorry, Robert, but she's adamant about this.'

Robert glanced again over Father John's shoulder to where Jenn sat on a rock, her arms wrapped around Andrew. The weather had been good to them all day, making the flight south a little more comfortable. Now, as the sun began to set, cold seeped from the ground and winter arrived again. The mountains in the distance seemed to chill the air. Fresh fallen snow was whipped up in icy clouds, visible even from this distance.

'But she won't say why?'

'You know she's not said a word since we left Clonnet two days ago,' John replied. 'We're lucky she's said this much.'

With a groan, Robert turned away and gazed out over the fields at Maitland Manor in the distance. 'She's mad. She knows that's the first place they'll look for her. Does she want Nash to find her? Without Eachern's small protection, she'll be Nash's first target. Is that what she wants?'

'I have no idea. All I know is we have to go to Lady Bella at Maitland.'

'Then I guess,' Robert sighed, turning for his horse, 'that's where we're going. But I'll tell you this now: I'm not leaving her there. I'll take her back to the Enclave kicking and screaming if I have to.'

Another dark approach, another night spent creeping in the shadows. So this was the life of an outlaw. If only he'd known.

But he had to admit that Maitland was an easy target. Few guards, lots of doors and, even though he'd never been there before, it was obvious where they would find Bella after supper. Even better – she was alone.

Robert tried to be as quiet as possible as he pushed the door open but Bella heard him and came to her feet in a rush. She'd been kneeling by the fire and its gentle radiance showed the shock on her face. He said nothing. He just let Jenn and the others inside, then closed the door and placed a warning on it.

'Is Lawrence about?'

Jenn stood before her sister, looking about the sitting room like a frightened bird. Her hands clenched and relaxed at her sides.

'No . . . he's away for a few days. What is this? What's happened to you?' Bella looked to Robert for an answer when none came from Jenn.

'There's been some trouble,' Robert began, but Jenn stopped him.

149

She took Andrew's hand and gave him into Addie's care. 'Would you take him over by the window, please. I have to talk to my sister.'

As they moved off, Jenn looked into the fire. For a long moment, she was silent, then, she gathered herself. 'Bella, I desperately need your help.'

'Of course.' Bella reached out and put a hand on Jenn's shoulder. 'Anything.'

At this, Jenn looked up. 'Eachern is dead. I . . . '

'Dead? But how?'

Jenn's mouth opened, but no words came out.

In the silence, John said, 'In a fall, my lady. Clonnet is burned to the ground.'

Uncomprehending, Bella looked to Jenn.

'He's dead and I . . . I've brought Andrew to you. I . . . I want you to look after him.'

'But why? What about you?'

'I'm leaving here, tonight. With Robert.'

Robert blinked and glanced up. What was this all about?

Jenn continued, her voice steadier now. 'Bella, Father John can fill you in on all the details later. I need you to take care of Andrew, take in Addie and Father John. When they come and ask you, you must all tell the same story. They know Robert was at Clonnet, but there was a fire. You can tell them he survived and brought the others here – but you must, *must* tell them I died in the fire. Can you do that?'

'I don't understand,' Bella said. 'You want the world to believe you're dead? And what do I tell Andrew? When will you come back?'

Jenn faltered at this. 'I don't know. It could be a while. As soon as I can, but I don't know.'

'Robert,' Bella appealed to him. 'What have you done? What's going on here?'

'Don't ask me. This is the first I've heard of it.'

'Then make her see sense. She doesn't have to leave.'

'But I do!' Jenn snapped, then took another breath. 'Please, Bella, do as I ask. Eachern's dead. Nobody will come for Andrew to take him away. You have the greatest claim on him. I know you'll love and care for him as I would myself. And don't worry, I can make sure he never tells anybody I brought him here. He'll keep the lie safe as long as the rest of you do. I don't have much time. We have to leave now. Please, will you do it?'

Bella looked from Jenn to Robert, then at the priest. Finally she said, 'I don't like this one bit, Jenn – you know that. But I won't refuse.'

Her shoulders stiff, Jenn gave a small smile. She crossed the room and knelt down by her son. Robert couldn't hear what Jenn said to Andrew, but twice, the boy glanced across at him. Then Andrew was nodding, his eyes full of unshed tears. He threw his arms around Jenn's neck and she held on, murmuring something. Jenn stood then and brought Andrew back to Bella. She said a quiet farewell to all the others, then, finally, turned to Robert.

'Let's go.'

He wasted no time – after all, he had little time to lose. They rode east all night and well into the next day, exhausting the new horses. Only when they'd crossed the border and were safely in Flan'har did Robert look for a place to stop. Jenn hadn't said a word, but as they travelled, her face grew more pale and her eyes dulled. More than once, Robert caught her grimacing at some silent pain. By sunset he could stand it no longer. He stopped outside a tavern on the edge of a village where a pretty river emerged from a crag in the forest. Large patches of snow covered the ground, roofs and treetops, and the entire street was a single lake of squelching mud.

'Why are we stopping?' Jenn murmured, looking around with little interest.

'We need to rest.' Robert carefully lowered himself from his horse. 'We're safe here. Nobody will come looking for us.'

'I don't need rest.'

'Well, I do – and so do the horses. Come on, I'll help you down.'

He reached up for her, but she pushed his hands away. Slowly, she swung her leg over the horse, but as her feet touched the ground, she crumpled. Robert caught her as people came to his aid. He lifted her and carried her inside. A room was found in no time; another innkeeper showing enormous kindness. Their horses were taken care of and food and drink brought to the room.

Robert spent a few minutes writing a coded message before

paying a courier to take it to Micah in Dromna. It was the only way to stop him returning to Flan'har once he'd heard of Jenn's supposed death.

As a new moon rose over the river, Robert sat down at the table and turned his attention to the meal. Jenn lay on the bed unmoving, probably asleep. The swelling around her eye had gone down a little, but still she looked unwell. Eachern's beating had done a lot of damage. After a while, her breathing slowed and steadied and Robert began to relax.

He drank his ale slowly and worked his way through a loaf of brown crusty bread and a hunk of strong cheese. His gaze shifted from the window and back to the bed every few minutes as he allowed himself to sink into the peace of the place.

Why had she chosen to come with him – a man she so obviously hated? What did she hope to achieve? Certainly she knew about the coming war, but at no time had she expected to play any part in it. But to leave her son behind like that?

Andrew had watched his mother kill his father with a power he had no way of understanding. Now he had lost both parents and still he wouldn't be able to understand. Bella would do her best, but that was no way to bring up a child.

By the gods, that flight had been a close thing – with the demon hedging at him to be let loose. And how had he managed to control it? Of course, he shouldn't have been surprised to find Malachi at Clonnet; in truth, it merely confirmed all his suspicions about Nash.

With a sigh, he refilled his ale from the jug on the table. It was a good brew, dark and full.

Bella would tell the story of Jenn's death and she would do it convincingly with substantiation from both Father John and Addie. Nobody would have noticed who'd left the burning castle in such chaos. As it was, they'd been lucky to even find a couple of horses in the mêlée. In all likelihood, Mass would be said for both the Duke of Ayr and his wife, prayers said for the new Duke, such a tragic young child. But nobody would take Andrew away – Bella would make sure of that. She would fight to her last breath for her nephew; Jenn had made a good choice there.

But was it the right one? She would never be able to go back, to come to life again. For the second time. To do so would arouse so much suspicion they would toss her in prison and throw away the key – if she was lucky. So, despite the fact that she had cut herself off from the Enclave, Jenn had relinquished all ties to her real life and set herself adrift . . . to where?

Robert glanced back at her once more to find she was awake, her eyes staring at the ceiling. 'You should eat something.'

'I'm not hungry.' She pulled the blanket up close. 'How long was I asleep?'

'A couple of hours.'

'Will we stay here long?'

'Till tomorrow. Then we head south again.'

'To Bleakstone?'

'Yes.'

'How long will it take?'

'Three, perhaps four days.'

With a muffled groan, she sat up, leaning her back against the wall. 'Will the Bishop be there?'

'Yes.'

She nodded. 'How is he?'

'I don't think he's ever been better. He doesn't want this war, though.'

'Who does?'

He drank again and rested back in his chair, wincing involuntarily as his wounds objected.

'Are you in pain?' She was looking at him.

'I'm all right. Nothing a good night's sleep won't mend.'

She didn't look away, but her eyes were distracted, clouded and dissolute. Abruptly, tears gathered and, one by one, they fell down her pale cheeks.

Keeping his emotions distant, Robert turned his gaze out the window again, lifting his cup to take another mouthful. He swallowed slowly and allowed his words alone to build a bridge between them. 'You've never killed before.'

Her answer was a sob as she curled up in a tight ball, her back to him. He watched her in silence for a few minutes then he rose and came to the edge of the bed. He sat on the side and reached out a hand to her shoulder. Immediately she pushed him away, but the effort lacked energy and this time he persisted.

'It's all right, Jenn, it's over. He can never hurt you again.' He pulled her close, but her body remained rigid and unyielding.

Slowly, so very slowly, he moved until his arms encircled her properly and her head was laid on his chest. Then her tears flowed again and he closed his eyes.

10

A dozen fat grey gulls squawked, chattered and launched sweeping attacks on the empty fortress of Clonnet. Their wings beat against the angry wind as they landed on a stone wall, blackened by smoke and fire. White against the black, light against dark. So little light, so much dark.

Nash stood in the centre of the courtyard, his gaze taking in the scene as a whole, but he couldn't absorb it. So much devastation from a simple fire. Everything of stone was charred, but still standing. All else had fallen. And once again rumours of sorcery had emptied the place. The castle workers – even the local people – had refused to come back here. Only Nash's squad of Guilde soldiers could be forced to rake through the wreckage – and that, unwillingly.

'Master?'

Taymar had come up behind him but Nash didn't turn to acknowledge his arrival. 'Yes?'

'We've found more bodies.'

'Is she among them?'

'I think so.'

Nash whirled around. 'She can't be! She could not have died in a simple fire, damn you! The Enemy was with her. There is no way he would have left her to die! Show me!'

He strode across the cobblestones as Taymar hurried alongside. The yellow of Guilde robes dotted the area as soldiers clambered gingerly over the scorched ruin. Before the husk of the gallery the bodies were laid out, uncovered but unrecognisable. Taymar stopped and pointed to one on the end, small and ravaged by the fire. No mark showed the identity, no clothing remained, no jewellery.

Nothing.

Was it possible?

No . . . it was inconceivable – and yet . . . The sister had said – and the priest. Why would he lie? The servant, too?

The boy.

The Ally was devoted to that child. He had always been the only thing she'd really loved, the reason why she'd put up with her oaf of a husband. She'd lived only to watch him grow. If she'd survived this fire, could she have just abandoned the child in her sister's care? Never to see him again?

Nash crouched down beside the small, blackened form. He reached out to touch the hand as though he would spark some life, but there was nothing in this shell, no laughter, no flashing blue eyes.

He stood and turned, calling for his horse. 'Taymar, you stay here and gather as much information as you can. Then bring the Duke's body back to the capital with as much state as you can manage under the circumstances. We must remember he was a cousin of our beloved King.'

'And the Duchess?'

As his horse was brought to him, Nash grabbed the reins. He swung up into the saddle and looked once more around the remains of Clonnet Castle. Empty. It was all empty now. 'Bring her as well. We have no choice but to bury them together. I'm going back to Marsay. If you find out anything more, let me know.'

Taymar nodded and Nash turned his horse through the gate. He might not know where the Enemy was right now – but at least Nash knew where he'd been. The Douglas was developing quite a penchant for destroying castles.

Governor Osbert wandered without purpose through the garden, paying no attention to the fact that his robes were collecting mud from the path. Every now and then he would be passed by castle staff on some business for the King; some murmured greetings, but nobody spoke to him. Not directly.

The narrow path led him to an insignificant little bridge which crossed the pond. The water was flat, mirroring the grey sky above and revealing nothing of its depths. He stopped there and placed his hands on the cold wooden rail. Bushes ringed the pond, their sharp, leafless branches spiking the edge like some great instrument of torture. None of them seemed to have yet noticed that it was spring.

This garden had been the Queen's favourite place, winter or summer. Almost every day, she'd brought her young children out here, Kenrick and the pretty Galiena. Now the Queen, like this garden, was dead. Her son, as spiky as the unruly bushes, growing more like his father every year. So where was the little Princess? Not so little now, of course. She would be sixteen and just beginning to blossom into her own spring.

Osbert turned from his pathetic fancy to pace back and forth across the bridge. In the distance he could see Archdeacon Godfrey enter the garden, hesitate, then change direction to head for the pond. He was dressed in his usual attire: the black robes of a priest, long chain holding a trium and the small medallion attached to it, denoting his position as Guilde Chaplain. Godfrey was a good man, forthright and honest. He'd remained steady throughout the last few years, yielding his honour to no man – regardless of the circumstances.

'Good morning, Governor.' Godfrey ventured a smile, taking only a single step onto the bridge.

'Good morning, Father,' Osbert replied. 'I'm sorry, but unless it's something urgent, I'm not really in the mood for casual conversation.'

'I apologise. I did not mean to disturb you. I thought only that . . . '

'What?'

Godfrey paused before replying. 'You appeared upset. I thought perhaps I might be able to help.'

Help? Wouldn't it be just wonderful if the damned priest could help?

Osbert resumed his pacing, unable to remain still. 'I'm in need of no help that you could give me, Father. I'm afraid my problems go somewhat beyond your role as Chaplain.'

'Nevertheless, I'm a priest, and I'm willing to listen.'

To what? A list of small but incredibly inconsequential events, all of which had brought him here to this barren spot? By the gods, he'd been such a fool, thinking he could use Nash's influence with the King to his own advantage. All he'd wanted was to be Proctor, to replace Vaughn – but Nash had known all along the partnership was flawed. Osbert had tied himself to Nash and now he couldn't get away. He was in too deep.

'You do yourself no good service,' Godfrey said into the silence, quiet and careful, 'by isolating yourself.'

'Isolating myself?' Osbert gave a bark of ironic laughter. 'I've *been* isolated by others, Father. Despite my position, I am cut off from the hierarchy of the Guilde, my duties almost removed from me completely. Vaughn sets the example and the rest follow. Even the court . . . ' He broke off. The whole catastrophic mess was simply insane.

'Troubles can often seem unsolvable when you stand alone in the middle of them. Sometimes we need other eyes to help us peer through the gloom. Are you in trouble, Governor?'

When the ground beneath you is so cracked it opens up, starts to suck you down into it – is that trouble?

The library was gone. He had no hope of finding out where. Years ago, when he'd drugged Vaughn and found the old empty room, the Proctor had said only one thing about the new hiding place: 'Where none shall look and none shall find.' A riddle designed to have no answer, nor was Osbert disposed to finding one, but Nash still wanted him to look. Trouble? The damned priest had no idea!

'My troubles are of my own making, Father, and as such, only I can find a way through them.'

'But can you?' Godfrey murmured.

Vaughn's little toy – it was supposed to sniff out sorcerers. But Osbert had been there when Nash had come before it. It had made no sign – how could that be? Nash was everything a sorcerer should be: evil to his core. Osbert had seen it with his own eyes; he had watched Nash as he'd tortured, inflicting pain and enjoying it. His powers were unbelievable – no man could stand against them.'

And certainly not Osbert.

Well, it was too late for him now, but at least he could gain some comfort from the missing books: Nash would never get his putrid hands on them!

He took in a deep breath and straightened up. He turned to Godfrey, his face calm now. 'I thank you for your efforts, but I fear I must bear this burden alone. I will, however, remember your kindness. In that, Godfrey, you stand alone.'

Godfrey frowned a little. 'If you do need help, Governor, you have but to ask. Good day.'

Watch Nash, Robert had told Godfrey. Watch him and beware of him. Show no sign that you know anything of him. Mind your thoughts or he will know them. Be careful.

As Godfrey hurried away from the garden, he looked back at the troubled Governor, still pacing the bridge. For many years now, Osbert had been something of an ally to Nash, bringing him up through the ranks of the Guilde, but despite Nash's success, Osbert appeared less than happy.

Robert hadn't said exactly that Nash was a sorcerer, but . . .

Osbert was indeed troubled and it was an easy guess that it had something to do with Nash. Well, if Osbert was about to fall, it could only help their cause if Godfrey caught him.

It would also help Osbert.

Vaughn kept track of the horse and rider from his small balcony overlooking the square. He saw them come up the hill, clatter across the cobbles before the Basilica and turn immediately through the castle gates.

Nash always appeared to be in a hurry, rushing here and there as though the slave of unseen masters.

Well, Vaughn mused with a smile, perhaps he was.

'He didn't stay at Clonnet long,' Godet remarked, standing beside Vaughn. 'I wonder if he found what he was looking for.'

'What makes you think he was looking for anything in particular? He was charged with finding the Duke's body to bring back here for funeral rites.'

'But the story about the Outlaw starting the fire, killing Eachern?'

Vaughn shrugged. 'Perhaps now Selar will do something. Now the Douglas has actually attacked a member of his own family, the King can hardly say the problem is only mine.'

'We've had no more Halls attacked for some time now.'

'No.'

'And the Bresail is finding fewer and fewer sorcerers.'

'Yes.' Vaughn pressed a finger against his lips. The city appeared to be clear of their evil for the moment, but still . . . 'We'll keep with it, however. One day, I know, as my blood runs through my veins, I will find Robert Douglas. Until then, perhaps we can find a few more ways to make his minion Nash more uncomfortable. Nash has used the Guilde for his own purposes. Now perhaps the influence of the Guilde can be brought to bear against him and whatever scheme he has going with Robert Douglas. Bring me that list of iron shipments, will you?'

The Basilica held an odd mixture of folk. Most obvious was the King, dressed in mourning for his dead cousin, sitting alongside his son. Behind them were arranged the most witless collection of courtiers Nash had ever seen. They each belonged to one of two groups: either they were so afraid of Selar that they dared not miss Eachern's funeral, or they had hated the Duke so much, they felt they had to be here just to make sure he really was dead.

Of course, the young Duke Andrew was present, his aunt, Lady Bella, holding the boy's hand firmly. Lawrence, Baron Maitland sat on the other side of him, a protective wall around the child. They had brought friends and retainers with them to mourn; though their loss was less likely the Duke than his wife. To his credit, the boy sat still and quiet, dry-eyed throughout the Mass. His gaze never left his mother's casket before the altar, which was draped in the Ross colours.

What was most surprising was the number of lesser folk who had entered the church behind the procession. Some had merely come to witness the spectacle. But the others? They appeared genuinely sad and sent sympathetic gazes towards the young boy and his stern but beautiful aunt. Were they mourning the death of one of the last of the Ross House?

These folk were Lusaran, after all. Not the wealthy merchant class imported from Mayenne after Selar's conquest; these people were poor and no doubt knew the strange story of how Jennifer had been abducted as a child, then found as an adult and returned to her lost family. Did they feel something for her, some vestige of loyalty to the old royal family? After all, there was a connection – going back generations – but it was all the connection they had.

Odd that such feelings could still persist in a people twenty years under the rule of a conqueror.

With the last prayer said, the choir broke into a chant and the sound rose high into the darkest recesses of the ancient church. People began to file out, quietly, as was fitting. Nash waited a moment, then left the Guilde bench and made his careful way through the throng to Bella's side. She saw him coming, but didn't move away.

'I'm very sorry, my lady,' Nash murmured, allowing his voice to be coloured by sadness. 'You've suffered a great loss.'

Bella lifted her head, but kept tight hold of her nephew's hand. 'Thank you, my lord Governor. I know you were one of the few friends my sister was allowed. I'm glad she had that much.'

'I too,' Nash murmured. 'So sad, too, that the man who rescued her from the forest and brought her back to you, was the same who was responsible for her death.'

Conflicting thoughts and emotions flitted across Bella's face, but all she said was, 'Yes, indeed.'

'And how do you fare, your Grace?' Nash gazed down at the boy who was watching him warily. He'd had the opportunity a number of times over the last few years to scan this child. It would have been an act of blatant stupidity if he'd not. He did so again now. The boy had an aura certainly – with a mother like Jennifer, how could he not? But there was nothing untoward about it. No suggestion of her power – nor any power at all. If this boy ever grew up to be a sorcerer, his talents would be virtually negligible, and therefore no threat to Nash.

Of course, if the boy's father had not been Eachern, but the *Enemy* – Andrew would, by this age, almost glow with the gifts from both his parents.

But he had no time for further study. Selar was approaching and the group around Bella shrank back, bowing as they did so. The King towered over them all. He put a hand on Kenrick's shoulder and opened his mouth to speak, but suddenly Andrew drew back, stumbling into the skirts of his aunt.

It was not Selar who had scared the child, but the Prince. Andrew let go Bella's hand and stood there, his face red with something that might have been anger. Bella leaned down to him. 'What's wrong, my love?'

Andrew shook his head, but didn't take his eyes off Kenrick.

'He's just scared, my lady,' Kenrick sneered, moving a little closer. Andrew didn't back away this time, but held his ground.

'Not scared,' Andrew spat. 'Not of *that*!'

'What did you say?' Kenrick demanded.

Andrew screwed up his face in clear disgust and shook his head again.

'*That*'s not worth being scared of.'

'How dare you! I'll—'

'Enough!' Selar growled. 'My lady, I trust you will teach your nephew the proper respect due my son when next we meet. Otherwise, I will be forced to do so myself. Come, Kenrick, Nash.'

Nash paused only long enough to glance once more at the young Duke, then turned and followed after the retreating King.

The fire in front of Nash crackled and spat, but in spite of its fierce heat, cold still worked through his bones, and deeper, where nothing could touch it. He stared at the flames and tried to ignore the posturing Prince as he stalked up and down the room between Nash and the chair his father occupied.

Was she really dead?

'I won't have it! That boy would have nothing without you, Sire!'

That body laid to rest beside Eachern's. Was it hers?

'Don't take it to heart, my son. He's just lost both his parents.'

The Ally no more.

'That's no excuse for his behaviour, Father, and you know it!'

He'd waited too long to Bond her. If he'd done it already, she . . .

'He's upset, missing his mother. Think nothing of it, son.'

She would still be alive.

'How can you say that? Should I accept such an insult to my honour?'

She would have been his.

Selar snapped, 'Duke Andrew is a child, son. A baby, no more. I will not allow you to exact revenge on a five-year-old the day he buries his parents.'

Kenrick came to a halt before his father, his face still suffused with imagined injury. 'But Father—'

'Enough. Wait a while, son. A year. We'll have him at court as your page. He'll learn a few sharp lessons, I'll warrant you. Until then, calm yourself. You'll find as you grow older, it's far wiser to make friends than enemies. You would do well, instead of berating him like this, to turn him into your ally. That's the greatest revenge you could have.'

Nash glanced up at that, but Selar wasn't looking at him. His entire attention was focused on his son. Kenrick bowed stiffly and left the room. Selar laughed indulgently and waved apologetically at Nash.

'He's young, Sire. He'll learn.'

'Still, damned odd of Eachern's son to react like that, don't you think?' Selar lounged deep into his chair, elbows on the arms, making a steeple with his fingers. 'I can't help wondering if the old goat said something to his boy, something not entirely nice about Kenrick.'

'Come now, Sire. What could he have said? The Prince isn't old enough to have done anyone harm.' That wasn't entirely true, but there was no need to point it out to the King.

Selar laughed. 'Of course you're right. Yes, I'll get young Andrew here next year. It's time he started his education anyway. Now,' he sat up and turned his expectant gaze on Nash, 'when do we ride north? I'm anxious to see how my army has progressed. Do we march in a month as planned?'

Nash almost sighed out loud, but restrained himself. This King, so powerful and so feared, only ever thought about two subjects: his son and his damned war against Mayenne. If it wasn't so necessary, Nash would happily have given the whole thing up as a tremendously bad idea. After all, it was costing a fortune – in gold and in even more precious time. But for it to work, it had to be done properly. The only way to flush out the Enemy was to give him a target so big he couldn't resist the temptation to stop it.

Ah, Robert Douglas, so powerful, even without the Word of Destruction at his fingertips. So strong, so driven by honour that it had become his major weakness: a weakness simple to exploit. The Enemy loved his country, would do anything to stop it being dragged into such a useless, hopeless war. *Such* a weakness, to want to save his pathetic people, so beaten and broken that they couldn't stand up long enough to save themselves. They needed a hero to stop Selar from drawing them into conflict with Mayenne.

Lusara could never win such a war and everyone knew it – except Selar. The natural result would be nothing but devastation – and Selar would be lucky to survive with his borders intact. He'd managed to blind himself to the greater strength of his brother, of Mayenne. No, Tirone would invade Lusara in response, kill his younger brother and rule both countries.

But it wouldn't come to that. The Douglas would stop them. Nash knew that as certainly as he knew to draw breath. The Douglas would stop the army before it got to the border – and when he did, Nash would have him at last.

Even if *she* was no longer there waiting for him. His prize . . . Could he still take the Enemy without her there?

Of course he could. He could do anything!

'I tell you, Nash,' Selar went on, ignoring the silence, 'I'm still not happy about bringing mercenaries from over the Sadlan border. I know they're mighty swordsmen and will fight well for their money, but it's not the same.'

'We can't recruit from the land more than we have. We've been over this before. If you'd sent out a general call to arms, Tirone would be well warned by now. As it is, all he'll have is rumours here and there, no more than he's had for the last five years. He'll pay no attention, and by the time he does, it will be too late.'

Suddenly weary to the core, Nash rose from his chair. 'As to your ride north, wait a week. I'm leaving myself in a couple of days. I'll prepare things for your arrival and tell you when you can come.'

'Good.'

Nash left the room and closed the door behind him. It was all very well having Selar Bonded to him, but sometimes it was very draining having to do all the thinking and planning. On the other hand, he never got a word of resistance from the King, and right now, that was much more important.

He headed down the stairs and found Valena waiting for him, her delicate perfume a balm to his ravaged Senses. There was something about her beauty that had drawn him in, from the first moment he had seen her in Karakham so many years ago. Now she awaited his approach, her eyes solemn.

'How did it go?'

'Are you asking me if the King is mourning his cousin?'

'Do I look that stupid?'

'No.' Nash glanced around to make sure they were alone in the passage, then drew her to one side. 'Have you spent any time with Kenrick?'

Valena smiled sweetly, secretly, just for him. Despite his purpose, a *frisson* of excitement flittered across his skin. 'Now why would I do something like that? Would you now have me share the son's bed as well as the father's?'

Nash forced himself to stand apart from her. 'I know you, my dear.'

A flash in her eyes was quickly gone. 'Why do you ask?'

'There's something not entirely right with that boy and no amount of digging gets an answer.'

'Well, it's obvious how he feels about you.'

'And how is that?'

Valena pursed her lips, no longer deliberately seductive, but even more alluring. 'I think he's jealous.'

'Of the time I spend with the King?'

'I don't think so. He is, after all, the heir to the throne. He thinks you're a young man with a long career at court ahead of you. I think he wonders why you don't . . . give him more courtesy, in your capacity as chief adviser to his father.'

'I thought he hated me.'

'Oh, he does – but I think the opportunity is there to do something with that hate – if you're willing to make the effort.'

Nash looked down the dark empty hallway. It was late and most people were in bed now, tired out after that damned long funeral. 'Go up to Selar now. Get him to sleep. I'll come back in an hour.'

'Why?'

'There's something I have to do.' Nash turned back, not failing to notice how the soft light caught her cheek, burnished her lips. 'Go on.'

With a dubious frown, Valena headed up the stairs. Deliberately, Nash refused to watch her go. Instead, he walked down the passage and turned the corner at the end. He stopped in front of the Prince's door. Huge bronze handles sank into twin wedges of oak, carved to illustrious heights to honour the resident within. Casually, Nash put one hand to the oak, pressed his fingers against the polished indentations. At first, he could Sense nothing but the wood, its hard fibres compacted and solid. But then . . .

'By the blood!' he breathed, his eyes opening in genuine amazement. 'Well, well, well! Now that is interesting.'

Briskly now, he removed his hand and strode back down the hallway, revelling in his walk. No limp, no shadow of pain any more. But he didn't think about how it was almost wasted now that the Ally was dead. He had to be quick. He had just enough time to grab something to eat before it would be time to come back.

The King's bedchamber was filled with the warm yellow glow of a dozen candles burned low, flickering in currents of air wafting about the castle. Valena waited for him, saying nothing. With a nod, he dismissed her, and she left reluctantly. For a few moments, Nash stood on the threshold of the room, steadying his breathing, focusing his mind. Then he stepped forward until he was kneeling beside the bed and gazing on Selar's face.

Carefully removing one glove, he reached forward and touched Selar's forehead. The man was deep in sleep, soft and shallow inhale and exhale, the brief shudder of the eyelids as some dream formed and then escaped.

Nash sighed. 'It's been a long time. You no longer remember when we first met. I was an old man and you, an angry young Duke with a score to settle with your father, your brother. You never knew how I made your life into what it is today. How I had men instigate the Troubles in Lusara, sowed the seeds for your invasion. You were an unwitting tool, but willing in your ignorance. I remember how terrified of sorcery you were. Now, you hardly believe it exists. I remember how you once loved the Douglas. Now you think of him as nothing more than a coward. And how wrong you have been – about everything. Yes, a perfect tool indeed – but I think the time has come for you to look elsewhere for your glory.'

Now Nash laid two fingers in the centre of Selar's forehead, pressing firmly, sustaining the power. 'You will fight to the end.

Understand, you will take no quarter. When the time comes, you will allow no hesitation. Do you understand me?'

Deep in thrall, yet still asleep, Selar's lips moved. Words barely breathed dropped into the room. 'Yes, Master.'

Taymar had bowls of water and linen laid out for Nash. The water still steamed; feathers rising from its surface to be caught by rays of bleak lamplight. Nash shrugged off his jacket and shirt, then plunged his head into the hot water. With eyes closed, he patted around for a towel, then found one pressed to his cheeks by a familiar hand. Its partner wound its way around Nash's waist to press against his stomach muscles.

'You have no idea how I miss you.' The luxurious voice caressed his ear like silk.

Nash couldn't help it. He dropped the towel and turned to Valena, holding her face in his hands. Before she could even take a breath, he kissed her, deliberately drowning her urge to speak further. It had been a long time and his body responded with an urgency he could no longer control. Eager, Valena dragged him to the bed.

His hands moved quickly even as his mind stumbled on the reality of what he was doing, what he had promised himself he would not do again. Why had she come to him again?

But mind and body did not communicate. Instead, his lust drove him to the edge of madness, and then beyond. Afterwards, as he lay beside her, he took the time to breathe in her scent, to feel again the smooth skin of her throat.

'You missed me,' Valena murmured against his touch, a smile in her voice.

'Why are you here?' Nash replied gently, wary, and yet unwilling to completely break the moment.

At his question, Valena rose onto her elbow and gazed at him steadily. All suggestion of seduction, of powerplay and betrayal absent. 'Don't try and tell me you didn't want me.'

'Answer me.'

Her reply was almost wistful. 'Even though you don't want to, even though you don't really know what it means, you love me – still.'

Nash stared at her for a moment longer, then got up from the bed. He grabbed a robe and threw it around his shoulders. He stalked towards the old fireplace, taking a deep mouthful from a wine flask as he went. 'We've been over all this before. You have your work to do, I have mine.'

'But you chose my work for me. You can't very well complain.'

'You chose your work by your own nature!' Nash snapped, then glanced over his shoulder to where Valena sat on the bed, still gloriously naked. It seemed that no matter how he tried, she still had this incredible power over him. And why? He wasn't that weak. He'd never even touched a woman until he'd met her – had never been interested. Lust had always been a problem other men had, not him.

'Samdon, please. We don't have to do it this way.'

'The King will wake soon and expect to find you at his side.'

Valena left the bed and came towards him. He did nothing to stop her moving her hands inside his robe until it encompassed them both and she shared his warmth. 'Sam, why can't you swallow your jealousy? I must share Selar's bed for your benefit . . . '

'Our benefit.'

'So why can't I share yours for our pleasure?'

'Isn't that what DeMassey is for?'

Valena looked up at that, her eyes golden in the firelight. 'I haven't slept with Luc for years.'

Nash didn't reply for a moment, but neither did he push her away. The touch of her against his skin awoke all kinds of things inside him and for the first time in years, he actually felt good. Could he stand sharing her? Wasn't that better than not having her at all?

Of course it was. Especially now.

'This used to be our dream, Sam,' Valena continued, now going on her toes to touch her lips to his chin. 'I miss sharing. You have no time to tell me how the work goes now. Luc used to tell me – but it was never the same.'

No, DeMassey could never fulfil a woman like this. Nash couldn't help smiling. DeMassey was a formidable sorcerer, a man of grace and beauty – but even so, all those years ago, Valena had chosen Nash over DeMassey, and still chose him now.

'Perhaps,' Nash murmured, his face against her fragrant hair, 'I was a little hasty.'

In response, Valena's hands moved and Nash forgot all about DeMassey, Selar – and the entire world.

11

For some reason, the weather could not make up its mind what it wanted. Aiden stood on the battlements of Bleakstone Castle, in the southern depths of Flan'har, and watched the sky warring between winter and spring. Huge blustery clouds tumbled together, alternately sprinkling the land with sunshine, rain and snow – and sometimes all three at once.

This place was oddly named. The fortress, little more than a century old, was ringed with a high wall of reddish stone. It sat between a fork of rivers as they roared from the sharp hills to the north. Beyond, in the east, was the shadow of tougher mountains, while in the south, on a clear day, a line of sparkling blue showed where the sea lay. The entire area was covered with forest, in places thick and dark, in others little more than a scattering of brush. All in all, it was a beautiful place and it was easy to see why Grant Kavanagh loved it so much – but why it was called Bleakstone was anybody's guess.

Kavanagh had wanted to give it to Robert outright, but Robert had refused, knowing that behind the gesture was a thread of guilt. Kavanagh had been responsible for keeping Queen Rosalind and her children safe from Selar, but the Malachi had killed the Queen and taken the Prince back to Lusara. Kavanagh blamed himself.

Princess Galiena and Samah, Rosalind's sister, had escaped safely on a ship south, but it had been a long time since Aiden had heard a word from their self-appointed guardian, George, Earl of Kandar. On the other hand, no news at least meant they hadn't been recaptured by Selar – not that the King cared a whit for his daughter.

'Hey, Father!' Patric scrambled up a ladder behind Aiden and arrived at the top, breathless, his long hair damp and matted around his face. 'I've been calling you for ages.'

'Why? What's up? Have you found something?'

'No, it's not that. Robert's back – and he's brought Jenn with him! You won't believe what's happened . . . '

Robert had long ago chosen a room in the south tower for his own. It sat only one floor up, a huge circular apartment with walls so thick the doorway was almost a corridor in itself. The six windows were long and narrow, while the embrasures fanned out wide, only a step up from the floor. An area to one side was curtained off with huge red tapestries hiding a bed and washstand. A heavy table, usually covered in piles of papers and books, dominated the centre of the room, which was lit by candles standing tall in spaces around the wall.

Aiden had to step aside to let people out as he entered the room. A bustle of activity and noise, the huge space appeared crowded. He waited to one side as Robert, travel-worn but otherwise in one piece, gave out orders, listened to reports and generally tried to control the chaos. It seemed that every man in the castle had business with him. He'd washed and changed and seemed to be trying hard to get some food into his mouth. Nonetheless, order eventually reigned and the room began to empty, slowly, until the last left, closing the door behind him.

In the sudden silence, Robert met Aiden's gaze and laughed. 'You'd think I'd been away six months!'

'You have.'

'I see everyone arrived safely from the Enclave. Other than that, the preparations seem to be coming along well. Deverin and Owen really are a mean force between them. It looks like we'll be ready when the army begins to arrive. If it does, that is.'

'Why, have you doubts?'

Robert's attention was on the papers, his answer nothing more than an ambiguous shrug.

Aiden took a chair beside the fireplace and allowed the fierce heat to sear his feet. It had been damned chilly up on the battlements. Robert remained by the table, eating, drinking and looking at the papers left there by the others.

'You're late back,' Aiden began, lacing his fingers together on his lap.

Robert nodded. 'I had a few problems.'

'I know. Patric told me as I was coming in here, so you don't have to repeat the whole story. One question: What's Jenn doing here?'

'I have no idea. She won't talk to me.'

'Oh.'

'Oh, indeed.' Robert left the table, bringing his wine with him. He sat on a chair opposite Aiden, leaning forward with his elbows on his knees. 'She's not well. I think she's had a fever for the last couple of days, but it's past the worst. Mother has taken her in; she knows what she's doing. I just wish I did.'

Aiden framed his next statement carefully. 'And Eachern is dead.'

Robert met his gaze for a long moment, the green eyes flinty and hard. 'Yes.' After a breath, he continued, 'Jenn will get over her injuries, but I think she could do with some of your priestly wisdom right now. I dare not go near her. She had enough to blame me for before this. Now?'

'I'll do what I can,' Aiden replied.

Robert sat for a moment, gazing at the fire, his expression hiding everything but the hint of some dark memory. Before he could ask, Robert's aspect changed abruptly and he relaxed back to study Aiden with a measured gaze. 'This all bothers you greatly, doesn't it? The sorcery. You've still not quite come to terms with it, have you?'

'Of course I have.'

'Don't lie to me, Bishop.' Robert wagged a finger at him. 'Those priests at Elita started you asking questions again. Questions you now realise you never properly answered. Go on, deny it.'

Aiden sighed. Some days it was impossible to hide anything from Robert. 'I didn't know what to say to them. There you were, the embodiment of everything they've been taught to fear and hate, and yet, they knew you. If they hadn't, it might have been different.'

'Go on.'

Aiden idly formed a trium with his hands, brought them up to eye-level. 'I was always taught sorcery was evil in itself, that it was the sorcery which governed the evil – not the hand which wielded it. You've shown me otherwise. You've let me see and know things no other priest has ever before been aware of. I've studied the history of sorcerers, read their books, learned the processes. I know as much about sorcery as any human could know and yet, while I would never condemn it, in my heart . . . ' He couldn't finish, and glanced up.

'In your heart, you're still not sure.' Robert smiled lightly. 'I know, I've wondered the same thing myself.'

'You have?'

'Of course. I learned the same lessons as you and was immensely shocked to find I was a sorcerer myself. Then the Key gave me the prophecy and the Word of Destruction to play with. How could I not question if it was evil?'

'And your answer?'

Robert raised his eyebrows, his eyes twinkling with humour. 'Again, that same blinding faith. You amaze me sometimes. What on earth makes you think I ever found an answer?'

Aiden raised his hands in misery. 'Well, you're not much help then, are you? What chance do I have when you, the most powerful sorcerer ever born, can't give me a clue? In a matter of weeks, those priests and a whole army of soldiers are going to be looking to me to explain why they should support your war. What am I supposed to say to them?'

Robert laughed easily. 'I've told you before, Bishop, you worry too much. You'll know what to say when the time comes.'

'And I don't know how many times I've told you – *don't* call me Bishop!'

She sat in the corner of the room, her feet up on a second chair, her arms wrapped around her knees. The window beside her was wide, with a narrow lintel, and from her seat she could see the courtyard below where Deverin and Owen were busily organising something with the aid of a dozen men brandishing tools in their hands. Voices and hearty laughter floated up towards her on the blustery breeze and disappeared into the recesses of her room.

Beyond was the red castle wall, topped with an open walkway where three or four guards patrolled at a leisurely pace. If she leaned forward, she could see the gate to her right, while on the left was the imposing south tower. From its top flew the standard of the Duke of Flan'har, as though he were in residence.

The room had undecorated walls and sparse furniture: just two beds, a table and a few chairs. Colour came from the rich ochre bedcover, the glowing coals in the fireplace. All the rest was grey.

Two weeks and still she could remember every detail, every second.

Where had that power come from? She'd never used anything like that before, never even suspected she was capable of it. But it had come, nonetheless. It had killed. Him. He was dead, and she'd killed him.

In a moment.

Without thinking.

Andrew had seen it all. She had held him in her arms the next day as he'd shaken with the memory. But he hadn't cried for his dead father. Instead, he'd spoken of the man who had saved his mother.

She could have wept at the irony of it all.

Was he all right? Would Andrew suffer torments from that horrible night, or would Bella be able to calm and comfort him? Would he be happy at Maitland – would he be free?

And they all wondered why she'd left him there. Why she'd insisted on the story of her death. Was it not obvious?

Perhaps none of them knew of her . . . relationship with Nash. Robert hadn't said a word.

If Robert was right.

If Nash was Carlan. The Angel of Darkness. The same man who had abducted her twenty years ago and hidden her in the forest of Shan Moss. She'd been a child then, remembering nothing of her previous home in Elita.

What did he want from her?

By the gods, what did *any* of them want from her? Did she really have to be a part of all this? And now her life had been destroyed completely.

It would be different if, like Robert, she had some idea of what she was supposed to do within the prophecy. She was supposed to be the . . . guiding light against the Angel of Darkness . . . not have him become the only friend she'd known outside Clonnet for the last three years.

But what did a guiding light actually do? So far her only accomplishments – apart from her son – were to become close to the Angel and to drive to despair the only man capable of stopping him.

Some contribution!

There was a quiet knock at her door. She called out a response and the door opened, revealing the gentle Bishop.

'Good morning,' he ventured, closing the door behind him. He stood before the fire with the palest of frowns, comfortable and yet hesitant. 'How are you feeling today?'

'Much better, thank you.'

'Lady Margaret tells me you've finally been eating properly. That is surely a sign of impending recovery.'

'She's very kind,' Jenn replied, her voice muted.

'Yes, she is,' Aiden agreed. 'I often wondered how she managed to produce a son like Robert. I hardly know Finnlay. Is he an improvement?'

Jenn wasn't in the mood for casual chat, but she could hardly be rude to this man. There were qualities in him impossible to ignore. 'Not really. At times, I think he could even be worse.'

The Bishop rolled his eyes in exaggeration and left the fireplace to stand by the window opposite her. He looked out, folding his hands together as though all the storms of winter could be stilled in that simple gesture. 'Your wounds mend, but those on the inside do not.'

Jenn frowned.

He looked down at her. 'Perhaps I've been around sorcerers too long. I'm learning to recognise the signs. I saw what Robert was like after he used the Word at Elita – despite all his promises to himself that he would never do such a thing. Though the circumstances are very different, you suffer in the same way.'

No, I don't want to talk about that. At all. Ever. 'I'm sorry, Father, I know you're only trying to help, but—'

'I can't. Yes, I know,' he replied easily. 'But really, the only person who knows what it feels like is Robert. Still, I won't force the issue. I'll leave you alone to get some rest. If you do want to talk, I have a study at the end of this hall. There are some books there you might be interested in taking a look at.'

He moved to the door and pulled it open, then paused. 'I know you aren't . . . kindly disposed towards Robert at the moment, but I

173

think you should know – he didn't desert you at Clonnet. Perhaps I'll see you at supper this evening.'

As the wind rattled the casements, Aiden got up from the table and shoved another piece of folded paper into the gap between wood and stone. It wasn't so much the cold that bothered him, but the noise. Both windows of the long room were littered with his attempts to keep them quiet, but the determined wind blithely found some other damned brace to target.

Returning to his seat, he once again picked up the document he'd been reading. This was long, tedious work, but oddly intriguing. Certainly a strange thing for a priest to be doing – and yet, who was to say it wasn't time for the Church to re-examine the question of sorcery? Didn't sorcerers have souls? Were they any less in need of the gods' grace than those without powers?

And if the teachings of the Church were correct – well, perhaps they needed it more.

Patric, as usual for this time of the day, was nowhere to be seen. He preferred to work long into the night – anything to avoid getting up early. Still, he was a bright colleague, more than capable of making his own contribution even if he was a little . . . difficult to contain at times.

A creak from the doorway made Aiden look up in surprise. Jenn stood there, her hand on the latch as though she would just as happily leave again. He stood quickly. 'Please, come in.'

She paused for a long moment, her pale face catching the flickering candlelight. The gown she wore was borrowed, making her seem even smaller inside it, shrinking away almost, to avoid touching it.

Carefully Aiden ventured a smile. It would be too easy to scare her away now. 'Please, sit down.'

Jenn left the door and came towards the table, her fingers lightly touching the rough surfaces of dozens of books laid out. 'What are you doing?'

'Well, we're researching a little of sorcerer history. Some of these Patric brought from the Enclave, but the rest are books we have . . . collected recently, so they're all new ground.'

Jenn frowned a little and pulled a chair closer to the table. She sat, drawing a few books closer to her. 'What did you mean when you said Robert didn't desert me?'

Oh dear. Well, he'd just have to tell her the truth. 'He went back to Clonnet.'

'When?' Jenn murmured, not really believing.

'About every three months or so.'

'What?'

Quickly, Aiden continued, 'I'm ashamed to admit I kept telling him not to – but he paid me no attention, as usual. He would tell me how he'd seen you from a distance, that you looked well.'

'So that's how he knew about . . . ' She paused, delicately removing a wisp of hair from her face, changing the subject. 'So, how did you get these?'

'Er . . . Robert . . . ' Aiden swallowed – but there was no reason not to tell her. 'Robert has spent a lot of the last five years chasing up any lead he can find to learn more about your history and the prophecy. Most of these tomes have been . . . liberated from the libraries of the Guildehalls. Both he and Patric are convinced there are answers to be found simply by looking in the right place.'

'But what answers are you hoping to find? How can these help?'

'They cover the period six hundred years ago, before sorcerers were anathema, and go right through the war with the Empire and the last battle at Alusia. Actually, we've found some very interesting things. Would you like to see?'

Jenn looked up. 'Yes. I would.'

He took a seat beside her and piled a few relevant tomes together. 'Well, this one is a list of sorcerer Cabal Palaces, dated seventeen years before that last battle. You see there beside the name of one Palace in Alusia, Felkri, some notes made to keep its activities under close supervision because of discipline problems. This here shows notes from a meeting between a Prince and a Cabal leader from Bu, in the west. No details are given, but the Prince is assured there is no danger to Alusia and that the problem is merely a difference of opinion. Later, another note, about a year before the battle, talks about how Felkri was to be left to it – as if all attempts at reconciliation with Bu had failed.'

'So there could have been one surviving Palace not drawn into the war the following year?'

Aiden smiled. 'It's a nice idea, isn't it? Unfortunately, there doesn't seem to be any evidence to suggest that more than a few wounded sorcerers ever left Alusia. No record of any subsequent attack on Felkri, nor any further rising of sorcerers against the Empire.'

'No mention at all? But doesn't that suggest that Felkri managed to stay so far out of it that the Empire ignored it completely – or perhaps didn't even know anything about it? Or perhaps those that did know were killed in the battle.'

'Not necessarily . . . '

Jenn stood up and wandered around the table. 'Do you know the cause of the rift between Felkri and Bu?'

'What's going on here?'

Aiden spun around in his chair to find Robert standing in the doorway. He came to his feet. This was not good. 'I was just . . . '

Robert glanced once at Jenn, then gestured to Aiden. 'Can I see you outside?'

Aiden moved into the passage and closed the door behind him.

'What are you doing?' Robert asked.

'I'm explaining our work to Jenn,' Aiden replied evenly.

'And you just decided that, did you?'

Aiden pursed his lips and leaned back against the wall for some kind of moral support. He framed his response with great care. 'You can't keep her in ignorance forever, Robert. One day you're going to have to explain things to her.'

'I don't have to explain anything.'

'Really? Regardless of how the prophecy affects her?' Aiden shook his head. 'Jenn has no idea of who she is, or even why she is part of this whole thing in the first place – and now she's separated from her son. We can try as hard as we can, but until we include her in this business, she's never going to feel as if she belongs.'

'She doesn't belong.' Robert's reply was dark, not giving in at all. 'I don't want her involved. The less she knows, the less likely . . . '

Aiden stopped him with an abrupt gesture. 'Do you really think keeping her in ignorance is going to have any affect on the outcome of the prophecy? I know you're trying to protect her from your destiny, but this is not the way to go about it. Gods, Robert, you really amaze me sometimes. One moment you refuse to believe in the prophecy, and the next, you're doing everything you can to prevent it. Doesn't that dichotomy bother you?'

'Look—'

'No, Robert.' Aiden took a step closer, as though pressing his point. 'This is the very behaviour you hate so much in the Guilde. Keeping people ignorant for their own good. If you don't tell Jenn what's going on, how the prophecy is supposed to end, how is she to know what to avoid?'

There was a long pause. Robert gazed at him steadily and Aiden felt frozen to his place, unable to speak. Finally, Robert spoke, his voice low as though he would contain something still raw. 'It's not that simple. I can't just tell her. She wouldn't understand.'

As Robert looked away, Aiden was released from that gaze. His voice soft, but determined, he replied, 'Then I can tell her. I am, after all, the only other person who knows.'

Robert shook his head. 'No.'

'Because of the demon?'

At that, Robert straightened up, his shoulders stiffening immediately. He turned back. 'You will not tell her the rest of the prophecy.'

'Then,' Aiden took a breath, 'at least give her a chance to fight it as you have done. Let her be involved.'

'Even if doing so will only take her closer to the danger?'

It was impossible to ignore the undercurrent of despair. With a sigh, Aiden reached out a hand to Robert's shoulder. 'Years ago you gave her the opportunity to make a choice about her future. She chose to go home to her father – sparking off all the events since. To take that choice away now is not only immoral, but dangerous. You know her as nobody else does. She can fight. Give her the chance to – and something to fight *with*.'

With an ironic smile, Robert said, 'You're supposed to be on my side.'

'But I am. Come on, I can tell you what we've found as I tell Jenn.'

Robert sat with his back to the fireplace, his feet up on the low window ledge, counting the pieces of paper Aiden had used to stop the casement from rattling. Outside, a few flakes of persistent winter snow flew past, caught up in the nasty wind. Aiden droned on in the background, answering Jenn's questions one after another. Robert deliberately kept his attention diverted. It would be bad enough for her to have to be in the same room with him; he didn't want her to also have to put up with him watching her.

And it was hard not to, hard not to notice the change in her. Now that he knew the cause, he could see how she had withdrawn into herself, never reaching out to others as she had always done before. Her laugh, the light in her eyes, had gone. Was it just Eachern's beating that had done this, or was there more to it? Like the fact that she had killed him – or the truth about her friend, Nash?

All the same, it appeared Aiden had read her correctly. She was captivated by their work, involving herself without even realising it. Was there no other way to do this, to keep her safe and stop Nash at the same time? Surely this would only play right into the hands of the prophecy.

She believed he didn't trust her, and the worst part was that he couldn't find a way to assure her that he did – because he *wasn't* sure. He couldn't afford to be, not when he knew of the time she'd spent with Nash, time she claimed meant nothing.

There was simply no way to be positive that Nash had held no influence over her, and even having her here was a danger. Even though he *wanted* her here. Even though, if the choice were entirely his, he *would* trust her.

And after all, wasn't that what Aiden had just said? To trust her with the truth of their work, what they were looking for? Would giving her what she needed – information – give her the chance to prove that she *could* be trusted?

By the time he got an answer to that, it might very well be too late. Still, the only choice he really had was to try.

Try to forget that he loved her still and that she no longer loved him.

He took in a deep breath and let it out, allowing his thoughts to subside, to be replaced with the subject under discussion.

'So we come back to what I was saying before,' Jenn continued. 'The absence of information about Felkri doesn't mean it must have been destroyed. It could still be there. If there'd been some disagreement between them, there might be some record of it remaining at Bu.'

Robert kept his gaze out the window; his voice was soft as he answered her. 'I've been to Bu and it's completely empty.'

'You didn't expect to find anything in the caves at Nanmoor – but you found that silver rod,' Jenn said harshly. 'Not that you've done anything with it since.'

Robert didn't reply. Anger was so much harder to ignore when it dealt with the truth. He kept the rod with him always, certain, in some strange way, that he would know what to do with it when the time came. Silly, really.

'And,' Jenn continued relentlessly, 'you've been to Alusia, but you never knew there'd once been a Palace there, did you?'

'What's your point?' Robert asked.

'There was a serious split between the premier Cabal Palace at Bu and Felkri. That split might have guaranteed the survival of Felkri while Bu fell. Surely it would be in our interests to find out if Felkri still exists. To discover the reasons behind the split. Otherwise, none of this makes any sense.'

'Why should it?' Robert murmured, still without turning. 'We're operating here with only the sketchiest records. I know there have to be more around, but I can't see us finding them in the near future. Not before it's too late. Besides, even if we did discover what happened to Felkri, would that really tell us more about the prophecy?'

Jenn didn't reply immediately, so Robert glanced over his shoulder. Her gaze was on the book in front of her. Eventually she said slowly, 'It would if the prophecy itself were the bone of contention.'

Startled, Robert sat up, swinging his legs from the window ledge. She ignored him and continued, 'The Key was created at the Palace of Bu and we know that's when it got the prophecy. Let's assume for a moment that there were two different versions of the prophecy – Bu having one, Felkri the other. If they were both adamant they were right, that would make perfect grounds for Felkri to be outcast. Can you think of another reason why there would be a split at such a sensitive time? And if Felkri had already been outcast by the time the Key was created, then it's possible the Key's version of the prophecy could be in error. So grave an error that Felkri was prepared to stand aside and take no part in . . . By the gods . . . ' Jenn came to a halt.

'What?'

For a moment she said nothing, then, her voice slow and steady, she continued, 'The Cabal lost that battle because, as legend goes, an incarnation of the goddess Mineah appeared out of nowhere and fought for the Empire. But what if she'd actually been a sorcerer from Felkri?'

'Now wait a moment,' Aiden interjected, his face suffused with red.

Robert quickly got to his feet and came around the table to stand between them. 'But why would she help in the annihilation of her own people?'

Jenn held up her hands, her eyes alight with excitement. 'To preserve their version of the prophecy. What else could be so important?'

Could she be right? Was it possible that the prophecy had become infected over time? That it had existed long before the Key?

Would the ending be different?

'Look, Robert,' Jenn continued, hesitating at his silence, 'I know this is all guesswork, but . . . '

Robert began to smile. 'It's all right. I'm convinced.'

'You are?' She blinked up at him, surprised.

'Yes.'

'Well, I'm not,' Aiden growled. 'More than once Mineah has blessed us by taking on human form and helping us when we most need it. I've heard nothing that makes me believe otherwise about the battle of Alusia.'

Robert almost laughed. 'And what makes you think she didn't take on the form of a sorcerer? The two theories aren't at odds with each other. Besides, I have another reason to think Jenn might be right.'

'Oh, what?' Aiden was obviously unhappy.

'I've seen the battlefield with my own eyes. There are scars on the landscape to suggest arcane involvement far beyond what the Cabal could have managed, stories handed down through the centuries of what Mineah was alleged to have done.'

'But that doesn't mean . . . '

'We have to go there,' Jenn interrupted. 'We have to find out if there is anything left. Any*one* left.'

'You might be right,' Robert said, 'but we don't have time to go searching for a Palace when we've no idea where to start looking. I have a war to fight, remember?'

Jenn gazed at him steadily, the iron-clad determination of old back in force. 'Are you going to tell me the rest of the prophecy?'

'Jenn . . .'

'Then you're willing to risk it, are you? Willing to face the possibility of having to fight Carlan on the battlefield, aware he knows more than you do . . .'

She would have gone on, but at that moment, the door banged open and Patric entered, looking more of a mess than usual. His fair hair was all over the place, grey smudges sat beneath his eyes and his clothes possessed more creases than they had a right to. 'Robert – thank the gods you're here!'

'Why, what is it?'

'That other Palace,' Patric began, all a flutter, 'the rift was all to do with the prophecy. I have it here.' He waved a scroll before Robert's nose. 'It doesn't use the word prophecy, but speaks of the true path and heresy and diverging destinies and all sorts of stuff. It was written six months before the battle at Alusia – but – it was found at Bu two years *later* by a squad of Guilde soldiers sent to clear the empty Palace of dangerous documents. The gods alone know what else they found. It's taken me all night to translate it.'

Half-frozen, Robert reached out slowly and took the scroll, opening it to see the faded script. 'Are you sure it's referring to the prophecy?' he asked, suddenly short of breath. If this was true, if the Key *was* wrong, then his destiny might not be . . . he might not have to . . .

'I'm positive, Robert.' Patric couldn't stand still. 'It's incredible! It documents the early troubles between the Cabal and the Empire and regrets the split that sent Felkri on a different path. Most important, though, is a reference to the "path carved in stone".'

'What?' Jenn started. 'You mean the prophecy is written somewhere? In stone?'

'I think that's exactly what it means. The only way we'll know is if we go to Bu and look for it. Or perhaps to Alusia and see if we can find the remains of Felkri. One way or the other, it looks as though there is another source to the prophecy. We have to find it. Robert?'

He looked up from the manuscript, moved by Patric's bald enthusiasm, then noting Aiden's gentle scepticism. Finally, he looked at Jenn. She was watching him closely, waiting for him to back away, to give in.

Abruptly, he turned back to the window. He didn't have time to go to Alusia – and yet, could he risk not going? Jenn was right, damn her. But he just didn't have the time. In a few weeks, the army would start to arrive, spring hot on its heels. And what would they all do if Micah sent word Selar's army was marching and Robert wasn't here?

But the prophecy might be wrong . . .

'How long would it take to get to Alusia?' Jenn spoke to Patric and instantly, Robert's skin began to tingle with warning.

'No,' he said, then turned to face them. 'Patric can go to Alusia – but you're staying here.'

'Robert . . . ' Aiden began, but Robert didn't let him continue.

'I know Alusia and it's the last place I would let Jenn go without an experienced escort. Patric has done a lot of travelling over the last six years. He can get by much better on his own.'

Jenn glared at him. 'Then I'll go to Budlandi.'

'By the gods!' Robert raised his hands in frustration. 'I told you, I've seen the Palace. The building still stands, but there's nothing else there. It's empty!'

'But the walls remain and that's where the prophecy is written. Did you see anything like that?'

'Of course.'

'Could you read it?'

Robert bit his tongue – but he couldn't avoid answering. 'No, I couldn't read most of it – but you still have no idea of the dangers involved. Until a week ago, you'd never even been out of Lusara. What are you trying to do?'

'Find a way out of this mess for both of us!' Jenn snapped, her eyes flaring. 'If there is a record of the prophecy, then I'll find it.'

'You'll get yourself killed first.'

'You can't stop me.'

'No?' Robert took a step forward. Involuntarily she shrank back until the table stopped her.

By the gods, what was he doing – treating her the same way as Eachern had?

But she wouldn't survive five minutes in the rough cities and deserts of Budlandi.

Robert tried to still that overpowering instinct to keep her sheltered and safe from anything that might harm her. She had a very good point and he couldn't afford to ignore it. If there was an alternative path to the prophecy, it was in everybody's interest that he find it – and soon, before he had to face Nash.

He didn't have a choice. And Bu was a lot closer than Alusia.

With a sigh, he said, 'Very well, I won't try to stop you. I'll do something better. I'll go with you.'

Margaret hurried across the courtyard, trying desperately to keep pace with Robert as he strode ahead with Deverin and Owen. Robert issued instructions, made changes and re-organised plans. He listened to what they had to say, but if there was an objection, he moved right on.

'The rest of those supplies should arrive in about a week. Get them stored then chase up the fletchers – and check their work. I don't want our archers flying north when they want to go south. When the other magnates arrive, tell them I'll be back soon. Payne and McGlashen should have bought us some time with their interference, more than a month at least. Micah's last message said that everything was quiet – but if he sends word that Selar's army is moving early, send out those letters I've prepared and leave a message for me at the port. Move what you have of the army down to the ships – Kavanagh has promised me they'll be ready and waiting. Even if we start out late, we can still get there long before Selar's army. Whatever you do, don't wait for me. It'll take you a lot longer to get to the border of Mayenne than me travelling alone. The chances are that I'll be back long before you need to do any of this.'

'And how long is that?' Owen asked, obviously unhappy with Robert's decision.

'No more than two weeks – probably less.' Robert came to a halt on the steps of his tower and faced them. 'Don't worry. It's taken me twenty years to get to this point. I'm not going to miss it now, and I promise you, I wouldn't be going to Budlandi at all if it wasn't important.'

With that, he disappeared inside and, despondent, his men went about their business, shaking their heads.

Margaret followed Robert into his room. He'd left the door open and she watched while he shoved clothes and things into a saddlebag.

'What is it, Mother? I don't have a lot of time. I leave in a few minutes.'

'I understand your rush – I fail, however, to understand your reason. How can you possibly leave now?'

'Father Aiden will explain.'

'But must Jenn go too? I can't see that a trip like this can be good for her.'

'Mother,' Robert said as he continued packing, 'you have no idea how much I wish she wasn't going.'

'But you must be able to stop her.'

Robert came to a halt at the other side of the table where his mother was sitting. For a moment, he concentrated on buckling up his saddlebag. 'I can't without hurting her – and I'm sick of doing that. Sometimes it seems the more I try to protect her, the more she pays for the privilege. And let's face it, I haven't been too successful so far.'

Margaret reached out and took his hand, held it tight between her own. For five years she'd hardly known anything of this son of hers and now, only days after his return, he must run off again. She touched the side of his face where a new scar was still healing and smiled. 'You're still in love with her.'

At that, he looked up, for a moment looking terribly young. 'What is this? Does everybody know? Am I suddenly so obvious?'

Margaret began to laugh, but Patric came in and Robert turned to face him.

'Now you be careful in Alusia, my friend. Make sure you keep your head down and listen to what Solcar tells you. You can trust him. If you can't find him at the port, wait a few days and he'll appear. Have you got everything you need?'

Patric nodded, his own smile wide. 'And to think that up until a few years ago, I'd never set foot outside the Enclave. You take care, Robert – and bring Jenn back safely. If I find anything, I'll send word.'

'Let's both hope you do.'

12

Micah made his brisk way along the street of what had been, until a few months ago, a sleepy village. Now Dromna had about it the energy a place gets when it's had to grow too quickly. Makeshift shops and market stalls overflowed the wooden town wall, spilling the populace further into the valley. The noise and bustle of the place was incredible and never seemed to quieten down, even in the dead of night. Almost on the hour, the village watch was forced to intervene in some dispute, armed or otherwise.

He walked with purpose, his hands thrust deep into his pockets. Birdsong filled the dawn air, full of spring joy – and some despair. The forest south of the village had been taken over, little left now but the tall trees which gave some cover to the forces amassing in the next valley. This was about as secret as an army ever got.

Micah turned off the main street and into the doorway of the tavern. Two men lay prone across a table in the opposite corner of the taproom, their faces oblivious. One even snored.

''Morning, Micah,' a voice called from the back room. Immediately a grinning face stuck its head around the door, followed quickly by a broom and the rest of the body. 'Would 'a been a nice walk this morning.'

'Aye, it was, Ciaran. Couldn't you get rid of these two?'

'I thought I'd leave them for you. I can't lift them on my own.'

Micah stood before the biggest of the drunkards. 'Of course you can. Here, give me that.' He took the pail of water from the lad and doused the man's head with half of it. As he rose, bleary-eyed, Micah took his elbow and ushered him to the door. A minute later and the other was outside as well.

Ciaran was grinning at him as he said, 'I wish I could think like you.'

Micah laughed and clapped the boy on the shoulder. 'Come on, we've got work to do. If this place isn't cleaned up in the next hour, Duffy will have our heads because he can't open up on time. You start sweeping and I'll get some more water.'

Despite the hour, Ciaran managed to keep up a constant stream of conversation as they worked. In between sweeping and mopping, shifting heavy tables out the way, spreading fresh straw on the floor, Ciaran chattered. Over the months working here, Micah had grown accustomed to the constant noise. Ciaran was young and working in a tavern had taught him some strange things.

'Duffy'll be hauling in the gold from this army – not that you and me'll see it. Never seen a body drink like them Guildesmen – except mebee the Sadlani. Wish they weren't here. They should go back where they belong. S'not a soul in town who don't hate'm, doesn't remember them coming over the border to fight us. I don't see how they can be our allies now. It don't mix with me. I tell you, one day there'll be a big fight between them and the Guilde and us'll be caught in the middle. Still, I'd rather die like that than in some stupid fire like that Duke Eachern.'

Micah glanced at him, but said nothing. Robert's note had arrived almost simultaneously with the news about Clonnet. Jenn and Andrew were safe. That was all he knew – but that was enough for the moment.

Ciaran continued, hardly taking a breath, 'They was all talking about it again last night. They say the sorcerer Dunlorn single-handedly attacked the Duke's castle, killed him and the Duchess, then torched the place.'

Half-smiling, Micah asked, 'And do you believe that?'

'Well, we all know what them sorcerers are like don't we?' Ciaran scratched his black cropped hair. 'And Dunlorn did far worse at Elita. He's a wicked one, that man.'

'Aye, he certainly is,' Micah nodded, chuckling. One day he'd have to sit down and tell Robert all the things he'd heard about the renegade outlaw. It would certainly give Robert a good laugh, if nothing else.

Micah picked up the bucket and headed out the back to pour the dirty water into the gutter. With gusto, he gripped the pump and refilled the bucket to clean the mop.

There was a certain rhythm in doing this work, day after day, a kind of peace in knowing what he had to do each hour, how to do it, what the results would be. Not that he would be happy working in a tavern for the rest of his life, but as a respite from roaming the countryside, it had its charms. The people of Dromna were good folk, like those he had grown up with at Dunlorn. Their patience was sorely tested by the presence of the army, certainly, but they hadn't become tarnished by it, just a little bruised here and there. It would be nice to come back here, after the war, and meet up with the friends he'd made.

After the war.

Micah squeezed the mop out, emptied the bucket and put them both away. Leaving Ciaran to finish inside, he headed towards the stables, collecting a pitchfork along the way. Picking up the chime of birdsong, Micah whistled as he set to clearing the hay out into the yard.

There'd been little activity in the valley that morning. The army, for what it was worth, appeared in no great hurry to move. It was still difficult to gauge the size of it, nestled as it was, in the thick of the forest. Five, perhaps six thousand. But it would be more later. As the time grew near. Not even a fool like Selar would march on Mayenne with only five thousand to fight for him. As long as Micah was able to find out when they were moving. As long as he kept vigilant watch, and got away as soon as he knew.

And how many men would Robert have? Would any come at all – or would they, after long consideration, decide they didn't want to fight alongside a sorcerer? Ciaran was right: rumours were still flying about the fire at Clonnet, as well as a dozen other crimes the Outlaw was supposed to have committed. Sometimes it was hard not to blurt out the truth, to tell people what Robert was really trying to do. So many of them felt betrayed that a man they'd once hailed as a hero – fighting these very Sadlani mercenaries now attached to this army – that he had turned his hand to the evils of sorcery. What they believed was unjust, and it sat cruelly on Micah's shoulders; but it was an injustice born of ignorance and he was in no position to change that.

And would they really be comforted by the truth – a prophecy nobody really understood, except perhaps Nash?

Micah sloshed water over the cobbled floor, swept it out, then filled each stall with fresh hay.

'You there!'

He paused and turned, squinting from the dark stable into the broad sunshine. 'Yes?'

'Can you stable my horse?'

Micah took a few steps forward – and stopped completely. A young woman stood before him, holding the reins of a fabulous black gelding. But the horse paled to insignificance beside its mistress.

Almost as tall as him, she glowed with colour that made the stable appear more drab than usual. Bright blue jacket over a rich crimson gown. Her face a perfect oval with eyes of crystal ice, fair eyebrows and hair like burnished gold. At least, that's what he'd always thought burnished gold would look like.

His stomach gave a single, not-unpleasant flip and settled again. He swallowed and did his best not to stare at her. 'Er, yes, my lady, I can stable your horse. Are . . . you staying at the inn?'

For a moment, she didn't reply. Then she glanced around at the shabby but sturdy buildings with a little smile. 'No. I just want to walk around the town for a while. Can you take him? I don't want to leave him in the street with all these people around. He can get a little skittish.' Her voice was warm and soft and melted into the birdsong.

Micah moved forward and placed a hand on the neck of the animal. 'He's a beauty.'

'Yes, he is.' Her face coloured a little. 'My father breeds horses. I've had this one since he was a foal.'

With a brief nod, Micah turned back to the horse. It was getting very difficult to concentrate on the conversation with her standing so close. His mouth was dry and words he could have spoken evaporated like a summer shower.

'He doesn't ride any more.'

'Who?' Micah murmured, risking another glance at the girl. She didn't appear to be in too much of a hurry to leave.

'My father.' Then she smiled – and Micah's knees felt suddenly weak. 'He broke his leg years ago, near the hip, and now he can't ride. So I get the best of his horses.'

Was it his imagination, or was she talking just for the sake of it?

'That . . . must be . . . er,' Micah fumbled for words, abruptly lost in her gaze, 'a great challenge.'

'I manage.' She shrugged, reached up to pat the nose of her horse, then glanced back at him. 'You will take good care of him, won't you? I'll be back before dark.'

She was about to leave; already his body sensed the wrench parting would be. As she turned to go, he almost reached out to touch her – then stopped himself in time. 'Your name?'

Another smile, and he was glad he was holding onto the horse for support.

'My name is Sairead. You'll be here when I come back for him, won't you?'

Micah could only nod dumbly as, with a brief wave, she walked out of the yard, past the high fence until he could see her no more. Without thinking, he rushed after her, but she was already lost in the crowded street. As he stood there like an idiot, a noise from the other direction made him turn.

'Serin's blood!' He swore under his breath: a column of soldiers in Guilde colours, Nash riding at their head. The street cleared before them as they made their way through the town. Micah stepped back, but continued to watch. Nash didn't look happy. He wore only a token of Guilde yellow: a fringe on the dark cloak around his shoulders. His hair was cropped short and black as midnight, his eyes the same colour. But it was always the face that surprised Micah, whenever he had the misfortune of looking upon it. The features were neither ugly nor handsome, merely present, as though neither personality nor character slept behind them. If it were not for his position – and his real identity – one would barely notice Guilde Governor Nash.

Nothing showed of the awesome power buried beneath that nondescript exterior.

Micah heard nothing useful as the column rumbled by. No carts of supplies accompanied them, there appeared no haste. They were merely arriving, not planning to leave in a hurry. It seemed Selar's army was not yet ready to march.

Good. Robert needed all the time he could get.

Micah turned, took the girl's horse and led it into the stable. He might just take another wander through the forest that afternoon. Just for a little exercise, of course. To get a breath of fresh air. Yes, a perfect idea.

As Nash passed through the camp, he made a point of picking up every detail he could. Sergeants gave him rushed reports as he rode along, giving him lists of things he didn't want to know and trying to hide the things he did want to know. One thing was blatantly obvious, however: this army wasn't ready to pop a sling-shot, let alone fight a major war. That's what you got for hiring mercenaries and recruiting farmers.

He came to a halt outside his pavilion, barked a few orders about increased training schedules, then ducked inside. He tossed his cloak onto a chair, poured himself a cup of wine and collapsed onto his bed.

He was tired, bone-weary from too many days in the saddle, too many years plotting and planning, too many decades waiting for something . . . for someone . . .

Tired yes, but not beaten. Over the next few days, he would take it easy for a change, try the old kind of regeneration: rest. It worked for everyone else – and it couldn't do him any harm.

'Taymar!' he bellowed, not bothering to get up. He did lift his head high enough to take a sip of wine, then plopped back onto his pillow. He heard the tent flap open. 'Taymar, have you got the supply reports yet?'

'No, he hasn't.'

Nash sat up in a hurry as DeMassey sauntered into the pavilion, his sky-blue cape sweeping behind like a royal train. He passed the table with a casual glance. 'What are you doing here?' Nash asked.

'Just dropped by.'

'Didn't Aamin recall you?'

'He did.'

'So you've come here to spy for him, have you?' Nash lay back down, but propped his head up so he could keep an eye on DeMassey.

'Nothing of the kind.' DeMassey feigned hurt so well. 'I have come only to commiserate with you on your recent loss. The little Duchess? Such a tragic end to one so promising. What will you do to replace her?'

'She can't be replaced, as you well know!' Nash snapped, then gritted his teeth. He had to control his temper, even when faced with DeMassey's usual irritating demeanour. Getting angry would only spur DeMassey on.

'And you were so close to Bonding with her. I remember you were on the point of going to Clonnet to do such a thing when word reached you of her untimely demise. Did she really simply go up in flames – or was she . . . helped along?'

'Damn you, DeMassey! Get out of here!'

'But I've come to help you.' DeMassey spread his arms wide innocently.

It was sickening. 'And what about your precious Chabanar?'

DeMassey shrugged and resumed his casual inspection of the tent. 'I'll admit I can't be as much use as before, but there's no reason why I can't help you here and there. To be honest, I expected a better welcome. Things aren't going exactly as planned, are they? Certainly you managed to flush out the Enemy – but I doubt you expected the Ally to die as a result. Unless I miss my guess, Jennifer Ross's death creates quite a problem for you, doesn't it? Not to put too fine a point on the matter – is there any reason to continue without her? You did say she was the key to all this.'

Nash swung his legs off the bed. He didn't have the energy for this tonight. He stood and looked around for the wine flask. 'What do you want?'

DeMassey shrugged. 'I came back to warn you. My spies have reported some movement in Mayenne.'

'Tirone?' Nash looked up. 'Does he have an army?'

'Not yet – but he suspects something. If you leave your departure too long, he may just decide to invade Lusara. And once he's over the border, you can say goodbye to your entire power base here. Tirone is simply too strong for any army Selar could muster in the next few weeks.'

Taking a step back, Nash bellowed, 'Taymar! Get in here!'

Pounding feet heralded the young man, panting for breath.

Nash paced back and forth. 'Taymar, I want the army ready to march in one week.'

'Yes, master, but . . . '

'But what?'

'We can't. There've been some problems.' Taymar swallowed and continued, 'We have no supplies.'

'What do you mean, no supplies?'

Taymar took a breath. 'Just that, Master. With the men idle here, they've consumed all our stores and used up just about everything within thirty leagues. The town has no food left bar a few days' worth. There was a fire yesterday, which destroyed the hay store. We can't feed the horses. The deliveries we expected haven't arrived. I just got word that a major shipment of arrows has gone astray. They were attacked on the road here and robbed.'

'Robbed?' Nash almost shrieked.

'Half the army is still not properly armed. They'll be fighting with pitchforks and wooden clubs. Vital supplies of iron have simply never arrived and the smiths have had no work to do. The army could march in a week, but by the end of the second day, they'd starve and be in no position to fight anyone but each other.'

Nash sank onto a stool and shook his head. The Ally gone and now no hope of striking towards the border before Tirone could react. Selar was going to have a fit. 'So, how long will it take to be ready?'

Taymar replied, 'I'll be able to give you a proper estimate tomorrow, Master. But my guess is something around four weeks. Perhaps even longer.'

'Broleoch's teeth!' Nash muttered.

'It will take a week or two just to sort out the mess.'

'Very well. Just get to it.'

Four weeks! Would it be too late?

'DeMassey, do you still have that man in Tirone's court?'

'Of course.'

'Get word to him. He has to do something to slow Tirone down, allay his suspicions or something. We must have more time. Send some of your spies down to the ports and to the trade road north of the Goleth range. I need to know which way the Douglas will get there.' Nash drained his cup of wine and glanced up. 'Taymar, send the mercenaries back over the border. We'll recall them in two weeks. In the meantime, organise some foraging parties – go as far afield as you need to. We'll give the Enemy plenty of time to be ready to meet us.' Now Nash paused, staring into his empty cup. 'Leave me, both of you. I don't want to be disturbed again tonight unless the Enemy comes walking into this camp. Go.'

For the third time that night, Micah straightened his best jacket and ducked out into the yard to see if she'd come back. Dusk had fallen an hour or more since and she still hadn't returned for her horse. The inn was quiet, with only a few locals in, softly chatting and drinking. Duffy kept them company, bellowing at Ciaran to serve the tables, leaving Micah the odd few moments to keep watch on the stables.

By the gods, what was it about her that had him jumping every few minutes? All afternoon, as he'd wandered around the perimeter of the encamped army, she'd been in his thoughts, her smile, her words, that look in her eyes. All so . . . captivating.

And Nash had sent the mercenaries back to Sadlan. Very good indeed – but they would be back. It appeared Payne and McGlashen had done their part in interrupting the supplies to Dromna. All the better. Yes, excellent.

So where *was* she?

He shut the door behind him and stepped onto the hard cobbles. The gate was half-closed and the street was almost empty. With a sigh, he turned for the stables, losing himself in the warm gloom to be nuzzled at by the first horse he touched.

'There you are,' a soft voice drifted towards him. 'I thought I might have to leave without thanking you.'

Micah peered into the shadows, but it was too dark to see anything. She laughed softly and came closer where a dust of moonlight could catch her face. Micah tensed, not knowing why, not quite understanding – and not caring.

'I was getting worried,' he breathed. 'You said you'd be back before dark. I thought something might have happened.'

She smiled, both hesitant and confident at the same time, as though she were trying desperately to overcome a sudden shyness. 'You didn't tell me your name.'

'Micah.' He fell silent, unable to move, unable to take his eyes from her. Her gaze troubled him: warm and serious and very still. He was breathing shallowly, but couldn't seem to stop it. 'Would you like me to saddle the horse?'

'No.'

'No?'

Her gaze still serious, she took a step forward and reached out to his hand. 'I would rather stay and talk.'

His skin was on fire where she touched it. Unthinking, his fingers turned to grasp hers. He shouldn't be doing this – hell, he shouldn't be feeling this! Where had all his good sense gone? Vanished into the smile of a pretty girl? Nonsense . . .

And yet it had. Vanished completely. But she was not just some pretty girl. There was something unusual in the way she looked at him, as though she already knew him. It was altogether devastating.

Throwing caution out like that stale old hay, Micah lifted her hand to his lips. She brushed her fingers over his chin, his cheek, his eyes, until she was standing very close. Without thinking, Micah bent his head and kissed her, finding her lips cool and sweet and welcoming in return. On instinct, his arms moved to encompass her, drawing her close. Already he could feel his body respond to her touch, her scent. She was wholly intoxicating and he was giddy with it.

As she moved to hold him closer, he kissed her again – then drew back, murmuring, 'No. This isn't right.'

Her gaze was hesitant, a little fearful almost. 'Why not?'

'I . . . hardly know you,' he replied lamely.

'Do you need to? Or are you of that honourable kind who will not touch a maiden until they are married?' Again, her eyes were full of serious depths, a look he wanted to comprehend. It was as though – despite her openness – she was hiding something. He could almost see it, in the back of his mind. Almost touch it.

'Yes, that's it exactly,' he replied, half regretting the words even as he spoke them.

Sairead pulled in her bottom lip, her gaze dropping to his throat. 'But you feel what I feel, don't you? When I first saw you, I thought . . . but then I could see it in your eyes. I hoped it wasn't my imagination. I don't see why that's wrong.'

194

Micah groaned, pulled her close and brushed his lips over her forehead. Of course he felt it! What a damn stupid question! 'But I don't know anything about you – and I want to. How old are you?'

'Twenty-two. And you?'

'Twenty-eight.'

'There,' she smiled up at him, 'now we know something. We're not strangers any more.'

Micah had to laugh. This was all too much. Too strange, too unbelievable. 'And what happens when you leave here? When you go home? I won't ever see you again, will I?'

'But I can come back. Or you could come and visit me.'

'And what would your father say to that? To find a man who works in an inn is courting his daughter?'

Now it was Sairead's turn to laugh. 'I think he'd say you were an improvement on some I could choose.'

As her laughter subsided, Micah sighed and kissed her again, drowning in that cool softness until his mind was emptied of all thought, all objections. Yes, he could fall in love with this girl. Very quickly and very easily. It was a pity he couldn't see what she was hiding because there was something about it that felt important. It was as though . . .

By the gods!

He stiffened – then instantly forced his body to relax. He didn't let her go immediately, even though every muscle in his body screamed warning and danger.

Such an idiot not to have noticed before now! Serin's blood, if she knew he'd guessed, she'd kill him – regardless of how she felt.

But her? This glorious creature? *Why?*

Gently he let her go. 'I'm sorry, Sairead, really I am. I think you'd better go before I forget why it is wrong.'

She shook her head slowly, leaving him with a soft smile to remember. Then he turned and saddled her horse and led it into the yard. She followed him out, but before she mounted up, she kissed him once more, briefly, as though to remind him of what he'd refused – as if he needed such a reminder!

'I'll come back, Micah, and perhaps next time you'll change your mind.' With that, she swung up into the saddle and turned her horse through the gate. He stood and waited until the clatter of hooves was swallowed up in the ordinary noises of the town. Only then did he let out a long-held breath.

Yes, he could fall in love with her as easily as blinking – but even if he'd been free to do so, free to live a normal life, to marry and have a family, he could never marry Sairead. Not next week, next year – not ever.

Because Sairead was Malachi.

13

The wind, harsh and abrasive, came from the west, whipping up sea spray into white peaks. Between the gusts, another, lighter breeze blew from the north, warmer. Amidst the sounds of oak creaking beneath her feet, Jenn stood on deck and gazed back the way they had come.

Nothing of Flan'har could be seen now. The ship had moved so slowly away from the dock she'd been afraid they would never leave. Then the wind had caught the sail and suddenly, like a child running uncontrollably down a hill, the ship had rolled before it.

Again Jenn lifted her face to the sky, into the icy wind. Again she breathed deeply of the air, salty and sticky. And it smelled of other things, too, things she couldn't name. Tart and sweet, spicy sometimes. A banquet on the breeze.

She allowed the scent to fill her lungs, seep into her flesh and bones, let it settle there, sharp and burning. It was so big, this ocean. So enormous, wide and vast. And the ship so small on it. With its mast rising high into the air, the heavy sail full of wind, the ship creaked and groaned ceaselessly, sometimes shuddering, at others, almost gliding. It rolled and dipped against the waves and Jenn swayed with it. The motion was not unlike riding a horse, but more as if the whole world were riding. Ropes and cords, wooden pulleys and iron rings sung and clattered. Sailors called out to each other: orders, questions, jokes and laughter. The passengers were more solemn, but still laughed with the seamen. All of them had come on deck, a few at a time, but all of them had gone below while Jenn stayed above, revelling in the incredible experience.

Andrew would have loved this.

Under any other circumstances, so would she. So much of her life had changed since she'd encountered Robert in that forest so long ago, and there was still a small part of her which longed for the freedom to roam she once so enjoyed. This kind of freedom, to wander and experience, to live from day to day without consequences and reasons and mistakes dogging her path. But this, this was nice, just as it was.

'You should be getting below, lassie,' the captain called to her. 'It'll be getting cold soon. The sun is about to go down and the air will be wetter than rain.'

Jenn flashed a smile at him. 'I'm fine, really. I want to watch the sunset.'

He gave her a toothless grin and returned to his watch, standing behind the wheelman.

She turned back to the sea – and then there were hands on her shoulders, a cloak being placed there.

'If you're going to stay out here,' Robert murmured, 'you'll freeze.'

Jenn didn't look at him, but she did pull the cloak further around her shoulders. The truth was, she was already cold; most of her face had lost feeling – but she just couldn't go. Not yet.

Robert didn't leave. Instead, he stood beside her, leaning his elbows on the railing as he gazed northwards, just as she had done. She tried to ignore him, to pretend he wasn't there. She'd not seen him all day, since the ship had left harbour. Deliberately, she faced the west where the sky was already turning gold. Gradually other colours appeared, as though the gods had dropped an almighty paint-pot to splash pink, orange and purple across the heavens. Never before had she seen a sunset so big, nor one so exquisite.

And then the last of the sun died, leaving only the shadow of brilliance in the sky.

'Come, lassie,' the captain called again. 'Let your husband take you below to warm up.'

'My husb—'

Immediately Robert took her elbow and steered her away from

the railing. 'I'm sorry. I had no choice. It was the only way I could get a cabin for you. I thought you might prefer to be alone rather than share a room with the other passengers. It can get quite crowded on these ships and a three-day voyage can seem like a month. I'll sleep with the crew.'

As soon as they got down the steps to the mid-deck, Jenn twisted out of his grasp. 'Why didn't you say anything before?'

'Because I didn't want another argument. Come on, I've made some food. We have to eat before it burns.' Without looking at her, he led her through a tiny doorway and down another flight of stairs. Beneath decks, this ship seemed too small for a man like Robert. He was too tall, his shoulders knocking against walls – but he moved about as though he'd been born on board.

A sharp turn to the left took them down another narrow passage and he pushed open the door at the end. He stood aside to let her through first, then closed the door behind him.

'This is a cabin? For a whole person?' she murmured. The side of the ship took up one wall, curving in towards the low ceiling. Along it was a bed barely wide enough for an adult, which doubled as a seat at the narrow table in the centre. On the other wall was a cupboard and bench on which stood a tiny brazier with a pot bubbling on top. The end wall had another cupboard from floor to ceiling – and that was it. If she'd taken two big steps, she would have hit her nose against the opposite wall.

'Actually,' Robert replied, giving the pot a quick stir, 'you'd normally have four people sleeping in here. The table folds down and that tall cupboard opens up. There're also hooks to string up a hammock.'

'What's a hammock?'

'A kind of hanging bed. Great as long as you don't have to sail through a storm – or get seasick. Sit down.'

Jenn squeezed between the table and bed and sat. Robert put plates on the table and spooned large quantities of stew onto both of them. He put the pot back on the brazier and dumped a loaf of bread on the table between them. Then he pulled out a stool from under the table and sat. Without another word, he commenced eating.

After the scent of the sea, the stew smelled wonderful, but for a moment, she didn't move. 'Why do you keep looking after me?'

Robert didn't look at her. 'Good question. You'd better eat up. This is the last fresh food you'll get until we dock the day after tomorrow.'

'Why?'

'Because it won't keep.'

'No, why do you keep looking after me?'

Robert chewed, swallowed and lifted his spoon again. 'You know why.'

'Because,' she paused, frowning slightly, 'you swore an oath to protect me?'

After a moment, Robert nodded, still keeping his attention on his plate. 'Yes, that's right.'

'But you swore an oath of allegiance to Selar – and now you're going to war against him because he was fool enough to release you from your vow.'

'Yes.' For the first time, he looked up, his expression hooded. 'Why, do you think you'll do the same?'

After the briefest moment, his gaze dropped again to his plate, almost empty now. 'If you do, I'd suggest you wait until we get back to Flan'har. Budlandi isn't exactly the safest place in the world.'

He finished his meal in silence, then got up from the table. He put his plate on the bench and collected his cloak. 'Get that food into you and get some rest. Goodnight.'

With that, he was out the door, shutting it firmly behind him before she could say a word.

It was cold on deck, but Robert didn't mind. So much better than the stifling atmosphere of that cabin. Much of the wind had dropped, leaving the sail flapping now and then. He swung his cloak over his shoulders and went aft, where he found a comfortable bulwark and sat, leaning back.

'Aye, it's a good moon to be sailing in,' the captain grunted, taking a seat beside the wheel.

'It is,' Robert agreed. The sky was perfectly clear now and the moon hung above like a transparent paper cut-out, blue and enormous.

'I've heard you're sleeping in with the crew,' the captain continued amiably. 'Trouble at home, eh?'

Robert had to chuckle in answer.

'Well, never mind. Perhaps a wee trip to Budlandi'll bring about a miracle. On the other hand, a spot of rum might do the same, eh?' With that, he held out a small flask.

'No, thank you.' Robert smiled.

The captain shrugged and took a mouthful himself, then settled back. 'You're from Flan'har?'

'Yes.'

'Do you go into Lusara much?'

'I've been once or twice.'

'I was born there.'

'Really?' Robert glanced at the captain. 'Where?'

'In the west, near the border. You wouldn't know the place. It doesn't exist now. That bastard Selar wiped it out as he was passing through, twenty years ago. I haven't been back since.'

'Why not?'

The captain took one more swallow of rum before putting the flask away. 'Why have rolling green hills when you can have rolling green seas?'

'You've got a point.'

'I try to stay away from Lusara now and only put into port when I have to. Don't like the merchants there. A greedy lot, from Mayenne. Won't pay a proper price for cartage and certainly not for shipping. Most skippers won't go near'm nowadays. Tell me, does your Duke ever get worried?'

'About what?'

The captain shrugged. 'Selar's greedy, just like his countrymen. Maybe one day he'll look at your nice little country and decide to put it in his pocket. Flan'har is too small to put up much of a fight. Look how quickly and easily Lusara fell. I tell you something,' the captain leaned forward and dropped his voice, 'I think that's why there's so many folk going on pilgrimages these days. I take hundreds every year to Alusia. I'm making a fortune out of Lusara's ills.'

'Are there more pilgrims now?'

'It's been steadily growing for a long time. Ever since they had that trouble a few years ago.'

'What trouble?'

The captain laughed and settled back again, 'You know – with that sorcerer fellow. I tell you, no other country has a problem like that. I think all the sorcerers in the world must live in Lusara. I wouldn't go back now if you paid me.'

Robert turned his gaze out at the ocean and folded his arms to keep warm. 'You must hear a lot of stories, travelling as you do.'

'Lately, all I ever hear is Lusarans telling me what they'll pray for when they get to the shrine of the goddess.'

'I suppose they're all afraid of sorcery.'

'Yep,' the captain said. 'Isn't everyone? You know they're all worried that one day this fellow, this . . . what's his name . . . Douglas, yes that's him. They're all afraid he'll use his evil powers to take the throne.'

'I should think if he wanted the crown, he would have taken it by now.'

'A good point, my friend. All the same, I have to wonder though.'

'What?' Robert murmured.

'Is there a difference? Between the evils of Selar and the evils of sorcery? I mean, if you had to choose? If you were Lusaran, and had to pick between them – what would you choose?'

Robert glanced away but couldn't help smiling. 'I think,' he said softly, 'I'd choose neither.'

The ship bucked and rolled again, just as it had done all day, and Jenn groaned. She twisted over on her side and held her stomach tightly, but nothing helped. The bed beneath her rose with the ship as it climbed another almighty wave – then crashed down to the bottom. Even from here she could hear the wind moaning in the sail, screaming past the mast and ropes. How could this little vessel keep going on such an enormous sea – and how could she have ever thought travel on a ship could be so wonderful? Surely they were doomed to sink.

The cabin door opened, but she didn't dare open her eyes. She could hear Robert come and sit on the side of the bed, his calm voice serving only to highlight the turbulence around her – and inside her.

'Here, drink this. It might help.'

'I can't. It won't stay down. Just go away and let me die.' The ship crashed down again, making her stomach lurch a step behind. This was torture! How could he stand this?

'Come on,' he said gently, 'just try it. A mouthful. It's an old seaman's recipe the captain gave me.'

'You told him I was sick?' Jenn moaned, holding her stomach against the next roll. Of course Robert was fine, wasn't he? He would never get sick like this. It would be beneath him. No, instead, he could be perfectly well and still be able to look after her, protect her, just as he'd promised – *because* he'd promised.

'You haven't been on deck all day, Jenn. He noticed all on his own. Now come on, sit up and try to take a drink. You'll find if you get outside, you won't feel so bad.' His gentle insistence was too much. 'Just leave me alone!' She swung out her hand and knocked the cup across the table, sent its contents flying.

Abruptly Robert stood up. 'Fine. Go ahead and suffer.'

He turned and left the cabin, banging the door behind him.

By the gods, why had she done that? Why couldn't she keep rein on her anger any more? She would just have to try much harder. He was only trying to help her, only—

The door suddenly crashed back against the wall and he stood in the frame. He took one step inside and shut the door again. 'I know you don't want me protecting you. I'm sorry, but that's the way I am. Would you rather I enjoyed people suffering – like your friend Nash?'

Her face abruptly flushing – she hoped with anger – Jenn sat up and pushed herself against the wall.

'Yes,' Robert continued, his low voice and menacing, 'your friend. The man who would gladly, even joyfully, kill me to get what he wants. The man you sacrificed your son to get away from!'

Jenn opened her mouth, but nothing came out. But Robert hadn't finished. He took a step closer. 'If you don't want me protecting you, then you should start by learning to look after yourself. And while we're at it, you can learn to be civil when other people are around. This whole ship is talking about the fact that I sleep with the crew and we're never seen talking. You and I may know the truth, and being within the safety of the ship is one thing, but tomorrow we dock and we'll be in a foreign country, with strange customs. A country you've hardly asked me about.'

He paused, reaching back for the door handle. 'I don't give a damn whether you hate me or not. My only concern is that we get through Budlandi and find some answers. You should try doing the same.'

With that, he turned and left, slamming the door with a force that rattled the walls.

Damned infuriating, insufferable, stubborn woman! How could he have been such an idiot, such a fool, to fall in love with her? That's right, it was just the Bonding. The Bonding and not real love. He had more sense than that. If only he'd had enough sense to avoid the Bonding, too.

Robert stormed onto the deck and strode the full length of the ship before he realised people were watching him. Passengers and their children, sailors at their work. They couldn't have heard him, could they?

He paused by the railing and looked out to sea for a moment, taking deep breaths to calm himself. The demon rumbled inside him, aching for release, but as usual he contained it, forcing it into silence. Another minor battle, another minor victory. Another mark against the prophecy. If he could just manage to go the rest of his life like this, he could win, and defeat the prophecy completely.

A movement to his left, a presence more than a touch. Jenn reached the railing and held on, keeping her face straight ahead. 'Are we going to sink?'

'That depends,' Robert replied, turning to look at her, 'on whether you mean the ship or our purpose here.'

Her head dropped a moment, then she looked up again. 'Why didn't you tell me about Nash earlier? Why did I have to hear it by default?'

'You wouldn't have believed me.' Robert laced his fingers together. 'Let's face it, you hardly do now.'

'I suppose . . . I wasn't sure you were right about him. Not until I saw those Malachi at Clonnet, and then—' She paused, dropping her head again. 'Why did you follow me back home?'

'And why do you only ever ask questions you already know the answer to?' Robert's voice was hard, but he couldn't help it. From the corner of his eye he could see people glancing in their direction, paying too much attention. There was nothing for it. 'Give me your hand.'

'What?'

'Just give me your hand and try to look like we've had a fight but we're making up now. Try not to do it as though my touch makes your skin crawl – even if it does.'

She put out her hand, but said nothing. He wrapped both hands around it, absently trying to warm her fingers. Then, just to make sure, he put an arm around her waist, pulling her a little closer, until they were almost touching. Nobody would see the way she tensed.

The wind tossed clouds together haphazardly, blown like boulders across a sun desperate to peek through. With a sigh Robert glanced at Jenn. Her expression was wary, her face pale. Strands of hair were caught by the wind, framing her face, but even so, there was nothing soft about her. The emptiness of lost years opened up before him then. 'It's been too long, hasn't it? Too many years. We've forgotten how to talk to each other.'

'Did we ever know?' she whispered.

'I thought we did. Once. Before . . . ' But he couldn't finish, didn't dare go down that path. Memory, like a pervading evil, doggedly followed him despite his will. The only thing that had made the last five years bearable was the belief that she had loved him in return. But she had suffered from her choice to stay, imprisoned while he had been free, when the sin had been his, not hers. And despite everything that had happened since, she had not once reproached him for it.

Perhaps it would have been easier if she had.

He looked away again. Now, at last, they were no longer the focus of attention on deck. 'Is there any chance that Nash somehow influenced Eachern to beat you?'

'I . . . don't know. Is there a way to do that?'

'Yes. A single thought, a purpose, can be placed in a person's mind. You've done something similar yourself, though by accident. I'm sure Nash is equally capable.'

'But why would he?'

Carefully, Robert met her gaze, containing everything dangerous behind a blank expression. 'You tell me.'

Jenn blinked at that, but quickly looked away.

'And you put up with it for Andrew's sake?'

Her voice, cold and tight, was almost hidden in the blustering wind. 'What else could I do?'

'You could have asked for help.'

'And endangered others? Father John? Patric?'

'Andrew will only ever have one mother.' Robert stopped. No, he should never have left her, never have allowed her to suffer like that, not when he had sworn to protect her. How could she trust him again after what he'd done?

And yet, she did.

Suddenly overwhelmed, Robert worked to contain the horror, the regret. There was no way he could give her back the last few years, but surely there was something he could say to let her know that . . . that he understood what he'd done. That at least, he was prepared to acknowledge it. 'I'm sorry. I . . . '

She gazed up at him, her blue eyes deep and grey with the sky.

'You didn't deserve . . . any of that. I'm sorry.'

'I know, Robert,' she whispered, her gaze softening a little. 'So am I.' She flicked a glance to the folk wandering the deck. 'I suppose we must keep up the façade. If you give me an hour, I'll see if I can't make something edible out of the rest of that salt beef – but don't get your hopes up. In the meantime, you might want to collect your blankets from the crew deck. I found what looks like might be a hammock in the cabin cupboard. If you really want to prove to me how brave you are, you can always try sleeping in it tonight in this awful sea.'

'Awful?' Robert forced a smile, 'but this is just a wee swell.'

She shrugged, her expression lightening a little. 'Then it won't bother you, will it?' She turned to go, but paused. In a gesture of artful complicity, she rose on her toes and kissed his cheek. He was left to watch her cross the deck and head back to the cabin.

Damned infuriating, insufferable, stubborn woman. How indeed could he have been such a fool to fall in love with her?

The port of Noru Imbel on the north coast of Budlandi seethed with activity and noise: what seemed like a thousand people all arguing at the same time, pushing and squeezing past one another, hauling

205

carts, carrying luggage, unloading freight. Seagulls swarmed all over the ships, squawking above the noise, while snapping dogs chased after them.

Jenn hurried after Robert, desperate not to lose him in the crowd. He strode ahead purposefully, his cloak flowing along behind him like a huge black wave, their bags over his shoulder. He had about him an unusual air, almost of arrogance.

'Remember what I told you,' he spoke over his shoulder without stopping. 'Don't look any man in the eye and only speak when you're asked a direct question. Keep your hands clasped in front of you and don't talk to another woman if I'm with you. Above all, don't touch me to get my attention.'

A cart pushed between them and Jenn stopped. Pulled by a white donkey, the cart was loaded with three boys dressed in bright colours, flashing in the sunlight. Each was juggling something high in the air, keeping balance as the cart bumped along the quay.

'And don't stare,' Robert came back with a smile. 'You'll have plenty of time to look around once we're settled. Come on.'

The press of people fell off a little once they left the quay. The streets beyond were wide and spacious, with a myriad tiny lanes spinning off in every direction. Some of the buildings were broad and squat, with windows curved to a point at the top. Others were made of stone and had no windows at all. Every structure as far as the eye could see, was daubed with white and glared in the midday sun.

Jenn began to get hot as she followed Robert, but he had warned her against removing her cloak in public. He strode along, seeming to choose streets at random, and now the feigned arrogance was explained. All the men in this strange city walked the same. More than one challenged Robert with a look or a word. At times she could feel their eyes upon her, but Robert never gave way. He would speak briefly, using words in a language she didn't understand, and the challenge would die away, leaving them to continue on.

How had she thought she would be able to do this alone? Mineah's teeth, Robert must have thought she was the greatest idiot alive!

'It's funny, you know,' Robert said, leading her down another, less crowded street. 'Micah never could quite get the hang of this place. He tried so hard, but I've never seen a man get into more fights than he did while we were here. It became almost a daily chore, getting him out of some scrape.'

Jenn would have smiled, but she couldn't remember if it was permitted or not. Better not to take the risk.

The street ended and they came to a stop. An enormous square spread out before them, lined with tall leafy trees and bedded with an ochre gravel. In the centre of the square was a knot of people, all dressed in blue. Every one held a flower of some colour. Unthinking, Jenn moved closer, and Robert didn't stop her.

These – indeed, all the people she'd seen here – had the same look about them: all dark hair and dark eyes, skin tanned in a relentless sun. The women were beautiful – the men, not so tall – but all walked with the same arrogance Robert copied.

In the middle of the group was a ring of people sitting on a blue mat. On one side were women and the other, men. One woman had a circlet of flowers on her head but none in her hands. The women seated beside her held large bunches of the same blooms.

'It's a wedding ceremony,' Robert murmured in her ear. 'The woman in the middle is choosing a husband from the collection in front of her.'

'Women *choose* their husbands here?'

'Yes.' There was laughter in his voice. 'Not before the age of twenty. She'll sit there until she's made a decision. It's been known to take hours, occasionally, even days. At one time, of course, this was the first she saw of her suitors, but these days, a wealthy woman will receive all kinds of attention before her wedding day.'

'But how does she choose?'

'I suppose wealth and position play a part – but a man chosen for those virtues alone wouldn't live long. She must look for other things. A strong man, but not necessarily a fighter. One who will protect her in the street without a daily bloodbath. One who has a sound mind and can advise her well. A man to whom family is important and who will give her many children.' Robert laughed a little before adding, 'Quite simple, really.'

'And she can tell all that by just sitting there looking at them? But who chooses them to sit in the first place?'

'Any man interested in marrying her may take a seat. You'll see a dozen of these ceremonies in this square every day. If you watch long enough, you'll see the same few men appear every time without luck.'

As they watched, the woman came to her feet and took the first bunch of flowers to a man seated opposite. He took them and dropped his head. She then collected another bunch and handed it to another man. One by one until all the flowers were gone and only one man remained empty-handed. He then stood, bowed to her and the crowd cheered.

Jenn began to smile. 'Everyone seems happy.'

'She must have chosen well. It is said the wisdom of the Goddess will guide her hand. His test is to be the one picked; hers to pick the right one. It is her test of character to know, understand and appreciate the qualities in her future husband. It's an important thing here. Women never remarry. Come on, we have things to do.'

Another maze of streets and alleys brought them to a market devoted to cloth. The brilliance of colour made Jenn gasp and she found it impossible not to finger the soft materials as she moved by. Again there was this strange line drawn between men and women. On one side of the market, the sellers were all male, on the other, female. Robert paused in the path between the two.

'I have to leave you here to do this alone. You need a dress in the local style. If you go right down to the end, you'll find stalls with gowns and everything else you need. Get something you can travel in, but lightweight. It'll get pretty hot as we go east. Whatever you do, don't be tempted to bargain. Women don't bargain. They'll give you a fair price, even though they know you're a foreigner. Unfortunately, the same can't be said for the men. Be as quick as you can. I'll meet you back here.'

'But,' Jenn almost reached out to catch his arm, but stopped herself in time, 'I don't know what to do . . . '

Robert smiled. 'Of course you do. As far as I can tell, a woman buying clothes does so the same way no matter where you are. Don't worry. I won't be far away. Mindspeak me if you get worried. Now, go on. Enjoy yourself.'

He waited for her to turn away, and she immediately sensed him disappear into the other side of the market. Clasping her hands together tightly, she proceeded down to the end of the square and wandered along the lane. It was impossible to take it all in. The colours, the sounds and smells. She was hungry and something delicious wasn't far away, but these dresses held her attention: they were exquisite. The style wasn't too different to what she was wearing, but the cloth was filmy and the hues much brighter than anything she'd dared wear before. There were scarfs too; most of the women were wearing one.

Robert was right, there was no real difference, in this respect at least. She paused before one stall to touch a gown of sunshine yellow – and a dozen women descended on her, urging her to buy from their stalls. Their noise and delight was infectious and she couldn't help laughing, though barely understanding a word they said. In the end, the most difficult thing was making a choice; she settled on a sky-blue gown over a deeper blue skirt. A simple plain white scarf completed her purchase and she went back to join Robert, oddly at ease for the first time in this strange land.

He waited for her with a bundle tucked under his arm. 'Well? How did you go? Start any fights?'

Jenn lifted her chin, hiding a smile. 'If it weren't culturally taboo, Robert, I would hit you for that. Now, what else do we need, because I'm hungry.'

Robert leaned back in his chair, ignored the creaking beneath him and swung his feet onto the low stool. He took another long mouthful of the delicious lemon juice and gazed in satisfaction at the courtyard in front of their room. Closely resembling a monastery cloister, the compact square let in breeze and shade and kept out the worst of the heat. Three rooms opened out onto each side, all with a view of the scrawny trees in the centre, desperately clinging to life.

He glanced at Jenn as she sat at the small table beside him. She was leaning over the platter in the centre, peering at the collection of raw greens and other vegetables arranged there, crisp and refreshing. 'What do you think?'

She took another leaf, crunched into it and said, 'Strange but nice.'

'Those little round things aren't meat, but some kind of grain. That flat bread is the best they can do here. You might like it, but to me, it tastes like baked sand.'

She sat back and gazed at the trees. As soon as they'd got here, she'd washed and put on her new gown, though now the scarf was pulled back from her head. The colour was perfect for her, complimenting her eyes. Was it the dress or the light in this place that brought out her beauty so much? She appeared quite content for the moment, but she was still too pale, too quiet at times. For hours on end she would not say a word, and often he caught her gaze going inward.

He could guess what was wrong. He could even try to get her to talk about it, but from his own experience, he knew there was no point. She was not ready and until she was, nothing he said would make a difference.

'You remember that wedding we saw?' she mused, staring at the courtyard, a leaf held to her lips almost in a caress. 'Did anything strike you as odd?'

'In what way?' he replied, entranced, unable to look away from her.

'The woman gave flowers to all the men she rejected, leaving the man she wanted with nothing.'

'He got her.'

'Yes, but . . . I couldn't help thinking how similar it was to the way the Key chooses a new Jaibir. At first it lights everyone Standing the Circle, then, one by one, the lights go out, leaving only the chosen lit. Whoever is left unrejected becomes the Jaibir. It's interesting, don't you think?'

'Very,' he murmured absently, utterly distracted.

She turned and caught him watching her, so he quickly busied himself pouring more lemon into his cup.

This had to stop! He couldn't risk her seeing the truth, couldn't have her knowing how he felt. The last thing she needed was to discover his unwanted attentions. They'd built a bridge so they could work together again – that was enough, and better than he'd hoped for. Anything else was sheer foolishness and could quite possibly get them both into a lot of trouble.

No. Enough was enough. What he felt didn't matter. It never had. Besides, they had work to do. He dropped his feet to the floor and got up. He went into the room, collected his bundle and put it on the table. 'I got something for you.'

With a frown Jenn unwrapped a pair of boy's trousers and a shirt. 'I suppose it would have looked odd if I'd tried to buy them myself.'

'They would only have thought you were a foreign harlot and no man would have spoken to you unless to . . . engage a transaction. I wouldn't have bothered, except there are parts of this country not wise for women to travel even when *not* alone.'

Jenn put the clothes down and sat back. 'So where do we go from here?'

'South for a while, and then east. It will take a little longer, perhaps three days, but it's the safest route to the Palace of Bu.'

'But how important is safety when we have so little time? Are you sure that's the best way?'

Robert glanced sideways at her. 'Tell me, what do you think I did in those three years after I exiled myself from my beloved country? Just lay about here in the sun, keeping Micah out of mischief?'

'Well,' Jenn mused idly, 'you were tanned when I first met you – and Micah did have something of a sheepish look to him.'

Robert laughed. 'Micah always looks sheepish. I've never quite been able to work out why.'

Jenn reached out for another crisp vegetable. 'You know, I really miss Micah. I'm sorry he's not with us now.'

'Yes,' Robert replied, drawing the word out. 'I hope he's all right in Dromna.'

'Are you worried?' Jenn faced him.

'Not really – at least, not about that.'

'Then what?'

'I know he's not the same bright-eyed lad who came to work at Dunlorn. He's grown up, matured, just as he should. But sometimes I can't help thinking his father was right. Micah was too young back then to really understand what he was getting into with me. When he gave me his loyalty, I thought I was right to take it.'

'And now?' Jenn asked softly.

'He deserves better. More.'

Jenn sighed and laced her fingers together. 'Robert, Micah is your friend – for all that he worked for you – you know it was friendship that kept him there. Not only that, but it is friendship that makes you wonder now. Don't question, just accept the gift as freely as it has been given. Is there anything you would not do for him?'

'Nothing.'

'Well then.' Jenn stood and stretched. 'I like this place – especially now the worst of the heat has gone.'

'It'll get hotter tomorrow in the desert. There's a saying about this place: when Broleoch plans his evil schemes, he goes to Sahobe for inspiration.'

Jenn's jaw dropped, then abruptly her face creased up in a smile, the first real one he'd seen so far. 'Oh, that's just perfect! Now you tell me!'

'Well, you never asked.' Robert sat back and sipped some more lemon juice. Yes, it was a lovely fine evening, of the kind only found in this part of the world. It was good to be back. 'We'll leave before dawn.'

14

Within hours of leaving the coast, it seemed all of Budlandi was covered in dusty, lumpy hills of hard stone and sand. On top, the sun beat down mercilessly, but in the narrow valleys it was worse, like riding inside a furnace. Small settlements would crop up now and then, stone shacks huddled around a vital well and a few scraggly trees. Jenn and Robert were ignored by the people living in these places and only the goats seemed even remotely interested in the travellers.

By the end of the first day, Jenn was very grateful she'd thought to buy the scarf. For most of the time she rode with it wrapped around her face, leaving only a slit to see through. It helped keep the dust out of her nose and mouth. Nevertheless, she remained constantly thirsty, even though Robert made her drink every hour.

And she missed Andrew, couldn't stop herself thinking about him, knowing that he woke in the morning without seeing her, that he slept each night without her kiss on his forehead.

Of course, Robert didn't let her alone long enough to worry. He talked, easily and comfortably: he told her stories of this country and others he'd visited with Micah, years before he met her. She knew he was trying to keep her thoughts away from other, less pleasant things, but she found it impossible not to laugh at some of the trouble both he and Micah had got themselves into from time to time.

And at no point whatsoever did Robert talk about a single thing close to them. Nothing about prophecy, sorcery, Nash, Selar – nor even the war he was about to fight. Especially not that. It was as though he wanted to forget – if only for a few days – why any of it was so important.

But as much as he kept apart from the troubles they'd left behind, in the quieter moments, when she looked at him, his conversation couldn't blind her to the presence of the demon still living and breathing inside him. He made no reference to it, acted as though it didn't exist. She had been, after all, the only person who had ever been able to see it – an added blessing to her Healer's Sight. But what kind of blessing was it? It seemed five years had done nothing to erase the demon's existence – in fact, there was a sharper edge to it now, as though it were looking out through Robert's eyes.

In many ways, she welcomed the relative peace of the journey, of the conversation on such safe topics – but there was a part of her which longed for him to talk to her as he'd once done, where there had been no barriers between them, when she'd felt she alone had deserved his trust, was worthy of hearing the thoughts which filled his quiet hours. This was the Robert she'd missed most, in the years he'd been gone; the man who'd anchored his soul to hers.

She missed him – and she missed the self he loved, the woman who had sent him on his way that morning, five and more years ago. She had held onto her anchor, the promise of his love, but his return had taken it away, leaving her lost.

Now, she was nothing more to him than an inconvenience, a bird trapped in the net of prophecy, somebody he had to watch out for, to protect, distracting him when his purpose lay elsewhere.

She wanted to help him, wanted to play her own part in freeing their country, but in the end, what possible use could she be? In trying to find her own path, would she obscure his?

Surely *that* was not to be her destiny.

Towards the end of the day, as they left the desert, green began to appear on the distant hills: not the bright, fresh green of Lusara, but a depressed green, littered with centuries of dust. These patches of colour became trees as they approached and, for the first time, she could smell water.

Robert led her down into a steep valley where first bushes then a spiky grass appeared on the ground. Finally, as the sun left them, he stopped before a tiny stream, almost clogged with trees desperate for drink. They made camp and settled down beside the fire as the meal cooked.

Robert lay back on the ground and laced his fingers across his stomach, completely at ease. He had always seemed more at home with himself when away from castles and soldiers, all the demands on his time. If he'd ever had the choice, would he have preferred to live the life of a wanderer?

It was not exactly the kind of question she could ask. It felt too personal a subject for them these days when they had to choose their words so carefully. Instead, she sat opposite, her knees up and her arms wrapped around them. The night was growing cold and soon she'd have to pull a blanket around her to avoid freezing.

'Can I ask you a question?' Jenn said after a while.

'Of course.'

'You really don't trust the Key at all, do you? And it's not just because it banished you from the Enclave six years ago.'

'No,' Robert replied, keeping his gaze on the stars. 'To be honest, I've never been able to understand why anyone would trust it – but then, I admit my perspective is a little different to everyone else's.'

Testing the ground, Jenn added, 'Because of the prophecy?'

In response, Robert chuckled a little. 'You must think my life is driven by the prophecy.'

'Are you telling me it isn't?'

He glanced once at her, then returned his attention skywards. 'You have the gift of objective analysis – you tell me. The Key was created by a dozen powerful sorcerers who objected to the war with the Empire. Together they formed it, giving it power and, I suspect, some degree of life. Then they gathered their friends and family, left Bu and headed north to escape the coming carnage. Somewhere amongst them was the man who created the Word of Destruction – and he gave that to the Key. Whether it was deliberate or accidental doesn't really matter. But think about what kind of mind forms a weapon of that magnitude. What was it designed to do – and for what reason? To simply protect?'

'That's what you did at Elita.'

'No, I wasn't protecting anything. Don't ever mistake my actions as altruistic. I was driven to destroy.'

'By the demon,' Jenn whispered, a little afraid even to move, but Robert wasn't provoked. Instead, his voice was calm, almost detached.

'The Word was designed to destroy – nothing else. When the Key gave me the prophecy, it gave me the Word as well. Now, I ask you – what kind of thing gives a weapon of that power to a nine-year-old boy? A talisman with only good at its heart? And according to Finnlay, the man who created the Word was a direct ancestor of Nash's.'

'That alone doesn't prove the intent was evil.'

'No, but knowing all this, would you, in my position feel any great affection towards the Key? If I just trusted it, just went along with everything it said, then I would lose the ability to think for myself. I'd be giving up a freedom we were all born with. A freedom as dear to my soul as anything on this earth. But that's exactly what the Key demands of me. You tell me: do you really think I should trust it?'

Buying time, Jenn reached across to the bags and pulled out a blanket. For all that he had told her, there was still one glaring omission: the end of the prophecy. The one thing that affected him more than anything else. Was that why he wouldn't tell her? Because he didn't want to admit such fear?

She sat back again, drawing the blanket over her shoulders. 'You don't know any of this for sure. For all you know, the Word might have been created to destroy something like Nash.'

Robert began laughing again, but she continued regardless, 'Wouldn't that prove it was a weapon for good – and that's why the Key gave it to you?'

'If you want to believe that, please, go right ahead. You asked the question, after all.'

Yes, but had he really told her anything she needed to know?

'I know you probably don't want to hear this,' Robert said quietly into the dark, 'but I still find it hard to believe you could leave Andrew behind like that. Especially after all you put up with to keep him safe. I have to assume you feel he's in no danger from Nash.'

The abrupt change of subject – and the direction – made Jenn pause. However, she managed a quick breath and replied, 'None.'

'Then he doesn't have powers?'

'Yes . . . I mean, no. I mean—' Jenn stopped. This could be awkward.

'I'm sorry,' Robert said evenly. 'You miss him. I thought you might like to talk about him.'

Jenn glanced at him, but his gaze was still firmly fixed on the growing stars above. He couldn't know how that made it easier for her. 'I do miss him, but I know he's safe where he is. Andrew does have powers, but Nash won't ever see them. He'll never think of Andrew as a threat until . . . '

'It's too late?' Robert murmured, smiling. 'I take it you don't have too much faith in my ability to dispose of our Angel. But that's good, healthy, to look forward, to plan in the eventuality of my failure.'

Jenn stared at him, her mouth suddenly dry. Fail?

Robert – *fail?* Against Nash?

He couldn't be serious . . . and yet, he'd spoken with the same dismissive air he always used against himself, like a caustic weapon, ever present, ever vicious.

But if he believed he was going to fail, why go into the fight? What had he said – that Nash would joyfully kill him to get to the Key?

And Robert *still* refused to tell her the rest of his prophecy.

'Is there something you're not telling me? About Andrew?'

Jenn's heart stopped. When it started again, it pounded so hard she couldn't hear her own words. 'What do you mean?'

'Well, why won't Nash recognise his talents? Have you found some way to shield your son? He's too young to Seal, but I know of no other way to hide potential in a child so young.'

'He—' Jenn swallowed hard, '—he shields himself. He always has. Even Father John couldn't see anything in him. I sensed Andrew had powers before he was born, but it wasn't until I got past the shielding that I realised he'd been doing it from the beginning.'

'Well,' Robert said, relieved, 'at least he's had the good sense to inherit something of real value from his mother – and he'll be immune to the Bresail. You never had to be taught how to shield, either, if I remember. He's a bright lad, I'll give him that,' Robert added. 'We had quite a few chats on the way to Maitland. Let's just pray that with Bella's influence your son won't, by some hideous twist of fate, turn out like his cursed father.'

Like a taut string snapping, Jenn began to laugh, softly at first, then louder, making Robert sit up.

'What? Did I say something funny?'

Jenn just shook her head, sobering quickly, lest he ask more questions. 'No. I just had an amusing thought. It doesn't matter.'

He frowned for a moment, obviously confused. 'I suggest you change your clothes tomorrow and put that dress away. We'll be passing through what was once the worst bandit country in the whole southern continent.'

He reached forward and checked the pot bubbling over the fire, talking as he pulled plates from a bag, but Jenn didn't really listen.

The prophecy.

Was that why he wouldn't tell her the ending? Because he was destined to fail?

Robert didn't know Andrew was his son – but in the end, it didn't matter one bit. Failure against Nash could only mean one thing for Robert.

His death.

Robert?

Yes, I'm awake.

Can you hear it?

Yes, keep still and don't make a sound. I think there're only three of them.

They're very close. I can almost hear them breathing.

Just don't move. If anything happens, jump on your horse and follow the stream down the valley. There's a village about a league away. I'll be back in a minute.

Jenn was frozen to the spot, her blanket almost covering her face. Her eyes were open, but the night was so black she couldn't see a thing. She didn't even hear Robert move until there was a grunt to her right as something heavy fell to the ground. Then suddenly the bushes began to thrash; there was a clash of steel, another cry – and silence.

Then footsteps coming towards her.

'It's all right.'

Jenn sat bolt upright as Robert stood over her. He gave her a grim smile, then went back to his own bed, tossing his sword on the ground beside him.

'All right? How can you—'

'Go back to sleep, Jenn. It'll be sunrise soon enough and we have to get through that village.'

Sleep? After that?

Jenn loved the village. It was wonderful, like the port, only not so noisy, full of travellers carting goods, traders in jewellery and cloth from the south, rugs from the east. Very alive.

They bought food and more of the flat bread and were out of the gates before midmorning. Nobody paid her any attention, never questioned her boy's clothing or noticed her hair tucked beneath a cap. An hour on and the valley continued, the hills on either side rising sharper again, more rocky. There were more trees here, and the stream was wide though still not deep.

'Robert?'

'Yes?'

Jenn pulled her horse alongside his. 'I want to ask you something, but I don't want you to get all annoyed.'

'Very well, I'll do my best,' he replied seriously. 'What is it?'

'Would you teach me how to use a sword?'

He came to an abrupt halt and wheeled his horse to face her. 'Is this some kind of joke?'

'Now,' Jenn raised a warning finger, 'you promised you wouldn't get annoyed.'

'No, I promised I would try. *Not* the same thing at all.'

'Well, I mean it. I want to know.' When he didn't say anything she added, 'I was thinking about those men last night. What if something happened to you? You said I should learn to look after myself.'

He swung his leg over the back of his horse. With a thud he

218

jumped to the ground. 'Damned women,' he muttered to himself, detaching his scabbard from the saddle. 'Impatient, unreasonable and inescapable . . . my life's littered with them . . . what did I ever do—'

'Oh stop whining, Robert.' Jenn smiled as she dismounted.

'Well, don't just stand there. If you want to learn how to use this, you'll have to get a little closer than that. Here, can you even lift it?'

Without warning, he tossed the scabbarded sword towards her. She tried to catch it, but the weight was too much at such an angle. It fell to the ground with an ominous thud. She looked at Robert, whose eyes rolled heavenwards.

'Well, pick it up. We'll go over there, on that sandy bank by the water. That way, when you cut me to pieces, it'll be easy for you to wash my wounds.'

He turned and strode off, leaving Jenn to pick the sword up and scurry after him.

The sand was firm and flat, jutting out into a bend of the stream. Robert stood at the water's end and faced her squarely. 'Take the sword from the scabbard and hold it with both hands. No, not like that, like this.' He wrested it from her and placed it back in her hands, positioning her fingers along the hilt. 'Now, lift the point until it's roughly level with your eyes. No! Wait until I'm out of the way! By the gods, are you trying to kill me?'

Jenn had to stifle a laugh; Robert was so gruff. She did as she was told, standing with her feet apart, the sword before her.

'Hold it steady. Now . . . look at me, not the blade. As with most things in life, you only need two things to wield a sword. Strength and intelligence. The next few minutes will tell us whether you're missing only one or both of those ingredients.'

Jenn began to giggle, then quickly sobered at Robert's scowl.

'Think of the sword as an extension to your arms. Don't ever attempt to use a blade this size with one hand. Even if you don't drop it, you'll have no control over it. The first thing you need to learn is the most important. Defence.' With that, Robert picked up a solid stick from the stream's edge and held it before him like a sword. 'Your blade is as much a shield as a weapon. Never forget that. Now, when I swing at you, I want you to bring the sword up to block my blow.'

He lifted the stick high above his head and brought it down. Jenn swung wildly, caught the stick – and ducked as it shattered into pieces. She began to laugh, but Robert was unimpressed. 'I'm sorry, really. I couldn't help it.'

'So you think this is funny, do you? Very well.' He grabbed another stick and moved behind her, herding her into the water. 'Since you've mastered the first lesson, we'll move quickly onto the second. Balance.'

The sand quickly disappeared beneath her boots and suddenly she was slipping over boulders slimy with algae. The water came up to her knees and she stopped, wavering, with a foot each on a rock. Precarious now, she brought the sword up again until the tip was at eye level.

Robert faced her. He brought the stick up again and swung it, forcing her to defend. This time the blade snagged on the wood, banged against the water and bounced out of her hands.

'Don't drop it in the water! How is it going to fend off hoards of attackers if it's all rusty? By the gods, woman, pay attention. Pick it up. Let's start again.'

Another swing and this time she held onto the blade, but slapped the water so hard it splashed up at him, reaching his face. He froze, his gaze going down his wet clothes and . . . she couldn't help it. She bent down, stuck her hand in the water and splashed him again.

'Right! That's it!'

As he took a step towards her, she dropped the sword and, with a shriek of laughter, stumbled and splashed her way out of the stream. Robert didn't even pause to pick up the sword. She ran as fast as she could, but he was faster. Still laughing, she tried to stop him. 'I'm sorry, Robert, I couldn't help it. I promise I'll be good. Really I will.'

'Not until I teach you a lesson you won't forget,' he bellowed after her.

She ran, her laughter slowing her down. Suddenly his arms slammed into her waist and she screamed as they tumbled to the ground. Still she tried to get away, but he had her now, and rolled her over to face him, pinning her wrists down. When she turned however, there was absolutely nothing serious in his eyes.

He held her though she made no effort to escape and, for a moment, his face took on a different aspect, his eyes—

Abruptly he stopped, his grip loosened and she squirmed out from under him. Getting to her feet, she took off again, and he ran after her. She dashed around a tree – and came to a halt when she saw the four horses.

Robert stopped beside her.

Mounted above her, the four men were heavily armed and looking down at Robert with something that bordered on distaste. The first was a man of about forty, a grey beard trimming his stern expression.

'May the goddess be with you,' he said in ritual greeting.

'And Mineah's blessing with you, Sergeant,' Robert replied.

'You are not from this place? Foreigners?'

'Yes. From Flan'har.'

The man nodded sharply. 'I am the Constable of the Guard for this area. I must inform you that your behaviour is unacceptable.'

Jenn didn't dare say a word. She looked at Robert to find him frowning a little.

The constable went on, 'I don't know what you are accustomed to in your own country, sir, but we do not tolerate *that* kind of thing here.' He turned to Jenn. 'Now, boy, give me the truth. Has your master . . . misused you in any way? You may trust that any accusation you bring will be treated justly.'

Accusation? Misused?

Jenn opened her mouth to ask – and shut it again as the awful truth fell on her, like a rush of spring rain.

She looked at Robert to find his face warring with disbelief and incredulity. 'You think I was . . . '

Oh, it was hard, so hard not to laugh. Barely containing herself, she turned away. 'Thank you, Constable but I do not wish to make an accusation.'

'There's no need to protect him, boy. We saw him chase you to the ground, saw you barely escape his . . . embrace. If you are afraid, we will protect you.'

So very hard not to laugh. 'No, thank you Constable. It was not . . . as it appeared. My master was teaching me how to use a sword. Please, I am in no need of protection.'

'So you don't wish to leave him.'

'No, sir.'

221

'Very well.' The constable nodded, gave Robert another stern look, then led his men away down the valley.

Jenn waited as long as she could, but the moment she turned again and saw Robert's face, still mystified, she could hold it in no longer. With a gasp, she burst out laughing, doubling up as her knees grew weak. It didn't help that Robert was looking at her with an air of such wounded injustice. She sank to the ground holding her stomach, in real pain now, but utterly unable to stop laughing.

Oh, such sweet, delightful, unpredictable revenge.

'Well? What do you think?'

Jenn stood on the edge of the escarpment and gazed down at the wide flat plain forty feet below. The only features visible for a dozen leagues were the tiny clumps of green gorse – and the Palace of Bu. 'It's incredible!' she breathed.

It was also enormous, even from this distance. The word Palace didn't really fit, either. It was almost a village all on its own: long low buildings collected together in a kind of maze, with fine, twisting towers at every corner. The stone was of the deepest red, now glowing in the twilight. Buried somewhere in the centre of the complex stood a dome which reached above everything else, but from this distance, she could see no detail, no decoration. Sitting alone in the desert, the Palace was utterly deserted.

A shiver ran through her body. Years ago the Key had sent her a dream, telling her of its creation. This was the place where it had happened, and that domed roof, yes, that was the spot. Now she would see it with her own eyes.

And now she could hear it again, the chanting from the dream, the rumbled voices using words she didn't understand, deep and clear, soft and solid. A memory? Or—

'Jenn?' Robert's hand on her arm made her jump. 'Are you all right?'

She looked at him. In the last of the light she could make out his face quite clearly. Strong, familiar, and yet distant. His dark wavy hair sat about his shoulders like a monk's cowl, his eyes, the green she knew so well, open yet wary.

The prophecy had said he was the Enemy.

The prophecy had also said that they were Bonded.

Why?

When she spoke, her voice came out as distant as his expression. 'Robert, why won't you tell me the end of the prophecy?'

His horse danced around on the spot, abruptly agitated. When he calmed it, he met her gaze squarely. 'Why do you want to know?'

Jenn bit back the sudden flare of anger at his evasion. She took in a breath and answered, 'Because you won't tell me.'

'No,' Robert replied levelly. 'That's not why you want to know.'

For a moment, she thought he was baiting her, but then she paused, frowning, reading more from his expression than she had seconds ago. 'It . . . has something to do with me, doesn't it? And . . . it's . . . bad?'

He kept his silence, turning his head to glance up at the sky, to where the first stars were appearing in the east, then down to the Palace in the distance.

'Robert?'

'It will serve no good purpose knowing how the prophecy ends.'

'Does anybody know?'

Robert dropped his gaze to study his hands where they held the reins. 'Only Aiden, but he won't tell you.'

'No, I . . . wouldn't ask him.'

He glanced up then, something of a smile in his eyes, almost of relief.

'I just wanted to be sure you'd . . . ' she paused, not certain of what she wanted to say here or why, but she pressed on, 'that you'd shared it with somebody, that you weren't just carrying the . . . responsibility on your own.'

He stared at her a moment, tilting his head to one side. Then he drew in a deep breath, his smile real now. 'The responsibility remains mine whether I share the secret or not – but thank you anyway.'

He kicked his horse forward then, leading her down the escarpment. Feeling her own smile grow, Jenn followed.

For a long time, the only sounds she could hear were the horses moving across the desert floor. The darkness encompassed everything now. Not for the first time, she wished she had Robert's enhanced sight so she could see the Palace as it loomed closer.

And then he was coming to a halt beside her, dismounting,

reaching for her horse as she joined him on the ground. She looked up to find an enormous open gate before her, black and heavy.

'Robert?'

'What?'

'Are you sure about this place?' Jenn murmured, no longer certain she wanted to go inside, regardless of what answers they might find.

'What do you mean?'

'You're sure it's deserted?'

'Positive. I've been Seeking for the last hour. Why, are you Sensing something?'

Was she?

She frowned. 'No, not Sensing. It's just that . . . '

He reached out and placed a hand on her shoulder – and abruptly the vague feeling of disquiet she'd felt vanished into the darkness. 'Take your time.'

Jenn closed her eyes and did just that, allowing her Senses to stretch and roam, to Seek into the shadowed corners of this place, looking for whatever it was that had disturbed her. She found nothing, but her Seeking abilities had never been that strong. Even so, the disquiet didn't return, so she opened her eyes again. 'I'm just imagining things. Let's go in.'

He led her through the gate into what seemed like a courtyard of some kind. Sand scraped against hard rock beneath her feet, ancient cobbles marking their path. She desperately wanted to create some light, to illuminate the deep hollows she could see all around her, but somehow, doing such a thing felt strangely like blasphemy.

They came to a halt before a tall building which reached high enough to make a mark against the star-filled sky. Robert tied the horses up and pulled their bags down.

'Come, let's see if we can find something to make a fire. I don't know about you, but I'm hungry.'

Again she followed him, silent now, trepidation working through her bones like a cold wind. Her feet took her up steps, through a portico and then to a huge door Robert pushed open.

She could see nothing. Total blackness greeted her and she could move no further.

The Key. The prophecy. The Word of Destruction.

This was the place. She didn't need to see the domed roof above, didn't need sunlight to know the walls contained long narrow windows. This was the place, the same place where the Key had been created, the place it had shown her, the place where Robert's demon had been conceived five hundred years before his birth.

He was no longer at her side. He'd disappeared into the thick morass of darkness. She could hear him moving about, putting his load down, his feet smart and sharp on the weathered stone, his breathing almost hollow.

Something flashed before her and she blinked, her heart pounding hard. Then Robert's face appeared bathed in a golden glow emanating from his hand. He was smiling. 'Well, come in. It's still warm in here from the day. I don't think we'll need a fire after all.'

The Key. The prophecy. The Word of Destruction.

The Enemy.

Steeling herself, she took a step forward. The moment her foot landed, she heard it again: the chanting. Loudly now, as though the voices were still in this room, still singing, still creating the Key, still . . .

Too loud. Much too loud.

Jenn cried out, her hands flying to her ears, trying to shut it out. Even as she sank to her knees, she saw Robert rush towards her, but then the darkness folded in on her and the chanting took over.

15

The forest was sparse where Sairead stood waiting. A thin trickle of water splashed over a few rocks then disappeared into a green mossy bog. Her horse dipped its head to drink, taking small sips to recover after the long ride. She held the reins loosely in her hand and glanced over her shoulder once more. Uncle Gilbert and Baron DeMassey were still deep in conversation and it was all she could do to hide her impatience. She couldn't really go until they were finished. Not without them guessing why she was in such a hurry to get to Dromna.

Would *he* be there? Would he want to see her again after last time? He'd as much as said he thought her behaviour wanton and her cheeks had burned with the thought – still did now. But how could she explain to him that it wasn't wrong for those not brought up in a country like Lusara?

How green it was here, even though spring had barely taken its first faltering steps. The hills were so much softer than at home, the valleys more gentle, the people more open.

Like Micah. Open face, open eyes that seemed to look right into her soul.

A secret smile tugged her mouth and she turned away from the men so they wouldn't see it. Micah suited this land, this gentle green. He was entirely at home in it, while still retaining an air of some other place. Had he ever travelled beyond Dromna? Was his family here? Were all his hopes and dreams bound up with working in that awful tavern? By the blood, there was so much she wanted to know.

'And what do you want to do with the rest of the day?'

Sairead composed herself and turned casually. 'I thought I might see the market. I promised my mother I'd bring something back for her this time.'

Uncle Gilbert nodded and looked at DeMassey. 'My niece likes Lusara, I think. Her mother told her too many stories as a child. Half Malachi, half Lusaran. Leaves you with a foot in two worlds.'

'As long as she understands which one she belongs in,' DeMassey replied.

Gilbert laughed. 'You should remember that yourself. Good luck, Luc. If all goes well, I guess I'll see you in Karakham for the summer.'

DeMassey swung up onto his horse, waved a farewell and rode away, heading for the army in the next valley.

'What do you mean, if all goes well?' Sairead asked quietly. There was something strange about that goodbye left unsaid.

'You know exactly what we were talking about.' Gilbert smiled. He put a hand on her shoulder and kissed her forehead. 'Now you go off and do your shopping. I'll see you at the camp. Don't get too caught up either, my girl. We head back to Karakham tomorrow night and I'll be damned if I have to go out looking for you.'

Sairead nodded, but couldn't find a response. How could she possibly get caught up when the greatest likelihood was that Micah would have nothing to do with her?

Gilbert mounted his own horse and left her in the forest. Of course, she could just not go, and keep the memory of Micah in her mind, untarnished, perfect. But – what if he'd changed his mind, or better still, if she could convince him to leave this dull place and return to Karakham with her?

Her hands reached for the pommel and she swung up, kicking the horse's flanks until it moved at a brisk walk. Her stomach grew queasy as she got closer to the town, heard its noises above those of the forest, but she only slowed when she reached the market beyond the walls. Then, still mounted, Sairead wound her way through the chaos of people until she was inside the town, her heart now pounding with fear.

If he had changed his mind – would she have the courage to tell him what she was?

There was the tavern, closed this early in the morning. She rode around the corner to the gate and dismounted. With quick movements, she straightened her jacket, smoothed the hair away from her face, tried to tuck the strays into the braid coiled at the base of her neck, pinched her cheeks until there was a little colour. Only then did she lead the animal through into the yard.

It was empty. For a long minute, she stood there, suddenly unsure what to do next. She could hardly go calling his name.

But then the back door of the tavern opened up and Micah appeared, carrying mop and bucket. He didn't see her immediately, but the moment he did, his guileless face broke into an instant smile – which he tried to still almost as quickly.

Slowly he put his gear down. 'You came back.'

He didn't move. He simply stood there in the morning fresh, his curly hair touched lightly by the wind. He was so tall, his shoulders so broad, Sairead felt suddenly dwarfed. Only the light freckles across his cheeks brought any kind of softness to his strong face. His eyes watched her, as blue as she remembered, pale, like the dawn sky.

Swallowing, Sairead nodded, afraid to move forward. 'I said I would.'

He gazed steadily at her for so long she thought he might tell her to go away again. Then he glanced back at the inn and walked up to her horse. Absently he took the bridle, then looked at her again. 'Are you going somewhere?'

'No.'

'Well, if you can wait a moment, perhaps you would like to take a walk through the woods. I just have to finish up inside first.'

Sairead couldn't help it. Her smile simply took over. 'I'd love to!'

Micah deliberately headed directly away from the army, deep into the untouched layers of forest where narrow overgrown paths scurried around corners, laden with new spring flowers. Shifts of breeze blew their scent towards him; the air was moist here and alive with things he couldn't begin to see. He led Sairead on until they crested a shoulder of hill. Two more rose on either side, obscured by thick foliage. There he stopped beside a rushing stream, almost buried with new grass and bracken, baby green.

He didn't look at her. He couldn't really. He knew what would happen. His resolve would falter and he would begin to forget why he'd come out here, so far away from the town. 'Did you have a long journey?'

'Not really,' Sairead replied. She moved past him to kneel beside the water.

Now he could do it and she would never know until it was too late. Yes, he would do it now . . .

But wouldn't it be better if he first tried to find out where she'd come from? That would be a valuable jewel to take back to Robert: the location of the Malachi home.

His hand froze on his dagger as she glanced up at him with a smile. 'What's wrong?'

'Nothing.' Forcing himself to move, he chose a rock and sat on it, lacing his hands together. 'I suppose I was surprised to find you came back so soon.'

At that she blushed and glanced away. 'Micah, I know you must think I'm some sort of . . . well . . . I don't know. I'm sorry. I guess I didn't learn the same lessons as you did. Where I come from, women are allowed to choose the man they would love.'

He couldn't say anything for a moment. Then, taking a breath, he asked, 'And where do you come from?'

'A place far from here. A city perched on the edge of a plateau. Inhospitable. Blistering hot in summer, covered with snow in winter.' She smiled as she said this, her eyes reflecting the love she felt for her home. She would have met his gaze, but he looked away then.

'Does your father live there? And your mother?'

'Yes. I had a brother, two years older than me, but he died in a fight. What about you? Does your family live in Dromna?'

Micah stood abruptly and turned away, forcing air into his lungs. He couldn't do it – but he had to. She would keep coming back to see him and one day his resolve would weaken so much that he would endanger his whole mission here. If she'd not returned, it wouldn't have mattered, but that moment this morning, when he'd first seen her, he knew. Stupid, pointless, irrational feelings. Things he had no time for. He didn't know her, so how could he possibly love her? He was in Dromna for one reason alone: to watch that damned army, and to ride to Bleakstone when he knew the day of marching. Nothing else. Nothing at all!

Her hand touched his arm. 'Micah? Have I said something wrong?'

No. He had to remain firm. He had to resist.

'Micah?' Her gentle voice grazed against him, awakening all the things he'd tried the last week to be rid of. Such a fool. He should have known it wouldn't work.

'No,' he sighed, dropping his head, 'you've said nothing wrong. I'm sorry.'

Only now – now that he had lost – did he finally look at her. Her eyes reflected the polished green of the trees above, as deep and as bottomless as an ocean.

Yes, he'd been a fool to think he could just kill her. She might be Malachi – but she was perfection in every sense. How could he destroy such a thing?

'You're troubled,' Sairead began, taking his hand. Firmly, she pushed him back onto his seat and knelt beside him. 'Is it something to do with your family?'

With a wry smile, Micah said, 'No. They all live in the south. I don't get to see them very often.'

'Is it a big family?' Sairead tilted her head on one side, obviously hoping to distract him with simple talk.

'I have five brothers and two sisters. They're all married with their own children, so I suppose it is a big family.' Micah shook his head. Robert had always told him the best lie was buried in the truth. 'All I can say is they certainly make a lot of noise when they all get together.'

'So, why aren't you there with them? Why live here?'

'I . . . er, had a disagreement with my father. He disliked my choice of friends, what I wanted to do with my life. He's hardly spoken to me in years. My siblings got themselves caught up in it, so I thought it was best I leave.'

'But you will go back one day? Surely your father will forgive you.'

Micah managed a short laugh. 'You don't know him. He has a long memory – and I still have my friends.'

Sairead nodded and glanced down to where their hands were still joined together. Without looking up she murmured, 'Do you hate me for the other night?'

'What?' Micah started. 'How could I hate you? I thought you might hate me for making you leave.'

She laughed at that, but still didn't look up. 'That was the thing, you see. That's why I came back. Any other man would have simply taken what was offered, throwing his own mores and honour to the wind. But you didn't. You cared enough about me to use them as an excuse to turn me down. You didn't want to do anything to dishonour me in your own eyes.'

'I didn't?' Micah didn't know where to go with this. Everything had turned upside down since he'd met this girl, and now he was completely lost.

'No.' Sairead looked up shyly. 'You feel as I do, don't you?'

Silently, he reached out and brushed his fingers over her hair. With a deep sigh, he replied, 'You know I do.'

A few moments ago, he'd almost convinced himself he could kill her. Now he was prepared to do almost anything to keep her. By the gods – what a complete and utter mess! What the hell was he going to do?

Micah got to his feet, keeping hold of her hand. 'Come on. I have to get back to work or I'll be in big trouble. Go and find something to do in town. We'll have supper together later.'

Nash stood outside his pavilion and gazed across at the camp laid out before him. Work continued, brisk and determined, without a light word or even a suggestion of laughter. Not any more. And why? Because they knew the King was coming. Even though they knew Nash gave the orders, they were all terrified of Selar.

Almost ready. In another few days, Selar would be here, and a few days after that, they would march west. It was so close now, Nash could almost taste it, almost see that moment in his mind's eye. But would he come? Would he put himself between Selar and certain destruction?

Of course, the real problem with having a sense of honour was that it made a man predictable, right down to the smallest detail. Without doubt, Robert Douglas had spies here, in Dromna. A man with Lusara's welfare embedded in the depths of his heart would know what was really going on, would even now be making provision against the desolation of his country.

Yes. Eventually, he would come. And then Nash would kill him and there would be no Enemy left to stop him finding the Key.

Nash turned to go back inside when a flash of colour caught his eye. DeMassey, striding towards him with all the arrogance and confidence of one who believed wholeheartedly in his own abilities.

'I was beginning to give up on you,' Nash said in place of greeting. 'It must be a hard life running around after all your people.'

'No harder than having other people run around for you, I should think,' DeMassey replied, removing his cloak. 'At least I know they're doing as I ask.'

'In that case, since they've been so diligent, you must have a great deal of news for me?'

'Oh, plenty.' DeMassey carefully removed his gloves and ran

ringed fingers through his hair. 'If the Douglas is amassing an army, I doubt it's anywhere inside Lusara's borders.'

'You can cover the whole country in two weeks?' Nash asked, amused.

DeMassey ignored him. 'On the other hand, I'm fairly sure both Earl Payne and Duke McGlashen had something to do with disrupting your supply lines. I know there's a lot more to it, but I didn't want to spend too much time investigating. So far there's no word along any border or in any port to suggest the Douglas is bringing an army into Lusara but . . . '

'But what?'

With a frown, DeMassey turned his gaze on the army. 'I have a feeling he'll come.'

'Of course, he will!' Nash laughed. 'Wouldn't you?'

'Gilbert's on his way home with most of my people. There are a few left but not enough to do much damage should it come to that. I've only been able to sneak you this much help because Gilbert chose to round them all up himself, and slowly at that. If they stay a day longer, Aamin will have our hides.'

'I suppose Gilbert will take that lovely niece of his away with him? A pity.' Nash folded his arms, 'And what about you? Valena will be arriving with Selar in a few days. I'm sure she'll be delighted to see me again. I won't want to be disturbed that night, so I could use your help keeping an eye on the King. What do you say?'

DeMassey's gaze grew hard. Slowly he shook his head. 'Sometimes, I don't know why I put up with you.' With that he turned and stalked away as Nash couldn't help laughing.

The cellar was thick with smells Micah couldn't even begin to name, some, probably, dating back to the first days of its existence some eighty years ago. And it was impossible to breathe shallowly while he was hauling a barrel of ale from a rack halfway up the wall. With a grunt, he got it free and lowered it to the floor. Rubbing his hands together against the cold, he put his foot on the barrel and rolled it towards the door. As he got there, Ciaran appeared.

'Duffy said not to hurry. The place is empty tonight. Not a Guildesman, soldier nor even one of them Sadlani to be seen. May as well leave it for the morrow.' Ciaran leaned against the door with a toothless grin. 'Besides, there's a lady to see you.'

Micah stopped. Sairead was here? 'I'll be up in a minute.'

Ciaran chuckled and left, his feet slapping against the stone steps up to the inn. For a moment, Micah stood there in the gloom, the dank smells forgotten. What was he going to do? He wouldn't tell her the truth even if he could – even if, for one moment, there was some way he could trust her, a Malachi. But did he really have it in him to just turn her away? Could he hurt her like that – especially when he wanted, so badly, to do exactly the opposite.

By the gods, this was insane! How could he fall just like that? He'd met pretty girls before, yes, even been tempted – but never like this. Never had one girl stayed in his thoughts day and night, ghosting everything he did as though she were there watching him. Was it because she was Malachi – did she have some power over him he didn't know about?

And would her leaving make any difference to the way he felt about her? No. Nothing ever would. He was lost and he would simply have to live with it. It was his own fault, believing his heart was his to give or take as he wished. Still, many more before him had been fooled in exactly the same way.

Shaking his head, he smiled wryly and made for the stairs. At the top, he swung left and into the taproom. On the right, Duffy sat his great bulk in his favourite chair by the fire, sharing an ale with his two best friends. And there was Sairead, seated at a table opposite, a dusty grey cloak over her gown, her golden hair in a plait that fell over one shoulder. The glow in her eyes when she saw him was enough to blot out everything else in the room.

Then he was there, at the table and pulling out a stool to sit. 'Did you have a nice day?'

She smiled and dipped her head in a way he was beginning to recognise. 'Did you?'

'No,' Micah murmured, suddenly breathless with a desire to be honest with her. 'I missed you.'

Instantly her eyes were on his, searching.

'Are you hungry?'

'A little – but if you don't mind, I'd rather not sit here and eat. Those men keep watching me and I don't feel comfortable.'

233

No, neither did he. Not when there was a chance some Guildesman or Malachi serving with the army might walk in any second. 'Well, it's too cold to sit outside, but if you like, I can get us some bread and cheese, a piece of ham and a flask of wine and we can eat in my room.'

Sairead giggled. 'Well, that will certainly make them talk.'

'Good,' Micah said, standing. 'It'll keep them out of trouble. Come on.'

He led her through the kitchen, collected supper on the way, then headed outside to where a staircase led up to his room above the storehouse. He kicked the door open and ushered her inside.

It wasn't much of a room, but he'd done a few things with it, purloining the odd piece of spare furniture from other parts of the inn. He had a brazier in the corner which he immediately stoked up. In front of that was a three-legged table he'd made himself. A little unsteady, but it did the job. He had one stool and one chair, a cabinet against the wall under the window and the bed against the wall opposite. He'd even borrowed a rug for the floor. But now that he looked at it, it was all so very shabby and he wished he'd never suggested bringing Sairead here.

He quickly began to lay things out on the table, but his hands, suddenly clumsy, shook and he spilled the wine before he got any into a cup. Serin's blood! He was behaving like an addled boy! He took a deep breath, poured the wine out and turned to hand Sairead a cup.

She sipped her wine without shifting her gaze from him. 'Micah, do you really think your father won't forgive you?'

He raised his eyebrows at the unexpected question. 'Perhaps one day – but no time soon that I can see. Why?'

'I just couldn't see my father disowning me for the friends I chose. Are yours so bad?'

'No.' Micah turned away to cut the bread. 'Not bad. Just different to what he wanted. I don't agree with his judgement.'

'And are these friends here, in Dromna?'

'No.'

'So,' she mused, coming to stand by the table, 'you've lost both your family and friends. Your loyalty is . . . unusual.'

Micah had to smile. Yes, it would look that way to her. 'And if your father did disagree with your choice of friends, what would you do?'

'I . . . ' she paused, thinking. Then abruptly she grinned. 'I'd change his mind.'

'You must have a very understanding father.'

'These friends of yours,' Sairead continued, her voice musing and almost coy, 'they're not sorcerers, are they?'

Micah looked up sharply. 'That's not a funny question to ask,' he said after a moment, busily hiding his thoughts.

'I didn't mean . . . ' Sairead put her cup down and wandered to the brazier. Micah forgot the meal. He couldn't take his eyes from her.

'If you can't go back to your family or friends . . . then . . . is there any reason why you should stay here?' she asked, her voice soft.

His throat suddenly dry, Micah replied, 'Why?'

'I just thought you might . . . like to come home with me.'

Stunned, Micah could say nothing, but his heart pounded so loudly in his chest, he hardly heard her next words.

'I know my father would like you and I know you don't do things the same way here, but you'd have work and somewhere to live and we could . . . be together. We could leave tomorrow.' She turned around then, facing him with hesitation and fear.

Unable to stop himself, he caught her in his arms, burying his face in the scented heaven of her hair. She held onto him as though he were her life.

'By the gods, Sairead,' he murmured, and then he kissed her, forgetting everything else for a few, brief moments. When he looked at her again, she held his face in her hands, her eyes once more terribly deep and serious.

'Micah, do you believe in sorcerers?'

Suddenly he couldn't breathe. 'Forget about sorcerers, Sairead.'

'I can't, Micah,' she frowned, pained, 'because I am one. I am a Malachi. I know that doesn't mean anything to you, because you know nothing of my people. My father is a Malachi, a horse breeder for the Dariet D'Azzir. My mother is human. She was born in Lusara. I know my father would accept you if you came back with me, because he married a Lusaran. I just wanted you to know, before you made a decision.'

A decision? Which one? His heart was already lost. His body was hers – but his soul belonged to Robert and always would. There had never been a decision to make.

Carefully, he took her hands between his own, held them a moment, then turned away, his heart like lead. 'I can never go with you. I can never marry you.'

'Micah . . . '

'If it makes any difference, I do love you, but what you want – what we both want – is impossible.'

There was a sharp intake of breath and then she was in front of him, her hand gripping his arm. 'You knew! But how? How could you know? Tell me!'

He said nothing, but met her gaze without tremor. She could pick up nothing of his thoughts, worm no secrets out of him, gain no truths about his mission or anything else. The Seal Robert had placed upon him so many years ago protected him against exactly this, and it was that Seal which had told him she was Malachi in the first place. He could no more tell her anything dangerous than he could slit his own throat.

'Tell me!' Sairead gasped. 'How did you know? Yes, I can see it now, in your eyes. You didn't flinch when I said the word Malachi because you know full well what that word means – but you could only know if you were Salti!'

When he still didn't speak, she gripped his shirt, her eyes ablaze. 'I trusted you with the truth – why won't you do the same for me? How can you say you love me in one breath, then lie with silence in the next?' Tears filled her eyes, brimmed over onto her cheeks.

Micah was not made of stone. For all that the Seal protected him from her, it did nothing to protect him from himself. He could tell her one thing, enough to settle her mind if only a little. His voice came out heavy and grating. 'I am not Salti. I'm not a sorcerer of any kind.'

Abruptly she let go and stepped back, tears still falling, chest heaving with the effort of living. 'You must be – unless . . . By the blood! Your *friends*! That's what your father disagrees with. You work with Salti and that's how you knew about me and . . . '

She groaned with horror, her hands flying to her face as the whole truth fell upon her like a thundercloud. 'That's why you're

236

here!' She paused. 'And you think I'll kill you now I know the truth?'

His hands abruptly unsteady, Micah poured himself some more wine and emptied the cup in one mouthful. 'I would have done the same.'

Sairead strode up to him, swung her hand and slapped his face. 'You . . . you . . . By the gods, Micah! Why? Why didn't you say anything? Why, is this so . . . ' But she couldn't go on. Great sobs racked her body and she buried her face in her hands.

Instinctively, Micah reached out and instantly she flew into his arms. His voice soft, he murmured, 'I wish you'd never come back. I wish things didn't have to be this way. I wish there could have been some other way for you to understand without knowing the truth. I tried to convince myself that killing you was the best way out – but I couldn't do it. How could I kill what I loved so dearly?'

Her head came up then, her eyes glistening. 'And you think I could? Is that what you believe of Malachi?'

'Sairead, your people and the Salti have been at war for over five hundred years. What else am I to believe? That they are all like you? I wish they were. I wish there were no problems at all and that we could marry, but we both know the truth. Wishing will change nothing.'

'I don't believe that! Some day . . . '

'Don't! Hope is not a toy to be played with. Things will not change. Not in our lifetimes.'

Her sobs now harsher, she said, 'But you know as well as I do that we were meant to be together. I knew it the moment I first saw you. You love me and now you want me to go on for the rest of my life hating you and wanting you at the same time. You can stand it, you can live with it. You're strong, it doesn't bother you. But it bothers me, Micah! It bothers me!'

'And you really think I don't care?' With that, Micah caught her face in his hands, kissing her hard, tasting the salt of her tears. She melted into his arms as though she'd been born for that purpose. Suddenly all the tension, the doubts and fears broke inside him and the flood swept everything aside. Even as he kissed her, he wrapped his own arms around her, drawing her closer. She was still crying, but her hands held him tight, as though she was determined never to let him go. In one movement, he lifted her up and turned for the bed.

He hardly noticed when the lamp snuffed out, all on its own.

The morning chorus of birdsong wafted across the roof of the tavern and through the window of Micah's room. A breeze rattled the door, crept under the gap and made the air chill. He grunted and pulled the covers up further around his neck without actually opening his eyes. Then some idiot in the street started hammering, which started a dog barking and then someone had to complain about it – loudly. Then, to make it all worse, a dozen horses rode by—

Micah came fully awake with a start. Horses?

He stared at the ceiling for a moment, listening intently. Yes, something was going on. Time to get up.

Carefully he rolled onto his side, ready to waken Sairead – but he was alone. He glanced about the room. Her clothes, her bag, everything, gone.

Instantly he jumped up, got dressed and flung the door open. He could see directly into the stable, but her horse wasn't there. With a sigh, he closed his eyes and leaned against the wall. She hadn't even said goodbye.

A lark swooped by him, squawking in the dawn. Micah moved. He grabbed his cloak and headed down the stairs. He was late this morning and he'd have to be quick or he wouldn't be back in time to start work.

The town was already awake in pieces. A greeting here and there was called out to him as he passed, but it was all he could do to wave a response. Those horses were nowhere to be seen now, but he could follow their tracks along the dirt road heading for the south valley.

With long strides, Micah left the road and climbed the hill on his right, pushing his way through the forest undergrowth. Near the top, he slowed, paused and listened before moving further. There were never many sentries on the army's boundary, but he didn't want to encounter one now.

Yes, there was one, to his left, leaning against a tree – not very vigilant. Wait – another to the right – no, two! What was going on?

Carefully now, he crept forward until he could see down into the valley. This was one of his best spots. From here he could see Nash's pavilion and almost the whole camp spread out, albeit a little obscured by the trees.

But the leaves had only just come out and the cover was not thick yet. There was movement down there – and purpose and—

Carts. Lots of them. They'd never been there before. Oxen to pull them. Sadlani mercenaries lugging sacks of flour. Long pikes stacked up ready for transport – and another pavilion being erected opposite Nash's. There could be only one meaning behind all this: Selar was coming because the army was ready to march.

By the gods – it was time!

All those years waiting, all these months – and this was it!

Micah's stomach lurched and he almost gave himself away by jumping up. However, good sense guided him in time and with one last look, he squirmed back away from the edge, away from the dangerous eyes of the sentries.

Right. Back to the inn to collect his few things, saddle his horse and leave. It would be good to see Robert again – and the Bishop – and find out what had happened at Clonnet. Perhaps Jenn and Andrew would be at Bleakstone.

A noise to his right made him pause. His gaze darted from bush to bush, looking for some untoward movement. Then he heard it again. A horse, somewhere close.

Silently he moved forward, coming to a halt behind a tree – and then he saw her. She stopped, making no attempt to reach for her horse, no bid to speak. Instead, she simply gazed steadily at him, her hands held loosely at her sides.

Micah moved out from behind the tree. 'What are you doing here?'

'What, are we enemies already?' came her quiet reply.

'You tell me.'

Sairead said nothing for a moment, but her gaze went up the hill, then back to him. 'What would you have me say? Would you have me betray my own people? I have asked nothing of you.'

'And I've asked nothing of you,' Micah replied evenly. 'But now I do. Are you involved with this?'

'Why?'

'Are you?'

'What would you do if I said yes?'

'Don't play games with me, Sairead.' Micah moved forward until he stood before her. 'We've been as honest with each other as we can afford to be. I ask again: are you involved?'

Sairead shook her head slowly.

'Then—' Micah paused. Every part of him cried out to touch her, but he resisted. 'Promise me to leave now and go home. Have nothing more to do with any of this, I beg you.'

She lifted her chin, defiance in every inch of her body – except her eyes. 'And if I asked you to stay out of it, would you?'

He lifted up his hand. 'Please, don't fight. Go home. This is the only thing I can give you, a warning.'

'Then I ask of you the same thing,' Sairead replied, her courage shining clear. 'Go home to your father. Tell him you've renounced your friends. Don't fight. Don't get killed. Please.'

What could he say? She was right. The time for words had passed them by.

Already cold inside, he took one last look at her, at her glowing golden hair, her ice-crystal eyes. She said nothing. She remained as immobile as time itself. They both stood there for long, terrible moments and then, without another word, Micah turned and headed down the hill.

16

'Jenn? Can you hear me? Try to wake up. Just breathe deeply. You're in no danger. I'm right here.'

She felt something stroking the side of her face and she latched onto the touch, holding it in her mind as something real. She did as she was told and breathed deeply, the air dry and hot.

Her eyes blinked open. Robert was kneeling beside her, his hand brushing her cheek; his expression shifted from worried to relieved in a moment.

'Thank the gods!' He moved a little, then brought a cup to her lips. 'Here, you need to drink something.'

The water was cool as it slipped down her throat. She swallowed a little more, then tried to sit up.

'Just stay there for a minute. How do you feel?'

Jenn looked around, belatedly realising it was light now. 'I feel fine. What happened?'

'You blacked out. I couldn't wake you. All night. Are you sure you feel fine?'

'Yes. Help me up.'

She sat up, resting her back against a rough sandstone wall. Robert sat in front of her, watching her carefully. Still, it was the room that demanded her attention. It looked so different in daylight, open and airy. The domed ceiling rose high above, the walls to either side of them splintered with tall windows, only wide enough to step through sideways. The stone was a warm ochre, the floor, dark grey, each block fitted to the next with tight precision. No decoration of any kind adorned any surface, as though the building itself were sufficient in its simplicity. This was a hard room, without compromise, its sharp edges lasting so much longer than the people who had built it.

The room from the dream.

'This is it, isn't it?' Robert asked, keeping his voice low as if not to disturb her. 'The room where the Key was created?'

'Yes.'

'So . . . what happened last night?'

She looked down at her hands. It wasn't easy putting such a vague feeling into words, but she tried. 'I had this . . . feeling that I didn't want to come in here . . . and then, the moment I set foot inside this room, I heard the chanting. It was the same as the chanting in the dream about the Key – but it was just so loud. I don't remember much after that.'

'Chanting? From the dream? Was it a memory, or something else?'

'I don't know. It didn't feel like a memory.'

Robert frowned and got to his feet. He took a few steps away, his head tilting back to look up at the ceiling. The tension in his shoulders was not echoed in the tone of his voice. 'Could you understand anything that was being said?'

'No.' If only she had. If only this made some sense. Perhaps it had been just a memory, coming upon her suddenly because she was finally here, in the place where the Key had been created.

She stood and stretched, feeling blood return to her body. She felt good, as though she had a good night's sleep last night and nothing more.

'You seem to have this . . . affinity with the Key.'

She looked at him. 'Affinity?'

'Or a connection. Something. Have you had any other visions or dreams?'

'Visions? No, I don't think so. None that I remember.'

He turned back to her, his gaze steady, successfully hiding whatever other thoughts he had. 'So, do you think you're up to a little exploring? That's why we're here, after all.'

'Really, Robert, I feel fine now.'

'Well, if you start hearing things again, you just say so.'

'I will.'

'Come on, I'll show you where I think the library was.'

It was strange being back here after so long. Nothing had changed. There was more sand on the floor, and both he and the stone had aged a little, but nothing else that he could see had altered one bit since he'd last been here with Micah.

Back then, he'd been an exile, drifting from place to place without any purpose, determined never to return to his own home, his lands and family.

Then one night, camped outside this Palace, he'd decided to do just that – return to Lusara and face the consequences. He'd never really understood why he'd made that decision, where it had come from – but it was ridiculous to believe the Key could exert that kind of influence from such an enormous distance.

Wasn't it?

It was very strange being back: so much had changed in his own life and yet nothing had changed here.

He took Jenn through long dusty corridors where empty rooms branched off from both sides. It was warm inside, but the solid stone of the walls blocked the stark heat of the desert. Jenn walked at his side, wide-eyed and a little awed by what she saw. He kept close watch on her, mindful of her odd fit last night.

He'd not slept at all. Instead, he'd sat with her, fear his only companion, listening to her occasional murmur, hoping she'd awaken. She certainly seemed recovered now, but still the question lingered: why had it happened in the first place?

Why did she have this invisible connection to the Key?

'What does this say here?'

Jenn had come to a halt before a narrow wall. She pointed up to a series of glyphs that ran from floor to ceiling.

Robert ran his hand over the stone. 'It's not painted on. It's etched into the surface.'

'Can you read any of it?'

'No. A few of the symbols are familiar in form to some I've seen, but they don't fit the pattern of any language I know.'

She glanced aside at him. 'How many languages do you know?'

'I have a working knowledge of seven ancient languages.'

'A working knowledge?' Jenn smiled a little. 'That's not what Father Aiden said.'

'Oh?'

'He said you taught him things about Saelic grammar that didn't exist in any book he knew of.'

'Oh,' Robert waved his hand dismissively, 'I made those up so I could impress him.'

Jenn grinned and turned back to the wall. 'The rest of this corridor is bare of writing, so I suppose this is here to label this room as something important.'

'It could be.'

She moved to the door, put her shoulder to it to push it open. It swung aside with a groan. The room before them stretched out to right and left, but like the rest of the Palace, was entirely empty. There was nothing on the walls.

'Patric said a squad of Guilde soldiers came to empty this place of dangerous documents two years after it had been deserted. I wonder what they removed, how much the Cabal left behind. I can't think there would have been too much left of any value.'

Robert shrugged. 'Those who fled before the last Battle and founded both Malachi and Enclave took a lot of the library books with them. I'm sure they would have taken everything of serious value. Whoever survived the Battle might have come back here to remove the rest. Of course, there are also a dozen nomadic tribes who live in these parts. They would have picked the building clean long before the Guilde arrived.'

'So why send them in the first place?' Jenn murmured. 'And why Guilde? Why not Imperial soldiers?'

'The Guilde claimed the right to hunt down and destroy the Cabal. They would have seen it as their duty.'

'But they must have known that after two years there wouldn't be anything of value here.'

Robert turned to look at her and frowned, seeing where her thoughts were going. 'Unless they were looking for something that couldn't be removed.'

'Like a prophecy carved on a wall of stone.'

Robert pulled in a breath, his gaze returning inexorably to the blank walls of the empty room. 'How could they have known about the prophecy? Unless . . . '

Jenn took his elbow and ushered him back out into the corridor. As they walked, she spoke. 'For over a thousand years, sorcerers – known then as the Cabal – worked alongside the Guilde in partnership. When the Empire grew, they became an established part of it. Then, five hundred and forty-odd years ago, Cabal and Empire quarrelled. The argument ended with them facing each other on a battlefield in Alusia. The Cabal would have won but, as legend has it, aid arrived for the Empire in the form of a woman who was believed to be an incarnation of the goddess Mineah. With her help, the Empire won the battle and the Cabal was shattered.'

'I'm delighted to see all those history lessons weren't a waste.' Robert grinned as he took her down a flight of stairs. Windows high in all the walls gave them a constant glow of indirect sunlight, plenty enough to see where they were going.

Jenn ignored his interruption. 'What I want to know is, why the battle was fought in Alusia when most of the Cabal lived here, in Budlandi . . . '

'That's a good question.'

'And why the Guilde thought it necessary to find records of a prophecy that couldn't possibly affect them. I can't help wondering if it was the prophecy itself that was responsible for the quarrel between Cabal and Empire, as it was between Bu and Felkri.'

Robert smiled. He'd missed this with her, missed listening to her work things out aloud, ask the kind of questions those with more knowledge wouldn't think of. It had been one of the things that had drawn him to her back in the beginning, before he'd had any idea of who she was. Perhaps coming here with her hadn't been such a bad idea.

But it was an interesting idea: that the rift between Cabal and Guilde had all been due to a prophecy half-lost in the shadows of history.

He got to the bottom of the stairs and found the door there already open. This room was at ground level, but the windows were still high above, giving the room ventilation as well as light. This was the library: to him, the most amazing room in the entire Palace.

'Oh, Robert!' Jenn breathed as she threw him a short smile and stepped into the room. He followed as she wandered about, gazing at one wall after another, her fingers reaching out to trail across the still-bright paintings, symbols and pictures woven together in a complicated pattern, colours vivid, gold trimming glittering in the morning air. This room was a work of art and it seemed a shame that it was hidden here, away from eyes that could appreciate it.

'It's so beautiful! It must have taken years to finish. Robert, do you see where it looks so much like the walls of the Council chamber in the Enclave? A tradition of painting history on the walls. It makes sense. Even some of the style is similar – though this makes the Enclave look a little dull by comparison. Why didn't the Guilde destroy this?'

Robert was enjoying watching her, plain and simple. He'd already spent hours going over these walls. There was nothing here he didn't already know, but it was fun seeing it through her eyes, listening to the wonder in her voice. 'I don't know, but I would assume this was exactly the kind of thing they'd have been sent here to remove.'

'And this isn't the prophecy?'

'No. As you said, it's a pictorial history of the Cabal and this Palace in particular. Most of it concerns the comings and goings of this place, who the leaders were, which Princes were allies, that kind of thing.'

'And these symbols? Can you read them?'

'Yes. They're a different language to those in the corridor.'

'So, this isn't the prophecy.'

'No.'

'So where is it likely to be?'

'Jenn, I told you at Bleakstone I didn't think there was anything here to find. Micah and I went over this whole place in minute detail.'

'So,' she turned to face him, lacing her hands together, 'we're only here because I wanted to come?'

'Jenn . . . '

'No, let's not go back over that again. Instead, you can answer me this – if you lived here and wanted to hide a prophecy somewhere, on a wall where it would be safe for all time, where would you put it? You know this place well, where would you suggest we start looking?'

Robert spread his arms wide. 'I have no idea.'

'Well . . . ' Jenn frowned, walking towards him. 'How did you find that silver rod?'

'I focused in on the properties of the Key as though I was trying to Seek it.'

'And?' She was standing before him now, her face upturned to him, expectancy clear in her eyes.

'That's hardly going to work here, is it?'

'We won't know until we try.'

'But we're looking for a wall, not some . . . '

'Or are you afraid that if we find the prophecy, you'll only discover that what the Key told you was right all along?'

Robert closed his mouth, silencing his objections.

Yes, he'd missed this. Missed the way she could talk him into a corner without even trying. Sometimes missing something was actually quite pleasant.

'Robert,' Jenn began, her voice soft and earnest now, 'I keep asking myself the same question: why keep the prophecy secret? No, I don't mean the ending and why you're keeping that to yourself – but the rest of it. Nobody we know had heard of it until a few years ago, when we found out you'd known for twenty years. But *nobody* else knew. Why?'

Robert blew out a breath. 'Somebody else did know. Nash.'

Her gaze clouded over then and idly she reached out a hand to trail her fingers down the wall. Standing there in her boy's clothing, her long hair braided down her back, she looked too much like she had the first day he'd seen her, being chased through the depths of Shan Moss. Back then, she'd had the heart of an explorer; now, once again, she was indulging her curiosity, her need to question everything around her.

She made a formidable ally.

He winced at the word his mind had unwittingly supplied, then smothered it with a grin. 'We know so little about all of this. For all we know, there might have been a very good reason to keep it secret.'

'What do you think is the most likely reason?'

'Information is usually withheld from the people because it will either encourage enemies to attack or encourage the people to revolt. That is, of course, not counting the seamier secrets some Kings keep to themselves.'

'So it's an act of protection.'

'That's right.'

'Well, *you* knew the prophecy for twenty years and didn't tell anyone. Why?'

'The Key put some kind of block on me. I couldn't tell.'

'And if it hadn't?'

Robert didn't answer that one – but he didn't need to. Jenn's eyes were alight with possibilities; her mind was firmly attached to this entire mystery. Abruptly, she smiled, then laughed a little.

'Robert, don't you see it? All this,' she spread her arms wide, 'it *does* make sense. The prophecy has been around much longer than we thought, perhaps a thousand years. It was handed down through one generation of sorcerers after another. Over that amount of time, it was bound to become corrupted here and there – enough to cause a split between Felkri and the people of Bu. And over that time, word of it was bound to have got out, so it makes sense that it could be the prophecy that drove the Empire to turn on the Cabal.'

'I'm not disagreeing with you – but that's still all supposition.'

'Perhaps – but think about this: why do we keep looking for answers? Why are we here?'

'Because we need to know what Nash knows . . . '

'No, Robert,' Jenn took a step closer, placing her hand on his chest. 'Why are *we* here? You and me?'

His thoughts came to an abrupt halt. He had no answer, so he waited for hers, with an odd intuition that whatever she said would be right.

'We keep pushing this, looking for ways to understand it, reading books, travelling to places, following up the smallest of clues – and why? Because that's who we *are*. That's *what* we are. As though we have it built into our souls, from the moment we were born, to do this, to solve this, to open up the mystery. And the prophecy – it was never meant to be seen by others, because it was for *us*. You and me and yes, even Nash – because we *need* to know what we are. Robert, the prophecy isn't the question – it's the *answer*.'

Stunned, Robert couldn't take his eyes from her, his voice coming out harsh and breathless. 'The answer to what?'

'To what's about to happen, to what's been happening.' She gazed at him a moment, the blue of her eyes reflecting things he couldn't see. 'Some day, somebody would be born to do this. And we were.'

'So, it's our fate?'

'If you'd never heard the prophecy, you'd still be doing what you're doing now, fighting Nash, fighting Selar, wouldn't you?'

He could only nod, however reluctantly.

Her hand dropped to her side. 'Why does it bother you so much to think you have been fated to play a role?'

He stared at her a moment, then turned away, his feet taking him to the door. 'Perhaps some of us have a fate we want no part in.'

He felt her move up beside him. 'And perhaps, like everything else, your fate is not what you think it is. Come on, show me around the rest of this place and then we should try that trick you used to find the silver rod.'

Jenn was thirsty, her feet hurt and her eyes ached, but for the first time in so long, she felt good, really good. As though she were doing something valid and solid and positive and real. She followed behind Robert, walking from room to room, down one corridor after another, picturing the life of the people who had once lived here, building an image she knew she would never forget.

There was something about the place which reminded her of the Enclave, the way the passages twisted and turned, how light was ingeniously filtered from outside, how everything led to and was centred around the great chamber she'd woken up in.

Whatever strange feeling she'd experienced last night had gone and not returned. Fortunately.

As the day wore on, Robert grew more quiet, but for once, she didn't press him to talk. He was thinking, she hoped, about the things she'd said that morning. Or perhaps he was simply not looking forward to trying to Seek the wall supposedly holding the prophecy.

They ate in a room overlooking the hall. Robert had insisted they move their meagre belongings up there after taking care of the horses. Apparently those nomadic tribes still passed by here now and then and he didn't want to be caught unawares.

The little room was one of a number of galleries which looked down on to the open space below. Sitting there, eating, Jenn could see the dream the Key had given her, see in her mind's eye, the men standing around, chanting, giving the Key its purpose, its power, its life.

Had they really known what it was they were creating?

'Have you had enough?'

She looked up to find Robert putting the food away. She finished her mouthful and helped him to pack up. 'When do we need to leave?'

'Tomorrow morning. Any later and we'll run out of time.'

He said nothing else as he led her back down the winding staircase to the main chamber once more. He stood there for a moment, his back to her, hands on his hips, not saying anything at all.

'Robert?'

'I don't even know if I can do it. Last time I tried it, I still used an *ayarn*.'

'But you don't need one any more.'

'Perhaps.'

'Please, Robert,' Jenn murmured, 'just try.'

His shoulders slumped a little and he nodded. Then he straightened up and she heard him take in a deep breath. He did not let that breath out.

In the back of her mind, she could hear something faint, something almost whispered, as though it were a shadow of a thought, a memory of one. Seconds drifted by as she watched him, too afraid to look away, too scared even to breathe for herself. As she waited, that frail murmur grew a little, took on shape and form, even though it was still a handful of nothing.

'It's here.' Robert's voice broke into the creaking silence. He turned, his eyes a little wild, a little pleased, a little confused. 'It's here – and I think I know where.'

Jenn grinned. She couldn't help it. 'Where?'

'Um . . .' He frowned for a moment, then pointed towards a doorway. 'Down that way.'

He headed off for the door and she ran after him, trying to keep up with his long strides. Tension and excitement built up inside her, a twisting pair of mixed emotions.

There was a short passage and then some stairs he immediately started down. There wasn't much light here for a change, but he continued, his sight more than capable of dealing with the shadows. At the bottom, he came to a halt and Jenn kept her silence. Another moment later and he was walking again, this time down another corridor. Turn after turn the maze continued on until Jenn was sure she was hopelessly lost. Abruptly, Robert came to a stop and she almost walked into his back.

This time he was quiet for much longer, and she stepped around him to see why.

A wall, blocking their way. Rough stone and mortar, completely unlike the rest of the Palace. She glanced up to find his eyes on her. 'What?'

'You wanted to know how to keep it safe? Well, there's your answer. It's behind there.'

'Well,' she turned back to the wall, 'I suppose if it was to be kept safe so that *we* would find it, we must be able to.'

'Your logic is impeccable – assuming you're right to begin with.'

'So what do we do now?'

He chuckled. 'I see. You do all the thinking and I do all the muscle work. Now I understand.'

Jenn lifted her chin and stepped back, leaving him lots of room. 'Well, go ahead. Impress me.'

Robert just rolled his eyes. 'Women!' Then, before she could comment, he raised his hand until it lay flat against the rock. He pressed and, for a moment, Jenn could see no effect at all. Then she heard something quite weird: a strange scratching sound coming, it seemed, from *inside* the stone.

'Stand back.'

She did, and, seconds later, he released the wall. As though it were made of sand rather than stone, the entire thing crumbled before her, making a mountain of small stones she could have held in her hand. Dust filled the air and she coughed a little, waiting for it to clear.

She whistled. 'I'll admit it, I am impressed. How did you do that?'

'A small trick I picked up years ago when I was reading about how the Enclave was built.' He shrugged, but was obviously a little shy about it. 'A lot of the Enclave tunnels are natural, but they weren't connected. Somebody worked out how to age rock before its time and – the next thing you know . . . '

'So you weren't joking about blowing the top of the mountain off?'

He laughed at that, then turned back to the pile of rubble. 'Be careful. The stones are going to be a bit sharp.'

He went first, leaving Jenn to gingerly make her way over the crushed stone, the soles of her boots not much protection against the new edges. She reached out and steadied herself against the wall, pausing to look up when she realised she'd put her hand on a wooden door, left wide open.

Of course, why bother closing a door when you're about to block it with stone. This door, however, was different to all the others in this place. The timber was pale and drier to the touch, and it was carved, deeply, a motif around the border she was sure she'd seen somewhere.

'Robert? Did you see this?'

When she didn't get an answer, she looked for him. There was only one source of light: a single window in the centre of the ceiling, which dropped a shaft of dusty brilliance onto the floor. Robert stood to one side of it, his right shoulder slashed with white.

'Robert?'

He neither moved nor answered. Suddenly afraid, Jenn ventured across the room, her gaze not shifting from him, from the total stillness of him. She reached his side, her hand touching his sleeve, hoping to make some sort of contact . . .

'No!' His voice came out hollow and haunted as though a thousand ghosts had just returned to him. 'No . . . '

Jenn turned, letting her gaze follow his, to the wall – and to the floor. 'By the gods!'

The wall stood freely, touching neither the sides of the room, nor the ceiling. It was taller than Robert and about twenty paces wide. Its surface had once been smooth but was now a mess of chipped gouges, the floor beneath it still carrying the gravel so created. Here and there were spots left untouched, little places no bigger than her palm. These were still silky smooth and bright with paint, sharp with carving. Not a single symbol remained whole.

Robert sank to his knees, his hands scraping at the gravel on the floor. 'The Guilde. They found what they were looking for. That's why the library is still untouched, because it wasn't dangerous and this, this was. This . . . they destroyed it, Jenn. Do you see? They destroyed it.'

Jenn, struck by the note of horrified mourning in his voice, put her hand on his shoulder, slim comfort. She couldn't take her eyes from the desecration before her.

'Someone must have told them where it was and what it was,' she murmured, thinking out loud. 'But I don't understand why they would have destroyed it – it would mean nothing to them.'

Robert shifted, sitting back on his heels, suddenly still. His voice, low and bitter, echoed around the walls. 'No. They destroyed it because they would have thought that in doing so, they could stop the prophecy from coming about. Serin's blood, even I wasn't stupid enough to think that! Damn them!'

Jenn dropped her hand, her feet taking her back a step. The vehemence in Robert's voice was overpowering in this small space. She took a breath. 'Robert, I don't think . . . '

'Come on.' He got to his feet and was walking to the door before she could stop him. 'There's no need to stay here the night. Let's go.'

With barely contained force, Robert pushed one thing after another into the saddlebags. In the moments when his hands weren't moving, they shook with the effort to contain it.

Anger.

It was his own fault. He'd known all along there couldn't be anything of use here, but he'd let Jenn sway him with her ideas, her arguments. So he'd come and he'd found exactly what he was expecting – only he'd never expected to find the prophecy in the first place, let alone discover that it had been deliberately destroyed by somebody who couldn't possibly understand how important it was.

Damn it!

Finished, he picked up the bags, Sensing rather than seeing Jenn collect her things and follow him down into the chamber. He'd left the horses in the ancient stable, out of the sun, out of the heat, but now it was later in the day, the air would be cooler soon, dusk would fall and he could bury everything within blessed darkness.

Bury it. Bury it all. He had to. Anger, frustration, hopelessness all gave rise to the demon. One spark was all it would take. Just one.

Control had never felt so . . . essential.

He saddled the horses with a minimum of fuss, handing Jenn hers as they emerged back into the afternoon light. He didn't dare speak. Couldn't afford to say the words aloud, because they were horrible, nasty words and she didn't deserve them. It wasn't her fault the wall had been destroyed, that some poor tortured soul had told the Guilde where it was in the first place. She'd been trying to help, trying to give him something else to fight Nash with, but instead, what she'd given him was something else to fight – despair.

They were almost at the gate when she spoke, but the words weren't what he was expecting.

'Robert? You know you said I should tell you if I was hearing something?'

He came to a halt, turning to face her, but she wasn't looking at him. She faced the Palace instead, her eyes darting this way and that.

'What is it? The chanting again?'

'No. It's . . . different. Can't you hear it?'

'No.' He went to say something else, but then he did hear something and it didn't sound like any kind of chanting. Without pausing, he grabbed Jenn's arm and pulled both them and their horses into the shadows of the guard house. Only then did he extend his Senses.

Out and through the Palace, beyond the domed room to the other side, towards the south gate. There were perhaps twenty of them, maybe a few more. But . . . they didn't seem . . . right somehow. As though their auras were trying to escape his detection. They weren't Malachi, but nor were they human. Instead, they seemed somewhere in the middle and the urge to know more swept over him with such force he gasped.

Damn, he wished he could see them! Could he risk getting closer, risk Jenn's safety?

'Robert?' Jenn's urgent whisper brought him back, and he turned to her. Her face was white, eyes wide with a fear she tried to ignore.

'It's okay, I can hear them too.'

'Them?' She frowned, shook her head. 'There're people here?'

'You can't Sense them?'

'No but I . . . I can hear them speaking, but it's here.' She tapped her head, her voice tight and agitated. 'Can't you hear it?'

'I can hear them moving around, their horses – but they're not talking.'

'Yes, they are!' Jenn grabbed his sleeve, her face beaded with perspiration. 'Robert, I . . . I can hear them! They're . . . they're *mindspeaking!*'

17

As quickly as he could. Robert led the horses inside the empty guard house, soothed them until they were still, then turned to Jenn. His voice low and quiet, he said, 'Are you sure that's what it is? Mindspeaking? It's definitely not the chanting or anything else?'

She frowned in silence for a moment, then nodded, her gaze meeting his. 'Yes. Definitely. These are phrases and sentences, questions and answers, and each of the voices speaking sounds a little different to the rest. Like they were having a conversation. And they sound so nearby. Are you sure you can't hear them talking?'

Robert closed his eyes and concentrated. He could hear footsteps, people dismounting from their horses, bags being collected and placed on the ground – but no voices.

Serin's breath! Who were these people?

Opening his eyes again, he murmured, 'Can you understand what they're saying?'

Jenn shook her head. 'It sounds a bit like a different language – but there are a lot of words that I can recognise. Just let me listen for a minute and I'll see if I can find out what they're doing here.'

'And whether they know we're here.'

It was Jenn's turn to close her eyes and Robert left her alone, keeping his Senses extended to warn him if their hideout was about to be discovered. The air inside the guard house grew close and hot as the sun drew towards the horizon. The horses were quiet now, but standing here too long would only encourage them to move. If they had to make an escape, the sooner they started the better.

Of course, leaving the shelter of the Palace to cross a flat plain in daylight would give them away immediately.

His attention was caught by Jenn's sudden gasp. She turned to him, her eyes wild. 'They know we're here! They can . . . Sense us . . . no . . . *you!* They can Sense you, Robert!'

'How?'

'I don't know. They keep saying something about darkness desecrating the chamber and . . . and the Enemy. Robert . . . ' She fell silent for a moment, then grabbed his arm. 'We have to get out of here. Now! They don't know exactly where we are, but they're searching for us. They sound so . . . ugly! Like they want to kill you. Please, we have to go!'

'We can't until it's dark. Just a few more minutes. I can keep track of them and if they get too close, we can make a run for it. The Palace is a big place. If they can't Sense where we are, then we have a good chance.'

His voice was filled with a confidence he didn't really feel, but at least Jenn calmed a little. Once again, he extended his Senses, keeping track of which rooms and which buildings were being searched. It would take some time, with any luck, enough time for them to get clear before they were discovered.

That didn't make the waiting any more bearable.

Nor did the questions. Where had these people come from – and how could they mindspeak? How could Jenn hear them – and if Jenn tried mindspeaking, would they hear her?

Until Jenn had come to the Enclave, they'd all believed mind-speaking was a lost art. But then she'd spoken to Robert and he in turn had learned how to speak back to her. Since then, she'd spoken to Finnlay, who could reply if the distance wasn't too great – but nobody else could. *Nobody.*

He kept a close eye on the sunset, visible through the open doorway. Just a few minutes more and they could get away – though part of him still wished to stay and talk to these people. It seemed silly to just run.

But they had spoken of the Enemy, of darkness and a will to kill him. Would they really wait long enough for him to ask a few questions? And would their answers be anything he wanted to hear – or would this idea be like all the others, destined to end with failure?

No. The demon had had its feed this day. He would give it no more.

'They're called the Generet,' Jenn whispered, standing close. 'They've . . . travelled a long way . . . they've reached the library . . . no, wait . . . they've gone down to the prophecy room . . . I . . . I don't think they knew where it was. They're all gathered in there, looking around. They think that you . . . This would be a good time to . . . '

'Get moving.' Robert grunted. Of course, why shouldn't a people who had never met him blame him for it? Why not? 'Yes, I agree. I can't Sense any of them around at the moment. Let's go.'

The moon had long since gone by the time they reached the escarpment and the cold of night bit deep into Jenn's bones. Robert seemed to have no trouble finding the path to the top of the ridge, but he did so in silence.

Some animal howled across the plain; another responded in kind. Every now and then, Jenn would see a glow of red eyes in the night, hear the pattering of feet across hard dirt. She kept close to Robert, but he either didn't see them, or didn't care. But, animals or not, she preferred these noises to the close whispering of the Generet; a sound which had slipped under her skin too quickly, had breathed dry and dusty desert right into her soul.

For hours they rode side by side, skirting a ridge before dropping back into the valley. Only then did Robert finally come to a halt. Still without a word, he jumped down from his horse, kicked a few stray sticks together and, with a flick of his hand, forced them into flames.

If she hadn't known any better, she would have thought it a gesture of fury.

Carefully she dismounted, tying her horse to the nearest scraggly tree. 'Hungry?'

'No. Get your blankets out and get some rest. We only have time for a few hours' sleep before dawn. I'll keep watch.'

'Robert?'

'What?'

Jenn turned, her blanket across her arms, held there, she knew, just as much as a shield as for warmth. 'Just because we couldn't read the prophecy, doesn't mean the ending the Key gave you has to be right.'

'No? Then why else would it be considered dangerous enough for the Guilde to destroy?'

'But the people at Felkri might have the *right* prophecy. If Patric can . . .'

Robert simply shook his head. 'Just leave it alone and get some sleep. We have two days to reach the coast if we're to get the next ship back.' He tied his horse up, pulled his sword from the saddle and sat with his back to a tree. When she didn't move immediately, he folded his arms and rested his head back. 'Please, Jenn, just do as I ask. Don't worry. By morning, I'll be my usual arrogant, pig-headed, glib self. You'll never know the difference.'

With that, he closed his eyes, shutting her out. She stifled a sigh and unfurled her bedroll beside the fire. She lay down but watched him nonetheless. He hadn't exaggerated. By morning, nobody would ever be able to tell he'd just suffered an enormous disappointment, made all the more sharp because he'd allowed himself to hope – for however brief a moment – that he would actually find an answer, a solution to whatever it was that was eating away inside him.

He wouldn't talk about it. He never had. Instead, he would force the disappointment, the anger and frustration deep down inside, fuelling the very thing he was afraid of. He would call himself a fool for having believed that he might be able to change his destiny. He would hate himself for failing. Again. That's what he would do. That's what he had always done, because he couldn't let anyone else take the burden from him, wouldn't inflict the knowledge on anyone else. Wouldn't let another understand his curse.

Even though he needed to so badly.

Jenn rolled over and huddled under her blankets against the cold. At the rate Robert was going, if the Angel of Darkness didn't kill him, the demon certainly would.

The future, like the past, beckoned Robert with every step he took towards the coast. Long, hot, dusty days and cold, icy nights, empty but for Jenn's presence. A last few precious days when, for reasons of her own, she chose not to remember that she hated him. Instead, she kept him company, sometimes in silence, at other times, in talk. About Andrew or his mother or some other safe topic. He knew what she was doing – just as he'd done for her on the journey out.

But even as she talked she was holding something back, hiding herself just as he did – he could see it so clearly it was painful. She had shut her pain and fear away; nothing he could say to her would ever change that. The closer she got to returning to Flan'har, the more the memory of her actions would affect her.

One day he would have to address it, or she was unlikely to use her powers again, no matter what the reason. Such an attitude could quite possibly kill her.

Other matters, however, wouldn't wait. In just a few days, he would be back in Flan'har, a growing army preparing to follow him into a battle he would have given almost anything to avoid.

And still, Jenn told him nothing about Nash – or at least, nothing he could use. It was as though the man had never played any part in her life. Robert couldn't bring himself to ask again, and couldn't contemplate any image of Nash that didn't encompass Jenn. Couldn't begin to think of Nash without having to suppress some bitter rage at what he had done to Eachern . . .

. . . or without being jealous of the time he had spent with Jenn.

Soon he would meet the man, on the battlefield, with Selar's army behind him. A coward's act that, ravaging a whole country because he couldn't find the Key on his own. But how would Nash feel, believing Jenn was dead?

For once, the demon gave a little hiccough and subsided under the pressure of satisfaction. Yes, there was something to smile about. Nash would be devastated – though that might make him a more dangerous foe.

Oh, what the hell – what could possibly be more dangerous than the Angel of Darkness, in whatever mood?

Robert had smelled the sea a full day before they reached the coast. It floated on the air like an enticement. Noru Imbel hadn't changed a whit in the few days they'd been gone. The smells, noise, crowds and heat enfolded him in a blanket of familiarity. It would have been so nice to lose himself in it, to convince Jenn – with some miracle of words – to forgive him, for them both to just run away from everything. Leave all responsibility, destiny and all that other rubbish far behind them. Live as normal people, together, in peace, without some damned prophecy pushing them here and there – and forever away from each other.

Twice, as they rode through the town, the words came to his lips, but they remained unspoken. If there was one thing he had learned over the years, it was that he couldn't leave Lusara. Not really – and especially not now. How much he could really help the country remained to be seen, but there was no way he could desert Lusara and just hand it to Nash. Jenn would never care for him again if he did – and nor should she. The whole idea was laughable.

He sold the horses without any trouble, paying for a passage on the same ship north. The captain recognised them, winking at Robert when Jenn smiled a greeting.

They even got the same cabin. Predictably, Jenn remained on deck to watch the dock drift away. Robert stowed their gear and joined her by the rail as sailors and dockmen hoisted ropes, freeing the ship to go on its way. Wind caught the sails in snatches and the ship lurched out of the harbour, leaving Budlandi and everything else behind in its wake.

'I'd like to come back here one day,' Jenn murmured, her chin on her hands as she leaned over the rail. Even now she exuded an air of isolation, despite her easy conversation. 'I always wanted to travel and see places like that. I wish we could have stayed longer. I'm going to miss the warmth, that's for sure.'

'Well, Lusara is on the brink of spring,' Robert replied evenly. 'You won't have to wait long before the sun browns your face again.'

'Am I brown?'

Robert chuckled. 'It suits you, brings out the colour of your eyes.' When she frowned a little, he quickly looked away, studied the diminishing harbour. There were moments when it was too easy to forget. The past, the future, all washed away. She'd always had that effect on him; probably always would. He was just going to have to try harder to hide it.

'Robert?'

'Mmn?'

'How do you feel?'

For a moment, he froze, his hands silently gripping the rail as though the ship might toss him overboard. Slowly, he turned to find her eyes full of something – but nothing he could name. Had she guessed what he was thinking? Had he really become so transparent?

He forced words to come out. 'What do you mean?'

'I'm sorry – it's just that . . . well, you've been so quiet since we left the Palace.'

'I've had a lot to think about.'

'The Generet?'

Deliberately, Robert shrugged. 'Let's hope Patric finds something useful without getting his throat cut. I'm beginning to wish I hadn't let him go.'

'I doubt you could have stopped him. He's a scholar at heart and this is the biggest mystery of his life. Do you really think the Generet came from Alusia?'

He turned back to the sea. 'You seem to have some considerable faith in my ability to understand all this. But even if I could, would that make any difference?'

'What do you mean?'

Robert kept his voice low. 'It doesn't matter if we comprehend the prophecy. We do know what Nash is. We came here to arm ourselves against him, to be as prepared as he. We may have failed in that attempt, but even so, I must still face him. He *is* the threat we believe him to be, and whether we like it or not, he does know what he's doing.'

'Are you telling me you've changed your mind about the Key? That you've decided to accept the prophecy?'

'Never. I've always fought against it because I knew it was wrong. Now I cannot give in, even if I wanted to.'

'Why?'

'Because,' Robert paused, paring the truth, 'it conflicts with a vow I made.'

She frowned, obviously wanting to ask the question, but something held her back. In the end, she put her hand on his arm. 'So, how do you feel?'

'How do you think I feel?'

'It's just that . . . I was worried about . . . '

His head snapped up and he took a step back, unable to stop his reaction. Stiffly now, he said, 'Of course. You were worried about the demon. Well, don't be. I'm sure you can see it's well contained.' Damned idiot! Again. Once more, he'd allowed himself to be fooled by the prospect of a little hope – no matter how fragile. She really didn't care about him at all – all she was worried about was whether he'd lose control and use the Word of Destruction again. Blanching the bitterness from his voice, he added, 'Jenn, believe me, I feel absolutely fine.'

'By the gods, I wish you would stop doing that!' she hissed, her eyes flaring with sudden anger. 'How am I supposed to . . . if you keep . . . Oh!'

Before he could say another word, she turned and stormed across the deck to disappear below.

It seemed the past and the future were one and the same after all.

Jenn slammed the cabin door behind her, but there was hardly enough space to move, let alone to pace up and down. With a gasp, she lashed out at the wall and kicked hard.

Why, why, why? Again the same stupid, useless questions! Her whole life was filled with them, empty caverns echoing frustration and ignorance. No matter how hard she tried, nothing ever changed. The wallowing darkness gathered around her, draining her will to ask. What was the point? She'd never know, never be able to see what she was doing wrong until it was too late.

Calm. She had to stay calm.

But . . . dammit! Why? Why couldn't he just talk to her for a change? Let down those walls just a little. Was he really so conceited that he believed that nobody, under any circumstances, could possibly help him?

Her fists clenched, digging her nails into her palms. She had to stay calm. She'd done it so far, controlled that . . . seething mess inside her, and she would continue doing it, but she *had* to stay calm!

Robert would keep her in ignorance. He wouldn't talk about what he was thinking or feeling and he would certainly never tell her the ending of the prophecy. Hadn't he already admitted that she was involved? So didn't she have a right to understand? How could she do anything, how was she supposed to help if she didn't know what the hell was going on?

By the gods, why had one little thing he'd said set her off like this? How could she possibly be so angry at . . . at . . .

She came to a halt, wheezing in air, hot tears stinging her eyes. Fury snapped at her, goading her, taunting her.

She would lose control. One day she would, and when that happened . . .

The power had used her, torn through her body as though she were nothing. He'd arched his back, frozen in time as the blast hit him. In that second, she'd stolen his life, extinguished it for ever . . .

And Andrew had watched her do it, watched as she'd stood there and let her body be abused by a force she'd never guessed existed . . .

'Jenn?'

Her head came up, but she couldn't face him. She forced herself to respond, to get him away. Now, before she could be used like that again. Before she could kill again. 'Leave me alone, Robert.'

'No, not this time.'

The door closed, but Jenn's eyes were shut against him, against his presence and everything that it wasn't. He'd once loved her and now, now he no longer even trusted her.

Serin's blood, why was she here? Why was *she*, of all people, involved in this?

'Jenn, let me help.' His voice was soft but insistent, moving closer. Full of nothing but . . . but . . . certainty. Damned insufferable certainty! Nothing else. Nothing more.

'I don't need your help. Go away!' Sobs racked her body, but she wouldn't give in. Not until he left. He had to go or she'd . . .

'Jenn, please. I can help you. Just talk to me.'

His hand touched her shoulder – and she could hold it back no longer. She spun around, her whole body seething with rage. She struck out at him, her hands flailing punches he made no move to defend against. She pushed him back against the door, her breath rasping, tears blinding her, but it wasn't enough. Too much and not enough. She wanted to lash out . . . to let that . . . power . . .

'Let it go, Jenn. Go on, I can contain it.'

'No, you . . . you . . . I hate you!' she wailed, edging closer to a precipice she'd walked for too long. 'Should never have come to Clonnet! You . . . interfered and made me . . . I . . . '

'Let it go.'

And once again it ripped through her, blinding, breathtaking, awesome, until at the last she remembered who she struck out against. Only then did she draw back, killing the fire with a desperate thought. Empty, she collapsed to her knees, sobbing dry tears.

A movement. Hands beneath her, lifting her, placing her on the bed.

She hadn't killed him.

This time, when the wound opened up, it didn't bleed any more.

She hadn't killed him. She'd trusted him and he hadn't failed her. Even the ship continued to rock and sway, soothing and soft.

A cup was pressed to her hands, her head held so she could drink. She swallowed with difficulty, but he was patient, letting her sip. Gentle. More calming than a whole world of sea. No matter what she said to him, no matter what she did, he still looked after her.

And by the sheer grace of Mineah alone, she had managed not to kill him.

He brought something to rest her head on then settled on the edge of the bed. Softly, he began, 'You'll never know how sorry I am that I didn't kill Eachern. But it's not only that you killed him, is it? It's the way it happened. The moment, the shock, the surprise – and the power. An entirely lethal combination. It rips through you as though you were made of straw, caring nothing of what you really want, what you think – even whether you want to use the power or not. It simply takes over, robbing you of will, making you, in that second, a puppet, a slave to something you cannot control. And it's very personal, killing like that. Your power is a part of your soul. That's why we have combat training and the Malachi have the Dariet D'Azzir. That's why I carry a sword.'

He fell silent and she opened her eyes to find him staring at his hands. As though he sensed her gaze upon him, he continued, 'I'm sorry, Jenny. I've been a fool all along, and all I've done is hurt you. I never meant to. I only ever wanted to protect you – but it seems even that is beyond me. I should have told you more. Aiden was right, but I wouldn't listen. He understood what you needed much better than I did. But I was so caught up with . . . '

'Father Aiden . . . ' Jenn paused, swallowing to clear her throat. 'He told me I should talk to you about it because you knew exactly what it's like to be . . . used like that. I thought he meant when you used the Word – but it's not just that, is it?'

'No.' Robert shook his head. 'Not any more. And that damned priest sees far more than he should. Still, it's my own fault. I asked him to talk to you. It never occurred to me to ask what he'd said.'

'He's a good friend.'

'More than I deserve.' Robert reached out and took the cup from her. He rose and refilled it from the barrel in the corner. When he returned, he didn't sit, simply held the cup out. 'I'll leave you now and let you get some rest.'

'No, Robert.' Jenn ignored the water. 'Stay and talk to me.'

He looked, for a moment, terribly vulnerable. 'I think I've done enough damage for one day. I'll come back later.'

'No. Stay.' She reached out and caught his hand, saw him

grimace – then looked down. The flesh was red and raw – on both his hands. He tried to draw away, but she pursued him, sitting up. 'Did I do that?'

He snatched his hands away, hiding them behind his back. 'Please, Jenn, it's nothing.'

She studied him for a moment. Her face felt solid and crusty, as though parts of it hadn't woken from a deep sleep, but she wasn't going to back down this time. Not when she'd been the cause of this.

Taking in a fortifying breath, she slid off the bed and faced him squarely. 'Robert Douglas, if you don't sit down and let me look at those hands, I'll hit you with something considerably worse than that feeble blast you saw just now.'

'Feeble?' An involuntary laugh escaped him, to be suppressed beneath that awesome control once more.

'Sit!'

'Well, since you put it that way.' He sat on the side of the bed as Jenn turned to the water barrel. First, she splashed some on her face, drying it quickly on a towel. Then she poured some into a bowl and brought it back to him. She pulled up the stool and sat, taking his right hand onto her lap. She held it over the bowl and rinsed water over it. Immediately he hissed.

'How does that feel?'

'Still asking questions you already know the answer to.'

'Oh.' She kept her head down. The burns weren't bad – at least, not as bad as when she'd split his *ayarn*. They would be sore for a couple of days, but nothing more. She took his other hand.

'Ow!'

'Oh, don't be a baby!' It was hard not to laugh. Not at Robert, but the whole cursed situation between them. He hurt her – she hurt him. Back and forth like some bizarre fencing match. Perhaps it was time they stopped and drew a line. Not the line she wanted so dearly, but maybe one they could both live with.

'By the gods, Robert, I don't know.' Jenn got up to get some fresh water. 'I swear there's one person in this world who hates you more than Nash does.'

'More than you do, even?'

'Yes, even more than me.'

'Who?'

'You!'

She caught his frown of puzzlement before she sat again and bent her head to her work. 'You are a fool, Robert. You've spent your whole life trying to help people one way or the other, but you don't stop there, do you? You take their suffering onto yourself. You absorb it. Haven't you learned anything from the demon? Don't you realise that you just keep feeding it, making it stronger?'

'I nearly get killed trying to help you and in return I get a lecture. I suppose I deserve it. Very well, next time I'll just let you sink the ship. I don't care, I can swim.'

'You twist yourself up inside trying to protect everyone, to ease their fear, their discomfort, their pain, to make them laugh. Yet you never pay the same attention to how you feel.'

'Well,' Robert replied lightly, 'you can't have it both ways. Either I act according to other people's needs, or I do what I want – and they're unlikely to have the same effect. I can't find a place somewhere in the middle. Such a heaven doesn't exist.'

'But do you know what you want? Have you even paused long enough to ask?' She glanced up to find him watching her, a faint, whimsical smile around his eyes.

'Well, yes, occasionally. I want to live in a peaceful world. I want my country free from tyranny, my people to live in prosperity and justice.' He paused. 'And, for dessert, I'd like the Angel of Darkness to drop dead.'

Jenn smiled. 'Again, you're thinking of it in terms of other people. What do you want, for yourself?'

'Right now?' He lifted his head again to look at her, an eyebrow raised comically.

'If you like,' Jenn laughed.

There was a long pause before he answered, 'You won't like it.'

'Robert, you're in no condition to throw me out of the cabin.'

'Oh,' he murmured, as though crestfallen. For a long moment, he said nothing. Then, when she was about to insist, he drew in a deep breath and added, 'In that case, I'll have to settle for this.'

Without another word, he leaned forward and kissed her.

Jenn sprang to her feet and the bowl dropped to the floor. Heedless, she turned away, both hands to her mouth. Suddenly it was difficult to breathe and she had to concentrate hard to get air inside her, slow the pounding in her chest.

Robert stood, his voice full of apology and regret. 'By the gods, Jenn, I'm sorry! I never meant . . . I mean I . . . Oh, hell, I've done it again. I really think I should leave this time.'

The door was open before she could utter a word. 'Robert, wait.'

'No, Jenn, you don't need to say anything. I'm just very, very sorry. I'll stay out of your way until we dock.'

And then he was gone.

18

A jagged breeze swept across the deck, filling the sails as Robert strode beneath them. He kept away from the captain, the crew, everyone. He finally came to an empty spot by the railing where a huge bollard sat on the deck, rope as thick as his arm winding around its base. No mess, no tangle, just simple lines, easy to follow, easy to unravel.

What was wrong with him? After everything she'd just gone through – what was he, to take advantage of her like that, abuse the trust she'd only just placed in him?

Ignoring the pain in his hands, he gripped the railing hard. Damned, stupid idiot! Couldn't just help her, ease her pain and then leave her in peace. No, he had to go and spoil their tentative alliance by behaving like an adolescent! It wasn't her trust alone he'd betrayed, now he couldn't even trust himself to bury his feelings, just like the last time when he'd given into the Bonding.

He turned his face into the wind. The sea stretched before him, untouched, choppy and empty. The sun dragged towards the horizon and he watched every moment of it, unable to move, to find the will to leave. In silence he watched the passengers drift below until the sky grew pale, washed with undefined colour.

He'd gambled and lost. He'd come all this way to find nothing, allowing hope to lead him on, allowing disappointment to cloud his thinking. Once again, the only consequence was the pain of another. In trying to make amends, he had hurt Jenn. Now, in trying to save Lusara from Nash, he would hurt her too. Men would die, people he knew and loved. Those he'd never met.

In the act of salvation, you will become desolation itself . . .

What was the point of fighting it? Every action he took only hastened him towards the ultimate destruction.

No!

He would die first! He would never give in. *Never!* Even if it meant Nash would win. Even if it meant there was no one left to stop him taking Jenn . . .

But could he really do that? Leave her to her fate – just so he wouldn't be the one to kill her? Just so she could survive?

Her soft voice entered his mind, sinking him in a moment. *At the age of nine, you went before the Key. It gave you a prophecy and the Word. On that day, you learned to hide and the demon was born. You hid from your parents, your brother – even from Micah. You've learned to hate yourself because you think you're not strong enough to fight it. I warned you once before that the demon would kill you. Now you're rushing it on, almost willing it to happen. Is the pain of failure so terrible you would rather die than find some other way to live with it?*

Dark as the night, Robert shook his head.

You cannot hide any more, Robert. You can't afford to. The cost is too high. Isn't that why you wouldn't let me hide? Can't you see what you keep doing to yourself?

In the shadows to his left, a movement. She was there, watching him, but he couldn't look at her.

'You don't understand,' he replied dully. 'There is no other way to live with it. Don't you think I've tried?'

'No. I think you've always been too afraid to find out.'

'Of course I'm afraid of the prophecy.'

'Not only that.'

Hesitant, stilled, his voice was nothing more than a whisper. 'What else?'

'Of me.'

Robert couldn't move, didn't dare. Instead, he let the cool breeze brush against his face, forcing calm into him from without. He closed his eyes and dropped his head, but still he knew when she left him.

Jenn didn't bother lighting a lamp. She shrugged off her cloak and felt her way to the bed, sinking onto the end. She shouldn't have gone up there in the first place. She had only made things worse. Not just for him.

With a groan, she buried her face in her hands and failed completely to stop the shaking. Never in her whole life had she felt so alone.

A noise, outside the door. Then it opened. Instantly she sat up, furiously rubbing her eyes in the darkness. He didn't move for a moment, but his presence almost filled the room, until she thought she would suffocate. Abruptly the lamp hanging from the ceiling flickered into life and she almost jumped. Robert closed the door, then turned to the bench and poured some wine into a cup. With his back to her, he took a mouthful, straightened his shoulders and turned around.

His strong face was set with a determination she'd never seen before. When he spoke, his voice was both sharp and soft, as if he were holding on so tight he could hardly move. 'You want me to tell you the end of the prophecy? Is that the only way I can make you understand?'

Hardly able to contain the trembling in her hands, Jenn lifted her head and met his gaze without flinching. Courage. That's all she had left now. 'What exactly am I supposed to understand?' Jenn continued, relentless. 'Should I have run away and not married Eachern? Should I have killed him before you ever found out what he'd done to me? Actually, I think it would have been better if you'd just left me in the forest of Shan Moss all those years ago. You'd never have known what happened to me, never understood my part in the prophecy and I . . . I wouldn't have been around to give you so much cause to hate yourself. Perhaps,' she swallowed deliberately, 'I could have lied and told you Andrew was your son. I nearly did once, hoping to make you feel better about the Bonding.' She stopped at that, unable to continue. If she wasn't careful, she'd tell him the truth – and then he would never forgive her.

His gaze widened with horror and disbelief. 'No. You wouldn't have . . . '

Jenn dropped her gaze, fighting useless tears. 'What else could I do, Robert? When I've been the cause of so much pain in your life?'

'You fool!' he whispered. He came across the small cabin, dropping to his knees before her. He lifted her face with his hand, his eyes holding hers, searching, looking for something. 'You have never caused me pain! It's my weakness that does all this, nothing else. I'm sorry I couldn't hide it better . . . '

'Don't hide, Robert,' Jenn whispered softly. Her heart pounded in her chest, her stomach turned somersaults, but still she held on. She lifted her hand to touch his face in turn, to brush the backs of her fingers over his cheek.

He caught her hand, hard. 'Don't! I won't have you sacrifice anything more for me. You don't know how little it would take. You can't trust me, you know that.'

'The sacrifice,' Jenn swallowed again, 'would be to *not* trust you.' She turned his hand in hers, bringing it to her lips. His fingers clenched, his mouth moved, but no sound came out. Finally, he frowned.

'You're mad!'

'Yes. And that is your fault.'

He snatched his hand away, his breathing ragged and unkempt. He blinked, trying desperately to regain some kind of control. Jenn wanted to laugh and cry at the same time, wanted to reach out to him, ease that frown, touch him, and let him share, give him something – anything – to hold onto other than the pain.

'Robert, please believe me . . . '

He flinched. 'Damn you!' Then his mouth was on hers, crushing and sweet, salty with her tears. When they parted, he rested his forehead on hers, his eyes closed.

'How can you hate me so much and yet . . . '

'Oh, Robert, I never hated you. I was just . . . angry because . . . because you didn't love me any more and you'd promised and . . . ' She couldn't mention trust. Not now, not at this moment. 'I . . . I blamed you for coming back to Clonnet. And, Robert, you stayed away for so long even though I knew your damned sense of honour would keep you away because I was married. But then, you didn't stay away, did you?'

Slowly, his head came up. 'You knew about that?'

'Father Aiden told me.'

He took her hands, his gaze dropping. 'Then you don't hate me?'

'No.'

'Not even a little?'

'Why, do you want me to?'

His eyes lifted, forming the shyest smile she'd ever seen. 'Then I guess I really have been a fool.' He kissed her again, long and deep this time, aching and tender. His arms came around her and she held onto him. Carefully, without letting go, he rose a little and sat on the bed beside her, pulling her closer.

His lips brushed her forehead, his fingers lifting the hair away from her face. His green eyes were filled with wonder and awe. 'You have no idea how much I've wanted to do that. So many times I came so close.'

Jenn gazed up at him. Relief, pain and longing all rushed through her, so swiftly it took her breath away. 'That day by the stream – I thought you were going to kiss me, and then you didn't.'

He smiled, gently. 'Would you have stopped me?'

'I don't think so.'

He grinned. 'Damn! But I suppose, as it turned out, with that constable watching, it was a good thing I didn't.' He allowed her a small laugh, then his eyes held hers steady. There were questions there, hesitations, doubts.

He took her hand, pressing the palm to his lips. 'You are so beautiful,' he murmured against her skin, his eyes on hers. Her hand shook in his, but still she couldn't move. Then he drew her close once more, kissing her, drowning her words, her thoughts, every sense she had. She fell into that place, willing the peace to fill her, build her again, into what she had been before.

One by one, the layers of distrust and anger were peeled back and she saw herself, not as a creature, pathetic and lonely, but strong and loving, determined and independent. She became once more the one he loved. Returned to it, refilled it – and found she had always been there, beneath those layers. The loss of him had put her in that prison, and now the return of him set her free. She emerged whole, luxuriating in the taste of him, his smell, his touch. How could she have lived so long without this?

With a moan, he drew her down, wrapping his arms around her. She burned with his warmth. Unconsciously her body moved in to fit against his. She could feel his heart beating as hard as hers, feel the urgency of his kisses match hers, growing stronger every moment. So many years, so much time lost. So empty. But now he was here, and he loved her, just as he'd said he always would.

Without thought, her hands moved inside his shirt to feel the hard flesh, yielding and firm, solid and very real. Her fingers traced a scar on his chest and she moved to kiss it, tenderly, over the smooth edge. He shuddered, a reluctant groan escaping as his mouth found hers again. Deft and sure, his hand slipped the gown from her shoulder. His lips moved down her throat, gaining new ground. Fingers reached her bodice, unlacing it slowly, brushing his skin against hers, sending shivers over her whole body. He moved gently, as though afraid she would change her mind, as though this would turn out to be nothing more than a dream. His breathing was short, rapid, matching hers. The touch of his skin against hers ignited feelings inside her she thought she'd forgotten.

After a moment, he drew back, his eyes seeking hers. He took her hand and kissed her fingers. He held his breath a moment then a look of pain washed across his face. 'No.'

'No?'

'Yes but no.' Those eyebrows rose, vulnerable again. 'It'll probably kill me – but I'd rather wait.'

'What?' Jenn wanted to laugh at the idea. 'Haven't we waited long enough?'

'Too long, my love – but just a little longer. If you don't mind, I'd rather have a priest's blessing *first* this time.'

'A priest?' Jenn whispered, wide-eyed.

Robert grinned. 'We could arrange it for the day after we get back to Bleakstone. Aiden would do it – he'd love to. He's just an old romantic at heart.'

'But . . . what about the prophecy?'

'My dear, sweet, lovely Jenny. I'm going to love you for the rest of my life, whether we're married or no. It won't matter a whit to the prophecy.' He kissed her forehead and brushed his lips down to hers. She could feel his body warming against hers, despite his words.

Could she wait? A few more days, after so many years?

She smiled and pulled him close again. How could she not?

'But whatever you do,' he murmured into her hair, 'don't start all over again, asking me what I want to do right now.'

Huge white gulls swooped down across the path of the ship as it dipped and swung its way towards the shore. Their cries rang out against the flapping sails, caught in a cross-wind blown between the crusty cliffs either side of the approaching port. The green of Flan'har greeted them with sunshine, but little of the warmth of the southern continent. Instead, the breeze had a chill to it, but it was familiar, like home.

Robert stood with Jenn in the prow of the ship, gazing at the shoreline, counting the fishing boats. He had one hand on the rail, the other around her waist. She was trapped between him and the sea, her head back against his shoulder. Without even looking, he knew there was a smile on her face.

As there was on his.

Miracles were such odd creatures, never warning you when they were about to strike. But who cared, as long as they did. As long as this one did.

As long as this one affected the demon in this manner. Never in his life had it been so quiet. Unless he looked really closely, it was almost invisible, having no more power over him than those seagulls. A miracle indeed.

'I think I love this ship,' Jenn laughed. 'It's odd to think I'd never been on one before this trip. For some reason, I feel like I've been sailing all my life.'

'So you've managed to forget how sick you were the first time.'

'But of course! Memory is good like that. You should try it some time.'

'Don't worry, I will.'

'I know this is going to sound strange,' Jenn said, her face half-buried against his cloak, 'but if you don't mind, I'd rather keep this quiet for the moment. If nothing else, we have to remember I'm still officially dead. I don't want people to get all distracted about what is really going on at Bleakstone.'

'To be honest,' Robert replied easily, 'I don't really want to share this with anyone just yet either. I'm still not sure I believe it myself.'

She laughed softly, the sound dying away in the wind. Without moving she added, 'You do realise, don't you, that when we get married . . . Andrew will be your son?'

'Yes. Why? Do you think I'd disown him simply because he happened, by some terrible twist of fate, to have the wrong father? Careless of him, I'll admit – but he's just a boy. He can't help it. Between us, however, I think we can make sure he becomes something considerably better than the monster who sired him.'

'I'm not sure that's possible.'

The words were so soft, Robert wasn't sure he'd heard right. 'What did you say?'

'Nothing. What's that? There, on the horizon?' Jenn asked, pointing east. 'It looks too big to be a fishing vessel.'

Robert squinted into the distance at the tall masts of the galleon. No colours were flying, but that was quite deliberate. 'One of Grant's ships, I'd say. There are six in all, though only one sits on the horizon at a time.'

'Why?'

He gestured towards the taller cliff. 'See there? It's a beacon. When we get word from Micah that Selar's army is ready to move, that beacon will be lit. By the time our army reaches the port, the ships will be in, ready for the men to board. They'll sail from here west to the port of Aaran and there the men will march north to Shan Moss.'

Jenn twisted around to glance up at him, her hands holding his around her waist. 'Kavanagh's risking a lot helping you like this. Does he really feel so bad about Rosalind?'

Robert grinned. 'That and a few other things.'

'What?'

He pursed his lips – but just looking at her made him want to laugh. To be able to watch her, hold her like this, just simply be with her was more than he'd ever hoped for. Was it possible to make this moment last for ever?

'A few years ago, I helped him out with a small problem he had.'

'Small? Why, Robert Douglas, I think you're not telling me the whole truth.'

'I quake when you use that tone on me, you know. Shiver right down to my boots.'

She giggled, going up on her toes to kiss his cheek. He turned his face in time to catch her, allowing the fire inside him to be ignited by that small touch. She put a hand to his chest, raising her eyebrows in warning. 'Don't you think you can get me all distracted now. And it's too late anyway. We'll be docking in a few minutes. Tell me about Grant.'

He laughed, pulling her close again, but behaving this time. 'Before my father died, Grant came to live at Dunlorn, to learn about courts and government and such. It had always been something of a tradition with the Dukes of Flan'har and the Earls of Dunlorn. My father didn't like Grant very much – Mother is still wary of him – but really, he's as harmless as they come. Just before Caslemas, Grant got a letter from his father, telling him that he was to be betrothed. He was to leave Dunlorn inside the month and return home to meet his bride.'

'Did he know her at all?'

'Actually, yes. In fact, he had always kind of hoped his father would choose her. The problem was that Grant, being such a contrary creature, disliked being ordered around like that, so he spent the entire Caslemas celebrations wooing every lass he could get his hands on. We used to hold a big gathering in those days, so you can imagine how busy he was. Of course, like an idiot, he managed to court a young lady who was far too clever for him. Fortunately, I was the only one who came across them hidden in an alcove. I caught them just as she was telling him he would have to marry her first.'

Jenn began to laugh, the movement against his chest filling him with warmth despite the cold. 'Oh dear.'

'Exactly. Anyway, when she'd gone, Grant took me to one side. I've never seen anyone look more sheepish. He confessed he felt little for this lady and really wanted to go home, but now he was trapped. He couldn't tell her the truth or her family would hold him to his reluctant promise. Remember, he wasn't actually betrothed as yet. He practically got down on his knees and begged me to help him.'

'And did you?'

'What else could I do? I found the girl a little later in the day and quietly set about wooing her myself.'

'What?'

'It might come as a surprise to you, my dear,' Robert replied, convincingly wounded, 'but some girls, occasionally, have found me quite attractive.'

She bit in her lip to stop her laughter. 'Poor souls. So what happened?'

'Well, of course, she found my attentions far preferable to those of Grant. She ran cold on him within a day and by the end of the next, was preparing the same speech for me as she'd given him. I'm ashamed to admit, I took her to my father. He, naturally, hit the roof.'

'You would have married her?'

Robert paused to brush a strand of hair from Jenn's face. 'I did.'

All laughter vanished from her eyes. 'Berenice? But I thought you were betrothed as children.'

'We were little more than that, but that's only Finnlay's memory of the thing. He was a child when it all happened. I was fourteen. Old enough to think her pretty, too young to realise what an idiot I was.'

'What did your father say?'

'Oh, once she was out of the room, he didn't spare me. Mother was no help either. They just told me that if I was foolish enough to get myself involved like that, then I would have to face the consequences. We were officially betrothed within a week, by which time, Grant was well on his way home. Berenice and I didn't actually get married until long after that, once Selar had thrashed his way across the country. For a while, Finnlay got it into his head I was relieved to have an excuse not to marry her. But he was wrong. I did want to marry her. I thought she was lovely.'

He glanced down to find Jenn was watching him, a soft smile on her face. 'I'm glad.'

Robert nodded. 'Me too.'

'But you never told Grant?'

'Actually, I've tried to, many times – but he just thinks I'm trying to be noble.'

'Obviously he doesn't know you as well as the rest of us.' Jenn laughed lightly and turned back towards the dock, now very close. 'And don't worry, I won't mention a word of it when I meet him. Will he be at Bleakstone?'

'Probably, though I keep trying to get him to stay away. It's bad enough I'm marshalling an army within his borders; there's no need to have Selar think Flan'har is a threat on its own.'

Jenn raised a hand to point at the dock. 'Look at that. Isn't that Owen?'

'Where?'

'In the blue cloak, by the nets. I think he's waving. He doesn't look happy.' She paused. 'Could Micah have come back already?'

'No. The beacon would be lit to bring the ships in. It must be something else. Come on, let's get the bags.'

The press of people on the dock bordered on the dangerous but Robert was tall enough to steer Jenn clear and down the end to where Owen waited.

'Welcome back, my lord. I have horses waiting. Don't worry, we've not heard a word from Micah.'

Without insisting on further explanation out here, in the open, Robert took Jenn's arm and followed behind Owen until they reached a hostelry set back from the dock. There, Owen took the bags and slung them over his horse. His lined, familiar face was grave as he glanced around to make sure they were alone.

'What is it?' Robert murmured.

'Bad news, my lord. About the Duke of Ballochford.'

'McGlashen?' Cold fear gripped Robert's stomach. 'What about him?'

'He's all right – it's his family. Two weeks ago . . . they were all murdered.'

Jenn's hand swiftly covered her mouth while the other reached for Robert. Immediately he put his arm around her shoulders.

'By the gods! How?'

'The details are sketchy. Apparently, the Duke was moving his family somewhere safe before coming here. He rode on ahead with only his little boy. The rest never arrived. He found them hours later, slaughtered on the road. Every man, woman and child. He sent us a message. We're expecting him at Bleakstone tonight.'

'Serin's blood, poor Donal!' Robert breathed. He glanced down at Jenn. 'Nash knows what we're doing. He's trying to scare off anyone who'll support me. We've run out of time. I just hope Micah's still safe. Let's go.'

19

The forest around Bleakstone Castle was so pretty that, now spring had finally warmed the ground a little, Margaret found it impossible not to escape the stone walls, go beyond the camp fires of the army and roam among the trees. Almost every day she rode out, choosing a direction at random, stopping when the moment felt right, walking until she'd had enough. After five years living within the closed caves at the Enclave, this small freedom seemed too precious to waste.

It was a shame Finnlay, Fiona and the children couldn't be here too. Finnlay had now been at the Enclave almost seven years and although he hardly mentioned it any more, the time was wearing on him. As a boy, he'd never found it easy to sit still for more than a few minutes at a time, quite the opposite of Robert. Finnlay had always been out, running around, getting into mischief, breaking things, offending people, arguing with his teachers and his father. All his life, he'd been active; no surprise, then, that all his efforts at the Enclave failed to completely fill that burning energy he'd been born with.

Margaret turned her horse onto a path which wound by the stream. When she reached the rock pool, she dismounted and let the animal wander, nibbling for sweet grasses among the stones. She was about to sit when she realised she wasn't alone. A tall figure came along the path towards her, hands folded together, head bowed a little in contemplation, paying no attention to the beauty around him.

When he saw her horse, he stopped and looked around, finally noticing her with a smile and a wave. 'Good morning, Lady Margaret.'

'Good morning to you, Father Aiden.'

The priest came to the edge of the rock pool and crouched down to dangle his fingers in the cool water. He wore simple clothes, brown trousers, jacket and boots. The only sign of his vocation was the wooden trium hanging close to his throat.

'It's hard to believe this place was covered in snow only a few days ago,' he began, glancing up at the trees with their new green buds, fresh and eager. 'I came down here the day after I arrived and this pool was solid ice. I walked from one side to the other and not a crack appeared.'

Margaret sat on her rock and watched him. After a moment, she said, 'I wonder . . . do you enjoy the freedom you have now? After two years in prison?'

He glanced up quizzically and she hurried to clarify the question. 'I mean, you've not really been able to go back to your life, have you? The work you do has little involvement with priestly matters. You can't live in your own country or take up the mantle of Bishop. Although you are no longer confined within dungeon walls, is this freedom enough for you?'

'Freedom,' he replied, sitting on a rock opposite her, 'is subjective. Very often, it's nothing like what we think it is. To a child, freedom is being able to play all day, with no thought of lessons or chores, of responsibility or work. Then there are degrees of freedom. Being able to do some things, but not others.'

'Is there no such thing as complete freedom?'

'Well,' Aiden gave a half-smile, 'that depends on what you want to do. I suppose if you were really well disciplined and managed to contain your ambition within things you already knew you could do, then I guess you could be completely free. However, I've never met such a person. It appears to be a characteristic of freedom which requires you to want something you cannot have – at least in the short term.'

'And what would you do, if you were completely free?' Margaret asked gently.

Aiden frowned. 'I don't know. It's not really a fair question for a priest. As a young man, I chose a life with limited freedom. I can hardly go back on it now.'

'But you're older, wiser . . . '

He began to laugh softly.

'And you're not that young man any more.'

'If you're asking whether I'd still choose the cloister, then I'd have to say yes.'

'Why?' Margaret asked.

'Because . . . ' he paused, looked at her then back at the rock pool, 'it's what I am. Inside. Perhaps now more than ever.'

Margaret steepled her fingers together. 'You take your responsibilities very seriously.'

At that, Aiden smiled. 'In that alone, I do have complete freedom.'

'But do you have answers?'

The smile faded a little as he turned a measuring gaze on her. 'Now I see where your son gets his perception from.'

Now it was Margaret's turn to smile, and she coloured a little. 'I'm sorry, I didn't mean . . . '

'No, it's I who should apologise. But, if I may ask, I know of your years at Saint Hilary's and the close kinship you've always felt for the Church – what answers have you come up with? It must have come as a shock to find out both your sons were sorcerers.'

'I don't think,' Margaret rose from her seat and Aiden followed her to her horse, 'that shock is an adequate word for it.'

Together they walked along the path back towards the castle. 'For some reason, Robert thought I'd guessed. He was afraid of telling me simply because of my relationship with the Church. As usual, he was trying to protect me.'

'It is a failing he has, I admit,' Aiden replied.

'To be honest, after I recovered from the initial horror, I found it rather easy to come to terms with. After all, it answered so many questions – about Robert in particular, but also about his relationship with Finnlay. You have no idea how they used to fight. Those two could keep a cold silence going for a month or more. When Trevor was alive, he tried to force them to make peace, giving them horribly difficult tasks to do, which they had to complete together or fail. In some ways, I think that only made it worse.'

'How so?'

'Finnlay is demanding, quick on his feet, often expecting things to happen instantly. Robert, as I'm sure you've noticed, is quite different. He has a patience I can't begin to emulate – but that very patience served only to irritate Finnlay more and drove him on to provoke Robert. It was exhausting being around them.'

'I'm sure it was. However, I find we're talking once again about your sons. What about you?'

Margaret glanced at him as they emerged from the forest. 'It's not a fair question to ask a mother. I learned early on that it didn't matter whether I could reconcile sorcery with my faith. I love my boys, no matter what they are.'

'But,' Aiden stopped her with a hand on her arm, '*what* are they?'

'I don't know. Does sorcery make a man evil? But you tell me – you know Robert very well, better than I do. Is he evil?'

'A few years ago, I would have said yes, without hesitation.'

'And now?'

'There are people in Lusara who would swear he is – even knowing him as I do.'

'But what do you think?' Margaret pressed on. 'You were at Elita when he used the Word of Destruction. Was that an act of evil? So many people died – and so many lived. It's not a choice I'd like to make.'

'But that's the point. He didn't make it – the choice made itself. If I hadn't been there, seen it for myself . . . it changes so many things, you see.' Aiden paused a moment to look around, unseeing, then he resumed walking, putting his hands behind his back. 'You don't know the hours I've spent rolling it around in my mind. Now I've run out of time. In the next few days, I'll have half a dozen rebel priests to deal with, all asking me the same questions – questions I still can't answer myself. But I've got to tell them something. After five years living and working with a powerful sorcerer, they'll assume I have those answers. Whether I like it or not, they'll look to me for some kind of lead in this matter. What am I to tell them?'

The castle loomed before them, already surrounded by more than four thousand men. Tents scattered across the green fields, punctuated by fenced enclosures where horses danced around in the spring afternoon. For an army preparing for war, the place was remarkably quiet, though certainly not silent. Music, laughter, shouts and dogs barking drifted across the air. This was a busy place, filled with men driven by a common purpose. Too soon, Robert and Jenn would return and lead them all into war.

To a man, they would all know they were following a sorcerer.

'Must you?' Margaret murmured then turned to look at the solemn priest. 'Give them answers? Would it really do any good if you did?' She continued, 'If you had answers, would these priests understand them – not having the exposure to Robert you have? You must see there is a chasm between you and them. You've had five years to think about it, day after day. On the other hand, so have they. Perhaps . . . '

'What?'

Margaret smiled and dropped her gaze. 'I'm sorry, I'm in no position to be offering you advice.'

'Nonetheless . . . '

'Well, perhaps you should give these men the chance to see for themselves – much as Robert did for you. I mean, if he'd just come out and told you sorcery wasn't evil – and then used the Word – would you have believed him? Wanted to go with him? I know things work differently in the Church, but really, you know as well as I do: matters of faith and belief can't be taught, only felt and sensed with the heart. Just as you know you would still choose to be a priest. Just as you have chosen to stay with Robert, despite your questions about what he is. Let them form their own answers, Father. They will, if you give them time.'

'But will they be the right answers?'

'Well,' Margaret shrugged, 'you're still here, aren't you?'

Aiden nodded slowly and smiled. 'You're a wise woman, my lady.'

'Not wise – merely practical. After all, if you don't have any answers, what else can you do?'

He took her arm and they walked towards the castle gate. 'Exactly.'

The courtyard was full of people as Aiden escorted Margaret to the door of the hall. The moment she left him, he turned and asked the nearest man, 'What's going on?'

'The Duke. He's back!'

Aiden's jaw dropped. 'Where is he now?'

The man pointed towards the round tower and Aiden murmured

thanks, his feet already moving. He had to pause at the door as half a dozen men pushed past on their way out.

Robert, as usual, stood at the centre of the chaos, an unusual degree of urgency about his demeanour. He glanced up, saw Aiden and immediately ordered the rest out, with instructions for a meeting in the hall in no more than an hour.

The noise of their departure echoed around the circular room as Robert briskly shut the door. He studied Aiden for a moment. There was concern in his eyes – and something more: an energy Aiden had never seen before, bristling beneath the surface, crying out to be expressed.

'Did you . . . ' Aiden paused, hardly daring to hope, 'find out what you needed to know?'

An involuntary smile flashed across Robert's face, but he turned too quickly for Aiden to catch it.

'More than I bargained for.'

'Where's Jenn?'

'In Mother's rooms. Away from prying eyes.' Robert tossed two more logs onto the fire and waved his hands above it, encouraging the flames with a little of his own. 'By the gods, this place is cold after Budlandi. For the life of me, Bishop, where did all these soldiers come from? How the hell are we feeding them? Aren't they bored yet? You've made a superb impression on the magnates – so much that they were all ready to follow you instead of me if I arrived too late. And where's my mother?'

Aiden came across the room, chuckling hopelessly. 'I'm sure she'll be here any moment.'

'And?' Robert swiftly turned and poured them both some wine, handing a cup to Aiden as he waited for an answer.

'And . . . ' Aiden frowned and concentrated. 'Er . . . I've no idea. You'll have to ask His Grace. And Lusara, of course. In reverse order.'

'The best way.' Robert nodded, draining the cup in one mouthful. 'I've just sent a couple of men north to check on Micah – just to make sure nothing untoward has happened to him. In the light of this terrible business with McGlashen, I don't want to take any risks. Have you heard anything more? Anything from Patric?'

'No.' Aiden paused, taking a sip of wine he didn't really want. He couldn't take his eyes from Robert. 'Tell me, are you feeling all right?'

'Why?' Robert almost buzzed around the table, pulling across bits of paper from every direction. It was as though he couldn't actually bring himself to sit still. In all the last five years, not once had Aiden ever seen him like this. Was it the impending war – or something else?

'Did you get hit on the head while you were gone?'

'No. By the gods, Bishop, what are you on about? I have a meeting in less than an hour and I need to know what I'm talking about – or at least, be able to make the others think I do – which is about normal for me. If you've got something on your mind, come out with it.'

'You've changed.'

Robert glanced at him from hooded eyes. 'Yes. But don't ask me to explain now. I can't – for reasons that will soon become obvious. Just be happy, all right? If it makes you feel any better, I believe, for the first time in five years, you might have actually been right about something.'

Aiden nodded vaguely. 'And Jenn? How is she?'

Again, the involuntary smile. 'Jenn is just fine, Aiden. Now stop dithering and help me get this stuff organised. If I'm not prepared, not one of those magnates is going to follow me into supper, let alone into a war. Come on, don't just stand there.'

Aiden came around the table and put his cup down on an empty space. Unless he missed his guess, something much more important than the prophecy had been discovered in Alusia. If that was indeed the case, he could wait a little longer to find out. If this is what it did to Robert, it was worth the wait. Hiding a burgeoning smile, he said grumpily, 'I've never met a man who treated me with less respect than you do – and you're the one who keeps calling me Bishop!'

'Now keep your temper, Aiden,' Robert laughed, clapping a big hand on his shoulder. 'We don't want the folk out there to think we've quarrelled. It wouldn't leave a very good impression at all. So, tell me, which of these lists has all the new arrivals on it?'

In the cool evening, the valley disappeared within folds of mist, leaving only the highest treetops visible from the window, like craggy rocks in a river of grey. A dozen crows flew low, sweeping down and over, together and separate, weaving in and out. Their cries were an echo of the invisible army settling down for the night. Now and then the mist would move, revealing a glowing fire, figures seated, or moving about. No urgency, no rush. Simply a calm, quiet readiness.

Jenn leaned as far out of the window as she dared, but the sun was gone now and the candlelight behind her wouldn't show her face to anyone. Her fingers were already cold, but she clasped her hands together and blew on them.

'If you're not careful,' Margaret came up behind her, 'somebody will see you.'

'No they won't – and even if they did, who would know it was me?' Jenn turned and smiled. 'I'm sorry, but do you mind if we build the fire up a bit?'

'Not at all, my dear,' Margaret smiled and turned back to the hearth to place two more logs over the flames. Jenn left the window to stand beside her, watching the fierce glow.

'I'm certainly glad you two made it out of that place alive,' Margaret said, picking her sewing from the table. 'What does Robert think about these Generet?'

'He thinks it's possible they might have something to do with Felkri in Alusia, but without talking to them, there's no way to be sure. Perhaps Patric will be able to tell us, when he returns.'

'Let us hope he *does* return.'

'Indeed.'

'It is amazing that you were able to understand so much of what they were saying. And it was all mindspeaking?'

'Yes.' Jenn nodded. 'That was the strange part about it. We'd always believed that mindspeaking only occurred between people who were Bonded, but the Generet were talking to each other, not just in pairs. Robert said he Sensed no other powers around them, that they weren't sorcerers as such. I think he wanted to stay and learn more, but they really did want to kill him.'

'Because he was the . . . Enemy?'

Jenn smiled at the innocent way Margaret used terms she had only recently begun to understand. 'They must know something about the prophecy. What else they know is anybody's guess.

Perhaps when this is all over, we could go back and see if we can find them again.'

Margaret sighed. 'I have to say, sometimes I have trouble keeping track of all this.'

'No you don't,' Jenn laughed. 'You see right through all of us – but you have enough sense to keep quiet about it.'

At that, Margaret turned a completely innocent expression on her. 'I'm sure I don't know what you're talking about.'

Jenn smiled and shook her head. *Robert?*

Yes?

How does it go?

Slowly. What about you?

Your mother keeps looking at me with veiled suspicion. I'm afraid I'm not as good as you at hiding my feelings.

Well, we'll have to tell her after this meeting – and Aiden. If, of course, you still want to go through with this preposterous wedding idea. You must be insane agreeing to marry an old failure like me.

If it is preposterous, you only have yourself to blame. But if you've changed your mind . . .

Are you joking?

Have fun.

You too.

As Jenn's silent voice faded from his mind, Robert sat back in his chair and once again studied the men arranged around the long table. Of course, he'd had no choice about sitting at the head of it. The place had been left for him by every other lord as they'd come in, stating loudly for all to hear – including Robert – exactly who they expected to lead this fight.

The hall was a wash of light, thanks to some twenty huge candles arranged along the tables and on stands in the corners. Torches stood out from the wall opposite the fireplace and in the soft glare, frowns of worry, pale concern – and not a little fear – could be seen on almost every face.

Most of these men he knew. McGlashen, of course, sitting halfway down the table, saying little, but watching carefully. Dark shadows framed his eyes and Robert would rather have released him from this meeting than have him have to hide his pain in such a manner. But Donal wouldn't have gone. He'd paid a high price to be here. Too high for Robert to argue.

Payne sat beside McGlashen, as always, languidly elegant in his attention. Grant Kavanagh – who perhaps stood to lose the most, harbouring a rebellion within his borders – did his best to inject a little humour where he could. Far from keeping quiet, Deverin and Owen had fielded most of the practical questions, only occasionally looking to Robert for confirmation. And there were others, too: men he'd not seen for a long time. Daniel Courtenay, Harold Holland, Kem Raskell and Walter Mauny – friends from years past who'd never known he was a sorcerer. Every now and then one would glance in his direction, a little querulous, a little puzzled.

Only Aiden remained wholly silent, seated close at the opposite end of the table, as though he'd not necessarily wanted to be seen to have any particular influence over the proceedings. The other churchmen sat near him, noisy in their questions, their objections and their problems.

Then there were those Robert had never met before, some of them too young to have been at court with him, others too old. It was these men who provided the greatest difficulty. Some were once-wealthy merchants whose trade had been quartered over the last twenty years. Others, like Bergan Dunn, Earl of Cordor, Robert knew by repute – as he in turn knew Robert.

But strangely, despite the call that had brought them all here, there seemed, on the surface, little of the common purpose that bound the men camped beyond the walls. In this hall sounded little more than voices of dissent.

'That's all very well and good,' Dunn was saying, 'but you can't really expect all of us to go into this without any kind of assurances at all. How do we know what we'll end up with? I've used all my resources to bring almost a thousand men with me. How do I know I'll not end up a pauper?'

Laughter came from the end of the table as a voice replied dryly, 'When the rest of us are grovelling in the gutter, Berg, you'll still be riding on a saddle of gold.'

'I'm not just talking about money, you fool,' Dunn growled. 'We are all staking our lives, some of us the very survival of our Houses, on this venture.'

'And you want guarantees?' Harold leaned forward and placed his meaty hands on the table. 'This is war we're talking about. If you weren't prepared to gamble, you shouldn't have come at all.'

Dunn opened his mouth but a priest interjected, 'While you men quibble about coins, you might also take into account the state the Church will be in once this is over. What do we do about Brome? He sits without proper mandate in a Bishopric which, by rights, belongs to Father McCauly. No true churchman will support this rebellion if there is no guarantee you will all support his reinstatement.'

'Well, I won't support any Bishop,' another man added, 'who won't promise to return my lands to me – those Brome took in his first year!'

A howl erupted at this, men bawling over the top of each other to plead a more desperate case, a greater tragedy, a harsher injustice. Robert allowed the noise to roll over him, his gaze drifting down to meet Aiden's. The priest raised his eyebrows a little, a subtle gesture of patience and encouragement.

With a nod, Robert drew in a breath and pitched his voice to carry over the noise. There was instant quiet. 'It appears I've not made my intentions clear enough for you all to understand.'

Robert got to his feet and stood behind his chair, placing his hands on the carved back. 'While I appreciate the risks you've all taken, what you stand to lose simply by being here, I must however, point out that this is not an invading army we have gathered here. We have a purpose – a single purpose, and one of far greater importance than placing a Bishop on his throne or the return of certain lands. I promise you, if that's all I wanted, then I would have taken Dunlorn and Haddon back from Selar the day I lost them. Now, we have a choice in front of us. Either we sit here and argue who gets the spoils, or we go out of this place and stop Selar's army from invading Mayenne and bringing chaos down on our whole country. The choice is yours.'

The fire crackled and Jenn stepped back, pulling her gown out of the way. She returned to the table and sat, taking her cup in one hand.

Margaret sat opposite, a candle before her, stitching slowly and carefully. 'Do you think Finnlay will be all right?'

'Why do you ask?'

Margaret sighed. 'I know you only saw him for a few days. You couldn't see how restless he's become. And now, with the prospect of Robert fighting this war without him? I fear he'll never recover. It's been bad enough that he can't leave the Enclave and go wandering, but he idolises Robert. He wants to help.'

Jenn watched her carefully. 'And what do you think about this war?'

Margaret looked up from her needlework. 'About the war – or Robert's part in it?'

'I suppose Robert's part.'

For a moment, Margaret stopped stitching. 'Some days, I find it difficult to believe it will really happen. At others, I can't help feeling that he's been heading in this direction since the day his father died. He's trapped in the same way Trevor was. In the end, Trevor died trying to do what was right.'

'Trapped how?'

Margaret resumed her work. 'The best and worst possible way. By love for his country.'

'This is all nonsense!' Dunn bellowed over the rabble of voices clamouring the smallest corners of the hall. 'I'm sorry, Your Grace, but it's simply not practical to focus only on the task immediately before us without taking into consideration the consequences. Armies are not made out of thin air . . . '

'I'm well aware of that,' Robert replied evenly. 'The point is, unless we can come to some agreement, the only consequences we will have to face will definitely be the worst.'

He waited until the noise subsided once more. 'But you are correct in one respect, my lord – this is ridiculous. We've been sitting here for three hours now, throwing things back and forth, scoring points as to whose life has been the hardest hit. For a start, I think the whole concept is sickening, considering Donal's recent loss. I know you've not all come here to simply talk. What I want to know is: why won't anybody ask the question you're all dying to have answered?'

The silence now was complete. Each man found somewhere new to look, with the exception of the priests; as one, they all turned to

Aiden. In response, he stared at his hands a moment, then set his level gaze on Robert.

'You tell them the truth.'

For a moment, Robert had to control a smile. Then he left his place and moved down the table. Men turned to watch him, enthralled. 'The truth is a marvellous instrument and sometimes the most powerful weapon imaginable. But I've already lied to many of you for years, claiming it was the truth. Can you now believe anything else I say?'

At this, McGlashen finally sat forward. 'Come out with it, Robert. You know as well as I do what all this dissent is really about. Are you a sorcerer or not?'

'You know I am,' Robert replied easily, ignoring the rustle of movement around the table. He reached the other end and stood there, his hands clasped together behind his back. 'Some of you have known for a long time; others only suspected it. Deep in your hearts, you both wanted it to be true and hoped it wasn't. Either way, the time has come to face up to the reality. I am a sorcerer and nothing is going to change that.'

'And will you use sorcery to win this war?' Father Chester asked openly, without fear.

Robert had to smile. 'I can't answer that.' When the noise threatened to rise again, he raised his hands to add, 'Only because I don't know. I do know I don't plan to. Does that make a difference?' At this, he leaned forward and placed his hands on the table. 'Does it make a difference at all? I promise you, I would be here, doing this, if I'd never heard of sorcery. Can all of you say the same thing?'

Margaret brought the jug of warmed wine back from the fire and topped up Jenn's cup. For a moment she stood there, her hands clasped around the jug.

'What is it?' Jenn murmured.

'I want to show you something.' Margaret went to her bed and pulled something out from underneath. She brought it back to the table: a long, cloth-bound object, tied with ribbon in three places. Her fingers shaking a little, she pulled at the ribbon and opened the cloth to reveal a sword.

'Where did that come from?' Jenn asked softly, moving closer.

The scabbard was black leather, beautifully cared for, with silver at point and hilt. The sword's handle was strong and heavy and inlaid with gold. No jewels adorned it, save for the black eagle embossed on the blade just peeking out from the cover.

'It belonged to Robert's father, and his father before him. I don't really know how long it's been in the Douglas House. It used to sit in a place of honour in Robert's council room at Dunlorn. He put it there after he married Berenice, swearing he wouldn't wear it again unless in battle. He always promised himself he wouldn't take it down except to clean it or to put it in the hands of his son.' Margaret looked up at Jenn, her fingers resting lightly on the cold steel. 'I brought it with me when I left Dunlorn. I've kept it all this time, hoping Robert would want it back.'

'Does he know you have it?'

'No. I can't help wondering if he hopes it is lost. Do you think I should give it to him? Now?'

Jenn reached out and touched the hilt, felt the smooth working of the black eagle, the sign of the House of Douglas. 'I don't know. Perhaps not today, but before the battle, yes. I think . . . he would like to be reminded that his father also fought for the same cause.'

Margaret nodded with a brief, sad smile. She began wrapping the sword up again.

. . . Jenn . . .

What?

. . . Jenn . . . for pity's sake, help me . . .

Robert? No! Finnlay? What are you doing?

Thank the gods! Have you any idea how hard it is for me to go so far? Where, in the name of Serinleth, are you?

Jenn moved to the window, keeping her face averted from Margaret. *In Flan'har. What's wrong? I didn't think you could reach this far.*

Neither did I – but I had to. I'm under orders. What are you doing in Flan'har?

It's a long story. Why are you calling?

I'm sorry, Jenn but I have no choice. You have to come back to the Enclave. Right away.

But why? What's happened? I can't drag Robert away now! He's in the middle of . . .

Not Robert. Just you. And Patric if he's there. You have to leave tonight to get here in time.

Jenn's heart lurched. She could hardly bear to ask the question. *Tell me what's happened.*

I'm sorry, Jenn. It's Wilf. He died last night. There's to be a gathering in eight days. And you . . . have to Stand the Circle – just as you promised.

Aiden didn't dare look at Robert. He had to keep his eyes on his hands, trying to calm the twisting in his stomach. In the silence, McGlashen slowly came to his feet, scraping his chair on the stone floor as he pushed it back. He looked at each one of the men seated around the table, slowly, as if to make sure of each one, before he finally reached Robert. He took in a deep breath and drew himself up to his full height.

'You're right. I don't think it makes one jot of difference to our cause whether you're a sorcerer or not. I confess, I was one of those who wondered, until you wreaked havoc on Elita. However, unlike some, I rejoiced that you had some other power we could use to bring the usurper down.'

Now Aiden looked up to find Robert frowning. 'I have no intention of . . . '

'Forgive me, Robert, but the truth is, you don't have a choice in the matter. The moment you decided to take arms against Selar, you put yourself in the game, so to speak. It's a moment some of us have been waiting for this twenty years or more. Yes, you being a sorcerer does make things a little more complicated, but I'll come to that in a moment. What you need to understand is that the men gathered here, both inside and outside these walls, expect you to lead us into battle . . . '

'But . . . '

'And they expect you to take the throne afterwards.'

Robert shut his mouth and took a step back from the table. Aiden began to shake his head slowly, then stopped himself. Why hadn't he seen this coming?

McGlashen continued, with another glance at the silence faces, 'I know your objections, Robert, but unless you become King, these men will not willingly follow you into any war. Why should they?

They could just as easily run after Selar and help him conquer Mayenne and become rich from the spoils. But that's not what they want. They want their own country back, in the hands of a man they can trust not to betray them. Even if that man has turned out to be a sorcerer.'

The silence was different this time, as muffled agreements filtered towards Aiden.

'You must see, Robert, there is not another man who could unite the whole country. We don't have to advertise what you are—'

'And base the whole thing on a lie?' Robert interrupted.

'Better that lie than the tyranny under Selar,' Payne added, coming to his feet beside McGlashen.

'You too?'

'I'm sorry, Robert, but most of us feel the same.'

One by one, Robert looked at each of them. This time they didn't look away. His voice was low and harsh. 'But I can't be . . . King. I don't want the throne.'

'It doesn't matter.

'Doesn't matter . . . ' Robert said, 'but I have no claim to it. The last connection of my family goes back seven generations. Hell, yours is stronger than mine!'

'Nevertheless, you must take it,' McGlashen went on, 'and you can strengthen your claim, remove doubt from anyone who would argue.'

Without pausing, he turned towards the door and nodded at the guard standing there. The soldier pushed the door open and a man entered, walking calmly into the room amidst murmurs of surprise – and horror.

'Kandar?' Robert murmured.

'Greetings, your Grace.' The man nodded, ignoring all those around the table.

Aiden couldn't sit any more. This man . . . George, Earl of Kandar, was Selar's own cousin. He'd betrayed his own blood to get the Queen to safety, had held her as she'd died in his arms – but what was he doing here?

It seemed that Robert already had a suspicion though the other faces around the table betrayed only mystification. McGlashen answered all their questions in one go.

'Six years ago, our sainted Queen deserted her despot of a husband, striking out for all Lusarans. Her son was stolen back and now sits at his father's side. But her daughter still lives in freedom.'

'No . . . ' Robert breathed.

McGlashen continued inexorably, 'Your marriage to Princess Galiena will provide a legal alternative to Selar's occupation of our throne. Queen Rosalind was of the House MacKenna, tied to the royal House of Ross, only five generations back. This marriage will give you all the claim you need. Marry Galiena tomorrow and this army can march united.'

Aiden couldn't take his eyes from Robert, saw the colour drain from his face. In an effort to turn the flood, Aiden spoke. 'But the Princess is only a child.'

'She's sixteen,' Kandar replied. 'Of legal age. She follows her mother's heart in her loyalty to Lusara. I have spoken to her of the marriage and she is willing to make any sacrifice necessary to win her country back.'

Aiden could almost feel the pressure radiating from Robert. His eyes were pits of green fire. But there was nothing Aiden could say or do. It was Robert's choice to make.

No choice at all.

Abruptly, Robert's gaze left McGlashen. In turn, each of the men around the long table flinched as he looked at them, as though he'd hit them. 'Are you telling me you won't do this unless I marry that child? Unless I kill her father and take his crown? Is that why you're all here?'

'Robert, please.' Payne took a step towards him, but a look froze him in his place.

'Don't!' His face barely moved for a moment, so contained was he. Then he turned for the door. Within seconds, he was gone.

20

Robert strode through the castle, paying no attention to where his feet were taking him. Nobody followed him, which was fortunate. He climbed stairs three at a time, storming along the battlements, only to descend at the next staircase. He had to get rid of it, wear it out, burn it away.

But it was useless. He knew where he wanted to go – where he had to go. He would have kicked the door to his mother's room down if he dared to indulge the fury just a little bit. Instead, he knocked and entered.

'I'm sorry, Mother, but I need to talk to Jenn.'

Like a ghost, Margaret rose, her face showing concern, but he barely glanced at her. Instead, he turned immediately to Jenn, standing by the window, her hand resting lightly on the small stone pediment.

As the door closed behind his mother, Robert came forward, but only as far as the table. Jenn didn't look at him at first. Her face was turned towards the cold night, the darkness beyond the window.

Despite his mood, his words came out gently.

'What's wrong?'

'Nothing.'

'Don't lie to me.'

'And will you tell me the truth?' She turned until he could see her face clearly. Pale, her eyes glowing huge and blue. 'I know now how the Generet saw you coming. The demon has almost taken you over. You stand there, reeking of it. Why?'

She was breathing hard, as though she had to contain something equally awful. And there were unshed tears in her eyes. Had she heard somehow? Did she know why he was here?

With a sigh, Robert crossed the room and took her in his arms. She was brittle in his embrace, holding on almost in desperation. He gazed down at her, brushing his fingers across her forehead. The tears were gone now, though her eyes still glittered.

'Tell me,' she whispered.

In answer, he kissed her, sustaining the moment. 'McGlashen and the others want me to marry Galiena and take the throne.'

Jenn's eyes widened. 'By the gods! When?'

'In the morning – so it's all done by the time we have to march.'

Jenn didn't move, not so much as to blink. Robert reached for her hand. 'Jenny, I could marry you and have a much greater claim to the throne, but I won't put you in such danger from Nash. He'd come straight for you.'

'Then you must marry Galiena,' she replied vacantly. 'You have no choice.'

No. He wouldn't let her get away so easily. He grabbed her shoulders tightly. 'I don't want this – any of it! I don't want to kill Selar and I don't want his cursed crown! I don't even want this damned war! It's all wrong. If I marry her, then . . .'

'But you must, Robert.' Jenn was cold in his grasp, her body rigid, as though she'd already given up. Her voice came, cool and detached. 'You know Lusara is more important than what we want. We can't sacrifice our whole country and all its people for love. We'd never forgive ourselves. How could we be happy then?'

'Are you saying you want me to marry her?'

'If you married me, if you told everybody, after they'd believed I was dead, how would they look upon their future Queen? How long would it be before the whispering began, how I would have to be a sorcerer – that I had killed my own husband so I could be with you. And . . . and Andrew has dark hair, like yours. They would assume he was your son – that we had plotted between us all along. Do I have to spell it out for you? You have no choice, Robert, and we both know it.' It took a moment for her to meet his gaze; what he saw there only mirrored his own despair. In desperation, he pulled her close again, feeling her arms go around him, needing to remember this feeling, needing her. He kissed her again, holding her as tightly as he dared, not ready to move on to the next moment.

But that moment came nonetheless. Jenn watched him steadily, the despair now hidden. Lightly, her fingers brushed over his mouth. 'Go and tell them.'

'You know I love you, but you won't fight for us. Why? You talk about me finding another way and yet . . .'

Carefully, she stepped back, leaving his arms. 'Please, Robert, go now.'

She turned away then, to the window. For a long moment, Robert couldn't move, couldn't find anything else to say to her. She had given up. What could he do?

Without another word, he turned on his heel and left without looking back.

The hall was almost empty now, and those who did remain spoke quietly. After the hours of noise, this hushed murmuring was balm to Aiden. He sat alone at the end of the table, feeling useless. Idly, his fingers traced letters carved into the wood, an emphatic lesson in Saelic grammar Robert had given him years before.

A scrape of wood on stone gave warning that the others were leaving. He heard the door close, but Payne stayed behind, drumming his hands on the back of his chair. After a moment, he coughed slightly and walked along the table to stop opposite Aiden.

'You think we're wrong, Bishop?'

Aiden raised his head. 'You're asking me? Now? What difference will my opinion make?'

'So you do think we're wrong.'

Payne was a handsome man, well dressed without gaudiness. He had a reputation for female dalliance rarely surpassed in court circles and while it would be possible to pass a harsh judgement on that score, almost everything else the man had done was done out of honour. For love of his country. He'd even helped Aiden escape Selar's prison. He'd endured ten years on Selar's council, ducking, diving and weaving to keep both his place and some influence for the good. Now he was here. His would be a harsh punishment indeed if Selar ever caught him. Perhaps that was why he – and McGlashen – were willing to push so hard to get what they wanted.

'Yes, I think you're wrong – but not for the obvious reasons. But what does it matter, now? Robert's agreed to marry the poor Princess. When this army marches, it will do so united.'

'Would it have done so otherwise?'

Aiden got to his feet and pushed his chair carefully under the table. 'Do you want absolution?'

'You tell me, Bishop.' Payne raised his hand to wave at the empty table. 'Those men sat here for hours, arguing over nothing in particular, and all because they're afraid. Not of going to war, nor even of losing – but of what will happen afterwards. It's like a man being afraid of the afterlife. Surely you, as a priest, can understand that.'

Aiden turned to leave, but Payne pursued him, stopping him with a firm hand on his arm. 'Did Robert ever tell you how he saved Selar's life?'

'No.'

'It was during the battle of Seluth. His father had sent him to round up reinforcements. As he returned close to the battlefield, he came across a man drowning in the river. Of course, Robert waded in and dragged him to safety, not realising who it was. A few hours later, that man crowned himself King and Robert's father lay dead at his feet.'

'Why are you telling me this?'

'Because I want you to understand,' Payne replied earnestly. Lines of fatigue around his eyes made him look older than his thirty-five years. 'Very few people know that story, but Robert told me because my brother had fought alongside Selar in the beginning, in an effort to retaliate for the Troubles. I felt so guilty because my brother had betrayed our country.'

'I still don't see . . . '

'I asked Robert if he was sorry he saved Selar's life. He told me no – and why? Because, he said, Selar's forces would have won that battle if Selar had drowned, but instead of a ruthless King to forge a new nation, we would have had years of civil war, far more damaging than anything before. Lusara would have become a bloodbath.'

As the hand on his arm dropped, Aiden reappraised the young man. Yes, there was guilt there, in those eyes, but it was new. 'Robert will not willingly kill Selar.'

'Perhaps he won't have to,' Payne replied. 'And perhaps this army would have united behind him anyway. But I'm not talking about the men gathered here. They've already committed themselves. I'm talking about the people of Lusara, whose one real hero has become the thing most forbidden by both Church and Guilde. Would they still follow him? Aid his army? Help the wounded? Hide them afterwards if necessary?'

As Payne stepped back, he rubbed both hands over his face, and shook his head. 'And if we lose this time, they'll still have some kind of hope.'

'Galiena will not make the sorcery go away.'

'No – but she will mask it, and for the moment, that's all we need.' Payne turned then, and headed for the door. He pulled it open and paused, his hand on the latch. 'Explain it to him, will you? And tell him I'm sorry.'

It had rained just before dawn and now, as the sun peaked over the first edge of hills, Margaret could smell the fresh air born of a garden waking from the long winter. As she took another path, her back ached and her eyes itched from too little sleep, too many hours spent wondering what this day would bring.

Nobody knew where Robert had gone. The castle was buzzing with the news. With so much tension building as the order to march drew nearer, this wedding was like a spark in a patch of dry tinder. She'd heard the army was preparing a salute in honour of the occasion and already the timber was being laid for a huge bonfire by the river. The men needed something to celebrate.

And Margaret was expected to do her duty – along with everyone else. With so few women in the castle, it was up to her to make the hasty arrangements for the ceremony, to make sure everything went smoothly. With so many eyes watching for signs and portents, it wouldn't look good if the whole thing fell apart.

Margaret lifted her head and straightened her shoulders. Then she turned the final corner of the path, around the last of the trees. There, sitting on a bench, were two women, with a tall man standing behind them. One of the women wore a quiet gown of grey, her hair hidden behind a pale scarf. Samah was still so very beautiful, looking more like her sister, Rosalind, as she got older. Beside her was the child, the Princess Galiena. Both stood as she approached. The man, George, Earl of Kandar, greeted her with a short bow. She had never known him before this, but everything about him spoke of a man of honour.

'I'm sorry,' Margaret murmured, finding a smile from somewhere, 'but things have been a little hectic.'

Although only sixteen, Galiena was already as tall as her aunt, her hair auburn, but her eyes hazel, like an autumn forest. Considering the situation she found herself in, she appeared remarkably calm and held herself with the kind of dignity her mother had been known for.

'Bishop McCauly is preparing as we speak,' Margaret continued. 'The chapel is ready and everyone will be there as witness. Tell me, my lord,' she turned to address Kandar, 'will you travel with the Princess into Lusara?'

'No.' It was Galiena who replied, firmly, as though in response to an older argument. 'He and my aunt will stay here, as guests of His Grace of Flan'har.'

'Galiena . . . ' Kandar tried to protest, but the girl shook her head, turning to face him.

'It is too dangerous. You are my father's cousin. You know what he would do to you and Samah if he caught you. Please, I will be safe enough – and much happier if I know you are both here, out of harm's way.'

Kandar shook his head, obviously unhappy.

'My lord,' Margaret tried to ease his concern, 'the Princess will be well taken care of. I myself will travel with her. She will have a whole army to protect her, not to mention my son.'

'I would rather fight,' Kandar replied stiffly. 'I have matters to settle with my cousin.'

'Even so,' Galiena placed a hand on his arm, soothing his ire. 'You will stay here and protect my aunt, as you have promised.'

'Of course, Your Grace. If you will excuse me?' He bowed briefly, then turned and left them.

'He is a proud man,' Margaret observed.

'He is indeed.' Samah nodded. 'My sister's murder changed him. Only his vow to keep us safe from Selar prevented him from returning to deal out justice.'

Margaret could see Galiena wasn't at ease with the subject, so she changed course. 'I'm sure Grant will take good care of you both while you're here. He's been the most generous host to Robert. I'm sure Robert would tell you himself, except . . . '

'What?' The Princess spoke quietly, her eyes watching Margaret with an intensity that was strangely soothing.

'I'm sorry, but my son appears to have vanished for the moment.

He will be in the chapel for the ceremony, but he did say he wanted to speak to you this morning, beforehand. I don't know what's become of him but I'm sure . . . '

'It's all right, Mother.'

Margaret turned around to see Robert slip through the garden gate. As usual, he wore black, but this morning, the darkness was nothing compared to that in his eyes. He stopped beside her and nodded to Samah. 'You look well, my lady. The southern continents have been kind to you.'

'Thank you, Your Grace.'

Then he turned to Galiena and she stood to face him. For a long moment, neither of them said a word. Then Robert frowned. 'I have to ask you this. Are you willing to go through with this wedding of your own choice? Have you been coerced into it by Kandar or McGlashen or anyone?'

'No, Your Grace,' Galiena murmured, her gaze suddenly dropping under his scrutiny.

'Then why?'

'Because . . . ' The girl paused, glanced at Margaret and Samah before continuing. 'I know my father and my brother. My mother lost her life trying to find some way to save Lusara. If I don't do this, how can I say I tried my best? I have little to give, but I'm willing to do what I can. I . . . want to go home.'

'Do you want your father dead?' Robert's voice was harsh in the quiet morning.

Galiena looked up at him again, the brief hesitancy gone now. 'No!'

Robert's shoulders were rigid, his expression entirely shuttered. Eventually he nodded. 'Very well. Mother, will you walk with me?'

He was already down the path and around the corner before Margaret could bid the girls farewell. She hurried after him, but he hadn't gone far. He waited for her by the door leading back inside the castle. He looked around to make sure they were alone – but still he didn't look at her.

'Mother, I know this has all been pretty hard on you. Ever since I returned to Lusara with Micah so long ago, things have gone downhill almost without remission. I'd like to say I'm not to blame for a lot of it, but we'd both know it would be a lie. I'd also like to say it'll get better from here, but right now . . . '

He paused, taking in steady, even breaths, as though his body was starved of air. He studied his feet for a moment. 'I want to ask you a favour. I'd do it myself, but it would be better coming from you. I need to make her understand.'

Margaret reached out to him, but he backed away, shaking his head.

'Please, Mother, just listen. I want you to speak to . . . Galiena. I want you to tell her that our . . . marriage will never be . . . a real marriage. Do you understand?'

'Oh, Robert, don't do this to yourself – to her. I beg you.'

'No.' He held up his hands and met her gaze squarely. 'I'm well accustomed now to acting purely out of duty and I'm willing to go through with this sham simply because I must. But there are two things that will never change. I can never love that child – not in the way a husband should. Not now, and not in the years to come. And I simply cannot risk having children. I can't explain why. I beg you to trust me – and to do this for me. You're a woman, you can help her understand – gently. I don't want her to get hurt. Will you talk to her?'

Margaret bit her bottom lip, but couldn't stop the tears running down her face. She nodded mutely and he leaned forward and kissed her cheek, then disappeared through the doorway.

The ceremony could have been shorter, but Bishop McCauly was under orders to miss nothing out, to make sure the marriage was as legally valid as possible. There must never be any doubt. But still, Margaret longed for it to be over.

The chapel looked a little barren, decorated in only the few spring flowers she'd been able to gather so quickly. And the guests were perhaps not dressed in their very best finery, but even so, Bishop McCauly lent the occasion so much grace and warmth that the air lost a little of the coldness forced upon it by expedience. He was a rare man.

There was, of course, the banquet afterwards but the revelry was remarkably contained. The greater merriment was going on outside the walls. The army gave a great cheer when Robert and Galiena appeared on the battlements shortly before the sun drifted down behind the hills.

And then Margaret said goodnight to both of them. She felt weariness sink into her aging bones and though she'd hardly ever known a day of illness in her life, she felt every one of her fifty-two years. She finally returned to her room and sat on her bed, unable, for a moment, even to undress.

Reluctantly, her gaze turned to Jenn's bed, lying neatly against the opposite wall. She wasn't there. Hardly surprising, really. But where was she?

She had probably found some place in the castle where she could be alone. And who could blame her? It was obvious that something wonderful had happened in Budlandi. And now it was gone.

Margaret got to her feet, but as she turned to the table, she noticed a letter sitting there, a single word written on the outside. Robert.

She picked it up and turned it over in her hands. Was it really worth bothering him with it now? Surely the morning would be early enough.

She put it down again, and finished getting undressed. Yes, she would give it to him in the morning. Soon enough for more bad news.

Aiden didn't like the quiet. It was deathly, like a crypt in the middle of winter. So why did he seem to be the only one who noticed it?

Half a dozen of Robert's closest friends sat around the table, well into the wine now. Everyone else had gone to bed – including the Princess – though nobody was brave enough to comment. These last few men were trading stories, swapping jokes, laughing and carousing. Robert sat on the edge of the group, neither listening nor ignoring. He responded when spoken to, wasn't even impolite and, a few times, the frail suggestion of a smile had graced his face.

But he was so quiet it gave Aiden a chill.

While the others were noisy, Aiden leaned forward slightly and murmured to Robert, 'Are you all right?'

He nodded. 'Yes, I'm fine. I'm afraid it looks worse than it is.'

'That's not much comfort,' Aiden replied and was rewarded with an ironic smile. Carefully he continued, 'Have you spoken to Jenn?'

The responding glance was sharp. 'Not since last night. Please, Aiden, don't go down that path.' He sat forward and planted his elbows on the table, resting his face in his hands, effectively shutting the others out. 'I want to apologise.'

'For what?' Aiden asked, suddenly surprised.

'Sometimes I let my feelings get the better of me – carrying around a shadow of tragedy with me like it was a pet. As though I'm the only man here who's had to make sacrifices. I hate it, but sometimes I can't help it.'

Aiden ventured a smile. 'You're forgiven.'

'No, I'm not.' Robert frowned, his gaze turning inwards. 'And I never will be.'

'What does that mean?'

'Your Grace!' Deverin came across the hall, far more awake and sober than anyone else.

'What is it?' Robert turned – then saw the figure following in Deverin's hasty footsteps. Instantly he was on his feet. 'Micah?'

With a grin, the young man strode forward and Robert slapped him on the back. 'Am I glad to see you!'

'The feeling is mutual, my lord,' Micah laughed, taking the cup of wine somebody handed him. 'I just wish the circumstances were different.'

As Robert met his gaze and nodded slowly. 'Then it's time?'

'Yes. The army is moving.'

Robert smiled a little, almost to himself, then lifted his voice to ring about the hall. 'Go, get the other magnates out of bed! Wake them all up. I don't care how drunk they are – we've got work to do. This army marches in the morning!'

In borrowed vestments and refreshed by the cool dawn air, Aiden blessed the army before the first of it moved off, heading south for the coast. Five thousand men, with carts, horses, oxen and more pennants than he could count. For the first time in seven years, he'd performed the duty of a Bishop and the effort left him breathless and not a little awed. Fortunately, nobody but Robert seemed to notice. As they made their way back towards the castle, a drum beat sprang up, accompaniment to the marching men.

'Well, you can't tell me off any more, Bishop,' Robert said

quietly, walking past men who watched them both. 'It's official – or as official as it's going to be for a while. Look on the bright side.'

'Is there one?'

'It could be worse,' Robert replied. Unlike almost everyone else within a league of this place, Robert showed no signs of fatigue at all – quite the opposite. He had somewhere to focus his energy now, something he could push at. He had something real to do.

'You're right,' Aiden said as they finally reached the gate and crossed the courtyard. 'Though it could be a lot better.'

'Oh, you priests,' Robert smiled faintly, 'always complaining. Look, Aiden, you're finally doing what you were born to do. I've never met a man with a stronger vocation. Whether you like it or not, you are the anointed Bishop of Lusara. Only your death can ever change that.'

'That's not the point. It never has been.'

Robert waited until the others filed past, then held Aiden up at the doorway. 'Oh, I know you've always felt unworthy.'

'How did you . . . '

'I'm not blind, my friend. Why do you think I've spent the last five years trying to remind you what you are? Listen, you've waited a long time for this. I suggest you relax and enjoy it. It's what you're best at. You'll find it's not so bad once you stop fighting it.'

Aiden stared at him a moment. 'Oh, that's rich, coming from you!'

Robert laughed, unashamed. 'Yes, isn't it.'

Kavanagh was waiting for them inside the hall where a dozen men were packing up the last of the papers which had littered the table since midnight. Only Deverin and Owen, Micah and a few others remained.

'Well, I guess it's time,' Robert said, stopping before Kavanagh. 'You can have your castle back now.'

'Blast and damnation, Robert! How many times do I have to tell you, it's yours.' Grant spread his arms wide. 'I've got a dozen of them. A man can only live in one house at a time.'

'Especially when your guests leave such a mess.' Robert smiled. 'You take care, Grant. Watch your borders carefully.'

'I wish you'd let me send a squad of reinforcements, just in case.'

'If we need them, then the fight will already be lost – and you'll need them more here if we do lose.'

Grant nodded, tugging at his beard. For a minute, they stood watching each other, then Grant reached out and gave Robert a hug, slapping his back. Abruptly he let go, and left, taking his men with him. In his absence, Robert turned back to Owen and Deverin. 'Well, the first ships should leave on the afternoon tide. If the winds are fair, you'll be in Aaran in eight days, nine at the most. Send the scouting parties out the moment you dock. March north and stop two days' journey south of Shan Moss. If I don't join you there . . . '

'You'd better, my lord,' Deverin grunted. 'Or there'll be five thousand angry men scouring the country for you.'

As the laughter subsided, Robert turned, looking around the hall. 'Has my mother come down yet? I hope she's ready to leave.'

'She was helping Lady Samah,' Aiden replied evenly, 'and your wife.'

'Oh. And where is . . . ?'

His train of thought was cut off as Margaret, Galiena and Samah entered the hall, dressed and ready for departure. For all she'd gone through in the last few days, the Princess appeared remarkably composed.

'All ready?'

Robert asked the question generally and the girl nodded. 'Yes, my lord.'

With a glance around at the others, Robert crossed the hall to her, drawing her to one side with a gesture. Aiden couldn't hear what he said, but the girl nodded twice, her eyes watching Robert's every move.

'Father,' Micah murmured in Aiden's ear, 'is he all right?'

'I can't honestly tell you. Why?'

Micah frowned. 'I don't know, but . . . '

'Well, what are you all standing about for?' Robert asked, coming back to them. 'Haven't you got a war to attend or something?'

'Sometimes I wonder if you really are my son,' Margaret said with a smile.

Robert grinned. 'I told you to disown me years ago, Mother, but as usual, you paid no attention.'

'As I will do now. Here.' She handed him a piece of paper, folded and sealed. 'This is for you.'

He frowned as he took it – and suddenly there was something about his stance that made Aiden tense. Robert unfolded the paper and began to read. Like a cloud passing over the sun, his face went pale, his eyes dark and fathomless.

'Sweet Mineah, no!' he breathed, horror filling every word. His gaze left the paper and dwelled somewhere else. Only Micah was brave enough to approach him.

'What is it?'

Robert immediately snapped out of it, energy suddenly coursing through every word, every gesture. 'Owen, get my horse saddled and ready. I'm leaving immediately. Deverin, I charge you with getting the rest of the army away. All the rest of you go with him.'

'But what is it?' Micah insisted. 'What's happened?'

'Wilf's dead.'

'By the gods . . . '

'Jenn has gone to the Gathering. She'll Stand the Circle, Micah. She'll Stand and she'll be chosen.' Robert turned and strode for the door. 'I have to stop her!'

21

For day after day, Micah rode beside Robert, in a daze, most of the time. He had one thing in the forefront of his mind – to keep up. He had to. Robert wouldn't wait for him. The beautiful hills of southern Lusara rolled by, untouched by their passage.

Jenn had a day and a half head start and Robert was determined to find her before she could reach the Goleth, but she was not to be found. Every few hours Robert would stop and get that familiar look in his eyes as he tried Seeking her – but without success.

Father Aiden had told Micah about Robert and Jenn's journey to Budlandi, and what had awaited their return. But there was something else behind Robert's haste. Something other than his normal worry about the prophecy.

There were quieter moments, when they rested the horses by walking, or in the brief period before they snatched a few hours' sleep, when Robert would ask him about Dromna. Not about the army, but of his life in the tavern. It was difficult avoiding the truth; Micah was unaccustomed to lying to Robert. He wanted so badly to confide in him, to explain how he felt – but there was nothing he could say about a Malachi that Robert would want to hear. In the end, he told the simple story of meeting a girl called Sairead, how he had fallen in love and left her behind.

And Robert, feeling as wretched as Micah, voiced hope and concern. It was a poor distraction, but it worked for both of them – for a while.

Still they rode on, changing horses when they could, steering clear of towns and villages. They saw no patrols, no Guildesmen and no trouble. Shortly after dawn on the seventh day, they finally climbed into the foothills of the Goleth range.

And Micah began to pray.

Hurry. He had to hurry. He pushed the poor horse so hard, it was a miracle it didn't collapse under him. But the path was worn, with recent marks of others passing this way, perhaps only a few hours before. It had to be Jenn. Just about everybody else would already be here. He might not be too late, but still he had to hurry.

He had to stop her. She was blind and couldn't see the truth. It sat before her, plain as day, and still she wouldn't see it. She didn't want to believe the Key had changed the prophecy to suit itself. She'd made the promise to Stand and there was nothing else to it. And why shouldn't she go? He could no longer offer her anything else.

There it was, the gate, at the end of this path. The horse stumbled and was too slow to recover. Instead, Robert jumped down and ran the last few feet to the gate. He heard Micah following behind as he stepped into the darkness. He felt the mild tingle and then he was outside again, running across the field to the main tunnel. There was nobody about, no challenger, no one to ask his purpose.

He couldn't be so close and still too late.

Exhausted now, he swung around corners and tore down passages, his boots skidding on the stone floor. As he drew closer to the great cavern, he could feel it, building up inside him, like a weight ready to drown him. Already dreading what he would see, he came to a halt at the entrance.

The cavern was almost full. People stood well back, surrounding the Key as it dominated the Circle. The bell had already dissolved and in its place, a shiny black orb glowed, suspended in space. From it came a single light, flooding the face of the only person standing before it: Jenn.

'No!' Robert lunged forward, but somebody caught his arm. Without a thought, he shoved back, flinging the person away. He continued on towards the Key. As he crossed the empty space around it, his hands rose, automatically preparing a defence.

Jenn was frozen in place, seeing nothing. She was pale under the light, her eyes colourless. Without pausing, Robert stepped forward and reached out to drag her away and . . .

. . . Nothing . . .

He couldn't move . . . but he had no body to move with . . . gone . . . there was just the nothing.

No light nor dark, just emptiness, filling him, surrounding him, penetrating him.

Slowly, the nothing developed substance, colour. A swirling grey fog, almost black. He couldn't feel it, nor see it. He had no eyes and yet he knew it enfolded him, dying and breathing, shifting and swaying. He was alone.

Jenn?

Alone. Completely alone.

Jenn?

WHY ARE YOU HERE, ENEMY?

Jenn? Answer me!

YOU ANSWER US, ENEMY. YOU WERE NOT CALLED.

I don't care. Leave her alone. You can't have her . . . Jenny? Please answer me!

Robert.

Suddenly she was there, and yet wholly insubstantial. He couldn't see her – and yet he could, with Other eyes.

Please, Robert, go. You can't stop this.

But you can. You must leave now, before it's too late. Don't you understand what you're doing?

It's already too late. It always was. I know you love me but you must go. You must forget. Leave me behind.

Do you think that's why I'm here? Don't you see this is not the way? You don't understand.

THEN MAKE HIM UNDERSTAND, LITTLE ONE.

The booming voice of the Key drowned out everything else, made Jenn fade from his awareness. Then, slowly, everything vanished, the fog fading to nothingness again . . . only . . .

This time he wasn't alone. She was with him, as though she'd always been there, inside him, a part of him – as he was with her. Together, as one, they moved through the fog, but now it was lighter, as though her mind alone illuminated the darkness . . .

. . . and then she was gone again, with a wrench so complete it left him staggering, tumbling in the wasteland.

NOW GO, ENEMY. YOU HAVE DONE ENOUGH. YOUR DESTINY LIES ELSEWHERE.

Jenn – stop this now! I beg you.

I can't, Robert. I made a promise. The Key has chosen me.

The Key is insane, Jenn. You don't understand what it's done. Just ask . . .

WE ARE NOT INSANE, ENEMY. WE KNOW EXACTLY WHAT WE ARE DOING. DO YOU? DO YOU UNDERSTAND WHAT WILL HAPPEN IF YOU DO NOT LEAVE NOW?

I'm not afraid.

NO, YOU ARE NOT. YOU ARE THE ENEMY. YOU WERE NOT MADE TO FEAR US.

Suddenly Robert could feel his body again, drowning in the swirling grey mess, gagging and suffocating him, dragging him away from her.

Stop it! Leave him. I won't let you harm him.

WE WOULD NEVER HARM THE ENEMY, LITTLE ONE. ALLY. WE ONLY DO WHAT WE MUST. TO BOTH OF YOU. THE PATH BEFORE YOU IS LONG AND YOU MUST NOT BE TORN BY THE WASTE OF AGING BODIES. THE G'HARVZIN E MIRANI *MUST COME.*

Robert gasped in silence as pain filled his entire body, a pain so intense that the grey shifted to red. The agony was appalling, but he could do nothing to stop it.

Then leave him alone! I won't allow you to hurt him. You may be the Key, but I will stop you.

Flickering lights now filled Robert's vision and parts of the floor seemed solid beneath his feet. Desperately he tried to get back to wherever Jenn was, but it was too much effort. Was this the power of the Key?

WE HAVE NOT HARMED HIM, LITTLE ONE. QUITE THE OPPOSITE. AND YOU ARE MISTAKEN.

Robert's head was spinning, red, grey, white. Lights, flashing, on off on off . . .

Mistaken?

YES, MISTAKEN. WE ARE NOT THE KEY.

His body was his own again, but still he clung on to the last frail threads of the connection . . .

WE ARE NOT THE KEY, LITTLE ONE – YOU ARE.

Robert's eyes snapped open. Jenn still stood before him, held in thrall by the Key's light. He teetered there for a moment, unable to move, then, without warning, his knees buckled beneath him and the blackness came again, blotting out everything.

Micah finished checking the horses and spent more time than he needed putting together the rest of the supplies. Outside the barn the night cracked bitter cold, ignoring spring which was flooding the rest of the country. Here in the mountains, seasons changed slowly. Perhaps that was why the Enclave had flourished here. Change had never been thrust upon the Salti; instead, it had always crept inexorably, dragging even the most reluctant along with it.

Until now.

He put the last bag down and leaned back against a wall built by Dunlorn men over the last five years. Wilf was dead. Jenn was Jaibir and that was that. Never again would she be able to leave the Enclave and enjoy the freedom she'd once thrived on. Well, that had been her choice – but was that all that had happened yesterday?

He turned his head until he could see out of the door to where moonlight caught clumps of stubborn snow clinging to the rocky mountaintop. With a sigh, he left the horses and ducked outside, heading for the corridor leading below.

Everything had turned out different. Everything. This war, Robert and Galiena, Sairead – and now Jenn. For a long time, Micah had been able to see the way forward, see what they were aiming for, the goal in the far distance. The path had always been clear and true.

He wanted to see Robert . . . but he was afraid of what he would find. But why was he suddenly so afraid of a man he'd known and worked alongside almost his entire life?

Robert had changed. Slowly, as inexorably as the seasons, he had changed and there was now about him a layer Micah couldn't recognise – and it scared him.

The corridors of the Enclave were empty and very quiet, as though the air held something oppressive, like the eye of the storm. Perhaps there was nothing he could do for Robert, but that didn't mean he should stop trying – especially because he *was* afraid.

Arlie and Martha had waited supper for him and as soon as he entered their rooms, Martha began to serve up. As usual, her cooking smelled wonderful and his stomach growled in anticipation.

'How is Jenn?' Micah began, reaching for the bread.

Arlie's long face frowned. 'Still unconscious. Fiona's with her at the moment. I'm going back after supper.'

'You sound worried.'

With a nod, Arlie replied, 'I am. It's been too long. And there's something strange with her eyes. I just hope when she wakes up, she can still see.'

'You mean she's blind?' Micah asked.

'I don't know. I've just never seen anything like it before. We'll just have to wait. If she is, well, perhaps it will wear off in a few days. Her body's been under tremendous strain.'

There was a sombre silence after this, punctuated only by the sounds of eating. Micah found himself watching Arlie and how he dealt with a meal with only one hand. The other had been cut off years ago by a Guilde soldier because Arlie had tried to help some sick children. Robert had almost got himself killed trying to save

Arlie and, for a while, they'd wondered if the shock of the amputation would kill the Healer. But now, Arlie worked around his severed wrist. He paid it no attention. He lived with it.

After a few more mouthfuls, Martha pushed her plate away and sat back. 'Don't you think this feels strange?'

'What?' Micah murmured.

'Well, for five hundred years, we've been looking for a sorcerer powerful enough to wield the Key properly. How long is it since we had a woman Jaibir?'

'About a hundred and twenty years, I think,' Arlie replied, pausing with his fork in the air.

'Then it's about time.'

Micah looked down at his plate but his own appetite had gone. He pushed his chair back, ready to stand. 'Is Robert awake yet?'

Martha started and glanced quickly at Arlie. She shook her head. 'Not last time I looked. He's been sleeping pretty solidly for the last eight hours.'

'I might look in on him.'

'I wouldn't do that. Finnlay's in there with him.'

Micah's face fell. 'Oh. But is he all right now?'

Martha turned to her husband for an answer. Arlie nodded vigorously. 'Absolutely.'

'But the bleeding . . . '

'All stopped. Don't ask me to explain it. I don't understand what the Key did to Robert and Jenn, but there's not a mark on either of them now.'

'But . . . ' Micah hesitated, tapping the table edge. 'Every old scar he'd ever had was open and pouring blood when the Key finally released him! Are you saying they've all healed again?'

'I told you I don't understand it. But honestly, there's not a single mark on him now, as though he'd never had a scratch in all his life. Jenn's the same. The cuts she got from Eachern have vanished. Whatever the Key did to them, it hasn't done them any harm.'

'Not yet,' Martha said, then looked apologetic. 'I don't mean to sound callous, but ever since the first day Jenn came here, people like Wilf and Henry have wondered what she could do for us, given the chance. Ever since the Key was created, we've struggled to understand it, to use it properly, in the hope that it will, as legend promised, find the Calyx and let us out of this prison we all live in. Aren't either of you just a little curious what Jenn will say when she finally wakes up?'

Arlie got to his feet and pushed his chair back under the table. 'Actually, I think I have a damned good idea what she'll say – and I think none of it will have anything to do with the Calyx. I'm going back to her now. I'll see you later.'

Robert drifted through layers of warmth, each movement brought a corresponding ache, but as he gradually surfaced, the pain drifted away. He opened his eyes, but the darkness was so profound he could make out nothing at all.

Was he still enmeshed with the Key? No, his body felt the same, solid, alive. The bed surrounded him, held him, cradled him. There was no danger here. Not now.

He *had* been too late. The Key had taken Jenn and now she belonged to it, heart and soul. Now there was no going back. No pause, no hope for redemption. She'd done it, just as she'd been fated to do.

She was the Key. It had been there all along and nobody had noticed. Jenn, the Ally, stuck in the centre, her road not defined by action, merely by existence. Hers was the choice to make, and now she'd made it – even if she'd had no idea of the consequences.

No going back. For any of them.

It was too dark in here. And too quiet. What had the Key done to him? Left him bereft of his Senses? No . . .

'Who's there?'

'Me,' Finnlay replied softly from the other side of the room. 'How do you feel?'

Gingerly, Robert stretched and the blood flowed to his hands and feet, full of energy. 'Fine. Better than I expected.'

'Good.'

'How's Jenn?'

'Arlie's looking after her. He said she'll be fine once she's rested.' Finnlay's words emerged softly from the darkness. 'I Sensed you waking up. I caught your aura as it gradually revealed itself, but by the time you opened your eyes, you started shielding again – like you always do – and you vanished. I'm the strongest Seeker in the whole Enclave – stronger even than you, but although I'm only a few feet away from you, you're invisible to me. As always. Why don't you ever let me Seek you, Robert?'

Carefully, Robert pushed himself up in bed. Why was Finnlay sitting in the dark?

'Why did you come here? Is the army moving?'

'Yes. I came to tell you . . . ' This was ridiculous! Robert reached to the bedside and found a candle. With a brief flick of his hand, the flame came to life and he turned back to Finnlay. 'Serin's blood, Finn, what happened to you?'

His brother sat crookedly in a chair in the corner. A nasty bruise crossed his left eyebrow, swelling the lid. His left arm was bandaged, too, held against his chest in a sling. 'What did the Key say to you?'

Robert frowned and swung his legs out of bed. He pulled on trousers and a shirt, but he couldn't take his eyes off Finnlay.

'Well?' Finnlay's voice dropped to a whisper. 'You won't tell me, will you? Well, I hope it was worth it.'

'Are you going to tell me—'

'I tried to stop you,' Finnlay replied, lifting his head a little, his eyes dark and luminous. 'When you came crashing into the cavern, I reached out and grabbed your arm, because I knew what you would do. I was afraid you'd get hurt – that the Key might kill you for daring such a thing. I tried to stop you,' he paused, blinking a moment, 'and you pushed me away.'

'But I . . . ' He hadn't used any force to get free. How could he have done this much damage? This must be some kind of joke!

'You don't believe me, do you?' Finnlay's voice suddenly changed, harsher now, cutting. 'How could you hurt your little brother like this? Real, physical injuries? No, it has to be impossible. That's what you're thinking, isn't it?'

'Finn, you don't understand.'

'I understand plenty!' Finnlay lurched forward to the edge of his chair. 'I know better than anyone else how you drive yourself, day after day, year after year. And you drive all of us along with you, dragging us whether we want to go or not. It's you who doesn't understand!'

With that, he got to his feet, steadying himself and breathing hard. 'I know how much you love her, Robert, but you've become so obsessed with the prophecy that nothing else matters any more!'

'That's not true.' Robert stood and faced him squarely. 'Would I be going to war if it was?'

'Would you be dragging us all into it if it wasn't?' Finnlay took another step forward, his eyes blazing. 'Why bother going to war when all you really have to do is face Nash alone.'

'You know I can't do that.'

'No, I don't – and neither do you. You just let the prophecy drive you towards the least frightening goal.' Finnlay paused, his voice full of venom. 'You could have killed Jenn last night. And now you've hurt me – except that this time, I have the bruises to prove it. But you won't believe you did this. You won't even say you're sorry. I'm just another sacrifice to your cause.'

'But I am sorry, Finn.' Robert reached out but Finnlay slapped his hand away.

He stood there for a moment, unshed tears filling his eyes. 'You hurt me, Robert, and the truth is, I'm not sure I can forgive you.' With that, he turned and walked out, slamming the door behind him.

Martha looked up when Finnlay emerged from Robert's room. She rose to say something, but his visage was a stone wall. He went to leave, then paused a moment by the door, looking back at her.

'I'm sorry. You didn't want to hear that. I'm going up to make sure everyone's ready to leave. Knowing Robert, he'll want to be away as soon as he's had breakfast. There are other wars going on, after all.'

He would have left, but Micah rose quickly and stood in the doorway, blocking Finnlay's exit. The two men watched each other steadily for several long heartbeats, then Micah spoke. 'You shouldn't have done that.'

'What?' Finnlay grunted. 'Spoken my mind? Told him what I thought? Why not? He's my brother.'

'That's not the point.'

'Oh, stop protecting him, Micah!' Finnlay snapped. 'Trust me, Robert is more than capable of looking after himself!'

He pushed past Micah and left, the sound of his footsteps disappearing quickly down the passage.

Martha came around the table and took Micah's arm. 'Was that wise?'

Micah shook his head, utterly lost. 'I don't know. Hell, I don't know anything any more.'

Jenn lay in her bed, listening. A long time ago, when she'd spent her first night at the Enclave, she'd done the same, learning the normal noises of the place, the scent, the feel. Back then, people had been wary of her, an unknown quantity, a potential, nothing more.

Now she was the Jaibir, linked to the Key for the rest of her life.

Rejoice, little one. Ally. All is well.

Are you ever going to give me some peace? Let me alone for a while? This is what being Jaibir means.

Was it the same for Wilf? For Marcus and all the others before him? They were too weak to feel it as you do. Little one. Ally.

Yes, yes, I know that part. What about the rest?

In time. We will always be with you.

She could see very little, no more than a blur of light where the heat of a candle stood by the wall. If she watched carefully, she could discern movement, but nothing more.

Why did every muscle in her body feel like it had been stretched to breaking point? Her head ached as though somebody had hit it with a mallet, but she could feel no bruise. She felt rested, but unable to get up. Her body was dry clay and would crack if she moved.

So she lay there and listened and, slowly, the noises changed. Hesitant, quiet noises. The bedroom door opened and Arlie's voice came, warm and friendly.

'Feeling better? Ready to have something to eat?'

'Yes, but in a minute. Is Robert there?'

'No. I've got some broth here Martha made especially for you.'

'Robert is there. I can Sense him. Make him come in here, please. I need to talk to him before he leaves.'

There was a silence then and Jenn held her breath. A long silence filled with suggestions and weight and absolutely no words at all. Then heavier footsteps trod on the stone floor and the door closed.

He was in the room, though she could see nothing of him but a hint of shadow. Closing her eyes made it easier; she could Sense him approach, darker than her blindness.

'Arlie tells me you'll recover well enough,' Robert said levelly, not moving from the foot of her bed.

'How are you?'

'Fine.'

'When do you leave?'

'An hour. Everyone's ready.'

'Then we don't have much time.'

'No.'

She held out her hand, willing him to come closer. He hesitated a long time before sitting on the edge of the bed, but he didn't touch her. Eventually, he began to talk, his voice the only real thing about him. Rich and warm, but also bewildered.

'You wanted to know if I was afraid – but you never asked what I was afraid of.'

'No.'

'Why?'

'Would you have told me the truth?'

He sighed lightly, holding back even now. 'Do you have any idea how precious you are to me?'

Fighting the heaviness in her breast, Jenn reached out again until she found his hand. This time he took it. A silence then, with only the sounds from beyond the door as company.

Eventually he spoke again. 'Do you know that if the Key hadn't said you and I were Bonded, I would have found some way to win your father over. I would have convinced him to let us marry, years ago.'

'That would have been some feat. He despised you.'

'And now the Key has you. Now it says you are the key. I think it knew that all along.'

'How?'

He laughed a little, soft and bitter. 'I think the prophecy says as much. It wasn't until yesterday that I understood. I suppose I was hoping it didn't mean something like that, so I ignored it. What did the Key do to us?'

'I'm not sure. Something about aging, of sustaining us. It won't tell me more – but it hurt.'

318

'Yes.'

He paused and she opened her eyes again, hoping to see something of him.

'You have no idea how much I hate the Key for ordering my life,' he continued. 'I should have seen what would happen if I fought it.'

'Robert, you can't keep blaming yourself. You were only nine years old. You didn't have the skills to see into the future.'

'I *am* the Enemy, Jenn. You have to accept that as much as I do. I can see what I've become and I don't like it much. Finnlay . . . '

But he broke off, falling into silence again. A silence of regret, heavy and unbreachable. In the back of her mind, she could feel the Key hedging her awareness, waiting for her attention. She ignored it.

He let out air, slowly and noisily. 'Oh, Jenny, what a road this has been. Sometimes I think the biggest mistake I ever made was believing that it was the Bonding alone that brought us together. You always knew the truth, even as I refused to see it.'

'Well, you can't have all the best powers,' Jenn replied, trying to lighten the mood. Blind though she was, her Senses found the demon, a ball of blackness sitting deep inside him, wound tight, pulsing with readiness. Did he know what it was? Did he understand how it had been formed? How his struggles against his fate only fed it, made it stronger, wore down his ability to resist it? More than once, he'd lost control – and at Elita, it had controlled him so much it had forced him to use the Word of Destruction.

No, he didn't understand – and that was why the demon thrived. Why, in the end, despite his strength, his power and unbreakable determination, the demon would kill him.

And what could she say? There wasn't a power on this earth that could turn his eyes inward to see what lay there. She had always known that destroying the demon was something Robert had to do on his own.

He lifted her hand to his cheek, pressed his lips to her fingers. 'You know this is the end of us, don't you?'

She swallowed. Did he have to go on? 'Yes.'

'What I feel for you will never change but . . . ' He fell silent and all she could hear for a long time was his breathing, forced and uneven. She could feel his hand stiffen around hers, Sense the tension radiating from him. Finally, his voice harsh and leaden, he added, 'I can't trust you any more.'

Jenn took in a swift breath, and held onto it, not daring to let anything go. Tears would finish her. He didn't let her say a word. Instead, he leaned forward and kissed her gently, holding her as though she were a thing already lost. Then he stood and dropped her hand. She heard him reach the door.

Hold him here. Don't let him go. 'Robert?'

'Yes?'

Say something. Anything. Don't let him go. Not like this. 'I'll be there, I promise.'

'No, you won't. You can never leave this place again. And I'll never come back.'

He opened the door, but again she stopped him, keeping the fear from her voice. 'Robert? Will you do something for me?'

'What?'

'Tell Finnlay I don't know where the Calyx is. The Key won't tell me.'

'Why not?'

'I don't know.'

'Well, I'm afraid you'll have to tell him yourself. That's one bridge I've burned once too often.' Another pause and she could think of nothing else to say. The door opened. 'Goodbye, Jenny.'

And then he was gone and the emptiness was complete.

Do not fret so, little one. You are not alone. You have Us.

Jenn rolled over onto her side and wrapped her face in her hands. *Please – just shut up!*

There was a line of cloud across the sky, blanking out the deep blue and casting half the mountaintop in shadow. Where the sun fell, the grass was green and almost warm. The rest was grey, cold and untouchable.

As Finnlay brought Jenn out of the tunnel, the last horse was brought around and mounted. Forty of the Enclave's finest men and women were prepared to leave, anticipation and some eagerness showing on their faces. Alongside them were fifty fighting men who'd come from Dunlorn, waiting for this very day. Already the caves below felt empty.

Friends and family had gathered to bid them all good luck. Martha waited to one side, her children with her, watching Arlie as he fussed with his horse, looking anxiously at her. The same pattern was repeated everywhere. Micah worked his way through the group, keeping order and passing out encouraging smiles to everyone.

And there was Robert, standing in the centre of the group, talking to, of all people, Fiona.

'What's happening?' Jenn asked as he paused outside the group.

'They're just about ready to leave. How do you feel? Do you need to sit?'

'No, I'm fine. Feeling stronger by the minute. I think it was a good move to make myself get up.'

'I don't – you're still very pale.' She was more than that. Not fragile exactly, but the red around her eyes had nothing to do with blindness. 'How much can you see?'

'Nothing. Just light and shadow. No shapes.'

'Then why come out?'

'I'm Jaibir, Finn. Of all people, I must be here. Would Wilf have stayed below?'

'I sincerely hope you're not going to model your leadership on his.'

Jenn smiled at this, turning her face towards him. 'Not a hope in hell, as it happens.'

Despite everything, Finnlay had to smile back. Two people could not be more unalike.

'What's happening now?'

'Everyone is ready. They're just waiting for my brother.'

'But he's there, I can Sense him.'

'Yes, but he seems to be deep in conversation with my wife. The gods alone know what they're talking about.'

Then the conversation ended. Fiona gave Robert a hug and moved back to stand with Martha. Robert took his horse and looked around, his expression sombre. Finally he turned towards Jenn and Finnlay, his gaze steady and unflinching, as though he could stay like that forever.

'Are you sorry?' Jenn whispered.

Finnlay couldn't answer immediately. Then Robert turned his horse and led the others through the gate. He disappeared quickly and the rest followed behind. Nobody moved until the last had gone.

'Yes, I'm sorry,' Finnlay finally breathed.

'But you haven't changed your mind?'

'No.' He turned to face her. She had a little more colour in her face now and she no longer stood as though she was about to fall over. 'I just wish I hadn't let my anger get the better of me.'

'Oh, Finn, you are wonderful, you know that?'

Finnlay looked askance at her. 'Are you sure you're feeling all right?'

'Of all the brothers Robert could have had, I know he wouldn't have swapped you for anyone.' She smiled and took his hand. 'You're worried you'll never see him again, aren't you?'

'I thought you were blind.'

'I think I have been, for a long time. It seems that when my eyes no longer work, I can see more than ever before. I want to ask you something, but I need you to think about it carefully before you answer.'

'What?'

'Do you trust me?'

Trust her? After all this time she had to ask?

But it was different now – *she* was different. It was weird, but although her blue eyes were glazed over with a pale white, it was obvious she could see *him* clearly. And, as if for the first time, he could see her in the same way.

He nodded slowly. 'Yes, Jenn. I trust you. I think I've always trusted you more than anyone else.'

She smiled again, warm and genuine. 'Then believe me when I tell you, you will see Robert again. I promise.'

'But . . . he'll never come back here again. You know that.'

'Yes. But you will see him.' She turned him back towards the tunnel, still holding onto his hand. 'I'll take you to him.'

22

'By the gods, what a mess!'

Vaughn turned his horse onto the rise and surveyed the army before him, almost obscured by heavy rain. Soldiers and animals alike wallowed kneedeep in mud. Carts were bogged down and sergeants bellowed at men to free them. All sense of order and discipline had evaporated within two hours of the downpour. Now, after three days, this supposedly well-trained fighting force had become a gaggle of hapless farmers and enslaved country folk undoubtedly wondering what the hell they were doing here.

Godet brought his horse alongside Vaughn's and adjusted the hood over his head. 'How far have we travelled since the rains began?'

'I'd be surprised if it were as much as ten leagues. You're right, it is a mess. I wonder, however, if our talented Governor Nash is capable of fixing it.'

With a smile, Godet shook his head. 'I don't think any amount of sorcery in the world can control the weather. If I didn't know better, I'd say you'd arranged it yourself, Uncle.'

'I? You do me a great injustice, Nephew. You know there is no one who wishes the King more success in this venture than me.'

'Of course,' Godet replied, laughing. 'And it's a great pity about those supply carts getting lost, don't you think? It could take days to find sufficient replacements in this weather.'

'Yes, a great shame. A pity they misunderstood my directions.' In the rainy haze, grey men fought through grey mud towards a grey hill. Between them, almost obscured at this remove, was a river, wide where its banks were flooded. 'However, though we hinder, we cannot, it seems, bring about a halt to this march.'

'But every day longer it takes us to reach the border, the more warning Tirone of Mayenne will have. I can't see Selar invading if there's already an army waiting to meet him. Especially if his men are in this kind of condition.'

'The border is still more than a week away – longer, perhaps, with this torrent. But the rain won't last for ever. In the long run, all this will do is help to unite the men. Having endured a common hazard together, they will become brothers in arms and face the enemy more attuned to each other, more trusting and more dangerous.'

As he watched, a cart at the bottom of the rise hit a rock in the mud and creaked to a halt. At the first push to get it moving again, the axle groaned and snapped, the cart collapsed, lopsided, and half its load slid off.

'We must be prepared,' Vaughn murmured. 'We can slow this army down with small efforts here and there, but if we do reach that border intact and it does really come to war, the Guilde must be ready to do everything to aid a victory. I don't care how many sorcerers Nash now has working for him, we cannot stand by and allow Tirone of Mayenne to win. He has little respect for the Guilde. Our influence in that country has dwindled during his reign. I don't fancy our chances if he kills his brother and invades our beloved Lusara. The Guilde has suffered during Selar's reign, but I believe we'd be forced out entirely if that came to pass.'

'And what of the rumours?'

'To which rumours do you refer?'

Godet glanced around to make sure they were still alone. 'That there is another army marching from the coast to meet us. It's said the men come from Budlandi, paid with gold from the Outlaw. There's some speculation the Douglas will come to stand between Selar and his brother Tirone.'

'More likely,' Vaughn uttered a harsh laugh, 'the Douglas will come to join and aid his minion, Nash. Why else would Nash believe he can invade a country the size of Mayenne with a mere ten thousand men?'

From the wet curtain below emerged a single rider, skirting the worst of the mud and making good time towards Vaughn's little hill. The man wore no helmet and his pure white hair almost glowed against the backdrop, his blue livery the only colour to be seen.

Panting and blowing hard, the horse gained the top of the rise and the man saluted. 'Forgive me, my lord Proctor, but the King has requested you attend him. He wishes to speak to you on the matter of the bridge.'

'But the bridge is down,' Vaughn replied with a shrug. 'Washed away by the flood. Does the King expect me to go and rebuild it personally?'

The man didn't reply, only waited patiently.

'Very well,' Vaughn sighed. 'We will go and attend the King. Where is he?'

'An open pavilion has been erected for him on the river bank, there to the right.'

Vaughn nodded, led Godet down the rise and deliberately took the longest path towards the river.

Nash stood at the edge of the pavilion, in the lee of the wind and untouched by the rain. With his hand resting on the pole, his gaze absently passed over the army as it struggled towards the river. Those who had made it gathered on the higher ground, out of danger of the floodwaters.

Selar paced up and down behind him, paying no attention to the meal or to the glowing brazier set up for his comfort. His impatience was almost palpable as the sergeant continued his report.

'We've lost more than fifty horses since the rain began, my liege. Almost half the supply carts have been damaged in one way or another. Our store of hay is now sodden and in a few days will be so rotten the animals won't eat it. The oxen pulling the carts are exhausted. They won't last much longer.'

'Are you telling me we should turn back?' Selar almost bellowed and Nash feigned a flinch. He couldn't be bothered turning to watch.

'No, Sire,' the unfortunate man replied. 'But we do need to stop and rest for a day, complete repairs to equipment, restock on lost supplies. Perhaps by then the rain will have stopped. We're making no distance as it is.'

'Go!' Selar thundered. 'Get out of my sight!'

Nash turned in time to see the man scurry out of the shelter into the rain. He wandered over to the table and poured himself some ale. 'Don't kill the messenger, Selar. He's doing his best.'

'Well, his best isn't good enough. I don't want to sit here for an hour, let alone a day! At this rate I'll be an old man before I see the border. If we camp here, every man will be drowned by the morning. That river is only going to get bigger.' Selar kicked a chair that was in his way and snatched up a cup of wine. 'And where's my son?'

'Kenrick was rounding up stragglers last time I looked. Just in case any of them might have changed their minds about this mighty enterprise we're embarked upon.'

Selar eyed him acidly. 'You know, Nash, sometimes I don't think you are taking this enterprise as seriously as you ought.'

'Believe me, Selar, I take it very seriously indeed,' Nash said. 'You just need to exercise a little more patience. You'll get what you want in the end.'

'Really? With that kind of chaos surrounding me?' He waved at the mess outside. 'My destiny awaits me!'

'Yes,' Nash smiled, 'I know. All the same.'

'Where's that damned Proctor?'

As Selar prepared to issue further orders, the Proctor rode up with his minion, Godet, at his side. Vaughn dismounted and entered the pavilion, bowing low before Selar.

'Your Majesty wished to see me?'

'Damned right I did!' Selar instantly attacked. 'Where is my bridge?'

'Washed away, Sire.'

'Then how, in Serin's name, do you expect me to get across this river without it?'

'There is another bridge, Sire, a dozen leagues downriver.'

Selar stormed forward, but Vaughn appeared untouched by his anger. 'What kind of answer is that, you idiot? We'd have to navigate the worst of Shan Moss to get to it!'

Vaughn drew himself up. 'Sire, I fail to see what you expect of me. I cannot conjure a bridge from nowhere. I am not a sorcerer.'

Something at the back of Nash's neck began to tingle and he turned his full gaze on the Proctor. Vaughn paid him no notice at all, but that wasn't unusual. It had been a long time since Vaughn had deigned to acknowledge Nash's existence.

There was something in the way that Vaughn was ignoring him. As though he wanted Nash to know . . .

The Bresail. Vaughn must have brought it from Marsay with him. So he would know, wouldn't he? About DeMassey and the other Malachi hidden in the army. Men who had escaped from Karakham in secret to help Nash, believing in him, sharing his goal.

What else had Vaughn done?

'For heaven's sake, Vaughn,' Selar spat, 'will you get off the damned subject of sorcery! I don't give a pig's ear about your difficulties. The Guilde builds bridges. I want one. Now!'

'Sire,' Nash murmured, not moving from his place, but dropping his gaze to his ale, 'not even the Guilde can produce a bridge from nowhere. I fear the Proctor is right. Our only option is to march south along the river and take the bridge in Shan Moss. In an hour, we'll be on higher ground and travelling much faster. We can be across the bridge by nightfall. The forest will afford us some shelter and the men can rest.'

Selar huffed and fumed some more, but, though he no longer remembered it, he was Bonded and had absolutely no will to oppose anything Nash said. 'Very well – but you, Vaughn, can give the orders. It's time you got your pristine vestments muddy like the rest of us.'

Vaughn didn't flinch. Instead, he bowed gravely. 'As you wish, Sire.'

As he disappeared into the rain, Selar said, 'One of these days, Nash, I'm going to make that man pay for the last twenty years. I've never known a supposed ally to act so much like an enemy.'

Nash nodded absently. Even as he watched, Vaughn was organising the men on the bank to begin the march south. Crisply, efficiently, calmly – above all, calmly. Not a quality Vaughn had ever been noted for.

'Where's Osbert?' he murmured, waving for his horse.

'How the hell should I know?' Selar grouched, gesturing towards the army. 'Out there somewhere.'

Nash pulled on his cloak and stepped out into the rain. 'You'd better get moving if you want to be at that bridge before nightfall, Sire.'

Night descended on the forest like a shroud, blanketing every movement, every sound. The worst of the rain had vanished, having done its work. As Nash left the camp, the noise of a relieved army remained behind to be swallowed up by the dense trees.

Shan Moss was the biggest and most feared forest in the country. It lay on the map in a diamond shape, one tip almost touching the border with Mayenne, the other lapping up to the foothills of the Goleth mountains. In between was a woodland sparsely populated and rarely travelled. There was a road which wound through it, but it was narrow and overgrown in places. People preferred to travel the north road towards Marsay, rounding the end of the mountain range. Almost nobody crossed those peaks, no matter the time of year.

Within the forest lay the occasional ruins, outposts of the old empire or scattered buildings of some brave lord who – defying superstition – believed the forest was not evil. Suspicion always ran free when fear was involved, that was why the Abbey had flourished: the gods making a stand against superstition. Laughable, really.

This had always been a special place for Nash. Dark, thick and a perfect place for solitude. On the northwestern edge stood one of a host of taverns, an inn once run by a man called Sev Halleck. He'd been Bonded to Nash, but was happy anyway to take on the three-year-old girl child Nash had brought him in secret. Halleck was to take care of her as though she were his own, to keep her there until Nash was ready to take her back. Halleck never knew where the girl had come from, had no idea she was the daughter of an Earl and destined to be one of the most powerful sorcerers ever born. Nash had believed Jenn would be safe in Shan Moss – and so she had been – right up until her 'father' had died.

Nash hadn't been able to visit for a long time. There had been a regeneration, which had taken almost three years to complete, to go from an old man to a young man. And after that, he'd joined the Guilde and worked his way towards Marsay – and Selar. Busy years, too busy to spend enough time with the child, to make sure her powers didn't develop before he was ready, to make sure he could turn her whenever he wanted.

Busy years indeed – and now he was paying for them. She was dead, beyond his reach entirely. No Bonding – and no child to give him life.

Nash came to a halt where a sloping cliff overlooked the river. Swollen and engorged, in the darkness it resembled a glistening snake of oil, bleeding the forest of life. DeMassey stood at the edge, looking down.

'Where is he?'

DeMassey jerked his hand towards the bushes to his right. 'In there.'

'Still?'

'Don't ask me, I just follow his orders, like you told me to.' DeMassey looked up and frowned. 'Isn't he just a little young for these appetites?'

Nash shrugged. 'He's nearly fifteen. Royal Princes take their pleasures where they wish. It's not for us to question.'

DeMassey laughed ironically. 'Right.'

'Any further news?'

'What? Since this afternoon? How many spies do you think I have roaming this damned country?'

Nash raised his eyebrows. 'As Master of the Darriet D'Azzir, I should think you'd have as many as you wanted. Didn't you tell me Malachi are flocking to train with you these days? Aamin's policies are not popular with all your people.'

'That's as may be, but I still can't use all of them to do your bidding.'

'This matter affects Malachi as well.'

'I know, that's why I'm here,' DeMassey said. 'Look, do we have to have this conversation again? Just be glad I did have a man in Aaran, otherwise you'd know nothing of the Enemy's army landing.'

Nash didn't have the energy to needle him any more. 'A week, no more. That's all we've got. One short week and he'll be mine.'

'You don't know that. My man said nothing of the Douglas leading the force. In fact, he was notably absent.'

'Oh, he'll be there, all right. This is not a fight he'll leave to anyone else. It'll be too late by the time he realises just what he's done.'

At this, DeMassey turned and looked at him. 'Are you sure? I find it very hard to believe that, after all this time, he has no idea who you are.'

'Why should he? His brother only ever saw my face once – and he was wounded and so desperate to escape at the time, I doubt he'd remember enough to pass on. It doesn't really matter anyway. What matters is that a week from now, I will finally face the Enemy.'

'And which enemy is that, Governor?'

Nash turned to find Kenrick emerge from the bushes, his hair and clothing giving no hint as to what he'd been doing.

'Why, our enemy from Mayenne, of course, my Prince.'

Kenrick appeared dubious, but didn't dally. He headed back towards the camp and DeMassey moved to follow him.

Nash dropped his voice. 'Just make sure nobody sees you bringing Vaughn out here.'

'You want him alive?'

'Of course – but use whatever means you must to get that nephew away from him. And afterwards? Find that damned Bresail and bring it to me.'

DeMassey nodded and vanished after the Prince. Nash turned back to the river where moonlight glittered off the water as it flowed towards the Abbey.

It was time to do something about that boy. He'd grown far too wilful for his own good. So young, and yet already so like his father. Still, as Nash had known how to handle the father, so did he the son.

Even more unsettling were the other activities Kenrick had been engaging in, experiments Nash had only heard about by the most indirect means. It was most inconvenient – and damned ill-timed – but it was entirely possible the boy was developing some powers. There was no other explanation for it. It was a shame Nash hadn't found some way to convert the Bonding process so the aspect of consent wasn't ultimately necessary. If he didn't do something to control Kenrick soon, he could have a big problem on his hands.

'I demand to know the meaning of this outrage!'

Nash turned slowly, a smile creeping across his face. DeMassey had bound Vaughn's hands behind his back and was marching him to the edge of the drop at the point of his formidable sword.

'I could say the same thing, Proctor.' Nash waited until Vaughn could fully appreciate the danger he was in before continuing, 'For example, I wonder what our beloved sovereign would say if I explained to him how you have worked to delay and hinder his army's progress.'

'I have done nothing of the kind!' Vaughn stepped back and

twisted his hands. 'I demand you let me go, immediately! I am your superior – how dare you treat me like this?'

Nash shrugged. 'It's your own fault. I never pushed you. I never forced you into anything. I was generous enough to leave you to your own devices – and yet, you've done so much to harm this war. Is that nice?'

Vaughn screwed his face up. He spat at Nash's feet. 'I know what you are. You are a viper who feeds off innocent people. You would bleed our country dry of life to get what you want.'

'Of course,' Nash replied offhand. 'It's not my country.'

'You don't even deny it?' Vaughn's voice was pure venom. 'You are a filthy, evil sorcerer . . . '

'There's no need to be rude.'

'And all along you have been in league with the Outlaw!'

'What?' Nash frowned, suddenly lost.

'You know who I'm talking about. For years you have stayed at court, doing his work. You have seduced the King and insinuated your foul minions into the sanctity of the Guilde. Your whore shares the King's bed. And now the Outlaw brings an army up from the south and you would hand him Selar on a platter. Deny you serve the Douglas!'

Nash opened his mouth, but for a moment, words failed him. He glanced at DeMassey, but the Malachi only shrugged, equally nonplussed. Nash turned back to Vaughn. 'Let me get this straight. You think I went to court, got close to Selar, urged him to this war, all because I'm working for Robert Douglas, Duke of Haddon?'

'I am *not* a fool,' Vaughn snapped. 'I have eyes. I can see you are both cut from the same mould.'

'More than you could possibly know,' Nash murmured, almost to himself. But then he couldn't help it: he burst out laughing, doubling up in an effort to contain his mirth. This was too rich by far! 'I can't believe it,' he gasped. 'All this fury – this ire – and for what? Oh, Proctor, I've made some big mistakes in my time – but you beat them all! I can't believe you've been so close all these years and never realised the truth.'

'What are you talking about now?' Vaughn refused to be swayed by Nash's laughter.

Should Nash tell him? The Proctor deserved to pay for his

331

meddling, and revenge would never be so sweet. 'You are wrong, Vaughn – you *are* a fool. Yes, the Douglas and I are very much alike, but we are the opposite sides of the same coin. I know you hate him, despise him, and have tried to do everything you could to destroy him. You have ruined your own reputation trying to get at him, but I am here to tell you, all along you were wrong.'

Nash stepped forward and placed a firm hand on Vaughn's shoulder, not allowing the man to flinch away. 'You are right about one thing: I am evil – more than you could possibly imagine. Oh, the tales I could tell you, if I had the time . . . But Robert Douglas is – and I mean this quite literally – the exact opposite of me. He doesn't have an evil bone in his body.'

'But he's a sorcerer . . .'

'Yes, but the sad truth is that not all are like me. Especially not the Douglas. Honestly, Vaughn, why do you think he was misguided enough to think he could do good on Selar's council? Why do you think he left Lusara ten years ago? Because he didn't want to stir up any more trouble with you. The only reason he stayed at home in Dunlorn was because his honour wouldn't allow him to break his oath to the King. I am sorry to tell you that the man has good written all over him from start to finish – which is why I am determined to destroy him. I know he's coming up from the south, but it is not to join me. He doesn't know it yet, but he's coming to fight me. Why do you think we're here, Proctor? I've no interest in invading Mayenne. I only want the blood of Robert Douglas, soaking into the soil at my feet. This whole effort has been simply to draw him out into the open.'

Nash began to chuckle again. 'You hate him so much, and yet all you've done is slow this army down and delay his inevitable end. Yes, my dear Vaughn, you are perhaps the biggest fool in the country!'

Vaughn had gone white. His mouth was open; his jaw hung slack and immobile. His breathing was slow and shallow, but he said not a word.

'You remember,' Nash dropped his voice to a conspiratorial whisper, 'years ago, just after Bishop Domnhall died? The synod elected McCauly primarily because of a story going around at the time. A hermit – from this very forest – received a vision that a dark angel had come to tear the Church in two. You – and everybody else at the time – wondered if it were Douglas, since he'd just returned from his exile. You know, Vaughn, I've been around a long time, more than a century. My birth was foretold in a prophecy dating back to the Dawn of Ages. In that prophecy, I have a name.'

Vaughn's eyes widened.

'I'm known as the Angel of Darkness.' Nash waited a moment, then dropped his hand. 'And for more than fifteen years, you have done your best to annihilate my Enemy, the only man who has the power to destroy me.'

Vaughn opened his mouth to speak, then his face twisted with some inner pain. Even as Nash watched, the old man's lips turned blue, his face red. Nash shook his head and once again placed his hands on Vaughn's shoulders.

'And that's my gift to you, Proctor. Something delicious to take with you to your grave.'

With that, Nash pushed hard. Helpless in his agony, Vaughn put up no fight as he stumbled backwards. With a silent scream, he fell over the precipice and tumbled down the slope. No rock nor bush halted his last journey. Instead, rolling in a broken heap, Vaughn fell into the river, his body immediately disappearing into the depths, drawn away by the raging torrent.

'What do you think they'll say?' DeMassey murmured, standing beside him. 'About the Proctor's sudden disappearance?'

'Who cares?' Nash turned away from the river. 'Look after that nephew of his, will you? A nasty accident or something will do the trick. You could even make it look like Vaughn murdered him and ran away. It'll give the masses something to talk about for a while. But do it tonight – before he notices his beloved uncle has vanished. I'm off for some supper with the sweet Prince.'

Help me!

Over and over he tumbled, tossed like a toy by the river, slammed up against rocks and fallen trees. Pain sliced through him, vicious and neverending, eating away at him from both outside and on. He was blind in the dark, inky treacle, torn down to the depths, then flung upwards to gasp in a lungful of air and water. He was dying: slowly, painfully – but dying, nonetheless.

His hand hit a branch and he struggled to hold on, then it broke away and followed after him. One last time he was pushed to the surface, but there was no time to look at the sky, to say a prayer for his own soul. He took in one more breath and sank. When his body crashed against the rocks, he felt no pain. When his head struck, the only sound he heard was his own plea for help.

Then there was nothing.

DeMassey strode nonchalantly through the camp, his Senses extended as far as they would go. Already the whispers had begun, rumours about Vaughn and his activities. By morning, everyone would know. Nash was busy with the King and while DeMassey kept a feather-like Sense extended towards the pavilion, he had a few moments' grace. He paused before a small tent, rich but simple. With a last glance around, he slipped inside.

There was no candle lit, only torchlight, gleaming through the walls. In the sudden darkness, a hand reached out to him, gentle yet demanding.

'I thought you were never going to come,' Valena murmured in his ear, her arms encircling him, her skin heady with her perfume.

Quickly DeMassey pulled her to him, kissing her with a passion he could only barely contain. Then he held her glorious face in his hands and spoke, his voice no more than a whisper. 'I'll have to tell him.'

'When?'

'Tomorrow night at the latest. I can't keep it from him much longer. If I do, somebody else will work it out and he'll have my head. I doubt it will take him too long to suspect you as well. I risk both our lives delaying.'

She nodded, fear brushing the edges of her gaze. 'I just wish you didn't have to say anything at all. Things have been different since she died, like they used to be before.'

'Don't be too sure. He's noticed that niece of Gilbert's. Sairead.'

'What's she doing here? I thought Gilbert was taking her back to Karakham.'

'She practically begged me to let her come. Not that she's trained enough to fight yet – I didn't think to refuse.'

'I see.'

DeMassey frowned. 'Have you changed your mind?'

'About us? Never! You know how much I hate Nash.'

'And he suspects nothing about the child?'

She shook her head. 'I have shared his bed but once since we left Dromna. I think now he'll be too distracted. The King as well. It's still early; I'm showing no sign.'

'Nevertheless, I want you to be careful the next few days. We're too close to ending this.'

'I can't wait until he fights the damned Enemy. I carry the bottle against my skin. He's never seen it, never wormed the knowledge from my mind. My shielding is very tight. He will never know that I was the one who killed him until it's too late.'

With a smile, DeMassey pulled her closer. 'And then you'll make sure he knows, won't you, my love? That it was both of us?'

She reached up and drifted her lips along his jawline, setting him on fire. 'It will be, I'm sure, the second greatest pleasure of my life.'

He woke to the sounds of a voice singing, an old, raspy voice, tuneless and incomprehensible. The words made no sense, but the song could have been a hymn. He opened his eyes. Above him was the sharp craggy outline of a cave roof, candlelight giving it some form.

He couldn't move. Not a single finger would obey his bidding. Only his eyes ranged about the immediate view. He strained to turn his head, even a little. Finally he had some success, but pain stopped him short. He opened his eyes again to see the source of light: two thick yellow candles on an ancient wooden shelf. Above, suspended on the wall, was a makeshift trium of river-washed twigs, smooth and interwoven.

'No! No!' The voice stopped singing and came closer. 'You not move, friend. Not good, not good. Stay still or you die.'

The man came closer. An ancient face, almost obscured by a long, straggly white beard, loomed above him. Deep wrinkles filled the dry flesh; the eyes were of pale yellow, bright and thinking. 'That's good. Just still. Good.'

His mouth worked strangely, as though he were unused to talking.

'You feel good?'

'I . . . ' It was hard to speak, his throat was dry. 'Who are you?'

'Who are you? Who are you? I'm hermit. Been here long time. Long time. On my own, yes. Always on my own. Talk funny, yes? No practice. Only singing songs of the gods. No talking. Not much.' He smiled, toothless and blissfully happy. Suddenly he turned and vanished, reappearing a moment later with a cup. 'You drink, get better.'

Swallowing, he kept his eyes on the hermit. 'Where am I?'

'Shan Moss, friend, Shan Moss, yes? Who are you?'

'I . . . ' He struggled for a moment, abruptly and completely lost. His name was . . . was . . .

What was his name?

'Doesn't matter, friend,' The hermit helped him drink some more, careful with every movement. 'You hurt bad in river. Broke your legs, arms. Hit your head. Cuts and blood. Very bad.'

'Am I dying?'

'Not now. I help. You get better one day.' The hermit rested back a moment, then raised a hand to sign the trium across the shoulders and up to his forehead. 'I know you come.'

'How?'

'A vision. Serinleth talk to me, tell me you come, you hurt. I help and you get better, yes? You get better and when I pass, you be hermit, yes?'

'No, I . . . ' Why couldn't he remember? He had to remember! He had a name. A real name – a life. Surely it would come back. With rest, as his broken bones mended, he would remember. He *had* to.

'This time you come to Serinleth,' the hermit murmured, his eyes bright. 'You come to gods' love and old life is gone. That's good. Very good. You do good. I promise. You stay here, become hermit. Do good. For the gods, yes?'

He closed his eyes against the urging. The past was an empty wasteland, invisible to his blindness. But every man had a past. What had he been doing in the river? Was somebody out there looking for him? When they didn't find him, they would think he was dead. Or would nobody notice he was even gone?

Who was he?

Pain formed about his head and he let the hermit give him more to drink. At least he was in no danger for the moment, and the hermit seemed sure he would survive. There was no urgency to leave, and perhaps his memory would return one day. Until he could remember, until he could even move, what choice did he have?

23

Finnlay sat back in his seat and surveyed the councillors arranged around the table. Martha and old Henry were there along with Acelin, the librarian, and the others, older, wiser perhaps, but none of them really prepared for the changes going on around them. At the end of the table sat Jenn: at twenty-five, by far the youngest Jaibir to be chosen by the Key, and only the fifth woman ever.

One for each century of the Enclave, as Martha had pointed out.

But there the similarities ended. For a start, there had never been a blind Jaibir before. Now, two days after the Gathering, Jenn moved about the Enclave with the aid of a guide, her eyes wrapped in bandages and ointments the healers assured him would help her regain her sight. For some strange reason, Jenn appeared completely unworried by the situation.

She was more concerned by the preparations, the scouts and reports from the west.

'And how big is this army Selar has gathered?'

'As far as we can tell, about ten thousand,' Henry replied, lacing his fingers together. 'At least half of them are mercenaries from Sadlan. It must be costing him a fortune to pay them. The gods alone know where the money will come from.'

'That's twice Robert's army,' Acelin added. 'I can't see how they'll have a chance. How can he win at such odds?'

'Is there any word where his army is now?' Jenn asked without addressing the question.

'They've landed – that's all we know. By now I should think they're a week's journey from Shan Moss. If they can move fast enough, they'll cut Selar's army off from the border at the western edge of the forest.'

Jenn nodded, turning her head as though her sight worked perfectly. 'I know this is a complete change of subject, but I wonder if Finnlay will now change his mind?'

'About what?' Finnlay sat forward again.

'Accepting a seat on this council.' Jenn paused, smiling. 'You turned it down once before, because you were afraid your loyalties would be divided between us and your brother. Now our purposes are joined. Will you now accept and give us the benefit of your wisdom?'

She managed to say this with a completely straight face, but when he glanced around at the others, they were also quietly serious. It was rare for someone to decline a council position – unheard of for it to be offered a second time.

'I . . . don't know what to say.'

Martha murmured, 'An affirmative response would do.'

Finnlay gave a short laugh. 'Why not?'

Jenn smiled again. 'Excellent. Welcome, Finn. Now, any other questions?'

'Yes,' Finnlay didn't waste time, 'the Key. What have you learned?'

Henry began to laugh. 'Patience was never your finest quality, my boy. Don't you know it takes time to assimilate joining with the Key?'

'It's all right, Henry,' Jenn raised her hand, 'I've actually learned a great deal so far, but I'm afraid none of it is any use to anyone but me.'

'What do you mean?'

The others shifted slightly, suddenly more attentive. Without doubt they were all thinking the same thing as Finnlay.

'I grew up knowing nothing of my powers or this place, so I have very little of the learning you all have, little of the assumptions you've had to make. But I can tell you the Key is not what we thought it was. In some ways, I suspect that's why it's always been so difficult to wield. I also believe my ability to mindspeak allows me to communicate with it more easily than my predecessors. On the other hand, that also makes it more difficult.'

'How?' Finnlay murmured.

'It never leaves me alone. It's with me constantly, would – given the chance – talk to me constantly. Sometimes it's an effort to push it into the background. It tells me this is just the beginning and it will get easier as we grow together. I've had some very strange dreams I'm sure come from the Key – partly because it doesn't deny it – but I remember none of them. What I can tell you is about the voice.'

'Voice?'

Jenn nodded. 'Did Wilf never talk about all this?'

'No Jaibir ever does,' Henry murmured, captivated. 'There's always been some reluctance. I guess it's always been assumed reticence was a characteristic of the joining.'

With half Jenn's face covered in bandages, it was difficult to read her expression. She was silent a moment. 'Well, Wilf was the only Jaibir I ever met, so I can't prove anything, but sometimes, when the Key speaks to me, it sounds just like him. But it also sounds like a lot of other voices as well. Many and one at the same time. And it always refers to itself in the plural.'

The murmur around the table ended when Finnlay asked, 'And you know nothing about the Calyx?'

'It refuses to respond when I ask.'

'Then it does at least know where the Calyx is?'

'I couldn't say. You have to understand, Finn,' Jenn leaned forward and rested her arms on the table, 'it's as though the Key speaks another language and I have to work through an interpreter. Sometimes it talks in riddles, knowing I'm not able to understand. It's often capricious, like a wilful child, only discussing the things it wants me to know about. I don't want to push it just yet. I don't want to break it.'

There was involuntary laughter at that and Jenn came to her feet. 'Well, if there's nothing else, I'll let you all get to your supper. Finn, will you take me back to my rooms?'

She made her way around the table on her own, then took his arm in a gesture of affection.

She was silent most of the way back, and beginning to speak only when they approached her door. 'Are you busy at the moment? Is Fiona expecting you?'

'Not immediately. Why?'

'I need your help with something.'

He pushed the door open and she moved inside.

'Will you light some candles for me?'

Finnlay waved his hand over the two candles standing on the table. As they flared into life, he looked up to find Jenn by the fire, ladling water from a pot into a bowl. Her hands moved deftly, she'd quickly become accustomed to blindness. She returned the bowl to the table and favoured him with a smile.

'Remember when I asked if you trusted me? Now I'm going to show you why.' She reached up and undid the end of the bandage. He took it from her and slowly unwound it until her eyes were uncovered. They were shut and smeared with something that glistened as though wet. He got a cloth and bathed them with the water, dried them and stood back. With a smile, she opened her eyes and looked at him.

'By the gods!'

'What?' she asked, a frown already appearing.

'You can see! The white's gone. Your eyes are completely normal again.'

'Of course they are!' She laughed. 'What did you expect?'

'I . . . ' Finnlay ran out of words. Some days . . .

'Poor Finn.' Jenn pulled out a chair and sat opposite him. 'I would think by this time you'd be used to these little surprises I keep springing on you. The blindness was never going to be permanent. The Key even apologised for it, said it was an unfortunate consequence of such a complete joining.'

He gazed at her. Her eyes were indeed the old azure, sparkling against the candlelight and full of understanding. She was really quite remarkable. 'Very well, go ahead and explain.'

She grinned and sat back, folding her arms. 'It's about the joining itself. I can't say I know too much about the Key just yet – but I have discovered one thing. I know how it works.'

'How?'

'Have you ever wondered how the Key's power works? Why it is that a new Jaibir must be chosen so soon after the last death and why the Jaibir can never set foot beyond the gate for the rest of his life?'

'Actually, no.'

'And I thought you had such an inquisitive mind, Finn! Do you know what the word Jaibir actually means? Life. When I joined with the Key, I gave it life. That's the way it works. The Jaibir sustains the Key with his own powers, but if those powers aren't strong, the link weakens with any kind of distance and both the Key and Jaibir would die.'

Finnlay's heart began to thump loudly in his chest. 'But your powers aren't weak.'

Jenn's smile dropped. 'No. So – will you help me?'

It was dark outside and just late enough for almost everyone to be underground, at supper. All the way across the field, Finnlay scrambled for some way to dissuade Jenn from this course. It was madness. Even if she were right – which he didn't believe for one minute – it was way too soon to be trying something like this. Surely she hadn't really recovered from the joining. She appeared to be in full health . . . but . . .

'I don't like this at all,' he said as they approached the dark void of the gate. 'If the Key hasn't said this will work, then perhaps you shouldn't try it. Not yet. Any number of things could go wrong. My shoulder is still injured – I'd never be able to carry you back inside if—'

'Oh, stop worrying, Finn. Life is full of chances.'

He stopped her, grabbing her arm and turning her to face him. 'And you can stop this act with me! I know you too well, Jenn. You have no idea if this will work, have you?'

'No. But I have to try. You of all people should understand that. I didn't want to come here, but the moment I made my oath to Stand the Circle, I knew it was my . . . destiny to become Jaibir. Your brother has always fought against his destiny, believing absolute refusal to obey was the only path forward. Perhaps, for him, it is. But not for me. I don't think you can avoid your destiny – but I don't believe it has to be a death sentence. I tried to explain that to Robert, but he wouldn't listen. I suppose with a destiny like his, reason is out of the question.'

Finnlay sucked in a horrified breath. 'You know the rest of the prophecy?'

'No, the Key hasn't deigned to tell me that much. What I do know is that so much of what Robert has done – and what he will do – is because he loves me. That gives me a kind of responsibility I can't honestly say I want. Try as he might, Robert has become a slave to his fate. I refuse to do the same. What would I be if I couldn't learn from his mistakes?'

'I don't understand.'

'I have a destiny, too, Finn – but I'm not just going to sit back and let it carve out my future. I'm going to push it along before me, bend it to my will, and make it do what I want. I may not have a choice about having this future – but I'm damned sure going to have a choice about what I become. It may use me – but I'm going to use it in return. Now, are we just going to stand out here, or are you going to help me?'

Her mind was made up. 'Very well, but I'll go through first, just in case.'

He turned and stepped into the darkness. After a few moments, a light tingle brushed over his skin, his Senses, and then he was into the tunnel, a corner of sky visible at the end. He stopped and waited.

Seconds later, Jenn shot through the gate, running as fast as she could. He caught her and they laughed.

'I gather you weren't all that sure after all. I doubt anybody has ever run through the gate before. I suppose I'll have to stop being surprised by anything you do. I might just assume the worst – then wait to see if you can match my best guess.'

She grinned. 'Come on. Getting past the gate was easy. I need to see how far I can get from the Key before it starts to panic.'

She took his hand and turned down the tunnel. At the edge, she let go and continued on her own for a few steps. Glancing over her shoulder, she murmured, 'Use your best Seeking abilities, Finn. Don't go too far – just the immediate surrounding area. I need to know if there's anybody but our sentries within a league of the mountain.'

Finnlay left the cave and stood beside her. He closed his eyes and reached out, Sensing his way down the path, up and over a dozen sharp ridges. The night aided his search, clearing the air, making all things equal. After a few minutes he came back and looked at her. 'Nothing. You're on your own.'

All humour had gone from her now. With a nod, she moved forward, slowly but surely. There was enough moonlight to see the path and her white-robed figure moving along it. Then she turned a corner and vanished. He didn't dare try Seeking her. Every attempt he made only increased the risk of Nash finding him – and the Enclave.

That didn't make it any easier to wait. He tried sitting on a rock, but impatience drove him to his feet again. He paced up and down to keep warm in the cool spring air. He waved his arms around, bounced on his toes and tried to pinpoint his favourite constellation in the sky.

I told you to stop worrying, Finn. Everything's fine.

He swallowed, but his pacing slowed. *I've changed my mind. I'm never going to get used to all this. Come back now, please. You're giving me a headache.*

Sorry.

Another long wait and then she appeared on the path again, her smile clearly visible in the moonlight. She ran the last few yards and hugged him.

'I knew it! I knew it would work. Oh, Finn, you have no idea!'

'Yes I do.' He laughed. 'And I hate you.'

'Perhaps, but not for long. Come on, we've got work to do. I don't have much time.'

It was one thing to convince Finnlay, but another entirely to make Fiona and Martha understand.

'You must be out of your mind!' Martha cried, then quickly moved to the children's door to make sure the noise hadn't woken them. Fiona's two were fast asleep, curled up together on a big comfy chair.

'Either that, or joining with the Key has finally done away with the last of your reason,' Fiona added, keeping her voice quiet. She stood next to Finnlay, watching him carefully. He almost squirmed under her gaze, but said nothing. 'I don't see the point. If you have to go anywhere, why go east? Surely you'd want to go west, to Shan Moss.'

'I will, but I have to do something else first, and if I don't leave tonight, it'll be too late,' Jenn replied.

'The Key's not the only one who talks in riddles.' Martha drew them all away from the children and faced Jenn squarely. 'I know how much your freedom means to you, but if you want our help, you'll have to explain properly.'

'This has nothing to do with freedom,' Jenn whispered. 'And everything to do with my son.'

Martha paused at that. 'What do you mean?'

Jenn took in a deep breath, holding her urgency at bay. 'Before I left Bleakstone, I sent a message to Father John. I asked him to get my sister to bring Andrew to the hills below the Goleth. With all the focus on the war, nobody would pay too much attention to them leaving Maitland for a couple of weeks. They'll be waiting for me now. If we leave tonight we can get there before sundown tomorrow. If I don't show up by then, they'll turn and go back home. I don't have the time to go chasing after them. I still have to . . . '

'So you do intend to go to Shan Moss?' Fiona murmured, expressionless.

'As soon as I get back. Now do you see why I have to hurry?'

Fiona nodded. 'Are you going to bring Andrew back here?'

'No, not yet. He's still too young.' Jenn studied the women, but avoided Finn's gaze completely.

'Very well,' Fiona said, turning to her husband. 'You'll have to manage the children on your own for a couple of days. It'll be a good exercise for you.'

It was obvious he wanted to protest, but he kept silent.

Martha said, 'Finn, if you can organise three horses while we pack, we can be away within the hour.'

'You're not going too?' Jenn hissed.

'Why not? I can have my aunt look after the children – and we won't be gone long. If we can get you as far away as the foothills, then you'll easily make Shan Moss. I'm sorry, but I have a vested interest in you being around for that battle. I want my husband back in one piece.'

'And you think *I'm* crazy. Well, come on. Let's get moving.'

Jenn had to admit it was a good idea having both of them along. Fiona rode in front, Seeking the path and leading with a confidence Jenn had to admire. Martha rode behind, using her Seeking abilities to watch for anyone who might approach them. As dawn rose, the sky turned pink, blotting out the stars and bathing the land in a grey glow of morning. Neither woman spoke much, concentrating on their work. Jenn had all the time to think.

There was absolutely no guarantee Bella and Andrew would even be in the wood, no guarantee the message had got through or that Bella would do as John instructed.

And there had to be a limit to how far the Key would let Jenn wander.

It was quite remarkable, really. There was a clear difference between the voice of the Key inside the Enclave and that outside the gate, as though, beyond the mountain, it spoke through a film of gauze. What was even more odd was how it made no attempt to stop her – even though it obviously knew what she was trying to do. No argument, no protests. Nothing.

But as each hour went by, the voice faded more into silence. She could still feel the Key with her, but its ability to communicate had vanished by midmorning. For a while she missed it and was besieged by a sudden desire to turn back, but Andrew might be waiting for her, and she kept her concentration on the link. If it too should start to fade, she needed to know right away. For all her temerity at taking these chances, there was no way to guess what might happen if the link broke completely.

It was near nightfall before they reached the edge of the wood perched on a hillside below the Abbey of Saint Germanus. From the trees, rows of grape vines were clearly visible, snaking their way across the slopes. Jenn paused a moment to study the place. Robert had told her all about his stay there after their Bonding, hiding from what he'd done, trying to keep himself from doing more harm. So strange that his effort to finally remove himself from the world had brought him into contact with the only man capable of helping him to embrace it again. Though she barely knew Aiden McCauly, it was obvious how close he'd grown to Robert, how much they depended upon each other, how similar their roles were – and how very different.

Robert needed someone around him with a bottomless faith. McCauly needed someone to help, to have faith in. What would have happened to both of them if they'd never met?

'I can Seek John from here.' Fiona interrupted her thoughts. 'He's not far.'

Jenn turned into the darkness of the woods, trying to hide her feelings completely. Now she was so close, she could almost see Andrew, his aura was so strong.

They led their horses between the trees, but before they even reached the clearing, Jenn dropped her reins and ran forward. Andrew saw her and, with a yelp, leaped into her arms. For a long time, Jenn just held onto him, ignoring her tears, the weight of him in her arms. Slowly she sank to her knees, not letting go of him.

'I knew you'd come, Mother,' he murmured into her shoulder. 'Aunt Bella told me not to hope too much, but I knew.'

Jenn held him back a little and looked at him, smoothing down his dark hair. His eyes were terribly solemn, but he was fine. Absolutely fine. She glanced up at Bella and John. 'Thank you for bringing him. Did you have any trouble?'

'Only with Lawrence,' Bella murmured. 'He doesn't understand.'

John smiled. 'I'll get a fire going.'

Bella now turned to Fiona, her gaze accusing. 'I know you. You came to teach Jenn at Elita, didn't you? Are you a sorcerer too?'

Fiona came forward and helped John. 'I don't think we should be discussing such matters out here in the open.'

'Oh, so my sister has managed to twist you to her purposes as well?' Bella snapped.

'Please, Bella.' Jenn stood, keeping hold of Andrew's hand. 'I know you're angry, but . . . '

'Anger doesn't even come close,' Bella hissed. 'I'm surprised you didn't bring Robert with you, just to complete the insult.'

'Robert is with his army,' Martha replied, her voice soothing, her demeanour warm and calming. 'He's planning to stop Selar's invasion of Mayenne.' She came and knelt before Andrew, a smile on her face. 'Hello.'

'Hello,' Andrew replied, suddenly shy.

'Did you enjoy your journey here?'

Andrew nodded. 'I never went so far before. Days and days and days. I'm a good rider.'

'I'm sure you are.' Martha smiled.

'Jenn,' Bella interrupted, 'are you going to tell me what's going on – or am I to remain in ignorance?'

Jenn sat on the ground by John's new fire and pulled Andrew onto her lap. 'It's as Martha says. The two armies are even now approaching the western edge of Shan Moss. Robert will find some way to stop Selar before he gets to the border.'

'Well, this is a fine time for him to decide to do something! And what happens when he does? Are you going to come home?'

'I can never go home,' Jenn murmured, keeping most of her attention on Andrew. He watched her with wary eyes, as though he expected her to run off at any second.

'And what about your son?'

'Please, Bella. Do we have to discuss all this right now?'

'I want an answer.'

'I . . . can't take him with me. Not yet.'

Silently Andrew's eyes filled with tears, but they were never shed. The boy had the courage of a man ten times his age. Jenn pulled him close and murmured in his ear, 'You know I love you. But there are things I have to do. Things for our country. People will die if I don't do them.'

'People like Duke Robert?' Andrew whispered. 'He saved you from Papa.'

'That's right, my love. He did.'

He stared steadily at her, his fingers playing with the cloak laces at her throat. 'Why can't I come and help? I won't get in the way. I want to help Duke Robert. He helped you. I promise I'll be good.'

Jenn looked away, suddenly finding it difficult to breathe. Both Martha and Fiona were watching her – with completely different expressions.

'Of course you'd be good,' Jenn whispered. 'And you can help. You can go home with Bella and learn your lessons. As soon as I can, I promise I'll come back and see you. Often. And one day, when you're a bit older, you can come back with me.'

'When?'

'Oh, a long time, so don't go counting days and driving your aunt crazy. But I'll be back to see you a lot before then. You like living at Maitland, don't you?'

He nodded. 'Better than Clonnet. Uncle Lawrence gave me a

horse. We go riding every day. He's funny. He tells me jokes and I laugh so hard my stomach hurts.'

Jenn glanced up at Bella, who shrugged. 'Lawrence was afraid you'd take Andrew with you. He wants the boy to grow up at Maitland. I think you can understand why.'

Though Lawrence had never said a word about it, it had always been obvious that the only great regret he'd ever had was that he and Bella had never had any children.

'And you?'

Bella frowned. 'You have to ask that? Of course I want him. I'd just be happier if . . . Oh, what's the point? I'm never going to get any sense out of you.'

'I'm sorry.'

'So you keep saying.'

'I never intended any of this to happen, and I don't really have a choice.'

The last of Bella's anger faded away and she looked tired. 'When this is all over and you come to visit your son, I'm going to get some answers out of you, whether you like it or not.'

Jenn turned back to Andrew, a small smile on her face. 'Well, perhaps by then I might just have some.'

A translucent half-moon hovered above the mountains as Jenn left the forest. Martha and Fiona rode on either side of her, quiet in the night. It had been so hard to leave him, so hard to put him into Bella's arms and walk away. He hadn't cried, but she had. Was it really such a good idea leaving him to grow up at Maitland? Would Lawrence and Bella make sure he had all the education he needed? He would never learn about his people from living at the Enclave – especially since he no longer had to hide there for safety.

'I just want to know one thing,' Fiona murmured, keeping her gaze on the path ahead.

'What's that?'

'Does Robert know Andrew is his son?'

Jenn pulled her horse to a stop, wheeling to face her. 'What do you mean?'

'I'm sorry, Jenn,' Martha held up a calming hand, 'we don't mean to imply anything . . . '

'Oh don't hedge, Martha,' Fiona said evenly. 'She knows exactly what we're talking about.'

For a moment, Jenn didn't know what to say. 'How did you know?'

Fiona gave one of her rare smiles. 'I've been married to his uncle for five years, Jenn. How can I miss the family resemblance? I know he's not Finnlay's son and you and Robert have been in love for years. What other answer could I come up with?'

Jenn turned to Martha. 'And you?'

'The resemblance is there – but to be honest, if I hadn't already been looking for it, I wouldn't have guessed. That's really why I wanted to come with you.'

'By the gods,' Jenn breathed, 'how many others will guess as well?'

'Not many.' Fiona shrugged. 'As Martha says, you've got to know what you're looking for. Andrew has your hair and eyes, even the shape of your face. But there's something about the way he tilts his head, something in his smile. I saw Eachern once. The boy looks nothing like *him* and too much like Robert. I just want to know if Robert is aware. It's obvious Andrew isn't.'

'No, Robert doesn't know,' Jenn snapped – then regretted it. 'I'm sorry. A few weeks ago, I was prepared to tell him, but not now. And now he's married again, I doubt I ever will. I have to put Andrew first and it would do him no good to learn the truth.'

'I see,' Fiona said. 'Who else knows?'

'Just Micah and Finnlay. They both guessed.'

'Well, suddenly a whole lot of things make sense.'

'And you want to keep it secret?' Martha added.

'Yes.'

'Great.' Fiona turned her horse back onto the path. 'Another secret. Just what we need. And I suppose you're determined to take Finnlay out of the Enclave and into Robert's war?'

'How did you know?'

'I'm married to the man, Jenn.' Fiona was mildly irritated. 'Do you think, after all this time, I can't occasionally guess what he's thinking? He's terrified, but he trusts you. He'll go through with it if you ask.'

'There won't be any danger, you know.'

349

'I love the way you say that,' Fiona replied dryly. 'As though you've already done it a thousand times before.'

'Stop it,' Jenn snapped, grabbing hold of Fiona's bridle and forcing her horse to a halt. 'I don't need this – especially not from you. If you love him, you must see how much he needs to get out of the Enclave, if only for a few days. What's more, he needs to be with Robert. Oh, I know they fought, and I know Finnlay is as angry as all hell with his brother – but that doesn't change the fact that Finnlay is eating himself up inside because he, above all others, knows the danger Robert is going into, facing the Angel of Darkness. Robert, bless his dear, misguided heart, has no idea at all.'

Fiona said nothing, merely lifted her chin against Jenn's on-slaught. Jenn continued, 'Now I want you to understand, I love Finn. He's like a brother to me and I'd never let anything happen to him – but if Robert fails against Nash and Finnlay could have done something to prevent it, it will kill him and you know it. You have to believe that I can keep Finnlay safe from Nash. I carry the Key with me. The protection it affords the Enclave, I can give to Finnlay. I'm the only person who can take him safely outside the gate. I beg you, don't oppose me in this.'

'I begin to see what your sister was talking about. You really can twist people around.'

'My sister is an ignorant fool,' Jenn snapped. 'You, however, don't have the same excuse. You knew what you were getting into when you married Finnlay. He's never made any secret of how he feels about Robert – and he's worked for almost twenty years to get Robert into exactly this war. If you pull at him from the opposite direction, you'll only make things worse for him. His soul is crying out to be at Robert's side. Don't tell me you can't see that.'

Fiona blinked rapidly. Her voice dropped. 'Of course I can. But I can also see my children without a father.'

'Believe me,' Jenn whispered, reaching for her hand, 'I'll keep him safe. I promise.'

24

Nash strode through the camp, idly counting the campfires which glowed against the forest backdrop. The wind was bitter, whistling through the trees and out across the plain. As far as he could see, the army was settling down for the night, quieter now, the closer they got.

They had no idea just how close they were.

He made directly for the royal pavilion. Guards at the entrance had the tent flaps open before he reached it and he walked straight inside. A long table stretched out before him, with Selar seated at the end. Around it sat his councillors, in various states of impatience. How it must kill them to have to wait for him before beginning the meeting. Nevertheless, he was the penitent servant. It was such a game now, though one he wouldn't have to play for much longer.

'Forgive me, Sire; I wanted to complete a perimeter survey before this meeting.'

Selar, gracious as ever, waved him to a seat. 'Just get on with it. Ingram? How do we stand?'

'Better than a week ago, Sire,' the Chancellor replied. 'We've managed to supplement our supplies from the two towns we've passed since reaching the forest. Horses are back up to full numbers and the oxen are rested.'

'Good. Any news from the border?'

'None since the last report. If Tirone is going to come across to meet us, he's doing it very quietly – or taking a route we can't cover with our scouts.'

'And which do you think is the most likely?'

'To be honest, Sire, the latter,' Ingram replied. 'I can't see how it's possible, with our march delayed by the rains, for your brother not to be aware of our approach.'

'Sire,' Bishop Brome insinuated himself into the conversation like a dagger between chain mail, 'I fear we have another, more immediate concern.'

351

'What?' Selar had a way of asking a simple question without volume, yet still managing to make a man quake before him.

When the Bishop didn't answer, it was left to Osbert to finish the sentence. 'The Outlaw, Sire.'

At this, Selar sat forward, pushing his wine cup out of the way. 'What about him?'

'The reports of his army have now been confirmed by a dozen of my people. He rides at the head of five thousand men and it's without doubt he intends to cross you before you can reach the border. We must assume he brings sorcerers with him.'

Selar looked at Nash and then at his son, seated beside him. 'More sorcerers? Please, Osbert, don't tell me that now you've become Proctor, you're going to harp on that subject as well?'

Osbert swallowed. 'Nonetheless, we must take it into account.' He paused, swallowed again, then continued, not looking at anyone, 'I fear I must also tell you of another piece of news which came with the scouts.'

'Out with it, man. I don't have all night!'

'Your daughter is with the Outlaw.'

'What?' Kenrick hissed, coming instantly to his feet. 'He would hold her ransom?'

'I don't believe that's his intention, my Prince. I . . . my scouts tell me that the Princess has . . . married the Outlaw. Already the rumours are flying about our camp. Everyone will know about it by morning.'

Now that was interesting. The Enemy has married the little Princess? An alternative now that the Ally is dead? Very clever, my friend, very clever.

'I'll kill him!' Kenrick swore, kicking his chair backward with a crash.

'Calm yourself, son.' Selar restrained him with a hand. 'There'll be time for that later.' He waited until Kenrick returned to his seat before continuing, obviously vaguely amused, 'So, we'll have to fight him – and perhaps it's time. How far away is his puny army?'

'Three days' march, Sire,' Osbert replied. 'I estimate he's intending to stop us within sight of the border. On the westernmost edge of Shan Moss.'

Selar was silent a long time, tapping his fingers idly on the table and completely unaware of how his son fumed beside him. 'So, Robert finally finds the courage to take a stand against me – but he needs my girl to gather an army. A bunch of criminals and malcontents, I'm sure. When they see what they're facing, half of them will run in fear. Well, it will give me a chance to see who's taken his side. I doubt there'll be many surprises. Payne and McGlashen, for a start. They were too quick to find an excuse not to join me.' He paused and nodded. 'Well, a brief scrap will harden my men to their purpose. The execution of a few thousand traitors will sharpen their swords. So be it. We ride to face the Outlaw.'

Nash sat back and smiled.

Godfrey finished his supper quickly, then returned to his door to watch the royal pavilion. It was only moments before the meeting broke up and Osbert emerged, his head bowed. Trying not to hurry, Godfrey left his tent and joined him. The new Proctor glanced up, surprised.

'Good evening, Archdeacon.'

'I'm sorry to disturb you, Proctor, but I was wondering if there was any further news on the investigation. The men have been asking.'

Osbert shook his head and paused before the door of his own tent. 'The investigation has finished, Archdeacon. I believe the news is about as bad as we could imagine – though I don't understand it for one moment.'

'Then you really think Vaughn killed his aide and then ran off with the Bresail?'

'What else am I to think? I'm sorry, Godfrey. I know nobody actually liked Vaughn – but who would wish something like that on any man?' Osbert frowned, his gaze on the royal pavilion. He paused for a few moments then dropped his voice. 'I think we're in trouble.'

'How?' Godfrey whispered, surprised at this sudden confidence from Osbert.

'The Douglas is bringing an army to stop us. Selar's taking it too lightly, not fully appreciating the danger. I remember Robert from old. He's a far better soldier than Selar could ever hope to be – and he's not blind. On top of that, he's married Galiena. Until I heard that piece of news, I thought Robert might only be playing a delaying tactic.'

'And now?'

Osbert looked at him, arid as wasteland. 'He means to bring Selar down, and unless the King takes that threat seriously, Robert might just succeed.'

Nash picked up his cup, swung his feet up onto the table and gazed across at DeMassey.

'I think I'll send for Valena tonight,' he said with the suggestion of a smile.

'Why?'

'Because I feel like celebrating.'

DeMassey responded typically. He grunted and stood, walking around the table to gaze out of the open tent door. 'You're damned lucky I tolerate your needling, Nash. I don't need you to keep reminding me of her choice.'

'But it is so much fun.'

'Well, I think you're ahead of yourself. The Enemy may well be only a few days away – but we haven't won yet. And his army is no pack of rabble as Selar would like to believe. It's a well-trained fighting force, under one of the best commanders this country has ever seen. I hardly have a scout return without stories of discipline, the training in camp.'

'I couldn't care less. I never needed this army to win a battle. It was only ever intended to act as bait.'

'But we will fight.'

'Of course. What's wrong, Luc? Afraid?'

DeMassey swung around, his face full of disgust. 'Sometimes you really make me sick!'

Nash began to laugh. 'Only sometimes?'

'You have no idea, do you?' The Malachi stood in the centre of the room, hands on his hips in an uncharacteristically inelegant stance. 'You think you know everything – but you'd be as blind as a bat if it wasn't for me! I've perjured my position in Karakham to be here, to help you – and all you can do is fire pathetic shots at me, hoping I'll do something to provoke you. I gave up on Valena the day she chose you over me. There's nothing more you can say to me that can make it any worse. On the other hand, unless I get some civility out of you, I won't tell you the news my latest courier brought me tonight.'

Nash burst out laughing. 'My what a fine performance! How long did that speech take to compose? By the blood of Broleoch, I'll bet you've been warming to it from the day I took Valena from Karakham. Rather typical of you to save it for now. Come, be a good lad and give me up your news.'

DeMassey set his jaw and said nothing.

Nash didn't bother to hide his smirk. With barely a wave of his hand, the dagger lying on the desk rose into the air and hovered against DeMassey's throat. Nash kept it there for a minute, enjoying the fear in the man's eyes, his inability to move away from the blade. Then, abruptly, he released it. He turned back to his wine as DeMassey staggered back.

'Sorry,' Nash murmured, leaning forward to pick up the dagger from the ground. 'I thought you might need reminding why it is that I give the orders around here and you don't. Now, tell me your news before I lose my temper.'

Breathing heavily, DeMassey pulled back his shoulders. 'It's about your little Duchess, the Ally.'

Nash glared. 'She's dead. Valena will have to take her place – regardless of how unfit she is to do so. What about her?'

'What if I told you Jennifer Ross didn't die in that fire at Clonnet?'

Nash froze. Slowly he turned and faced DeMassey. 'What are you talking about?'

A brief sneer crossed the man's face before he spoke. 'Remember you had a spy at Clonnet?'

'What of it?'

'I had one there, too. A woman.'

'She knows what happened?'

'I don't know. All I do know is that I've not heard from her since the fire. If Eachern recognised the Douglas and called the guard out, she would have gone to fight.'

'And the Enemy would have killed her,' Nash breathed, sitting up straight. Absently, he brought his cup to his lips, but he didn't drink. 'That was the body we buried in the Basilica. By the blood – I underestimated her! So the Ally could leave her brat after all – of course she could. He's not a child of the Bonding . . . But . . . if she's not dead, then where is she now? Why has the Douglas married the Princess?'

'Don't ask me,' DeMassey growled. 'You're the one who gives the orders around here.'

Nash looked up, then formed a smile. 'I apologise, you are right. Forgive me?'

'You still make me sick!'

Laughter grew in Nash's belly and he did nothing to halt it. She was alive! She was *alive*! And though something might have gone wrong between her and the Enemy, there was no doubt at all she'd be somewhere inside his army. She wouldn't miss it for anything!

Still chuckling, he came to his feet. Suddenly everything, even this wretched tent, looked so much better! 'On your way out, let Valena know I'll visit her tonight. It seems I have something to celebrate after all! I'm off to have a quiet word with the sweet Prince.'

Kenrick wasn't alone. He sat back in a chair, his boots upon another, shirt undone to the waist like a man twice his age. Half a dozen of his friends were arranged in similar fashion around the tent, all deep in their cups, oblivious to Nash's entrance. To the naked eye, there appeared present none of the usual pleasures the Prince indulged in. Perhaps it was too early in the evening.

'Well, my lord Governor,' Kenrick waved languidly, 'I'm honoured you stopped by. Wine?'

'No, thank you, my Prince.'

'Oh, well.' Kenrick lifted a bottle to his lips, swallowing deeply before coughing. He brought the bottle away, dribbling red down his chest. A few of his friends laughed.

'I would speak with you alone, my Prince,' Nash said, evenly, but loudly enough for the others to hear.

'Not in the mood, Nash. It'll wait until morning. I have another matter to attend to right now.'

'I won't take much of your time,' Nash replied, exerting just a little uncomfortable pressure on the others. One by one they sat up, rubbing faces and eyes as though they'd woken from some sleep. A little more pressure and, in a group, they rose, bowed and left. Nash waited as Kenrick watched him, obviously nowhere near as drunk as he appeared to be.

'What do you want?'

'I was about to ask the same question, my Prince.'

Kenrick's gaze narrowed. 'You can stop the act with me, Nash. I know what you are.'

'And I know what you are.' Nash paused. 'So, we're even. Now perhaps we can get down to business.'

Stony-faced, Kenrick waved him to a chair and Nash sat.

For several moments, Kenrick said nothing, but the wine bottle landed on the carpet beside him. 'How did you get rid of my friends? The same way you control my father?'

'The two methods are entirely dissimilar.'

'Explain.'

'Not tonight. This is about something else.'

'I want to know now. How do you control my father? He obeys every word you say and has done for a long time. I want to know how to do that. Tell me!'

'No.'

Abruptly, Kenrick sat forward, his eyes blazing. 'Do you have any idea what I could do to you?'

Nash ventured a calm smile. 'Actually, you can do very little to me – but I don't suggest you try just at the moment. Not until you at least hear what I have to say.'

'I don't give a damn for your arrogance, Nash! Nor for how powerful you think you are. All I have to do is yell for help and a hundred men will rush in here, swords swinging for your neck. Don't pretend that doesn't bother you a little. Now, you will tell me how you control my father or I won't listen to another word you have to say – because you'll be incapable of talking with your throat cut!'

This time, Nash suppressed the smile. The boy was provoked enough for one night. At least he had his attention. Nash smiled, generously. 'Very well. Your father is held by a process that goes back more than a thousand years. The original purpose was to bring two particular people together in marriage – to make sure they would marry. I have . . . perfected it to bring about a similar loyalty. The process is called Bonding. Your father is Bonded to me for the rest of his life. Nothing can change it or break it – so if you were thinking of trying it yourself, think again.'

Kenrick's eyes grew wide and abruptly he sat back, reaching for the bottle again. 'Now, was that so hard? Really, Nash, we don't have to be enemies, do we?'

It was very hard not to laugh. Nash simply shook his head. 'On the contrary, I think we can become allies.'

'And is this how you trapped my father? Would you do the same to me?'

'I cannot.'

'Why?'

'Because the Bonding process I just described won't work unless you give your consent – which I doubt you'd ever do. So, I return to my original question. What do you want?'

Kenrick shook his head, an immature chuckle escaping. 'You couldn't begin to imagine.'

'But those things you already enjoy with great abandon. I'm prepared to offer you so much more.'

With a snap, Kenrick's gaze was upon him again. 'Like what?'

'You have powers growing in you, things you can't control, no matter how hard you try. I've heard of your experiments, seen some of your failures. I can tell you, in all honesty, if you don't stop what you're doing now, you'll be dead within a month.'

'Oh? And how do you know that?'

'Because you are tampering with what's called the forbidden side of the art. It's hard enough to master those talents which are allowed, let alone to tread that dark path without tuition. I'm prepared to offer myself as your guide.'

Nash sat back and waited. Kenrick watched him for a moment, suddenly restless in his seat. He got up and went to the door, then came back, glancing once at Nash.

'What do you want in return? I won't give my consent to be your slave like my father.'

'Bonding,' Nash spread his hands, 'has its limitations. Your father has almost outgrown his usefulness. I don't want to Bond you. I merely want your promise.'

'And why should you trust me? Or I, you?'

'Because we need each other. Believe me,' Nash came to his feet, 'you will find no better teacher anywhere in the world. Everything you want to know, I can give you. And then more.'

'What more?'

'How old do you think I am?' When Kenrick frowned, Nash continued, 'Believe it or not, this body has lasted more than a century so far. No wound, no matter how severe, can kill me. No matter how old I get, I can renew myself, returning to this youth and strength, time after time. Is that not worth a promise?'

Kenrick's face worked hard against disbelief and a lust he only barely contained. 'I still don't know whether to trust you. How do I know you're telling the truth?'

'I will give you two forms of proof. First, I will show you a small trick you will find extremely useful. I believe you have enough power already to master it without trouble. Secondly, I will place my life in your hands.' He moved closer, stopping only a foot from Kenrick. 'In the coming battle against the Douglas, you will see things nobody has seen before. Oh, he is strong, I promise you, very strong. Certainly not a man you would want to fight on your own. But I can. I don't plan to, but I can. If it comes to that fight, I will be wounded – but I will still be alive. If I am so, you must promise to bring me back here, make sure I have what I need. Then, when I am well enough, I will begin your tuition. The choice is yours, my Prince.'

Kenrick struggled, but he was still too young to hide the greed in his eyes; desire almost leaked out of him. With a short jerk of his head, he agreed. 'Very well. You have a bargain.'

'Your promise?'

'My promise. If you still live, I will make sure you survive. If you don't give me what I want, I'll make sure you die. I think that's an agreement we can both understand.'

What was the point in trying to make him understand the depths of his misjudgment? Better to leave him thinking he still had some degree of control, Nash thought.

'Now,' Kenrick stuck the wine bottle on the table and rubbed his hands together, 'what's this little trick you want to show me?'

'Well, you might find it useful on some of your . . . night adventures. You never know who might be keeping an eye on you.'

25

A brisk wind whistled across the hilltop, bringing with it scents from the downs and a haunting suggestion of the forest in the distance. White birds hung almost motionless in the air above, their wings balancing against the unseen force.

Robert studied them without moving, afraid they would detect his presence and fly off. But his caution was unfounded as Micah cantered up the hill behind him, and the birds remained in the air.

'Serin's breath, but that can't be Selar's army already?'

Robert followed Micah's gaze out across the hills in the distance where the forest came to an end. A thin black line crossed from the trees to the western downs, a river passing through the only flat land for leagues. Beyond the water were small specks; men and horses, building fires, making camp. No more than five hundred of them.

'No. Selar has sent an advance party to stake out his claim to the battlefield. He's decided that's where we'll fight.'

'It's a good enough spot.'

'It's the *only* spot. I had Murdoch come out here yesterday. We're only eight leagues from the border. Murdoch said the river flows west for a bit, then angles back through the hills towards the sea. It's wide but shallow enough for a man to walk through.'

'Then it's no real barrier.'

'No.'

Yes, it was a good spot. With the forest for protection on the right, the hills on the left, the only place to fight, the only area big enough to move troops around in, was the plain in the centre. A captive space upon which to decide the fate of a nation?

He smiled at the fanciful thought. This place *was* as good as any.

'Is the land there dry?' Micah asked, still watching the soldiers, though they were too far away to make out any detail.

'Mostly, though a little boggy in places. Rocky too. All to our advantage.' He turned to look at Micah. Now the brown dye was gone, the red curly hair was ruffled by the wind, his beard trimmed along his jawline. He was his old self. At least, on the outside.

'Is something bothering you?'

Micah blinked and shot a glance at him. 'Now that's a stupid question. I'm looking at a battlefield where, in less than two days, we'll both be fighting for our lives. I didn't think dancing and singing would be appropriate.'

Robert grinned. 'Oh, I don't know.'

Micah didn't smile. Instead he looked back to the river.

'Come on, Micah. I'm supposed to be the one who bottles things up.'

Now Micah laughed, though it was harsh and bitter – completely unlike him, which made Robert frown. 'Tell me.'

For a long second, Micah said nothing, then, his mouth set in a grim line, he said, 'Nash has been planning on facing you for more years than you've lived. He undoubtedly knows more of the prophecy than you do, his army is twice ours and who knows how many Malachi are with him. I don't doubt your skills. Let's face it, I've seen a lot more of what you can do than he has, but all the same, he won't let you survive this.'

'And if I don't?' Robert murmured under the wind.

At that, Micah's gaze rose to meet his, both anguished and frustrated at the same time. 'I'm serious.'

'So am I. What happens if I don't survive?' When Micah didn't reply, Robert continued, 'It's not the sword that will kill you, my friend, but the fear of it. Face it. Now, while you can. What if I don't survive? There's nothing in the prophecy that says I must.'

'But you don't believe in the prophecy!'

Robert reached out and caught his arm, waiting until Micah looked up again before speaking. 'Micah, you *will* survive without me.'

'But . . . '

'That's not a request.'

Micah held his gaze for a moment, then an involuntary smile broke through and Robert responded with one of his own.

'Don't worry so much, Micah, or I'll start to think you've been taking lessons from our dear Bishop.'

'Now there's a thought.'

'Don't you dare.' Robert turned his horse to look south. From up here he could just see the fringe of his army making camp in a wide valley. The forest stood to his left now, curving away from this point. There would be good shelter for his camp here, below this hill. They could make the distance easily over the next day, be settled in long before dark, get rested and prepared for the battle. Yes, despite all the odds, the timing – and a lot of other things – had fallen very nicely into place.

'And Micah?'

'Yes?'

'You just make sure that you *do* survive.'

An aggrieved sigh partnered the wind. 'Oh well, *if* you *insist.*'

Aiden squeezed between two chairs and took his seat at the opposite end of the table to Robert. The pavilion was about as full as it could be without the sides actually bulging – and warm with it, despite the evening chill.

Outside, the army was encamped, fires already lit for cooking, beds made. The tone had changed subtly since Robert had joined them. More confident. More . . . certain. So far everything seemed to be going well – though it was sure Selar's spies had done their work well.

As the last men took their seats, Robert brought the meeting to order, his voice raised to gain quiet.

'As you know, I've been out to view the battlefield. It's not good, but we can make a few adjustments.'

Aiden quietly reached forward for the flask of wine and poured himself a cup. He let his gaze drift up the table, watching for the expressions, the unvoiced worries. They were all here, the magnates, knights and barons who'd thrown their lot in with the Outlaw. McGlashen and Payne, Bergan Dunn and Robert's friends from Dunlorn. Micah, as usual, had a seat to Robert's left, set apart from the table: aide as well as personal guard, a role he would allow no other man to take.

Inevitably, Aiden's gaze rested on the young girl seated to Robert's right. Galiena had attended every one of these meetings, perfectly attentive and yet gravely silent. She seemed too young to be shouldering such responsibility.

Robert continued, 'As soon as it's dark, a squad of fifty men will approach the battlefield with picks and spades. They'll dig trenches along the line of the river, then cover them over. When Selar's cavalry charges, they won't stop to see what condition the ground is in.'

'But surely the advance guard will see them work?' Dunn queried.

'They'll be invisible.'

A moment's silence at this, then Abbot Chester said, 'With the use of sorcery?'

'Yes.' Robert's reply was short and he went on, 'We have only five hundred cavalry ourselves, but our archers are more than double the enemy's. Another squad tonight will dig trenches halfway up the hill nearest the river. Tomorrow night, we'll hide two hundred archers there. When Selar's army crosses the river, they will be harassed from behind as well as in front.'

'What about the forest?' McGlashen grunted, folding his thick hands on the table. 'Selar is bound to make use of it.'

'I'll come to that in a moment. As for the rest, we'll go as we've already discussed. The army will be split into three forces, advancing as planned. The first will be commanded by Dunn, the other by McGlashen. The rest of you will fight alongside your own men. I know it's not customary, but we'll maintain better discipline and cohesion. Our weakest point is our rear, so a third force of five hundred archers will remain in reserve and guard the camp.'

'That's stretching our forces pretty thin,' Payne added.

'We have sufficient for the job. The valley is not wide enough to have fifteen thousand men all fighting at once – and besides, I want the Sadlani mercenaries to join first. The fewer Lusarans our men have to face, the happier we'll all be.'

'But you can't guarantee Selar will send the hired hands across first,' McGlashen pointed out. 'What if he doesn't?'

'He will.'

'But . . . '

'He will. Selar will want to treat with me first. I know it's hard to believe, but I can be fairly persuasive when I want to be.'

Muffled laughter greeted this comment and most of the men settled back, a little more relaxed.

Abbot Chester, however, had other ideas. 'I'm sorry, your Grace, but you did say you weren't planning to use sorcery in this battle. Was that another lie?'

363

Robert said nothing for a moment. Then, carefully, he leaned forward, folding his arms on the table. His voice, his expression, his words, all spoke of a great inner calm – and not a man present was immune to it.

'Not a lie, Father Abbot. It was the truth – then. Now I've seen the field, I know where our weaknesses lie. I don't mean to sound harsh, but I would rather use a little sorcery to increase our odds of success than hold back and risk defeat. I received a letter today, from Tirone of Mayenne. He is finally prepared to await the outcome of our battle before making any decision. He admits – and our scouts have verified – that he has forty thousand men ready to repel any invasion. Though the terms were cloaked, I'm convinced Tirone is prepared to invade Lusara if we fail to stop Selar.'

Abrupt murmurs were quickly silenced as Robert continued, 'There will be little time for sorcery during the battle. My . . . colleagues are as prepared to fight with swords as other weapons. They are also skilled in repelling sorcery that may be used against us – and I promise you, it *will* come, in some form. But we are not helpless in that area either.'

'The forest?' McGlashen enquired. Though the big man rarely smiled, Aiden was quite certain he was enjoying himself.

'Yes, the forest.' Robert stood and took the map Micah handed him, laying it out on the table before him. 'You see here the line of the river, the area where Selar will camp, the battlefield and the forest. We will camp behind it, allowing it to shield us from both the field and Selar's army. There have always been strange stories about Shan Moss, and they give us a unique opportunity. Tonight and tomorrow night, we will place inside the forest, along the edge closest to the river, fifty men armed with a few innocuous tools.'

'More sorcery?' Chester groaned.

'Actually, no.' Robert ventured a smile. 'These men, using sheets of white cloth and certain noise-making instruments, will convince the opposing soldiers that there are indeed demons and monsters inhabiting the forest. Since everybody in the country knows I'm a sorcerer, the enemy will assume the worst. Coupled with that, three of my colleagues have volunteered to hide themselves in Selar's army overnight and spread tales of the size of Tirone's army – and what they saw in the woods and how, on the battlefield, the gravest horrors will be brought against them from the pits of hell.'

Laughter had already sprung up before Robert had finished, and even Chester betrayed a grudging smile.

'We will play upon existing fears, Father Abbot,' Robert said easily. 'And perhaps, in the process, we can save a few lives.'

'That's very sneaky.' Payne grinned.

'Why thank you. Any other questions?'

When none were forthcoming, Robert looked down the table at Aiden. 'Our good Bishop here will say mass before the battle and oversee the work of the healers, along with my mother.'

He said nothing for a moment and his silence brought all eyes back to him.

'I know you have dreams of putting me on the throne,' Robert murmured into the quiet, his voice infused with a passion greater than Aiden had heard from him before. 'And you know how I feel about that. I am prepared to accept if there is no other alternative, but I want you to remember, to understand: our purpose here is to stop Selar crossing the border. In the end, it won't matter how we achieve it – only that we do.'

'We're agreed on that, Robert,' McGlashen began, but Robert held up his hand to silence the Duke.

'What none of you seem to have considered – and which you now must – is what will happen if I fall.'

For some reason, Aiden's gaze was drawn not to Galiena nor any of the others around the table, but to Micah. He sat forward, his face a mask of intensity, absorbing Robert's next words.

'I will not stop until I have achieved my purpose, but if I die in the process, you must fight on. Our men have their hearts set right. They know why they're here. Lead them and lead them well. They will not fail you – as I know you will not fail me. Now,' he paused, his voice gentle, 'go to your supper, be with your men. Make the most of the peace. With the grace of the gods, in three day's time, we will enjoy it again and for many years to come.'

'Amen,' Aiden added, joined resoundingly by every other voice. Slowly, one by one, they rose and left, their comments loud after the recent quiet. Aiden stood and gained Micah's side. Keeping his voice low, he said, 'He is not doomed to fail, you know.'

Micah frowned and turned so Robert, busy at the table, couldn't see his expression. 'I'm sorry, Father, but I have such a bad feeling about this.'

'What kind of feeling?'

He lowered his voice further. 'I wish I could explain. It's Robert – there's something about him.' He glanced over his shoulder and frowned again. 'Or perhaps it's just me.'

He met Aiden's gaze as though he would say something more, but then abruptly he hid his thoughts behind a smile. 'I'm sorry. Pre-battle jitters. I'll be fine – and don't worry, I won't let him see it.'

Only a little comforted, Aiden nodded, gave his shoulder a companionable squeeze and headed out into the night. His stomach was growling and if he didn't get some supper soon, it would start to embarrass him.

Robert took one last look at the map, then rolled it up and put it away. All the others had gone, leaving only Micah and Arlie. And Galiena. She kept her seat, composed as always. She'd not said a word during the meeting – nor any other that he'd had since rejoining the army, but she'd listened to every word.

'I suppose, my lord,' she said evenly, her hazel eyes grave, 'now would not be a good time to change your mind and turn back.'

'Your Grace,' Arlie began to protest, but Robert interrupted.

'Don't get all excited. My wife is joking.'

Arlie eyed Robert with asperity. 'I can't tell you how sorry I am to hear that. No offence, your Grace.'

Galiena nodded. 'None taken.'

Robert picked up the wine jug and moved to refill her cup. 'Arlie finds this waiting excruciating. He's never been part of an army before.'

'I think you'll find, my lord,' Micah said, 'nearly half your men are in the same boat.'

'Big boat.' Robert smiled so only Galiena could see. A slight shifting of her eyes acknowledged his remark. She rarely smiled. He turned back to Micah. 'Damned odd about Vaughn, though, don't you think? I can't say I'm sorry he's gone, but I had my hopes pinned on removing him myself. And Osbert is now Proctor. I should think he's a happy man. I just hope Godfrey is careful. Living in the midst of the spider's web is a dangerous job.'

'By the sound of it,' Micah ventured, 'he may win some protection from Osbert. Even with his elevation, it doesn't seem the new Proctor is any more popular than the last one.'

'No.' Robert paused by the brazier and scratched his chin. 'What kind of rotation are your people using, Arlie?'

'I have six Seekers patrolling our northern perimeter at all times, one league out. Two more keep track of the south. All of them are trained in combat. They each work in eight-hour shifts, giving full coverage, night and day. If Nash should try and sneak up on us, we'll know.'

'I want the patrols increased tomorrow. Double the men along the south. Put Murdoch with them. He's had battle experience.'

'Any particular reason?' Micah asked.

'Yes.' Robert looked up. 'Some time between now and engaging the enemy, when he thinks we're not looking, Nash will have worked a squad to come around our flank, possibly using the forest as cover, and most likely under cover of darkness, to harass and keep our men from their sleep. From dawn tomorrow, Arlie, I want you to make that your personal task. Ride with the vanguard, tell them what to expect – and fill in as much detail as you like about how only a sneaking worm of a general would do such a thing.'

'Or even think of it?' Micah replied, deadpan.

Arlie laughed – then abruptly stifled it.

'Go on, off with both of you. Stop by the Bishop's tent and tell him I'll be in to see him after supper,' Robert told them.

Still chuckling, Arlie took Micah's arm and herded him out of the tent. Robert looked at Galiena to find she was trying hard not to laugh.

'I'm sorry, my lord,' she murmured, hiding her smile with her hand. 'Sometimes your men are terribly disrespectful. They didn't see me laughing, I promise.'

He reached out and took her hand away. 'It would have been good for them if they had. That's a smile that should be seen.'

Her gaze dropped suddenly. 'Forgive me, my lord.'

With a sigh, Robert drew her out of her seat. 'You silly girl. I'm not angry with you. In fact, I'm very proud of you.'

'You are?'

'Of course!' He put her hand into the crook of his elbow and led her across the tent to their private chambers. A dining area and two smaller rooms led off: as civilised as a battle camp could be. 'I thought we might have supper together tonight.'

The table was laid out already and they sat.

'Forgive me, my lord, but . . . '

'You,' Robert paused, pouring wine for her, 'must call me Robert. Nothing else.'

She said nothing, only studied him with her usual composure a little ruffled. She made no move to drink her wine. He filled her plate from the dishes set out before them, then filled his own. Still she said nothing.

'Are you not hungry?'

Galiena shook her head. 'Am I supposed to understand?'

'What?'

'You.'

Robert raised his eyebrows. 'Why? Do you think you should?'

'Does anybody?'

'Micah – though he claims he doesn't. Bishop McCauly makes great noises about how he can read me like a book . . . '

'That's not what I mean and you know it.' She swallowed nervously. 'Please . . . Robert, I'd like an answer.'

He met her gaze then and put his knife down, resting his arms across the table in front of him. 'My dear, *I* don't understand me, so I'm never surprised when nobody else does.'

'Another evasion.'

'Yes.'

'Why?'

'My, you are persistent, aren't you?'

'No less than you.'

His gaze narrowed. 'Funny, I never thought of myself as persistent.'

'How else would you produce seven evasions in a row in order to avoid answering a simple question?'

'You're counting?'

'Eight.'

He burst out laughing and only a hurried mouthful of wine

sobered him. She was still watching him, waiting for another evasion. He took one more sip, then said, 'No, you're not supposed to understand.'

'Thank you.' She sat back and picked up a piece of bread, began to nibble on it. Not once did she take her eyes from him. 'I didn't think you'd give in.'

'How could I not?' Robert resumed eating. 'We're not at war, you and I. Are we?'

'That's a good question.'

He looked up with a frown, but she turned her attention to the meal, feigning interest in her food. He watched her for a moment, then continued his supper in silence. She didn't say another word, so when he finished eating, he refilled his cup and sat back.

She resembled her mother enough to hide the shape of her father's eyes. Her hair was a rich auburn and curled around her forehead despite all efforts to stop it. She moved with an inborn grace and elegance she was blind to – but her mind was something else again.

Selar had never been a dullard – nor had Rosalind, for that matter. But it seemed their daughter had inherited more than they alone could have given her – not to mention a healthy measure of courage, determination and . . . something else he couldn't quite define. If a man had to have a wife forced upon him by circumstance, he could do worse than this. Much worse indeed.

She knew he was watching her and a slow blush grew from the collar of her gown right to her forehead. She wouldn't look up. 'Please don't.'

'What?'

'You know what I'm talking about.'

'I'm sorry,' he said. 'But this is so strange for me. I remember when you were born. If my first wife hadn't died, I would have had a son almost your age.'

'And it's not strange for me?' Her eyes flickered over his then back to her wine. 'Especially with . . . what . . . '

'What my mother spoke to you about?' he whispered.

She nodded. 'I want to understand. You remember when I was born. You think you're so much older than me and you'll always think of me as a child. I'll be seventeen in a few months. Most girls my age are married by now, sometimes to men much older than you. They don't see their wives as children.'

'Yes, perhaps I do see you as a child,' he murmured, 'but that's not the reason.'

'I know,' she glanced up again, 'but if I'm to give you nothing but my name, will you at least allow me to understand why?'

He closed his eyes and put his head back. There was only one way to answer her questions, and that was to tell her the truth. It was a painful truth, but one which, after all, he owed her.

He came to his feet and held out his hand. 'Come, let's go for a walk. I'll tell you all about it.'

The camp was dark but friendly, warm and inviting in places, rowdy and boisterous in others. When someone recognised them, peace reigned, punctuated by quietly called greetings, which Robert was glad to return. Music floated up from a dozen different fires, sometimes singing, and there was enough laughter to make him relax a little.

'I've known since the age of nine that I was a sorcerer,' he began quietly, keeping his voice pitched so she alone could hear him. 'Being so young, I had no real idea of what it would one day mean. But before I could begin to understand, I was given a prophecy and a weapon of such incredible force that I would be unable to avoid my destiny. Understanding that small fact should go a long way to explaining most of what I've wasted my life doing.'

Galiena looked up at him, but said nothing.

'As was usual for one of my birth, I was betrothed at an early age. When your father conquered Lusara, the wedding was put off. Eventually, once I'd proven myself to him, I was given my liberty and married Berenice.'

'What was she like?'

'Delightful,' he answered simply. 'Quiet and thoughtful, funny at times. Very caring. My people at Dunlorn thought the world of her. Even my brother Finnlay gave her his open respect. If you knew him, you'd understand how rare that is.'

'And did you love her?'

Love?

The way he loved . . .

'I think I did. We were happy when we were together – which wasn't often. I spent too much time at court, trying to keep your father under control. And then, Berenice got with child.'

He came to a halt at the end of the camp. Beyond was darkness, lit only by a pale moon filtered with blue cloud, dusty and damp. Sentries patrolled the boundary, but he could see nothing of them. 'I returned one night from court, having lost my position on your father's council. Berenice was ill with a fever and the doctor was concerned. She was delirious, in a lot of pain, and I wanted to help her. I couldn't bear to see her like that. Some sorcerers have an ability to relieve pain, so I dismissed the doctor and took her hand. I did my best and, for a few minutes, it seemed to work. Her fever cleared a little and she looked at me with recognition. Then suddenly, before I could do anything about it, she cried out, holding the child in her belly. I felt the power wrenched out of me, twisted and dark, coursing through her body as though something else were controlling it. Within a minute, she was dead.'

No, retelling the story did nothing to ease it, no matter how calmly he spoke.

'Oh, Robert!' Galiena breathed. 'How awful!'

He turned to look at her, but her horror was not directed at him, but the tragedy. She didn't back away from him, nor did she take her hand from his arm.

'I'm sorry,' he whispered, 'I don't want you to get hurt, but either way, you will. I'll never risk having more children. Even if these men succeed in giving me a throne I don't want, there will be no heir to follow me. I don't understand how or why Berenice died, but I'm not willing to try again purely as an experiment.'

Galiena nodded and smiled. 'I understand.'

They continued walking, taking in another section of the camp before making for their tent. He took her inside and paused. 'I suppose I should have told you all this before we got married.'

She shrugged. 'It wouldn't have made any difference. What we're fighting is real now. Who knows what the future will bring?'

She turned to go inside her room, then abruptly faced him again. 'What?'

'Nothing.' Then she lifted her head and kissed him, lingering long enough to make him move.

371

He put his hands on her shoulders and looked into her eyes. 'Are you sure you understand?'

'Absolutely. Don't worry, really. I do understand, I promise.' She smiled a little. 'But perhaps, one day, given time, you'll love me a little. Perhaps as much as Berenice. I would rather that than nothing at all.'

And that's what happens when you don't tell the whole truth! But how could he now? One word about Jenn would destroy the little happiness Galiena had gleaned for herself. Why should he ruin that?

No. No more hurting, no matter the cost. He brushed his fingers over her cheek. 'You don't need to wait for the day, my girl.'

Her answering smile was glorious. He couldn't help it – he kissed her, holding her long enough for her to be really sure he meant it. Then he released her and stood back. 'I have work to do. You get some sleep.'

'Goodnight, Robert.'

'Goodnight.'

She vanished into her room and he stepped outside again. Women. Damned unpredictable women. How was a man to think straight with a woman around?

Aiden finished the last line and put down his pen. He ran his fingers through his hair, idly scratching his scalp in an effort to wake his brain. It didn't do much good.

'Busy?'

He glanced up to find Robert's head stuck through the tent flap. 'Yes. Go away.'

'Sorry,' Robert replied, coming in. 'I'm the ill-mannered Douglas. If you want polite behaviour, you'll have to see my mother. What are you doing?'

'Trying to write a letter to Brome.'

'Oh. Having success?'

'All I can tell you is the eleventh draft is only slightly less useless than the first.'

'So, a gradual improvement then? Got any of that nice sweet wine?'

'You hate sweet wine.'

'No I don't.' Robert rummaged around in the chest at the end of the table and brought up a flask. 'Is this it?'

'Fill two glasses.' Aiden sat back and clasped his hands behind his head. Robert played the servant, then sank into a chair, sticking his boots on top of the chest. He drained half his cup before wiping his sleeve across his mouth. Aiden snorted. 'I see what you mean about manners.'

'Tell me,' Robert said with a quizzical frown, 'do you understand women?'

'I'm a priest, Robert.'

'Yes, but do you?'

'Do you mean, have I ever broken my vows?'

Robert looked horrified. 'I'd never dream of asking you such a thing! I'm not *that* ill-mannered.' He paused a second, then glanced sideways. 'Have you?'

'No!'

'What? Not even been tempted?'

'No. Why, what's your problem now?'

Robert drained his cup and immediately refilled it. 'The child has convinced herself she's in love with me.'

Aiden began to laugh. 'Oh, such arrogance.'

'Hey, that's not fair!'

'Hah! "The *child* has *convinced* herself"? Really, Robert, you should be ashamed.'

'Why?'

Aiden took a sip of wine and rolled it around his mouth before answering. 'Plenty of people love you. Why shouldn't your wife?'

'But she hardly knows me!'

'So? She's an intelligent, well-educated, well-travelled young woman. She's not – as you're so busily trying to convince yourself – an innocent child. I think if she believes she loves you, you have to take her at her word, no matter how misguided she may appear to the rest of us.'

Robert half-laughed and dropped his gaze to his cup.

'And are you going to tell me you feel absolutely nothing for her?'

'Of course I *like* her. I just think it's typical that a girl I hardly know decides she loves me for no apparent reason, is prepared to

373

ride into battle beside me, against her own father – while Jenn didn't love me enough to fight so we could stay together.'

'You don't know that's what happened.'

Robert looked up. 'No?'

'She promised to Stand the Circle.'

'And she promised to marry me. Either way you look at it, I was less important to her.' He was more confused than solemn. 'I'm never going to understand women as long as I live.'

Aiden stared at him, only slightly disbelieving. 'You're never satisfied, are you?'

'Nope.' Robert emptied his cup again. 'You have me in a nutshell.'

'You know,' Aiden sighed, 'though I love you like you were my own son, sometimes . . . '

'What?'

'I could happily give you a good thump.'

Robert roared with laughter.

'And this is really developing into one of those times.' When Robert continued laughing, Aiden couldn't help but join in. 'I think I understand how your mother feels some days.'

Robert reached out and poured some more wine for them both, 'You know what's really scary? Sometimes I do too.'

26

The last day's march was solemn. The men moved in ordered groups, talking, but quieter this time, the next day's battle at the forefront of all their thoughts.

Hours before sunset, the army was camped by the ancient forest, but it was a long time before things settled down. Robert, with Galiena at his side, moved through the camp, sharing a few words with as many men as possible.

Galiena was subdued at supper. He tried to draw her into conversation, but she was immune. Instead, he left her early and went wandering through the camp again, unable to rest himself. Every hour or so, one of his aides would find him with the latest report on Selar's army, entrenched beyond the river, but there were no surprises as yet.

Robert climbed a hill opposite the forest and, almost immediately, was challenged by one of his lookouts. He identified himself and continued on until he could see the whole vastness of Selar's army spread out before him like a quilt, with only the river holding them back: a rare moment when his enhanced sight did him no good at all.

Samdon Nash was down there, somewhere. Probably eating his supper, drinking wine, much as Robert had done. He'd be giving last-minute orders, receiving reports, doing his best to try to guess what moves Robert would make first.

By the gods, why did he have to be fighting his own people?

But, damn it, facing Nash on his own would not stop this army! How many times did he have to remind himself of that?

So many years, so much time, all spent fighting the prophecy, proving it was wrong, fighting the demon – and still he had ended up here, on a hill overlooking two armies. Was this his destiny, to destroy his own people while trying to save them?

'I thought I'd find you up here.' Micah's voice came to him, quiet and undemanding. 'Not a pretty sight, is it?'

Robert shrugged. 'From the air, a bird would never be able to tell the difference between us and them.'

'What do you see?' Micah stood beside him.

'Trouble.' Robert turned, clearing his thoughts. 'You know, when this is all over you should go back to Dromna and see if you can convince the lovely Sairead to marry you.'

'What?' Micah started.

'Remember? Sairead? The girl you gave your heart to? Or are you suddenly so fickle, you've forgotten already?' Robert smiled and gave his shoulder a nudge.

'No, I've not forgotten her. I doubt I ever will – but going back to Dromna won't help.'

'Why not?'

'I . . . well, there are . . . '

'Complications?'

Micah gave a short laugh and nodded wryly. 'You could say that. Any suggestions?'

'From me?' Robert almost choked on the idea.

'Well, you're on your second marriage. You must have learned something by now.'

Robert grinned. 'I'm sorry, my friend, but I don't have any answers. I'm the last person to be giving advice on women. Were you getting bored down there?'

Micah screwed up his face, somewhere between a frown and a smile. 'Not exactly – but um . . . there's someone here to see you.'

Nash was restless.

He strode up and down the narrow length of his tent, stopping only to issue yet another order to Taymar, who waited patiently outside. He'd done with meetings and tactics and Selar. He'd had enough of them all. After so very many years pursuing this goal, he just wanted it to be done, finished with, over. Wanted the coming fight to be won already. Food had been brought to him, but he'd left it untouched. Now it sat on the tray, cold and stinking as though rotten. Anticipation and dread had swallowed his appetite.

He turned and stalked outside. The night air was cool and fresh, the darkness cloaking his mood without help from his powers. He walked between the tents raised for the rich and mighty, past the fires built for those of lesser import. Only when he was beyond them all did he stop, still inside the ring of sentries. Before him the river bent its way from the edge of the forest and across the valley to disappear into the cleft of hills to his right.

Of the enemy camp he could see nothing. The forest hid it all, though every man this side of the river knew they were there. Robert Douglas had prepared well.

Would he take the bait? See the needles Nash drove into him, know he was being weakened with every step? Or would the Enemy see the trap – and walk into it anyway? Even with all his own preparations, there was still no way to make sure. But one way or the other, Robert Douglas had to die.

Nash raised his head and scanned the nearest hilltops. Layers of cloud obscured the stars, but moonlight bled through in scattered patches of grey here and there. And on one hill, steep and towering over the river, was a shadow that could have been a man. Nash strained to see, but the harder he tried, the more the figure shimmered and refused to take form. Could it be him?

Was he restless, like Nash? Climbing to get his first glimpse of the man who would be his destiny?

Was Robert Douglas afraid?

The cold night shifted around him and the figure vanished into the darkness. With a sigh, Nash turned and headed back to his tent.

Stubbornly, Micah refused to say a word about the mysterious visitor. Instead, he led Robert back to the camp in silence. Rather than curiosity, Robert felt irritation grow within him and worked hard to control it. Micah led him not to his own tent, but to Aiden's. He lifted the flap and stood aside to let Robert in first.

The light hurt his eyes for a moment, then he was looking at the Bishop, who had a rather smug smile on his face. Then . . .

'Finnlay!' Robert drew in a breath, stunned to his core. 'Serin's blood, what the hell are you doing here?'

Finnlay shrugged. 'I didn't want to miss the fight.'

'But . . . but it's too dangerous.'

'Nash couldn't possibly have Sensed me leaving the Enclave. I left under the protection of the Key.' At that, Finnlay stepped aside to reveal a small figure waiting behind him.

Jenn.

Like a frail twig between his fingers, the irritation snapped. 'Get out!'

I tried to warn you I'd come, but you wouldn't believe me.

I said, get out of my camp!

I can't and you know why.

Of course, you're joined to the Key now. You have no excuse to be ignorant.

I have to be here, Robert.

No, you don't! But she didn't move. He drew in a forced breath and nodded once. 'Fine. Stay. But keep out of my sight!'

With that, he turned on his heel and, ignoring Aiden's call to wait, strode out of the tent, heading for any place where Jenn wasn't.

Blind, stupid, stubborn idiot! And she was no better! Why

couldn't she just stay where she was, where it was safe? She'd made her choice, but she still rode in here as though it was all some kind of joke!

'Robert! Wait!'

He didn't stop, but Finnlay caught up with him anyway. 'Don't blame Jenn, Robert. She only came because of me.'

'Don't kid yourself. She's here for another reason entirely.'

'What's that?'

'Because of *him*!'

Robert came to the edge of the camp where the forest stood, a curtain of pitch black only yards away. Breathing heavily, he faced Finnlay. 'She's the Ally, Finn. His Ally! Why is everyone so blind to that?'

'Robert, she'd never do anything to harm you! She loves you!'

'Oh really? She told you that, did she? Eh? Did she actually tell you she loved me?'

'She . . . '

'Because if she did, it was a damn sight more than she's ever said to me!'

Robert closed his eyes and dropped his head. The demon rumbled around inside, crashing against things, opening up new wounds, and older ones.

'You think . . . ' Finnlay said quietly, 'that she loves *him*? Nash?'

Robert grunted, 'I know she does. Even if she doesn't realise it. It's all in the prophecy. Why else would she be here?'

'She wants to help. That's all.' Finnlay took in a breath. 'As you were both told, she is the Key.'

Robert froze.

Finnlay continued, gently and carefully, 'She told me all about it – what happened in Budlandi, when she Stood the Circle. Everything. But she doesn't know how the prophecy ends, even now. Believe me, she just wants to help you.'

'Well, she could have done that by . . . by staying at the Enclave,' Robert whispered, suddenly drained. 'I don't have time for this now.'

Finnlay reached up and took Robert's shoulder. 'Come on. I think you need a drink.'

*

At first, Galiena ignored the noise, but then it came so close, she sat up in bed and looked around. Had Robert come back already? But he didn't normally sneak around like that – and this was definitely a sneaking noise.

A bottle scraping against the table . . .

'Who's there?' she called. 'Robert? Is that you?'

The noise stopped and footsteps came closer, breathing slow and heavy. 'Don't you know yet the sounds your own husband makes above those of other men?'

A pressure on the end of her bed and she scrambled away, pulling the blankets around her in a gesture she knew was futile. 'Who are you? What do you want?'

A sigh. 'Oh, how you hurt me. Do you not know your own brother after only six years? Sister, I'm wounded.'

Galiena gasped, 'Kenrick? How can I know you? It's so dark in here.'

'Then I'll light a candle.'

Instantly a flame sprang to life, a short squat candle held in his hand. His face was illuminated from below, oppressive and only a little familiar. 'Now do you know me?'

She stared at the candle, then at him. She'd seen Robert do the same trick a dozen times.

'Yes, wonderful, isn't it?' Kenrick laughed lightly. 'I had no idea until I found myself doing such things. Every day I learn a little more. Of course, Father knows nothing about it. Actually, it was something I wanted to share with you first. Wasn't that nice of me? To want to keep something just between us?'

Galiena didn't move. 'How did you get in here?'

He raised a shoulder carelessly. 'Another trick, nothing difficult. I even made it past the sorcerer guards your husband has out there. I suppose he'll be quite angry with them when he finds out.'

By the gods, he'd changed so much! As a child, he'd been petulant, sometimes selfish and always wilful. Now he was all of that full grown, and more. Mother would have been horrified to see her greatest fears realised. Galiena certainly was. Rosalind had died trying to prevent this very creature from forming.

'Are you happy then?' Kenrick continued, one hand snaking out to her ankle beneath the blankets. 'You chose a fine hero for a husband. A man the people look up to – even after so long in the wilderness, his ballads are still sung in taverns across the country. But I wonder if they'll sing when they understand the temerity of his ambition.'

He caught her ankle and pulled it towards him, firmly, so she couldn't escape. 'Are you expecting him, sister? Do you enjoy sharing the pleasures of his bed? Does he kiss you? Touch you and make you cry out in delight?' In one swift movement, his hand sought the warmth between her legs.

With a desperate shove, she kicked him away and crawled to the furthest corner of the bed. 'What do you want?'

'Nothing but peace between *us*, sister. Our Father and your husband, I fear, will have nothing but war. I can get you out now, if you like. You know I'll take good care of you.'

'I'm not leaving! You go – or I'll call the guards. Robert's close by. I don't care how many powers you think you have. They're nothing compared to his!'

'How proud you are of your sorcerer husband. I suppose that's only proper. Oh well, if you don't want to come with me, I can't very well drag you away kicking and screaming. You'd wake both armies with your noise – and we can't have them turning up to fight in the morning sleepy-eyed and grumpy, can we?'

'Just get out!'

He stood and grinned a moment. 'As you wish, sister. Don't say I never asked. Farewell!'

The light blinked out and his footsteps disappeared into the night.

Galiena sat on her bed for a long time, trying to listen for him over the thumping of her heart. Slowly, in the silence, she relaxed a little, sliding across the bed to put her feet on the rug. She took the blanket with her, drawing it over her shoulders. Unsteadily, she got to her feet and made for the table. With shaking hands she poured out wine, spilling some in the dark. Taking a deep breath, she swallowed until the cup was empty. Gradually the shaking stopped and she turned back to the bedroom. There was no point calling the guard; Kenrick would be long gone by now.

'Hey, steady with that.' Finnlay raised his hand, but Robert ignored him. Instead, he lifted the flask once more and took a solid mouthful. Then he rested his head back against the tree and closed his eyes.

The forest was about the only place Robert could really be alone. But there was no way Finnlay was going to let him out of his sight. He sat with his back to his own tree, at right angles to Robert, sipped his own flask of ale and held a modest mask steady against anyone coming past.

It was uncanny; Robert looked like a man without a care in the world. No frown, no lines about his eyes to give anything away. But Finnlay had seen him like this once before, seen enough to be frightened of it. The surface was there, unbroken, untouched. But Finnlay was no longer blind to what lay beneath.

'I believe,' Robert said lightly, 'that it's something of a tradition for generals to take a sup of ale before a battle.'

'But not to get drunk.'

'Why not? It could be my last chance. Yours too, for that matter.' Robert swallowed noisily. 'He knows I'm the Enemy, brother, but I'll bet any money he'd give a country or two for your blood. You escaped him three times. A man can only take so much before he buckles under the weight of dented pride.'

Finnlay snorted and put his bottle down.

'Don't worry, I'm not going to get drunk and embarrass you.' Robert chuckled, emptily. 'Have you met my new wife?'

'No.'

'You'll like her. She's very . . . tough. Her mother's daughter. I just hope I survive long enough to make her completely miserable.'

'You know, Robert, you're really unpleasant company in this mood.'

His brother gave another hollow laugh before replying, 'I'm surprised you never noticed that I'm in this mood most of the time. My problems, you see, never seem to come one at a time, so I can deal with them. They always fall on me in a big fat heap. I scramble and scramble but I just can't seem to get on top of it all. And things like that tend to affect a fellow's mood. Of course, I probably take them too seriously. But inside I . . . '

Robert was staring into the darkness, abruptly sober. There was too little light for Finnlay to see more.

'Are you afraid of Nash?'

'I don't know,' Robert whispered, 'I should be. I know he's out there, waiting for me. But I've been scared for so long now, I can't tell if this is new or not.'

Finnlay turned to look at him, but his gaze was elsewhere, puzzled, bemused and uncomprehending.

No, Robert wasn't afraid of dying tomorrow. He was afraid of losing.

As he watched, the gaze refocused, met Finnlay's squarely. A long silence ended when Robert said, 'I have to tell you something. Now, just in case . . . ' He swallowed but didn't look away. 'You were right.'

Finnlay snorted again, unimpressed. 'About what?'

Robert took another drink, then put the flask down, shoving the stopper in firmly. He settled back again. 'I should never have sworn an oath to Selar.'

'What?'

'You heard me.'

Finnlay stared. This had to be some kind of joke. There was no way Robert would say something like that – not after eighteen years. 'No. I don't believe it.'

'Nevertheless, it's true. I think I knew all along, but I couldn't bring myself to tell you. I didn't want you to think you were right. Pride, you see?'

Finnlay could find nothing to say, and Robert continued, relentlessly honest. 'You don't know how many times I could have killed him – and got away with it. But I was convinced I was doing the right thing. All I can say in my defence was that I was young. I kept trying to think what Father would have done in my place.'

'He wasn't a sorcerer.'

'And isn't it strange how that always makes a difference?' He paused, half a smile on his face. 'You and countless others wanted me to kill Selar and take the throne. Stubborn to the last, I refused to listen – and yet look at me now. Personally, I think you would have made a much better job of it.'

'What?' Finnlay lifted his head. 'Are you sure you're not drunk? Could you really see me as King? Impatient and headstrong and completely incapable of listening to reason? What a charming concept.'

Robert ignored the joke. 'You were right – I have become obsessed with the prophecy and, in the process, I've become blind to the hurt I cause. For years I've tried to convince people that sorcery itself was not evil – but I have this demon inside me and I know otherwise.'

Extremely uncomfortable now, Finnlay tried to object. 'Robert, you're not evil . . .'

'It was so easy to just blame the Key,' Robert continued, his gaze floating into the darkness, 'but it was never the Key, Finn, it was me. Even as I fought it, I allowed it to mould my character, devour my attention, infiltrate my every thought. And still my destiny awaits me, untouched by any of my efforts to stop it. All these years and I never realised I was fighting the wrong battle.' He turned and faced Finnlay again, his voice quiet. 'You have no idea how sorry I am, Finn. For everything. I've made a lot of mistakes and you – you've borne the brunt of most of them.'

Finnlay couldn't look at him then. Slowly, the fingers of fury unwound themselves from his stomach and he was left raw and hollow.

'It's always amazed me,' Robert murmured, his voice almost inaudible, 'that you continued to stick by me.'

Swallowing hard, Finnlay replied thickly, 'You know why.'

'We're quite a pair, aren't we?'

Now Finnlay looked up to find Robert getting to his feet. He held out his hand and Finnlay took it, standing a little unsteadily himself despite his words of warning to Robert. 'Come on, we'd better get back.'

Before either of them could move, a flash of light split the night. Following hard on its heels was a cry from the perimeter to their left and the unmistakable ring of steel.

Robert was already moving. 'Get Arlie's men over here now! That's a Malachi attack!'

Finnlay ran flat out through the camp, desperate to get back to Robert. Already the army was roused, men darting everywhere in a confusing mass, trying to find out where the threat was coming from. He caught sight of two more flashes, alongside cries of pain and the clash of steel. He broke free of the camp and arrived to find Robert in mid-battle, his sword ringing white against the night, illuminating the trees towering above. His opponent swung wildly and in a second, Robert had cut him down. Others still fought on as Finnlay dashed into the fray. Men, dead and dying, were scattered around the forest edge. A figure lunged at him from the darkness and he spun, ready to defend with fire if he had to, but this was no Malachi.

He parried and thrust, but the man was already wounded and died before Finnlay could even get a look at his face. He whirled around, ready for the next – but now there was silence.

'Bring those torches over here!' Robert's voice rang out and Finnlay joined him as he knelt down beside a wounded man – one of Payne's. 'Quickly,' Robert added. 'Bind up that cut before he bleeds to death. I'll see to the others.'

More men came from the camp now, doctors and Healers alike, carrying torches, bringing help. Finnlay left his man in better hands and joined Robert standing in the centre of the small battlefield, a deep frown on his face.

'You all right?'

'Fine.' Finnlay nodded. 'But you've got a nasty cut on your arm.'

'It can wait.' Robert turned as Arlie emerged from the forest, shaking his head.

'Both my sentries are dead. Arrows. I don't know how those bastards got past the others – but I'll double the guard for the rest of the night.'

By now, Payne had arrived, his face pale with shock and horror at what had happened to his men. He stopped before Robert.

'Sorcerers?'

'Malachi. The worst kind.'

'How many?'

'Twenty at best count, but only three Malachi. At least that's three fewer we'll have to face tomorrow.'

Payne spread his arms side. 'What did they hope to achieve?'

Robert sheathed his sword. 'A test of our resolve – and to see how good our defences are. Pass the word on, double guards on every station, another on backup. We can't afford another mess like this tonight. You've lost half a dozen good men, Payne. Look after the rest.'

Finnlay grabbed a bandage from the nearest Healer and took Robert's arm. He wound it firmly around the wound, but as he tightened it up, a voice came to him from the forest. He looked up to find Murdoch stumbling towards them, a body across his arms.

'I caught one, Robert!' Murdoch almost roared with triumph. 'She was keeping back, watching the attack. I knocked her out – but she's Malachi, all right. A Malachi prisoner!'

Murdoch stopped before Robert and laid the girl on the ground. She was unconscious and Robert knelt, waving a torch closer. She was young, golden-haired and very pretty, even with the wound on her head, already turning into a bruise.

'Well done, Murdoch.' Robert looked up with a smile. 'Well done indeed – and she won't have any powers for some time thanks to that knock to her skull.'

'Are you sure?' Payne asked.

'Positive. I've had enough personal experience. Arlie?'

'Yes?'

'Bind her hand and foot and put her in that tent over there, on the perimeter. I don't want her anywhere near the centre of our camp. Salti guards only, understand?'

'Perfectly.'

'Once she's settled, get her awake. I want to talk to her.'

27

Finnlay spent a few moments more checking the guards outside the tent. Before he could get back in, however, he saw Micah hurrying across the camp towards him.

'Robert?'

'He's fine. He's in there with the prisoner.'

Micah came to a halt. 'And is she a Malachi?' he asked warily.

'Certainly is.' Finnlay grinned. 'She's awake now and I can sense

385

her aura. Come, take a look.' He lifted the tent door to let him through.

The girl sat on a chair in the centre of the space, her hands bound behind her, her feet secured. She looked up as they came in, ignoring Finnlay, but looking at Micah as though he might hold some hope for her. When he said nothing, she turned back to Robert.

She was indeed young – and scared – though she did well hiding it. Nor was she giving anything away.

Robert stood before her, his hands clasped in front of him. 'I can't see what harm can come from telling me your name.'

Silence.

'Are you Darriet D'Azzir?'

Nothing.

Robert pulled up a chair, turned it around and straddled it. He studied her for a moment before continuing, 'You're in no immediate danger. I do have guards outside, but they're not about to come in here and cut your throat.'

The girl kept her silence, her eyes flickering once more over Finnlay and Micah.

'Come, I just want to talk, nothing more.' Robert was at his most reasonable, most likeable, and this girl was no more immune than anyone else to Robert's charm.

'I won't betray my people,' she said, her voice shaking a little.

'I haven't asked you to. Like I said, I just want to talk. Are you D'Azzir?'

'Why?'

'Well, it's just that I have met a few and none were so easy to catch as you. My guess is you've only just begun your training. Am I right?'

She gave a short nod, but said nothing.

Robert smiled encouragingly and leaned forward, resting his arms on the back of the chair. 'Do you know why you're here?'

'I was caught.'

'No, I mean, why your people are fighting this war alongside Selar?'

'Oh, and I suppose you're going to tell me how misguided I am. Give me your rotten side of the story. I've met your kind before, Salti monster!'

Micah shuddered, but Finnlay laid a gentle hand on his shoulder, whispering, 'Don't let her get to you. Robert knows what he's doing.'

'Yes, I suppose I do think you're misguided, but I doubt anything I have to say is going to change that. But, strictly speaking, I'm not Salti.'

'And I'm supposed to believe that?'

'I won't lie to you.' Robert paused. 'Do you know who I am?'

'I don't care.'

'Now who's lying,' Robert said indulgently. 'I am the Enemy and I don't want you to betray your people. I don't even want you to betray that damned idiot King you've set yourself to helping. Rather, I want to know about Samdon Nash.'

Her eyes widened, once more flickering to Micah, lingering a moment longer than before, but still giving nothing away. She wasn't to know there was no help at all to be gained from Micah.

'Nash?' The girl repeated, feigning confusion.

'Or Carlan, or the Angel of Darkness. Whichever you prefer. It appears those of us in the prophecy are cursed with a multitude of superfluous names. I'm told it's the nature of prophecy to be so unnecessarily complicated. Will you tell me about him?'

'I . . . I . . . ' She paused, a little more fear showing on her pale face. 'I don't know anything about Carlan.'

'You're afraid of him?'

She said nothing.

'Are you prepared to protect him?'

'I protect nobody but my own people!'

'Then Nash is not Malachi.'

She shut her mouth as though she'd let out a great secret.

Robert sat back. 'Just as I'm not Salti. Interesting. Has he told you about the prophecy?'

'He told us you would claim some great destiny drove you on. I'm not a fool. I know what I see.'

'Do you?' Robert enquired gently. 'I don't see how you can. I don't see how anyone can know what he is and follow him. Did you ever ask – or did you just follow your leaders, assuming they knew what they were doing? You're here because you're Malachi and you want the Key from the Salti Pazar. It's as simple as that, isn't it? No questions, no need to look with your own eyes, think with your own mind. You know what's really sad? If you had the Key, you would be no better off.'

'So you do know where it is?'

'And I would destroy it before I ever let a Malachi get his hands on it. Or Nash.'

With a sigh, Robert got to his feet and lifted the chair out of the way. 'You sit there a while and have a good think about all the things you've been told. Think about what you know is true and what you see in Nash. I'll be back later.'

Robert turned and ushered Micah and Finnlay out of the tent. They stopped a little distance away and Finnlay asked the inevitable question. 'What are you going to do with her?'

Rubbing a hand over his eyes, Robert answered, 'I don't know. I can't keep her here. I can't afford the manpower tomorrow. I need Salti on the field to combat whatever Malachi are left. I know she's young, but . . . '

Micah interrupted, his voice harsh, 'You would kill her?'

'I'm not a murderer, Micah, but I remember what happened to Ayn because I let Valena leave Dunlorn in one piece. How do I know this girl won't, some time in the future, bring harm to someone I love? I'm not sure I could face that again. What do you expect me to do?'

'Well,' Micah paused, his face hard, 'you can't be sure she won't change her mind and help you. It will be another few hours before she's any danger. Why don't you just ask Arlie to give her a sleeping draught. Keep her that way. She'd be no harm to anyone. And after tomorrow, you could let her go or . . . or kill her. Whatever.'

Robert raised his eyebrows and glanced at Finnlay. 'Certainly a better idea than any I've come up with. What do you think?'

Finnlay shrugged. 'She's done us no harm so far. And she could be a help if we can turn her. It's as good an option as any.'

'I agree . . . '

Finnlay?

Jenn? What is it?

Is Robert with you?

Yes, why?

Your mother is looking for him. She's frantic. It's Galiena. Something's wrong.

It took little time to gain Robert's pavilion. Finnlay hurried in after him, expecting to find chaos, but only Aiden waited, pacing, concern written all over his face.

'Thank the gods!' He waved towards the other chamber. 'Your mother's in there with her.'

Robert didn't wait to ask questions. Instead he strode through the open doorway to find Margaret just getting to her feet, a bowl and a cloth in her hand.

'I'm sorry, Robert, Galiena is very ill. I've sent for a Healer but . . .'

Galiena lay on the bed, her eyes staring up without moving. Her breathing was a harsh gasp, drawn in, held and let out again. Each one seemed more difficult, more laboured. Her eyes were ringed with red; a thick film of sweat shone over her white face. Her whole body was rigid, tense, as if ready to fight.

Robert knelt down beside the bed and took her hands. 'Galiena? Can you hear me?'

Slowly, she turned her head, her eyes wide and uncomprehending. Her mouth quivered, but the only sound to come out was a rasping breath. Robert looked up at his mother, then called, 'Finn, get Jenn in here. Now!'

Jenn? Come quickly!

On my way.

'Galiena?' Robert urged. 'Just hold on. You'll be fine. I'll stay with you. Just hold on.'

Again the girl tried to speak, but the effort failed and only weakened her.

'How long has she been like this?' Finnlay asked Margaret.

'I don't know. I was woken by the attack, but as things quietened down, I could hear her crying out – our tents are so close. I came in to find her like this.'

Galiena stiffened suddenly, closing her eyes with a grimace. Robert smoothed her hair down, trying to ease her pain with whispered words. 'Where's Jenn?'

'Here.'

Finnlay stepped aside to let her through. She came to a halt at the end of the bed.

'Tell me what's wrong with her,' Robert said through clenched teeth.

Jenn nodded, pushing her hood back. She stared a moment at Galiena, then looked with complete despair at Finnlay.

'Well?' Robert demanded. 'What's wrong? Doesn't your Healer's sight work any more?'

Jenn swallowed. 'She's been poisoned, Robert.'

'Poison?' Robert whirled around.

'She's . . . dying.'

Galiena gasped then and Robert turned back to her, putting his arm around her shoulders.

'Please, Robert,' Jenn whispered. 'Help her.'

'Go.' He cradled Galiena against his chest, his eyes shut tight against them all.

Silently, Finnlay drew Jenn away, then his mother. Only Aiden remained, murmuring prayers. Finnlay stayed in the doorway, unable to leave completely. He felt the power grow out of Robert, sensed it flowing through his body to Galiena's, swallowing up her pain, her torment. He heard her breathing ease and grow so quiet it was almost inaudible.

And he saw the tears.

As McCauly fell silent Finnlay stepped back, into the shadows. Then Galiena's breathing stopped completely.

Margaret sat in a corner of the meeting room, clenched her hands together and tried to force some calm, some degree of . . .

Oh, what was the use of it? Her eyes wouldn't obey. Tears fell down her cheeks without pause, as though they would drown the pain inside, wash it away.

'Here, drink a little of this.' Jenn approached and sat beside Margaret. Carefully, she placed a cup between Margaret's hands, guided it to her mouth.

'I'm sorry, I just can't seem to . . . '

'Don't apologise,' Jenn said softly. She glanced over her shoulder to where the men stood. Micah and Finnlay, the Bishop and now

Arlie. All talking quietly, as though there were a risk they'd wake Galiena.

If only they could.

'She was so young.' Margaret swallowed and sniffed. Jenn gave her a slip of linen and she wiped her eyes. 'She was too young to die like that. She wanted so much to do something, to fight the evil her father had become. And now, like so many women before her, she's been sacrificed for nothing. Just a child . . . ' Margaret's voice trailed off as Robert appeared in the doorway. He moved stiffly, his eyes grey and tired, his face ashen. Everyone turned to face him.

'Who else knows about this?' he said into the silence.

'No one,' McCauly replied, apparently the only one to retain the ability to speak.

'Then,' Robert nodded slowly, 'as far as everyone else is concerned, my wife did not die. She's ill, needs to rest. This army will not know what's happened here. Not tonight. Aiden, will you take care of her?'

'Of course.'

'Tomorrow night, no matter what, Galiena will lie in State as she deserves. Micah, find Deverin and tell him what's happened. Nobody else is to know.'

He said nothing more, so the others began to move, but Margaret couldn't find the strength to get up. Robert watched her for a moment, then came over, bending to kiss her forehead with barely a touch.

When Jenn made to leave, Robert raised a hand to stop her, calling Finnlay over.

'I can't imagine anyone hating my wife so much they'd want her dead,' Robert began carefully, 'so I'm forced to assume that the poison was intended for me. I drank from that flask myself earlier this evening, so it must have been added since Galiena went to bed.'

'Nash?' Finnlay asked, his eyes wide.

Robert frowned. 'Possibly, but I can't see him taking such a risk coming here on his own.'

'A traitor, then?'

'Or somebody who managed to get in here while we were fighting on the perimeter. Somebody powerful enough to make a mask he can move with. A dimensional shift.'

'But I've never known anybody to do that . . . '

'I can.' Robert ran his hands through his hair. 'The problem is tomorrow and keeping the truth from our army. Galiena was to ride with me before the battle. Jenn, since nobody knows you're here – or even alive for that matter – you'll have to take Galiena's place. Mother will find some suitable clothes for you. Wear a scarf or something so nobody close recognises you. You're shorter than Galiena, so you'd better stay mounted. You just make sure you stay out of the fight.'

Jenn nodded.

'Finn, I want you to keep your ears open. If you hear any rumour about Galiena, let me know. I trust everyone who's here. If word gets out, then it will only be from the mouth of the traitor. Where did this wine come from?'

'McCauly,' Finnlay replied. 'I tipped all the rest out.'

Robert nodded, then noticed something lying on the table. A long package wrapped in linen. For a second, Margaret didn't move – then she stood abruptly.

But it was too late.

'What's this?'

'I . . . It's your father's sword, Robert. I wanted you to have it for tomorrow.'

Hesitant fingers pulled at the ribbons, taking the cloth back to reveal the blade in its scabbard. 'I thought it had been lost.'

'I couldn't leave it behind at Dunlorn. I . . . '

He stepped back, his eyes still on the sword. 'Put it away, Mother.'

'Robert?' Finnlay began.

'No. I will not use it to kill my own countrymen.' With that, he turned for the door.

'Where are you going?' Jenn instantly sprang to her feet. 'You're not going to find Nash?'

Robert's gaze snapped to her, but his voice remained level. 'I'm going to do something I should have done when we first got here.' And then he was gone.

The night was cold, almost icy, but Robert hardly felt it. As he stole through the camp, soldiers complained about it, wrapped their cloaks around themselves against it, all a little more nervous than before. Fires burned glowing coals, rich and red, dotted about the darkness like fat stars in a bumpy sky.

He paused at the perimeter to check no one could see him. The forest sat on his right, bleak and full of movement, life unchallenged and uncaring of the forces gathered around it. With barely a thought, Robert reached down inside and gathered together the threads of his power, wove them into a tight ball against the demon. Even as his feet moved again, so he took the mental step sideways, crossing into a dimension he could never fully understand. From this moment onwards, he would be completely invisible.

A breath of warm air drifted towards him as he passed the forest. Nightjars and owls sang in echo, faintly calling to his intent. Then he came to the river. Selar had erected a bridge and his guards patrolled it, but Robert walked by unnoticed. Even his footsteps on the timber were silent. He reached the other side and ignored the Sadlani patrols. He walked through the slick black oil Arlie's men had poured along the enemy bank, ready for the morning. He picked his way past clumps of sleeping soldiers, Lusarans and Guildesmen, panting in nightmares of the day to come.

Then further and deeper into enemy territory he moved, where humble tents and mighty pavilions littered the land, scars on the once-clean grass. He could hear horses and dogs in the distance. Closer, the snoring of men, grumbles, moans and someone coughing.

He stopped and counted.

A patrol of four armed soldiers in royal livery marched by him, intent on their work, unable to see the danger within their boundary.

Forty-six. Malachi, every one. Foul putrescent canker, spread about the camp, hidden from fearful eyes, buried deep and ready for treachery.

And something else. Not Malachi, not Salti. Something else. Something so rotten, his senses recoiled from examining it too closely. Was it *him* – or the murderer?

Not Nash. Robert knew no scent of his aura. That was invisible to him, as his had always been to Nash. Just as it should be.

Yes, there was someone else.

He should go now, while he still had energy to hold the shift. He'd need all his reserves for the battle tomorrow but—

He turned and wandered between the tents, his head turning, listening, smelling for the rat who had left a trail wide as the river. It brought him to the door of a pavilion beside Selar's.

Kenrick.

Two guards stood outside and Robert paused before them. He raised his hand and they turned, imagining a noise to their left. In that instant, he ducked through the door and came to a halt before the bed.

A boy, no more. Fourteen, with the face of a baby as he slept on in ignorance. The sheets were a mess, tangled around his legs.

On the table was a bottle small enough to fit into his palm. Robert picked it up, carefully sniffing the contents. Then he reached the side of the bed.

Slowly Robert reached out to touch a single finger to Kenrick's forehead. 'Remember,' he whispered, 'every day of your life, remember with pain. Fear me.' He pressed hard for a moment, enforcing the command, then stepped back. Kenrick shifted and moaned in his sleep, but didn't wake.

No, not death for this little one. Not for the boy who had just murdered his own sister and could still rest in the slumber of the innocent. No death just yet. Instead, something much worse.

Robert turned on his heel, paused long enough to repeat the command on the guards, then strode out of the camp.

He waited until he was halfway across the bridge before releasing the shift. Let the enemy know he'd been among them, unhindered and unnoticed.

Let them be afraid.

28

Aiden rode in solemn procession towards the battlefield. At his side, her face veiled but her back straight, was Jenn. Half a dozen soldiers accompanied them, two in front and four behind, all proudly wearing the black eagle of the Douglas House emblazoned on their chests.

A bleak sun elbowed down on the silent battlefield, while a wind blustered back and forth, tossing threatening clouds before it. Pennants flew above the lines of men, topping the pikes and spears raised in salute. Row upon row of archers lined the hillside to the left, still and waiting. Horses snuffed and stamped, but kept their positions, as though they too knew what was about to happen.

Aiden rode along the ranks until he reached a small hillock where magnates and priests alike sat upon their mounts in a wide row, gazing out at the view. They were all there, polished armour glinting silver, faces grim and empty of all humour. So different to the reverent faces he'd seen at mass that morning.

He came to a halt beside Finnlay and turned to look out over the valley: five thousand Lusaran soldiers, gathered and ordered in their divisions, left and right. A flat green expanse empty to the river. The bridge, guarded by Robert's sorcerers. And the enemy, twice the men, tightly formed, pennants of black and red flying high above. Yellow too, for the Guilde. In the centre, high above the others, was Selar's banner, declaring, for all to see, his claim to this field.

'Sweet Mineah!'

The whispered words came from his left. Jenn fidgeted with her reins a moment, then settled her hands once again. Aiden would have reached out to her, but with this audience, such comfort was impossible.

'Yes, it's quite a sight, isn't it?' Finnlay replied, his voice betraying his own awe.

'And Robert?' Aiden asked, looking about.

'Over there.' Finnlay pointed to the left where Robert, walking ahead of his horse, reviewed the archers. Micah rode behind him, carrying Robert's banner. After a moment, Robert stopped, swung himself up into the saddle and cantered over to Aiden and the others.

He stopped before them, looking from one face to the next. 'Well, I suppose we'd better get on with it. If his Grace the Bishop is ready?'

Aiden swallowed and gave a firm nod.

'Then be my guest.'

Aiden spurred his horse into motion and headed out onto the battlefield, McGlashen, Dunn, his guard and half a dozen others following behind. Almost the moment he began moving, a delegation from Selar's army approached the bridge. Each stopped on their own side.

For the first time in almost eight years, Aiden saw the face of the traitor who had replaced him: Anthony Brome, overweight, slack-jawed, with tiny podgy eyes fixed in a round podgy face, puffing and wheezing at the effort of sitting on the back of a horse.

'In the name of the King, I charge you to hand over the Outlaw Douglas and have this army stand down!' Brome called.

Aiden took in a deep breath and replied, 'In the name of the gods and all Lusara, have the King's army stand down.'

Brome shook his head, finished with the formal declarations. 'You are a traitor, McCauly. You were imprisoned for treason and you've done nothing to disprove the allegations since. How can you, in all conscience, ride at the head of an army led by an acknowledged sorcerer?'

'How can you?' Aiden replied without pausing.

'I? Empty accusations, McCauly! Meaningless.'

'Very well, I'll leave and we can be done with this.'

'Wait.' Brome held up a podgy hand. 'The King wishes to parley.'

'Let him come forth.'

'Not with you. He will only speak to the traitor Duke.'

Aiden almost smiled. 'I'll pass on your request.' With that, he wheeled his horse around and led his delegation back to Robert.

The others were waiting, all grim-faced and patient, except for Robert. He appeared pleased.

'Well?'

'Selar wants to talk to you.'

'Of course. Did you see Nash?'

'I don't think so.'

Robert looked at the others thoughtfully. His eyes rested on Micah for a moment, then he turned his horse for the river. 'I'll go alone.'

'My lord,' Micah protested, but Robert was already moving.

'Don't worry, I'll be back in a minute.'

As his dark figure rode away, McGlashen began to laugh.

'I don't see what's so funny,' Aiden said.

'It's an act of defiance, Bishop,' McGlashen replied.

'So?'

Payne leaned forward and added, 'Not only for them – for us. Look at our soldiers. Robert is riding alone onto the field, unafraid. Suddenly, they're not afraid either.'

Aiden snorted and turned back to face the river. 'Well, I just wish it would rub off a little more.'

Arlie and his men were on either side of the bridge, waiting quietly, when Robert finally arrived. He pulled up. 'Arlie, take your men back out of the way now.'

'But that'll leave the bridge unguarded.'

'And if you don't, you'll get mown down within minutes. Go on, leave now.'

Reluctantly, Arlie collected his men and headed off towards the forest, leaving Robert alone before the river.

A small group detached itself from the army and made its way towards the bridge. Quickly Robert scanned the faces as they came closer, but he knew all these. Nash was not among them.

Coward!

But there was a Malachi there, tall, fair-haired and elegantly dressed, watching Robert with a mixture of wariness and suspicion. This close up, the man's aura was unmistakable.

Selar led the group, stopping on the northern bank. Surrounded by a dozen soldiers and Brome, he appeared completely calm and supremely confident. Robert swung down from his horse, walked onto the bridge and stopped midway.

Selar dismounted, waving the others to remain behind. He strode out to the centre. For a long time, he stood there, watching Robert, his gaze never moving to the army arranged out behind. Eventually, Selar raised his arms wide and spoke.

'And what have I done that you should come in arms against me? We were always friends.'

Robert shrugged. 'It's a dull life being an outlaw. What's your excuse?'

'You know full well my purpose here. I will wrest the crown from my brother and rule Mayenne as I was destined to.'

'No, you won't.'

Selar raised himself up. 'You have a weak and puny army, Outlaw. Do you really think you can stop me?'

'I know I can.'

Selar laughed meanly. 'Vaughn was right; I should have done something about you a long time ago. I was a fool to disbelieve him.'

'And you're a fool not to believe me now. Take your army back to Marsay. Do not approach the border.'

'Do you think,' Selar hissed, 'that you scare me? Do you think I care a whit that you're a sorcerer?'

Robert paused and looked behind Selar to where the Malachi waited. 'Where's Governor Nash?'

'Nash? Why? What do you want with him?'

'Where is he?'

'I'm hardly going to tell you anything you want to know, am I?'

Robert turned back to Selar, meeting his gaze levelly. 'I have to assume you know what he is.'

'Oh, what?'

'A sorcerer – like me, like that man sitting over there with your guard.'

'Why, that's rubbish!' Selar scoffed, laughing a little.

Robert shook his head. 'No, I suppose he's found some way to keep you ignorant. How else would he have survived so long? His name isn't Nash, either. It's Carlan.'

Selar paused, his mouth open. He frowned, his face working hard at something, as if struggling to remember. Slowly, however, a grim smile appeared. 'If this is some tactic to get me to turn back, then it's pretty pathetic, even for you.'

'I give you one last chance, Selar.' Robert moved closer. 'I can and will win this fight. No other adversary would give you such fair warning. Believe me, your army will not survive to fight Tirone.'

'Not survive?' Selar laughed and took a step back, gesturing widely towards his forces. 'We outnumber you two to one. How can we lose?'

'Will you turn back?' Robert asked again.

'Never!'

The guard by the bridge moved, unsettled and nervous. Behind, spreading as far as the eye could see, was Selar's host, anxious to move, to have the day begin. Already crows flew above, squawking in the heavy silence, swooping into the gusts of wind buffeting the army.

Somehow, the moment had come and gone, unnoticed. Now Robert could look at the distant faces and know so many of them would not live to see the sun set. Odd really; all along he'd thought he might turn back at this point.

'Very well,' Robert murmured eventually, his gaze flickering back to Selar. Carefully and deliberately, he put on his most arrogant expression. 'Might I suggest you send across the hired swords first? Sadlani have always made the most energetic of targets. My men will enjoy slaughtering them as a prelude to destroying the rest of your army.'

'Hah!' Selar crowed. 'How easily you underestimate your enemy! And how you will pay for it!'

Robert dropped his voice. 'Then so be it.' He turned and walked away, leaving behind the shell of the man he'd once known and loved. Selar had died long ago, killed off by his unholy alliance with the Angel of Darkness.

He swung up onto his horse, but didn't look back. Instead, he rode towards his lines. He gestured at Finnlay to ride forward and meet him a little distance before the others.

'How did it go?' Finnlay asked, nerves affecting his voice.

'Very well, as it happens. He'll send the Sadlani over the bridge first, just as we'd hoped. However, there's one thing I want you to do for me. You must give me your solemn oath, for I'll not believe anything else.'

'What's that?'

Robert paused, his eyes moving along the lines of magnates until they rested on the figure beside McCauly, dressed in the finest cloth, her face covered with a veil, her back rigid, proud upon her white palfrey.

'If I should fall,' Robert murmured, turning back to Finnlay, 'you must promise me to use whatever means necessary to get Jenn out of here. Take her, bound and gagged if you must, back to the Enclave. Brook no argument, no threat of violence. Knock her out or drug her if you have to – she must never fall into the Angel's hands. Do you understand me?'

Finnlay nodded, wide-eyed. 'Yes. I promise.'

'Good. Now let's go to it.'

'By the gods, I feel so sick,' Jenn murmured, swallowing hard.

'Don't worry,' McCauly replied quietly, 'not long to wait now.'

'Is that supposed to make me feel better?' Through the veil, she could hardly make out the army in the distance. It was just a blot, seething danger. But of Nash she could Sense nothing. Why? Where was he?

'Did you eat breakfast this morning?' McCauly asked.

'How can you think of food at a time like this?' She swallowed again and kept her focus on Robert as he and Finnlay came back to the command group. She couldn't hear what was said, but almost instantly the magnates turned and headed out to their own troops, leaving her, McCauly and their guard alone on the rise.

'Did you hear the last message from Godfrey?'

'No.'

McCauly dropped his voice once more. 'It seem Robert's tactics have already had a dividend. Godfrey estimates almost a thousand desertions from Selar's army since dusk last night.'

'A thousand less for the slaughter,' Jenn muttered, her eyes still on the battlefield.

Robert, with Finnlay on one side and Micah on the other, rode back out into the middle of the field. Without a word, Micah raised Robert's colours: a huge gold canvas with a single black eagle, its wings spread, talons arched ready to attack. In that moment, the wind caught it, spread it wide and an enormous cheer flew up from the whole army. Robert raised his left arm and the cheer subsided. A rumble of thunder gathered in the east and the sun disappeared completely.

As though on cue, the enemy advanced, two rows of knights crossing the bridge at a canter and spreading out to cordon off the river. Behind them marched the Sadlani, dark grim faces, long curved swords. On and on they came and still Robert didn't move. In response, his army began to chant, clanging swords on shields to a drum beat the enemy couldn't help hearing. The Sadlani filled the northern end of the valley, positioned in standard formation. After them came Selar and the Guilde soldiers, mounted and foot.

Robert raised his hand a little higher and the chanting became a bellow. Then he dropped it.

With a boom, the bridge exploded, scattering men before it. The air was instantly filled with arrows as the archers began the attack, deafening. Jenn's horse bucked at the noise, but she held it firm. The archers continued on, and, for a brief moment, it seemed they would win all on their own. The Sadlani knotted together, many falling where they stood. With their retreat cut off, panic threatened. Then Selar rounded on them, urging them to the fight. With a mighty roar, they charged – and the heavens opened.

At first the rain fell lightly. Robert's men, in ordered precision, advanced, their chant marking their footsteps towards the battle. At the last moment however, they broke formation and ran into the fray. Selar's cavalry came to the pits hidden on the field. One after another tumbled and fell, horses screaming, banners flying into the air. But still they came on.

The chant finished with a roar and the clash of steel, the demarcation between the armies fading until the entire valley was a seething mess of fighting men, slipping in the mud, chaotic and haphazard.

Rain poured down on the battlefield, obscuring the river and what lay beyond. The only thing Jenn could see with any real clarity was Robert. He wielded his sword left and right, cutting men down before him. Micah rode at his side, keeping the banner held high, cutting down Sadlani who would kill Robert from behind. They fought in the centre of the field, surrounded by men of both sides, already black with mud, crying rage and pain.

'I can't watch,' Jenn whispered.

'You must,' McCauly replied firmly.

'But where's . . . Finn? And Arlie? And . . . Mineah's teeth, I can't see anything with this damned veil on!'

'The archers hidden on the hill have begun firing. More men are trying to cross the river to join the fight.'

'Can't I take the veil off now?'

'No.'

'Damn it!' Jenn bit her lip, then felt Aiden's hand on her own.

Calm, reassuring. How could anyone have their wits about them at a time like this? 'But I need to see Robert. I have to know if Nash is near him!'

'Micah is there, and Finnlay, too. But the only enemies within their reach are Sadlani.'

'Nash probably isn't even going to fight.'

Aiden didn't say anything to that. Instead, he sat on his horse beside her, occasionally telling her of something new she couldn't see. The rain penetrated her cloak, its cold seeping down to her skin. She shivered but the weather only continued to deteriorate. As did the noise.

After what seemed like weeks, Aiden spoke again. 'It's not going well.'

Jenn tore the veil away. Robert was now dismounted and almost impossible to see in the confusion. Micah was still on his horse, the banner attacked from all sides. The mess was appalling, veiled by a thick curtain of rain.

And if Nash *was* going to attack, he would do it now.

'Do you know what Nash looks like?' she asked quickly.

'Yes.'

'Can you see him? Anywhere on the field?'

'I'm not sure I would, even if he were there.' Tension filled the Bishop's voice. So he wasn't so cool after all. 'Can't you Seek him? You sensed his presence when he was at Elita.'

'But he'd be shielding now . . . '

'Try.'

Jenn stifled any further objection. Hastily, she closed her eyes and sent her feeble Senses out onto the field. Robert, as usual, glowed across the horizon, but of Nash there was no sign.

Except . . .

There, on the other side of the river . . . behind the forest. Seething black and coursing with the same things she'd seen before. So clearly. He was coming this way. Hiding under cover of the woods. He was coming. Now!

'Oh, hell!'

'What?'

Jenn didn't have time to answer. She pulled her horse around and headed down the back of the hill. The Bishop sent a guard after her, but she didn't wait. She rode along the edge of the camp, almost empty now, and turned for the forest.

She had to get to Nash before he could do anything.

The noise was impossible, but Finnlay didn't need to listen to anything but the pounding of his heart. Instead, he focused entirely on the mêlée, swinging his sword, parrying, thrusting, trying to keep his balance in the mud. He couldn't see anything beyond the man in front of him, and he didn't stop to look. The press of soldiers made fighting even harder; every now and then they were blinded by the flash of lightning, deafened by the crash of thunder.

The smell of blood and mud mixed together in a heady perfume of fury and desire. Energy and hunger flooded through his bones.

His horse fell in the first onslaught. He tried to keep Robert at his side, but it was impossible. The Sadlani came on with a fierceness he could only match, not beat. They fell before him and vanished into the mire.

He was cut on his shoulder, but there was no pain. His knee was wrenched, but he kept to his feet. The chaos swirled around him and, one by one, his thoughts dried up, the only desert in this soaked battle. The man before him swung his blade sideways and Finnlay blocked, pushing forward. Before his foe could regain balance, Finnlay thrust, withdrew and the man collapsed before him.

Without pausing, he turned and faced the next.

'Look out!' Payne called. Scrambling forward, he ducked behind McGlashen and crashed straight into the Sadlani's stomach. In a tangled heap, they both fell to the ground. In an instant, the man had rolled over and wrested the sword from his hand. A knife grazed his throat – then abruptly the Sadlani stiffened and slumped.

'What the hell do you think you're doing?' McGlashen bellowed, dragging the man's body off Payne. He held out his hand and hauled Payne to his feet. 'Are you trying to get yourself killed?'

'That's gratitude for you,' Payne grunted, retrieving his sword. 'That's the last time I do you a—'

McGlashen stumbled sideways, a Sadlani sword half stuck in his back. Payne launched an attack, cutting the enemy down with two swift blows. Then he fell at McGlashen's side.

'How is it?'

McGlashen was already grey. 'It's nothing. Leave me.'

Payne put his arm under McGlashen's shoulder and tried to haul him to his feet. Pushed and elbowed by men fighting around him, he struggled and slipped. McGlashen groaned ominously.

'I said leave me! Go now. I'll make my own way off the field.'

'No.' Payne pulled harder this time, taking the big man's weight. 'You're always trying to push me around. This is hard work, so just shut up and save your strength.'

It was terrible the way it worked. Terrible, and so perfect. Micah held his horse with his knees alone, his left hand glued to Robert's banner, his right wielding the sword. Swing and cut, block, fend off. Turn and swing again.

Robert was on his feet, his horse long lost, but never did he leave Micah's sight.

So perfect.

Thrust and turn, pushing the horse to block any attack Robert couldn't deal with. Slice and jab. Another down. Another death.

So perfect.

And so terrible.

McCauly ducked back under the awning and passed a bucket of water to one of the Healers. Already there were more wounded than could be dealt with. Lady Margaret and the other women, boys and pages, together with the qualified doctors and Healers, moved from one man to another, binding wounds, saying a few words of comfort. Three open pavilions had been erected, but the rain beat down on them all, leaking, turning the entire camp into a swamp of bleeding, dying men. All the priests were busy either healing or giving last rites. Every one had a purpose, even those who were charged with carrying away the dead.

As another crash of thunder split the day, Margaret came to the table and washed blood from her hands in a pail of already-dirty water. Her hair was tied back but loose strands, wet from the rain, stuck to her face where spatters of mud contrasted darkly to her pale complexion.

'How are you coping?' Aiden asked, looking around at the organised chaos.

'Don't ask. What about you?' Margaret glanced up, drying her hands.

Aiden could only shrug.

'Have you seen the battle? Do you know how it's going?'

'Not for an hour or more. I'm just on my way back. Selar sent a small force to attack our rear, but they were repelled. I haven't seen anything since.'

Margaret nodded, turning back to her work. 'Be careful.'

The battlefield was a sea of black writhing bodies when Aiden finally returned. He could see the river and the men beyond, struggling to help their own. Banners had fallen, colours clouded by mud and rain, but this was no longer a universal disorder. Instead, the field was now littered with bodies, crowded and pushed aside by larger knots of fighters. It was absolutely impossible to gauge who was winning.

Aiden got down from his horse and gave it to a wounded soldier helping another off the field. When he turned back, Robert was stumbling through the mire towards him, his sword wet and covered in gore. Blood streaked down his face and his trousers were open at the thigh, revealing a deep wound.

'Have you seen him?' Robert demanded.

'Who?'

'Nash!'

Jenn hadn't returned. Should he say anything when the battle was so close? 'No, I've not seen him.'

Robert paused to catch his breath, surveying the field with a piercing gaze, no less alert from the hours of fighting. 'I can't see Selar – or Kenrick.'

'Could they have fallen?'

'This army wouldn't keep fighting if they had. Where the hell is Nash? What's he playing at?'

'Here,' Aiden moved, 'let me see that leg. You should have it bound before you—'

'It can wait. Selar can't.' With that, Robert turned back and faced the field. He raised up his left hand into the rain. Instantly a roar of flames sprung up along the opposite bank of the river, cutting off Selar's reinforcements. The sight of unveiled sorcery had the men behind in terror. Robert dropped his hand and disappeared into the fray.

Another rumble of thunder and Jenn gave up calling for the guard. Her voice was hoarse and he was nowhere to be seen. She was soaked to the skin and hopelessly lost.

How had they become separated? He'd been right behind her when she'd entered the forest. But then she'd not noticed after that, so desperate was she to keep hold of that trace of Nash.

A crack of lightning split the air, crashing into a tree before her. Sparks flew out and the trunk groaned before colliding with the ground. With a scream of panic, her horse reared and she slipped off its back. The ground came up hard, but she managed to keep hold of the reins.

'And you wonder why he thinks you're such an idiot, Jenn,' she grunted, getting back to her feet. 'Go out to face Nash alone, will you? Get yourself lost in the damned forest you grew up in, and then you can't even stay on your bloody horse! I swear, I'll never argue about it again.'

She reached up to calm the animal, but it skittered around, not letting her get close. 'It's all right,' she soothed. 'Just stay still.'

It jumped out of the way, almost pulling the reins out of her grasp, wrenching her shoulder.

'Damn you, listen to me!'

We always listen to you, little one, Ally.

She stopped. For a moment, silence reigned in the forest – as though the storm raged everywhere but this spot.

But you do not listen to Us.

I . . . didn't think you could reach me this far away.

We can reach you anywhere you choose to go. How else would we survive? But you did not want to listen so we kept silent, respecting your wishes.

Jenn heaved in a big breath, glancing at the horse. It eyed her with suspicion, but at least it made no move to get away.

Why do you tarry here?

It was so eerie, feeling that disembodied voice, so like mind-speech, and yet so different. Lots of voices, all as one, the same inflection and yet many.

Look, I don't have time for your pointless questions right now. You know very well why I'm here. It's all your fault. If you hadn't given Robert that damned prophecy, none of this would have happened.

On the contrary, we gave it to him so that it would happen — because it would always have happened. His destiny is written in his soul and you, little one, can do nothing of good being here. The G'harzavin e'Mirani is to come, but not now.

What does that mean?

To force destiny now is to endanger all. Come. The time has come for you to sever your connection with the Enemy. Darkness approaches you and we will not have harm come to you. Return to us now.

No. I've told you before: I won't do anything you tell me without reason. If you want me to desert him — now, when he needs me the most — then you have to tell me why. Jenn paused, forcing her concentration past the wet and the cold. *Give me the rest of the prophecy. Tell me what I'm supposed to do.*

You can do nothing now.

I don't believe you!

We are joined for ever. You cannot change what is to come. But it must not come now. Leave . . .

Tell me!

As you wish. Silence for a moment — and then, slowly, the voices changed, whispered, almost inaudibly, as though it were not the Key speaking. *By your very means, Enemy, that born unto your hands alone, you will be the instrument of ruin. In the act of salvation, you will become desolation itself, destroying that which you love most.*

The reins dropped from Jenn's hand as her knees buckled beneath her.

By the gods! A curse? That couldn't even come close! Oh, Robert! No wonder . . .

Now you must return to us, Ally. Darkness approaches.

Jenn couldn't move, but as the voices died away, heat grew within her, burning with a fury she had once been afraid of. Now she used it, with a fierce, hideous kind of joy. *Leave them? Now? Never! You*

*brought us into this, never asking what we wanted. If you'd never told
us the prophecy, none of this would have happened.*

*It would always have happened. It is the G'harzavin e'Mirani. That
which must come. Leave now, little one, Ally. Darkness approaches.
We are afraid.*

Afraid? How can you be afraid? What are you afraid of?

Afraid for you, Ally. Be gone from this place.

The voices abruptly dried up, like snow on a summer's day. In
the empty void, Jenn staggered to her feet and cast around blindly
for the horse. It stood a few feet away, but as she reached out to grab
the bridle, something moved in the corner of her vision.

'You never used to be so eager to get away from me, Your Grace.'

Jenn spun around – and froze – her only movement now the
deafening pounding in her chest. She swallowed once, twice, but air
wouldn't enter her, wouldn't sustain her.

Nash smiled, spreading his arms wide. 'And it is so wonderful to
see you again, alive despite all reports to the contrary.'

29

'Selar!' Robert bellowed, pulling his sword from the guts of another
royal guard. He pushed the man aside and once more dashed after
the retreating figure. 'Selar! Stand and face me!'

Slipping on the mud, Robert went down, but rolled and sprang to
his feet in time to meet the next man hindering his path to the King.
A blade came up to cut his head off and Robert ducked, spinning
around to slice his sword into the man's legs. The guard buckled,
but Robert didn't wait to finish him off. He ran again, splashing
mud as he went. 'Selar, damn you – you'll face me if I have to chase
you to the ends of the earth!'

Selar was heading for the forest, would run away if he could.
Robert dodged another attack and kept after him. When Selar
slipped and fell, Robert let out a yell of triumph and dashed forward
the last distance.

Surrounded by tall trees, Selar scrambled to his feet, drawing his blade. He brought it before him, ready to fight, his chest heaving with his thwarted effort to escape.

'Hah! So now you're ready to face me,' Robert yelled. 'Now you have no choice.'

'Get back, Dunlorn! My men will be here soon.'

'You don't scare me – why the hell should you? I should have killed you off years ago!'

Selar backed away, his eyes flaring with sudden, consuming fear. 'Then you were a fool!'

'Yes. I believed somewhere inside you was the heart of a good man. Fool indeed!' Robert came to a halt, filling his lungs with air, steadying himself, feeling the rage surge through his body. It felt good. So very good. 'Not going to ask about your daughter?'

Selar started, taking another step back, his eyes darting, searching for help from his soldiers. None was forthcoming. They couldn't see him amongst the trees. 'What of her? You married her to take my crown. The child is a whore, like her mother was.'

'The child,' Robert grunted with a smile, his voice pure venom, 'is dead. Killed by your own son. She was no whore. Like her mother before her, Galiena was a true patriot – something you were always too weak to understand.'

Selar roared and swung his blade high to crash down on Robert. With a laugh, Robert brought his up and steel crashed together, deafening.

'What's wrong, sorcerer?' Selar hissed, his face suffused with red. 'What of your mighty powers now? Too tired to kill me with a bolt of lightning? Or are you, in the end, too much the coward to kill me at all?'

'Oh, I need no sorcery to kill you,' Robert hissed gleefully. 'That's already been done for me.'

With a snarl, Selar shoved back, spinning on his foot to take another swipe at Robert. Again Robert caught the blade with his own, holding it long enough to drain Selar's strength. Selar twisted away, then advanced, clashing his sword against Robert's with every step. Robert gave way easily, parrying each jarring thrust and cut, unable to still his laughter. When had the demon become this much fun?

'Fight me, damn you!' Selar bellowed, lifting his sword again. One almighty swing crashed into Robert's sword. It broke in two, kept on – and carved into Robert's side, piercing his mail.

Without thought, Robert jabbed the broken steel up hard between Selar's armour. A final shove crushed through flesh and bone and buried it to the hilt in his chest.

Selar froze, his face draining of colour. His weapon fell to the ground and he staggered back, his hands going to the blade, words of incomprehension stunted on his lips.

Robert held his side, only now gasping as the pain seared his whole left side. The demon shrieked with delight, but the joy dried up with the pain. He bent over as blood poured between his fingers, but he couldn't look away from the other man. Still Selar remained on his feet, his knees weakening, but holding him up. His gaze lifted to Robert's. Suddenly his legs buckled and he sank downwards.

'You . . . ' he gasped, fighting for air, 'should have . . . come back.'

Selar fell backwards, his eyes darting rapidly to the treetops above. Gingerly, Robert moved to kneel beside him. Selar reached out and grabbed his sleeve. 'You too proud. Carlan . . . stayed . . . '

The breath drained away, the words faded and suddenly, Selar was still.

'What's wrong, Your Grace?' Nash murmured, immune to the rain as it slowed around him. The rumbling thunder drew back, as though afraid of the man. 'Have you nothing to say to me?'

Jenn gulped in air, forcing some shred of calm to fill her. Why did he look the same? Hell, there wasn't even any suggestion of threat about him!

So why was she so terrified?

'I can't say I blame you for running away. Eachern was no fit husband for you – never was. I would have stopped the marriage, but Selar moved without consulting me. Still, it doesn't matter now, does it?'

'What do you want?' Jenn managed, backing away towards the horse. Nash came to a halt before her, making no further move. 'Who are you?'

He smiled openly, without malice, 'You know very well who I am. Your friend, nothing more. A friend who is brave enough to admit deeper feelings than he has been allowed to show. I would have confessed all to you weeks ago, but events overtook me. You gave me quite a scare with your efforts as Clonnet. Tell me, were you wounded at all when the Enemy married his little Princess?'

Jenn gave a start, swallowing hard. 'How do you know about that?'

'Please. I haven't survived this long without some skills to play with. Was it his choice, or yours?'

'It's got nothing to do with you.' Jenn edged further towards the horse. Why had she come out here? Why had she thought she could deal with this?

'But if the Enemy has hurt you, I would like to know about it. Perhaps I can help.'

'How?' Jenn snapped. 'By killing him?'

'That's what he did to Eachern, isn't it?'

'No, I killed Eachern. Are you going to tell me you would have done it?' She backed up against the horse and, for once, it stood firm.

But now she had no place to go and Nash came towards her, still mystifyingly calm and gentle. He halted a pace away, a hand raised in a gesture she didn't recognise. Suddenly she couldn't move her legs at all. She was trapped, wholly and completely.

'I would never hurt you, Jennifer. I cannot. My heart would never allow it. I had believed I could be close to you and not be touched by you. In that, I was mistaken – but I rejoice in the error. Your beauty has lifted my heart every time you came within my sight. Everything I have done, I have done to keep you safe. You were never in any danger at Clonnet. Not even from the Bresail. Not until the Enemy came and stole you away. Has he kept you safe? Will his army protect you?'

'He didn't bring me here . . . ' Jenn began the protest before she could stop herself.

'He could have kept you away. If he really cared for you as I do. He has married another, leaving you alone – despite the prophecy. But more than that, he has kept you ignorant, hasn't he? How can that keep you safe? You must know your destiny if you are to embrace it. I am prepared to share everything I have with you. I can give you eternal life at my side. Can the Enemy make such a promise?'

He was so close now, Jenn couldn't look away.

'Has he never told you your destiny is to be with me?'

'No!' Jenn breathed a little cry.

'You know it's true, in your heart. That's why you never told him anything about me. Why you could never betray me.' He reached forward and put a hand under her chin, lifting her face. Frozen by his power, Jenn could do nothing to stop him. His face came closer until his lips pressed against hers, warm – not cold, as she'd expected.

'Please,' she moaned, screaming inside, 'let me go.'

'Of course.' He smiled, his hand leaving her face with a slight gesture. 'You have all the freedom you could want. But you will want to come back to me. Soon.'

He stood back, releasing her. Abruptly her legs turned to jelly, but she didn't wait. She scrambled onto the horse, afraid to take her eyes from him. Without another word, she pulled the reins up and kicked the horse hard.

As she tore through the forest, she looked back, but Nash had vanished.

Micah paced up and down before the pavilion, trying not to limp. His whole body hurt in a way he'd never experienced before, but, much as he would have loved to just lie down and rest for a while, he couldn't.

'Micah, will you please sit down and let me finish dressing your hand!' Lady Margaret tugged his sleeve.

'There're men who need your ministrations more than I.'

She smiled gently. 'They are being tended, Micah. Please, come.'

With another glance over his shoulder, Micah turned and sat where she put him. He placed his hand on the table and looked around at the others gathered. Sunset was little more than an hour away but already the sky was dark, still grim with heavy grey clouds.

As far as the eye could see, men lay on the ground, wounded and resting. Some would never rise again. A few fires had been lit, but only now the rain had stopped did they show any life. Other soldiers, weary from fighting, tended their friends or sat in silence. Priests moved about among them, saying prayers for both the living and the dying. But no matter their condition, they were all, to a man, aware of the sight arranged in the centre of the camp.

A sole pavilion, canvas walls rolled to the roof. Inside, two biers with a lighted candle at each end, two bodies lying side by side. Micah couldn't take his eyes from it.

'What are we going to do?'

Margaret removed the bloody cloth from his hand and rinsed the wound with clean water. The Bishop handed her a fresh bandage with one hand, and Micah a cup of ale with the other.

'There's nothing we can do,' McCauly replied.

'How can you say that?' Micah whispered, only too conscious of the men around them, discussing the situation. 'Can't you do anything?'

Margaret wound the bandage around his hand tightly, tying it with a knot. 'I've tried. He won't move.'

'But he's wounded! We can't just let him sit there.'

'I agree,' Dunn added, coming across the room. 'Robert has duties to perform. Someone has to get him out of there.'

'Well, where's Finnlay?'

'Don't ask me.' Finnlay approached from the other side of the tent, his arm in a sling. His right eye was puffy and swollen from a cut on his cheek and he moved like a man twice his age. 'I've tried already. Robert just told me to leave – in his usual gracious manner.'

'But we have to do something,' Micah insisted, getting to his feet. He tried to keep his voice low, but exhaustion was working against him. 'You didn't see his wounds. He'll bleed to death if he doesn't see a Healer soon.'

He would have gone on, but everyone turned as a rider approached the tent and dismounted. Jenn. All heads turned and immediately, quiet whisperings filtered among the magnates.

'What's happening? Is Robert all right?' Jenn asked, quickly hiding from them behind McCauly. Her eyes darted around as though looking for something, afraid she might find it.

'Robert is alive. The battle, for what it's worth,' the Bishop replied evenly, 'is over.'

'And?'

'Nothing either way. A truce has been called to allow both sides to recover their wounded and dead. There'll be no more fighting today.'

Jenn frowned, her eyes wide. 'Where's Robert?'

'In there.' Micah raised his hand and pointed. 'He killed Selar.'

'By the gods,' she murmured.

'He's laid the body in state, beside Galiena's. Serin only knows what will happen now.' Micah moved and put his arm around Jenn's shoulders, drawing her away from the others. 'Robert's wounded, Jenn. I can't tell how bad it is, but he's been in there an hour now and refuses to move.'

Jenn looked up at him, her blue eyes reflecting the grey sky, sombre and serious. She looked like she'd already seen a ghost.

'Are you all right?'

She nodded. 'I'll go and talk to Robert.' With that, she walked out of the tent and across the drying mud to the pavilion. She paused a moment, then stepped inside. Micah stayed in the tent and watched, almost afraid to move.

Robert was seated on a chair at the end of Selar's bier, looking at neither his old friend, nor his new wife. Jenn stood beside him, her gaze, for a moment, on the bodies laid out, cold and lifeless. Then she turned to Robert.

Slowly he looked up. Neither of them said a word. Jenn reached out and touched Robert's shoulder. For a long time, he didn't move a muscle. Then his hand came up and took hers. She let go and stepped back. Robert came painfully to his feet and walked out of the pavilion. Jenn began to follow then stopped, throwing a last look over her shoulder at the still, silent bodies. Then she, too, left them behind.

'I'm sorry, my lord,' Deverin reported, his voice husky and coarse. 'The news could be much better.'

Robert waved him to a seat and tried not to wince as his mother applied another bandage around his waist. The meeting pavilion was full of men, each bearing their own wounds, some worse than others. Finnlay would have had the walls rolled down, but Robert refused. His men were out there, in similar or worse condition. This was not the time to be withdrawing behind closed doors.

He'd ordered fires to be lit against the oncoming darkness and a small quantity of ale to be distributed, but there was little he could do at the moment to lighten his army's mood. A whole day of fighting and nothing to be seen for it but a dead King. If Kenrick was under the influence of Nash as his father had been, that army could still make an attempt to cross the border. Nash would still want to find the Key.

Robert nodded at Deverin and took a sip of the warmed wine Micah handed him. 'Go on. Tell me the worst.'

'If there is a fight tomorrow, we'll be lucky to field three thousand men.'

A murmur rose through the gathering, but Robert ignored it. 'What about the enemy?'

'They'll have four thousand or so fresh soldiers ready to fight, those that were kept back, alongside the three or more surviving today. We'll be worse than two to one.'

Robert let his gaze wander across the faces surrounding him. 'What else?'

Deverin swallowed. 'We've lost Alard Bain, my lord. Payne is wounded and . . . McGlashen is dead.'

Robert closed his eyes. How many more? More fighting. More death.

And the demon. How much more would *it* take?

He sat up as his mother finished and put on his shirt. He pushed himself unsteadily to his feet and held his cup high. 'McGlashen.'

To a man, everyone in the tent stood, raised their own cups and echoed his salute. As they all resumed their seats, Robert steadied himself with a hand on the back of his chair. 'Dunn and Harold, I want you to take the west side with your freshest men. Make sure we get everyone from the field, leaving no body behind. Set up a watch again on the hilltops. Father Chester, Daniel take the east side. Arlie and Murdoch, you'll have to set up a watch as well. I know your men are tired, but we have no choice. Keep our Malachi prisoner safely drugged. How many Malachi were slain on the field?'

'A dozen, no more,' Murdoch replied. 'It's hard to tell exactly, since we can't Sense them once they're dead.'

'I'll go out later and do a quick count.'

'Robert,' Margaret warned, 'you're in no condition to do anything for a few hours at least.'

He ignored her and turned back to the others. 'The rest of you, get some sleep. Stay with your men, do what you need to be ready for the morning.'

'What are you planning?' McCauly asked on behalf of the others. 'If we couldn't win today, tomorrow will be far worse odds.'

'Tomorrow we face a different army,' Robert replied quietly, his gaze dropping to the deep red wine in his cup. 'Kenrick is now King, a boy of fourteen. His army of Sadlani has been destroyed. He will try to scare us, but he won't fight.'

Another murmur filtered around the room, but McCauly silenced them. 'How do you know?'

'He's not . . . ' Robert looked up, 'capable. I don't know what else will happen, but I do know Kenrick won't stay on the battlefield long enough to do us any harm. Other than that? A squad of my sorcerer colleagues will be mounted up to attack their rear – yes, with as much sorcery as they can manage. I'm sorry, Father Abbot, but we can no longer afford to simply play upon their imagined fears. Now those fears must be realised. We'll form up as before, keeping a thousand men in reserve. We'll pull back with the first charge and let them think we're retreating. Then, when they're between those two hills, we'll box them in. The rest we'll have to take as it comes.'

'But,' a voice rose from the back, 'do you still believe we can win this fight?'

Robert took his hand from the chair to stand firmly on his own. It took an effort, but he managed, 'I don't believe, my friend, I *know*. With the terrain in our favour, we don't need as many men. We've come a long way for this, waited a long time. We've all lost people we love, but that which we love most is still in danger. As long as an army broaches the field tomorrow, we will face it. I will not leave this place until we have won. Now,' he paused, draining his wine, 'before you all go, there's something I have to do. The first of many, I'm sure, but this, I can't wait any longer for.'

Another rustle of movement at Robert's grim expression. He took a few steps to a clearing between the tables and chairs. 'Micah?'

'My lord?'

'Come here!'

'Yes, my lord.' Micah squeezed his way between others. For some strange reason, he'd hidden himself away.

'Where's my banner?'

'Outside, my lord,' Micah stammered, self-conscious before so many. 'I put it there myself.'

'That's what I thought. Daniel, hand me your sword, will you? I seem to have misplaced mine.'

Daniel froze for a moment, then swiftly drew the blade, cleaned now after the battle. He handed it to Robert hilt first.

'For some time now, it has occurred to me that I've been missing something amongst my ranks. Something important. I'm surprised it's taken me this long but I can only assume that with my mind on so many other matters, what would normally have been obvious has remained carefully hidden. However, this is not the case any more. Micah, on your knees!'

Micah swallowed, but nevertheless, he settled gingerly onto his knees. Even now his trust was absolute. So typical.

Robert raised the sword. 'For more than twenty years you have served me faithfully, saving my life on more than a few occasions. Today however, I counted no less than six opportunities when I would have been cut down if it hadn't been for your efforts. To make matters worse, you hold my banner high throughout the entire battle, then manage to keep it safe to bring back here. Any man having a tenth of your courage and loyalty would deserve this tribute.'

Micah gazed up at him, suddenly breathless. Robert smiled and slowly lowered the sword. With the gentlest touch, he lighted it upon Micah's right shoulder.

'I dub thee knight,' Robert said, unable to keep the tremor from his voice. Why had it taken him so long to get around to doing this? 'Live all your days with the honour you have carved into your soul. Your example is a light the rest of us strive to follow. Rise, Sir Micah Maclean.'

For a moment, Micah didn't move. Then slowly, his face a myriad conflicting emotions, he got to his feet. Instantly a cheer rose and men strode forward, clapping Micah on the back, calling out congratulations. As they gradually left, Micah turned back to Robert, completely mystified.

'But you never said . . . I . . . '

'You don't understand?' Robert smiled, put his arm around Micah's shoulder, and thoroughly enjoyed the hopelessly pleased look on Micah's face. 'I know. That's what makes you so special. Go now and get some food. You can come back later to tell me off. Go on.'

Micah turned to leave, paused and looked at Robert. 'Nope, I'm never going to understand you. Not if I live a hundred years.'

Robert laughed, 'Go!'

Shaking his head, but giggling like a boy, Micah finally left and Robert sank gratefully into his chair. Only McCauly, Margaret and Finnlay remained behind, and they were all smiling.

'That, Brother,' Finnlay said, raising his cup, 'was about the best idea you've had for years.'

'Thank you, Brother.'

'I thought the poor lad's eyes were going to pop out of his head when you raised that sword,' McCauly added. 'You are such a crafty bastard.'

'I beg your pardon!' Margaret looked perfectly offended and McCauly raised his hands, offering a hasty apology.

As Robert's chuckle subsided, he turned back to Finnlay. 'Where's Jenn?'

'Out of sight. Rumours are flying around the camp, you know. Between the two of us, people are starting to really believe in ghosts.'

Robert smiled. 'When you've finished your wine, can you go and bring Arlie back here?'

'Why?'

'I need him to get rid of this pain.'

'Is it so bad?'

What a question! 'Bad enough to stop me moving about.'

Finnlay's eyes became hooded and he sat forward. 'Are you sure about this?'

'Never more about anything else in my life. He'll come soon. I'm wounded, tired and will do anything to prevent another battle. The perfect trap. He knew I'd walk into it. As long as Nash is alive, there will be an enemy ready to face us tomorrow – perhaps even earlier. Go ahead, Finn, tell me I've read it all wrong.'

Finnlay met his gaze for a moment. With one swallow, he drained his wine and came to his feet. 'I wish I could. I'll bring Arlie back in a moment. And please, try not to knight anyone else while I'm gone.'

Long after darkness fell, Jenn put on a cloak and ventured out of McCauly's tent. The air was crisp and dry, the sky almost cleared of clouds, revealing pristine stars reaching to the distant hills. With her hood up to hide her face, she wandered through the camp, listening more than seeing. There was a quiet pervading the entire place that chilled her bones more than the night air ever could.

Occasional moans filtered below soft voices talking about the battle. Snatches of heroic tales came to her, words of friends who hadn't survived, of loved ones left at home. No word, however, of what might happen tomorrow.

She walked on, avoiding pools of mud as best she could. Firelight gave the camp a cheer it didn't deserve, but nobody seemed to be complaining. These men had long ago committed themselves to this war, for love of country and their people. But they were fighting their own, and they knew it.

Sometimes she would hear of men she knew. How Sir Owen had lost an eye saving two ordinary soldiers from a dozen Guildsmen. How Harold Holland had managed to keep his horse despite a hundred efforts to topple him from it. Even the gentle Lord Daniel Courtenay had done his part, credited with bringing home more of his men than any other, while still managing to inflict his share of damage. Of the loss of McGlashen, few words were spoken, and all with regret.

More than a few times, Micah's name was mentioned, always in the highest regard. To carry a commander's colours into battle was a position of grave honour and importance. Not only to that commander, but to the army in general, giving them a constant focus, a reminder their leader was alive and fighting alongside them. As a result, the banner was always the greatest target for the enemy. Micah's elevation to knighthood appeared universally approved.

Of the King and Princess dead, the murmurs were quiet and thoughtful.

But the one name mentioned more than any other was Robert's.

With awe, with respect – and something that bordered on worship. They spoke of his efforts on the field and of how he'd come amongst them tonight, sharing a moment with so many of them. Hardly a mention of talents he might have beyond his abilities as a general, his skills as a warrior. They believed in him because they'd seen it now, with their own eyes. But that didn't stop them being afraid – of sorcery, and of the people he'd brought with him.

For more than an hour she walked amongst the army almost unnoticed. Finally she came to the perimeter where guards patrolled the battlefield beyond and the hills hiding the river. Steeling herself, she reached out with her Senses, trying to pinpoint the aura. Even as she sought it, she cringed inside at the prospect of finding it. But she felt nothing. It was as though Nash had completely disappeared.

Why had he let her go? Did he really believe she would go back to him? How could he delude himself so?

About as easily as she had deluded everyone she'd seen since. Only Father Aiden had asked, and he had apparently believed the lie that she'd not found Nash. But she couldn't hide from herself, couldn't relieve the sick feeling in the pit of her stomach, the memory of him touching her. The fear.

'You shouldn't be out here.'

Jenn spun around to find Robert behind her. He wore a cloak, but the hood was down, revealing his face in the pale light. A cut above his left eye and another on his jaw were the only wounds she could see. Everything else was invisible, even the demon.

'How do you feel?' she asked nervously. Why couldn't she see the demon?

'Fine.' He moved to stand beside her, his gaze roving the hills, taking in minute details in a moment. 'But you really shouldn't be out here. You know the camp is awash with rumours about you. It's bad enough that Finnlay has appeared out of nowhere, but there were always doubts about his supposed death. Yours was another matter. There've been enough men who recognise you to tell the world.'

'Does it matter?'

'I don't know. It depends on whether you like the idea of being seen as a ghost – or worse.'

Jenn turned back to the view. 'I heard about McGlashen. I'm sorry.'

'He was a good man, and a good friend. The best. Payne blames himself. McGlashen was the one who pushed me to marry Galiena. Now they're both dead, the King along with them.'

'Robert, you . . . '

'Don't comfort me.' He turned to look at her, a frown creasing his forehead. 'Aiden told me what you did today.'

A sudden cold washed over her and she scrambled for a response. 'Oh, I know what you're going to say. Yes, it was a stupid thing to do, I admit it . . . '

'I was going to say impulsive, but stupid will suffice. I'd hoped the Key would work that kind of behaviour out of you, but perhaps it just needs more time. I don't suppose you'll tell me why you went?'

'You know why.'

'Yes,' he murmured stiffly. 'I do.'

Jenn met his gaze, but she could read nothing in his expression. His voice was level and soft, contained, but also resigned. And yet, he wouldn't allow her to reach out to him, no matter how much she wanted to. Needed to. The wall was impenetrable. 'Your men are talking about you, you know.'

He raised his eyebrows.

'Before today, you were only a hero in their minds. Now?'

'And what do they say about Micah and the others?'

'Good things.'

Robert nodded and looked once more at the hills. 'You could have come on your own, but you didn't. Thank you for bringing Finnlay. It means a lot to both of us.'

He turned and walked back through the camp, leaving her alone on the edge of a tired, wounded army.

No, he didn't trust her any more, just as he'd said. But was it just because of the Key?

Within the meeting pavilion, cool night drifted down with a gentle peace. The last order had been given for the evening, the last messages received and sent. Little more to do now but rest, recover and do everything possible to avoid thinking about tomorrow.

The brazier crackled, flames licking up over its edge. Robert leaned forward to put another log on, holding his bandaged side. Then he settled back carefully, easing his body around to keep the worst of his wounds from the hard chair. He could have got some cushions, but right now he was so tired, he couldn't be bothered with that much effort.

Micah sat at the table, fiddling with his sword. With a cloth, he worked away at the joins, cleaning, polishing, bringing it up to full shine. The bandage on his hand didn't hinder the work; the bruise above his eye appeared pale in the lamplight. He'd done well today. Not too many scars, not hurt too much.

At least, not yet. And not because of anything Robert had done for him. Micah had survived intact because of his own skill. All Robert had done was drag him into this war – along with all those others outside this tent. Micah had not survived today *because* of Robert, but in spite of him. And tomorrow, Micah could just as easily die.

By your very means, Enemy, that born unto your hands alone, you will be the instrument of ruin.

And now Jenn was here, in the camp, wandering around, paying no attention to the danger she was in. It was torture. How could he face Nash knowing she was close, that the prophecy could come true in a moment, simply because he might fail to control the demon?

Like he'd failed today.

Selar, Galiena, McGlashen and all those others: good men, fighting for their country – but why were they really here?

Why was Jenn here?

Because of a prophecy that drove power into the hands of two men born to fight a battle between them!

Selar had started this only because Nash had pushed him. Robert was only here because somebody had to stop the carnage . . .

Stop the destruction of . . .

In the act of salvation, you will become desolation itself, destroying that which you love most.

Robert sucked in a breath and frowned as the glowing coals burned truth into his eyes.

The prophecy was already coming true, already winning. It would always win because *he had already become the destroyer!*

Closing his eyes, he set his head back. It was too late. It had always been too late. Sweet Serin's breath, why hadn't he seen it before?

A noise, palely discordant, reached his ears. Whistling to accompany work. A familiar sound, aching back to his childhood.

He opened his eyes and looked across at the table. Micah was completely absorbed in his work, unaware of anything else.

Bury the thoughts, Robert, bury them deep. Yes, let the demon swallow them whole.

Robert laced his fingers together, took in as deep a breath as his wounds would allow and formed a gentle smile. 'If you don't stop that soon, you'll wear the damned sword out. A new knight can't ride into his first battle with some thin shrunken embarrassment dangling from his hand. You have ancient traditions to live up to now, my friend.'

A shy smile crossed Micah's face. 'Perhaps you should have warned me, then. You know I can't read your mind.'

'I know nothing of the kind. In fact, I have proof to the contrary. What I do know,' Robert paused, keeping his gaze on the head of burnished red hair, 'is that you've been around me too long.'

Micah finished with the sword, briskly sliding it back into the scabbard at his hip, but then he stopped, glancing up with a frown. 'What does that mean?'

'It means that it's time for you to leave me.'

'No.'

'I mean it, Micah. You and I have been together more than twenty years now. It's time for you to go.'

'No.'

'When we finish here, I want you to leave. You have to find a life for yourself. One that doesn't have my fortunes – ill or otherwise – attached to it. Go back to Dromna and solve your complications with Sairead. Have a family, settle down with a home. I really don't want you with me any more.'

Micah studied him for a moment, his blue eyes growing dark. 'You liar.'

Robert raised his eyebrows.

'If you want me to have some life of my own, you don't have to push me away to do it.'

'You're going to fight me on this, aren't you?'

'And what would I be if I didn't? Who would I be?' Micah stood, his eyes flinty in the firelight. 'Do you think I've learned nothing from you?'

'Micah . . . '

'No! Did you think I'd just walk away? No, Robert, I can't read your mind – but I do know you. You don't plan to survive tomorrow, do you?'

Robert turned back to the fire. 'Of course I do.'

'By the gods, you *are* a liar!'

'Don't sound so surprised. I've lied to you before, and you know it.'

'Don't you dare . . . ' Micah's jaw came up and he looked away, some glint in his eyes betraying his thoughts. 'I can't stop you, can I? I can't say anything?'

Robert got up slowly and put a hand on Micah's shoulder. 'You have no idea what your friendship has meant to me over the years. But no matter what happens tomorrow, I want you to promise me you'll do as I ask. I want you to have a better life than this. You deserve it. If you love me at all, you'll go.'

Working hard against himself, Micah's face screwed up as his head dropped. 'You don't understand. I can't.'

'But you must,' Robert added softly. 'If nothing else, it will bring joy unbounded to your father.'

A wry, involuntary laugh escaped Micah and he glanced up. 'I fear the shock would kill him.'

'Then you'd better break it to him gently. Killing your own father is not the best way to start a new life.'

Micah swallowed, the smile gone. 'I suppose that's what this was all about wasn't it? Making me a knight?'

'In a way, yes. But I've never met a man who deserved it more. Consider it a parting gift. It's not a lot to be starting off with, but unfortunately, I don't have much else to give you.' Robert turned back to the fire. He had to. This was harder than he'd thought it would be.

For long moments, Micah stood behind him, a flushed silence giving no hint of his thoughts. Then he spoke, his voice soft in the night. 'Twenty years is a long time, for both of us. After Elita, you gave me a choice, but now you take it away. You're right – I do deserve better than that.'

Robert heard nothing more until the tent flap lifted and fell and he was alone once more.

Jenn sat on her bed and stared at the thin canvas wall, plain and lit from without, a soft glow generated by the whole camp, darkened by one small spot twenty feet away.

She wouldn't sleep. Not tonight. Somebody had to keep watch on the demon.

All she had left was this cold silence. And memory.

If Nash came now, she wouldn't Sense him. He'd shield, hide himself in the black night, just like Robert.

Only Robert wasn't hiding any more. Not from the demon. It had almost consumed his aura. Soon, perhaps in only a few hours, there would be nothing left of his will to control it.

Are you there?

Always. Little one. Ally.

Can you save him? Can you stop this?

We must not.

But can you?

Nothing can stop it.

But he'll die!

Be comforted, little one. You have us.

But I don't want you!

Then you must make him survive.

How?

We do not know. We do not understand this demon you think of.

Understand the demon? Did she really understand it?

What does he love most?

We do not know, little one. He will not talk to us.

No. Not to anyone. He's surrounded by close friends, people he can trust his life with – but not his curse.

Holding back a sigh, Jenn pulled the blankets further around her shoulders and tried to shut out the fear along with the cold.

Dark night covered his movements. No stars now, no moon. The fires had died down as the army lay in slumber. In a few hours, the sun would begin to rise and he would lose this chance for ever.

Micah paused in the shadows and gazed across at the tent where two Salti guards stood watch. Despite their exhaustion, they were alert and would already know he was there. Straightening up, he strode forward, feigning confidence.

'Is she asleep?'

'Like a baby. She had another draught three hours ago. She won't wake until sunrise.'

'Good.' Micah nodded. He lifted the tent flap and stepped inside, giving no explanation, fabricating no orders. But it didn't matter. They didn't try to stop him.

It was dark inside. He could just make out the narrow pallet, had to almost imagine Sairead lying sleeping on it.

Carefully, he moved and knelt at her side, reaching out to where her hands were tied to the corners. Arlie had been kind, binding her hands with cloth beneath the rope. It wouldn't be comfortable, but it would cause her no harm. And she had blankets on her.

His fingers found her face, touched the smooth skin of her closed eyes, her lips. Then he leaned forward and kissed her, pressing his face to the side of hers.

Tomorrow. Her fate would be decided tomorrow – and he would have no say in it. Even if he told the truth.

And if Robert didn't survive tomorrow, Sairead would be killed for vengeance alone.

He would lose both of them.

By the gods, why had she come? To see him? Her training gave her no claim to fight. She'd come because of him – and she'd protected him, not giving away anything when Robert had interrogated her.

He had to move, or the men outside might come in. He had to leave—

He froze as a sound outside breached the walls of the tent. Scrambling to his feet, he turned and faced the door.

The morning sky was already suffused with the palest pink as Finnlay ran through the camp, ignoring the pain in his knee. Sharp gusts of wind whipped around his cloak, warning of another blustery day to come. Already the army was moving, quietly, but with dogged purpose. He dodged a troop marching out to take up guard duty and ducked inside Robert's pavilion.

The meeting room was empty, so he continued on through the antechamber. Still no one. Desperate now, Finnlay stepped through the door to Robert's bedroom. He was stretched out, a blanket covering his legs. His chest – where it could be seen above the bandages – was already purpling with bruises and scarred from a dozen cuts gained in the battle.

'Robert?' Finnlay put a hand on his shoulder and shook gently. 'Robert, wake up.'

His brother shook his head slowly, opening his eyes with an effort. 'What is it?'

'You have to get up. It's almost dawn.'

'Dawn?' Robert replied groggily. He sat up, swinging his legs over the bed. Instantly he let out a groan, holding the wound on his side. 'Why didn't anyone wake me?'

'I don't know.' Finnlay could hardly keep still. 'But you have to hurry.'

'Why? Is the enemy lined up ready to fight?'

'No, it's something else.'

Robert frowned and reached for a shirt. 'What?'

'There's been some trouble. People hurt.' Finnlay took a deep breath. 'And Micah. He's missing.'

30

The change came so quietly, Jenn almost missed it, but after a few minutes she could hear a distinct alteration in the pitch of camp noise. Not bothering with a cloak, she pushed the tent door open in time to glimpse a group of men in front of Robert's pavilion. Robert was issuing orders with rapid clarity. A horse was brought to him, and then her view was blocked by the Bishop striding towards her, his expression grim and determined.

'What's happening?'

'Get back inside first.' McCauly gently but firmly propelled her backwards, dropping the flap behind him. 'I'll tell you on the condition that you make no attempt to leave here.'

'Why? What is it?'

'Micah's been abducted. Some hours before dawn. He was with the Malachi prisoner, and she's gone too. Three perimeter guards are dead – and two Salti – but there are no visible wounds.'

'Malachi?'

'Robert's sure of it.'

Jenn opened her mouth to ask, but the answer was written all over McCauly's face. 'Robert's going, isn't he? Alone. Nash has Micah and Robert's going out there on his own.'

Before McCauly could utter a reply, a single horse galloped past the tent. Jenn didn't need her Senses to know who was on it. Unthinking, she took a step towards the door. McCauly caught her arm.

'No. You're to stay here.'

'But I can't.'

The door opened and Finnlay stood there, his eyes dark. 'Robert's orders are explicit, Jenn. I'm sorry, but I can't let you leave here.'

Jenn shook her head wildly. The longer it took her to get out, the worse it would be. 'You've got it wrong. Robert has it wrong.'

'You can't stop it, Jenn.'

'But I must! You don't understand.' Jenn gulped in a breath but it did no good. Her heart was racing and only leaving here would change anything. 'If I don't go, they'll kill each other!'

As though she'd slapped him, Finnlay took a step backwards, his face suddenly wiped of expression. He gazed at her with new eyes. 'So – Robert was right after all. Well, I don't care what you say, Jenn. Whether you deserve it or not, my brother loves you more than his own life, and you're going to stay here if I have to knock you out with my bare hands!'

Frantic now, she grabbed Finnlay's jacket. 'I know how the prophecy ends – but it's not *supposed* to end this way!'

'And that's why you're staying here.' Finnlay replied darkly. 'I don't care what you say. I gave Robert my word.'

'But they can't face each other yet. If they do . . . don't you see? Nash won't need to kill Robert *because the demon will!* You must let me go.'

Finnlay took her fingers from his jacket and stepped back, covering the door. 'You're not going anywhere.'

He rode as hard as he could, but, too soon, the forest closed in around him and he had to slow down. As though a strong silk thread rested in his hand he kept track of the Malachi touch, sharp and venomous, so clear he could almost taste it. Dawn enveloped the forest gradually, dusting the treetops with gold, glades with shafts of misty white. In any shadow, behind any tree, they could be waiting, hiding, drawing him further in, poised with expectation and bloodlust. He could feel it.

The ground dropped before him in a gentle decline, following the roll of the hills. He stopped and immediately the sense of urgency left him, vanishing into the folds of brush and new-grown moss. Tentatively, he reached out with his Senses, felt the trees around him, the movement, the air, the noises.

As though obeying some tacit order, the forest fell silent, piece by piece, until only the breathing of his horse broke the stillness.

This was the place.

He slid down, minding his injuries, and let the animal go. It wandered on its own, oblivious, pulling at stray stalks of grass pushing through the leaf-covered floor.

Robert moved forward cautiously, following the slope, touching trees as he passed, listening, almost sniffing the air. The tranquillity was unnatural, but he was attracted by it as much as repelled, inexorably drawn further down towards the bottom. A small clearing in the trees above filled the copse with a veil of light even his sight could not penetrate. He came to a halt while still in the shadows.

'Micah?'

His voice echoed around the wood and was then swallowed by it.

So this is where it would be. The answer. The end. The silence washed across the demon, chafing every surface of it awake. It sat around the edges of his eyes. Waiting.

'Micah?'

'He can hear you, but he cannot respond.'

Robert turned swiftly, his senses shrieking warning of Malachi blood approaching. At first, the figure seemed a part of the sunlight, pale and insubstantial. Then it moved closer, stopping yards before him.

'Who are you?' Robert said, still scanning the forest with his Senses.

'I am the Baron Luc DeMassey, Malachi and Master of the Darriet D'Azzir. Who are you?'

'We require no introduction. I didn't come here to fight you.'

'Are you sure about that?'

'Where's Nash?'

DeMassey smiled. 'Oh, he's around somewhere. I'd have thought you'd be more interested in discovering the whereabouts of your friend.'

'I doubt you'd tell me.'

'Most certainly I would. He's right there, in front of you. Of course, you'll have to move a little to see him.'

Robert went to take a step, but DeMassey held up his hand. 'The question is, will I let you?'

Moments before it came, Robert sensed the build-up of power emanating from the Malachi. On instinct, he raised his hand, deflecting the blast harmlessly into the ground, but the effort left him pale.

In the ensuing silence, an echo of laughter reached him, surrounding and vanishing too quickly for him to pinpoint.

DeMassey was no longer smiling. For the first time, Robert turned his full attention on this man. It seemed this was some kind of test.

'Darriet D'Azzir?' Robert murmured, deliberately curious. 'Supposed to be combat masters. Your sole purpose is to seek out Salti and kill them.'

'That's right.'

'How pathetic.' Robert laughed a little, mirroring the Malachi's arrogance enough to irritate him. 'I've often wondered if the D'Azzir had anything interesting to say, but those I've met never lived long enough to talk.'

DeMassey sprang forward, his sword appearing out of nowhere, blazing power crackling to its point. Robert had no time to draw his own. He ducked behind the nearest tree, then sprang back as the sword slashed through the trunk. He spun around behind DeMassey and ran into the clearing. The tree crashed down and the ground shuddered under his feet. DeMassey roared and raced after him. Before Robert could get too far, DeMassey was on him. He drew his sword just in time to parry the next blow. The power seared his hands and face. He couldn't hold it for long. With a grunt, Robert twisted, spun his sword around the hilt of DeMassey's and flicked it away. DeMassey would have gone after it, but Robert's blade stopped an inch from the Malachi's throat.

'Step back.'

'Why don't you just do it. Kill another D'Azzir.'

'I told you,' Robert said, 'I didn't come here to fight you.' No, not this man. Save the effort.

DeMassey glowered, but moved back, keeping clear of his now-cold sword. Satisfied for the moment, Robert lowered his blade and turned back to the centre of the clearing. The Malachi hadn't lied. There was something there. Solid. A figure, lying on the leafy floor.

Quickly now, Robert dashed forward and landed on his knees beside Micah. Blood caked around a shallow wound to his shoulder. His feet were tied, his hands bound behind his back. There was even a gag on his mouth.

'Micah?' Heart beating so loud he could hardly breathe, Robert reached out, already feeding Micah the power to ease his pain, help him wake. Micah opened his eyes, met Robert's gaze with an unspoken apology. Robert smiled gently. 'Don't worry, my friend. It'll be all right.'

He reached forward to remove the gag, loosened it over Micah's jaw. 'Serin's blood, Robert, I'm sorry!'

Robert moved to cut the bonds with his sword and froze when a sharp point touched the centre of his back. DeMassey hadn't stayed clear for long. Robert kept hold of his sword, readying to spin and face the Malachi once more but—

Like a serpent sliding across a dry desert, his Senses reacted to something he couldn't define. Every sinew, every fibre curled up, taut, opposing movement. Even the pain from yesterday's wounds faded into the background against this onslaught. His whole body –

no, his entire being drew inwards, defiant, full of expectation and . . . destiny . . . and . . . warning . . .

'Leave him be, DeMassey.'

Robert held his breath. The pressure at his back vanished. Deliberately, and so very slowly, Robert came to his feet and turned around.

Nash.

Plain, unscarred face, close-cropped black beard following his jaw, at his waist, a gilt and bronzed sword, gleaming red jewels, like the ring on his left hand. No Guilde emblem, no badge of office. But Robert didn't need his eyes to tell him this was the Angel of Darkness. Every nerve-ending in his body screamed danger.

Nash moved forward a few steps into the clearing and stopped, appraising Robert openly. With barely a flick of his fingers, he gestured DeMassey out of the way, his gaze never leaving Robert.

'So, Enemy, there you are.'

Robert said nothing. What, after all, was there to say?

'No words of greeting?' Nash added lightly. 'No curses? No joy that you've finally arrived at the moment your whole life has been heading towards?'

'I'm not in the mood for games.'

'Games?' Nash raised his eyebrows. 'How little you understand.'

He moved, circling the place where Micah lay. Every step he took, Robert matched, keeping himself between them.

'What do you want?' Robert asked eventually.

'I think it's more appropriate to ask what *you* want. The life of your friend, there? Simply taking young Micah was enough to draw you out into the open. So touching how you're willing to risk your own life to save his. You must know how feelings of loyalty, of duty and honour – of love—' Nash paused, savouring the word, 'only make you weak and vulnerable.'

'And you're so very strong without them?'

'Simply understanding them has given me an advantage you have failed to appreciate.'

'What do you want?'

'Your blood, Enemy.' Nash came to a halt, spreading his hands at his sides in a gesture of honesty. 'I believe your brother would understand.'

Out of the corner of his eye, Robert saw DeMassey move to the edge of the clearing, and then another figure emerged from the bushes.

The girl. Of course – they'd rescued her, hadn't they? He should have killed her when he'd had the chance.

Nash sniffed. 'It must be so galling to you, struggling your whole life against something you know nothing about. You stand there, every inch the warrior, your sword poised ready to strike. But you can't kill me with a blade of steel. You can't even blast me to pieces as you would have done to DeMassey. There is only one way you can kill me.'

Despite himself, Robert forced out a laugh. 'And I suppose you're conceited enough to tell me?'

'It's only fair,' Nash replied, equalling his smile, 'when I know so much and you know so little. It's simple really: you must sacrifice the Ally.'

Even though he'd known it was coming, Robert couldn't stop the chill that gripped his stomach. Of course. Jenn. He hissed as a sharp jab of pain stung his side. He pressed his hand to it, but his eyes never left Nash. 'Get on with it, Carlan.'

'So you do talk to your brother! How amusing! Then he must have told you all about me. Did the Ally?'

'She knows who you are, if that's what you mean.' Pain jabbed at him again, but this time he did it successfully. Nash was dragging this out deliberately, making him tire.

'Well,' Nash said, 'I would have told her myself before, but there was all that fuss at Clonnet. But don't think too harshly of me. I do understand what it is to love someone and be unable to show it. And you do love her, don't you?'

Robert nodded slowly. 'And you made Eachern beat her. That's about the only way you would know to demonstrate such feeling.'

'You're hardly one to talk, Enemy,' Nash snapped. 'You've pushed her away, deserted her, all in the name of love? You were Bonded from birth and yet, like a fool, you ran away, never realising the treasure you denied yourself. She is mine, Enemy, and there's nothing you can do to stop that. She will give me what I want, quite willingly, without a thought to you. She is my Ally and she will give me the Key.'

No. Never sacrifice Jenn. Never.

'You've missed so much,' Nash continued, his voice again like silky oil, insinuating itself into Robert's mind, into the demon. 'You've been played like a fool. I never intended Selar to invade Mayenne, I just wanted to bring you out into the open. All those men of yours dead, because I wanted you here. But wait, there's more. Remember your dear uncle, the Duke of Haddon? I sent a man along to that fight specifically to kill him.'

The demon blanched at each word, struggling to get free, smacking at Robert's wounds with every jerk.

'Of course, you know how I abducted all those children during the Troubles, our dear Jennifer included among them. But I'll bet you didn't know that I started the Troubles in the first place. I had to get an army into Lusara to find the Key. Selar was my best chance. He took it thinking the idea was his own. He was always so easily led, don't you agree?'

'Why are you telling me all this?' Robert desperately tried to control his breathing, every movement white-hot agony. He had to get control or . . .

'Because I want you to know how deeply, how badly and how completely you have failed your destiny. I want you to know all this before you die.'

Robert dropped his gaze to the ground at his feet. Come, gather the pain-deadening power he could use so easily on other people.

But it didn't work.

'Why don't you tend to your friend?'

Robert looked up, but DeMassey was nowhere near him and there were no other Malachi nearby except for the girl. Taking a chance, he turned warily and knelt down to cut Micah's feet free. Micah sat up, words on his lips, but then his gaze shifted—

'Sairead! No!'

Robert spun – but too late. The blade hit deep into his right shoulder and he buckled forward, blinded by the pain. Micah caught him, but Robert stayed upright, trembling on his knees, gasping for breath.

'Finnlay,' Jenn pleaded, turning swiftly, 'please, Father Aiden, you must believe me. I have to go out and stop them! I can't leave Robert on his own.'

The Bishop looked extremely uncomfortable, but didn't give in. 'He doesn't want you there, my dear. You must understand his fears for the prophecy.'

'Of course I do!' Jenn snapped. 'But the prophecy is not his enemy – the demon is. If I'm not there . . . '

Abruptly she gasped as a searing pain slashed through her body. She stumbled forward, unable to keep her balance. McCauly caught her, harsh concern thrown towards Finnlay.

Jenn fought back tears as the pain settled, angling into her shoulder. Robert. He'd been wounded. Somehow. By the gods, did she have to kill these two men in order to save Robert's life?

A wave of nausea swept over her as she held onto the Bishop. She lifted her head and looked into his grey eyes. 'I have to go.'

'No.'

'Hold on,' Micah hissed. Cloth tore, but Robert hardly heard it. His vision swam. Nash faded and came back again. Faded and back. Laughing.

'Take the knife out,' Robert whispered. 'Now.'

'All right.' Micah pressed something against the wound, took hold of the blade and pulled.

Robert groaned and fell forward onto his hands. Fire ripped up his spine, turned his legs to jelly. 'Give me the knife.'

Micah pressed it into his hand and he forced something to gather inside him. He didn't need much, but he needed it quickly. With aching sluggishness, some shred of power filtered through his fingers into the blade, growing painfully stronger. The blade began to glow a little and instantly Micah grabbed it, pressed it to the wound, burning it to stop the bleeding.

Robert bit back a curse as the pain intensified. He concentrated hard. Too hard. No. Not too hard. Not yet. No. Better now.

Slowly and painfully, Robert straightened up.

Nash was watching him. 'Well done, Sairead! Well done indeed.'

'Shut up!' Sairead snapped. 'I didn't do it for you.'

Nash laughed again . . .

Sairead? *This* was Sairead?

Micah was moving at his arm, helping him to his feet. Robert stood, his breath snatched away by something else, something he'd never seen, never known, never have believed – and yet should have.

He turned to Micah, his eyes wide. Then, without thought, he grabbed Micah's collar, the demon bubbling up from deep within.

'You . . . traitor!'

'No,' Micah pleaded. 'It's not what you think . . . '

'How could you!' Robert pulled him close, breathing the same air, just as they'd done for so many years. Micah, of all people . . .

He gripped hard and turned to the demon. With a blink, he let it go, let it course through him. Fitting that the demon should destroy this traitor. Fitting, yes. Let him die. Let him . . .

NO!

Robert froze.

What was he doing?

Just what he was supposed to do.

No.

Never.

Never give in!

Slowly and very carefully, he released the pressure in his hands until he had only a light hold on Micah's collar. He closed his eyes a moment, Sensing where the others stood, and those beyond the clearing. Yes, plenty of them to fight him, so Nash wouldn't have to.

A good trap. Only a fool obsessed with a prophecy he couldn't defeat would have walked into it.

'I'm sorry, Robert,' Micah whispered. 'I didn't betray you. I . . . '

'Fell in love with a Malachi,' Robert murmured, continuing his search. No, Jenn was nowhere near the clearing. She was still at the camp. Well done, Finn.

'Micah,' he hissed under his breath, 'when I tell you to go, run as fast as you can, take my horse and ride back to the camp. Tell Finnlay to gather every Salti and get Jenn back to the Enclave. He's not to wait a moment. Do you understand?'

Micah's voice was unsteady. 'Yes. But . . . '

'And *don't* come back.' Robert opened his eyes, enforcing his meaning. 'Do you understand?'

A mute nod was the only reply.

'You'll know when,' Robert added finally, letting Micah go. He closed his eyes again, ignoring the laughter from Nash. Agony ripped from his shoulder to his hip, enough almost to make him faint. He had to stop it. Had to do something. Taking the demon in hand, he faced the pain square-on, isolated it, singled it out from the other aches, as he had done so many times before, with pain less physical. So many years at war with himself finally gave him something to fight with. His breathing eased a little, his vision cleared and he opened his eyes to gaze back at Nash once more. The demon was under control.

'For someone who's lived more than a century,' Robert began unsteadily, 'who has had so many advantages, so much knowledge at his fingertips, you've made quite a number of serious mistakes, haven't you?'

'None that couldn't be remedied.' Nash appeared unconcerned. He was enjoying himself.

Mistakes, hah! How many mistakes had *he* made? Letting Jenn go. Loving her, knowing the danger it would put her in.

Robert kept his voice hoarse, but invisibly shifted his weight, gauged the distance to his sword. 'Putting so much effort into those abductions, hoping to catch me as a child.'

'A miscalculation of timing, nothing more.'

Miscalculation? Yes, plenty of those. So many years trying to fight the demon, with so little hope of success. It had used the Word once already. And next time, would it kill her? Would he really have no choice but to destroy the one thing he loved more than any other? Just so he could destroy this monster?

He swallowed. 'Then going out of your way to kill my brother – not once, but three times. Failing each time. Never knowing, until I finally revealed myself, that he wasn't the Enemy.'

'But you did give yourself away.'

Yes—

Self. Resigned self. The Key took his will away. The prophecy took his will away. The demon . . . the demon used it for . . .

Robert gasped again and almost lost his balance. Black spots flashed in front of his eyes, deep black spots, dredging up . . .

The demon?

By the blood of the gods! The *demon!*

Robert almost laughed, but caught himself in time.

There *was* another way, another answer!

A way to destroy the prophecy for ever – and the demon would help him . . .

Oh, he could have laughed indeed, but he held fast and kept the charade going, deliberately weakening his demeanour, rasping his voice. He didn't need to act much, not to kill this man. 'I've known for more than three years who you were. But I suppose what really must have stung deeply was to find your Ally stolen from under your nose.'

Nash merely shrugged.

Robert faked a cough, closed his eyes as though he were fading with every moment. So many years of wearing a face closed to the world made it easy. 'I've known about the prophecy since I was a child, had the Word that long. Doesn't it bother you – not the mistakes as such, but the gaps in your judgement?'

'I still have the upper hand.'

'Perhaps. But you don't have the Ally. And I'll never sacrifice her to you.'

'Then you lose,' Nash smiled, and for the first time, Robert smiled back.

'I know she's your Ally.'

Nash's smile faded. 'Then you know she is close to joining me. Should I tell you how yesterday, while you were fighting your battle, our lovely Jennifer came to see me?'

Robert allowed his knees to buckle at that – again, too easy to fake. *She'd lied . . .* Micah knelt to help him, but Robert paid no attention, instead making sure his hand landed close to the forgotten dagger. Oh, Jenny! Why?

'Yes,' Nash laughed again, 'so much for prophecy. In the end, you have been almost too easy to defeat.'

'I believe,' Robert said, coughing deliberately, 'that you said the same thing of my brother.'

In one fluid movement, Robert grabbed the dagger and threw it at DeMassey, hitting him square in the stomach. At the same moment, he let the demon go to fill him with new energy. Before DeMassey had even hit the ground, Robert had snatched his sword and reared to his feet. He spun around, sweeping the clearing with a searing flame pouring out of the point. Micah ducked beneath it and began to run. The Malachi ignored him.

Instead, they dodged the flame and raced towards Robert, each bearing a similar weapon. Nash moved back, yelling orders, but Robert wasn't going to waste what energy he had on these minions. He cut through the first few, leaving them behind as he took off after Nash. They pursued him, blasting trees in his path. He tripped, but kept his balance, spinning around to fling one single burst at them. He didn't bother to wait and see the effect. Nash was getting away.

Leaving all thoughts of pain behind in the clearing, Robert ran after Nash, dodging low branches and bushes in his path. The ground was flat but uneven, but Nash had to run as well. As Robert began to gain on him, Nash finally reacted. He stopped in his tracks long enough to hurl a blast of energy directly at Robert. Instinctively Robert ducked low, throwing up a hasty shield. Even so, he landed on his back, winded. By the time he got to his feet, Nash was on his way again – and Robert took off.

More blasts followed, but these were nowhere near him. It wasn't until he was between the tallest trees that he saw why. An ominous creak made him look up. Branches swayed and the trunk came toppling towards him. With Nash's laughter ringing in his ears, Robert threw himself to the ground.

At first, Finnlay thought the thunder had returned. He ducked his head out of the tent long enough to see the sky clear of clouds. Another boom and those left in the camp started to fling questions at him, expecting him to know what was going on. He turned towards the forest and saw a flash illuminate the depths. Another explosion was followed by the unmistakable sounds of trees falling, growing closer to the battleground. Suddenly a horse came galloping out of the darkness, right across the camp, skidding unsteadily before him.

'You have to take Jenn away. Now!' Micah almost fell off the animal, then Jenn was beside him, holding him up. 'Please. He said you had to go. The only safe place is the Enclave. Nash told us . . . what he's going to do. You have to leave. Now!'

'No!' Jenn turned to Finnlay, but as he caught her, she stopped, her gaze obsidian in determination. 'Finnlay, let me go. Don't make me choose between you and your brother. You said you trusted me.'

Finnlay reached out to catch her arm, but she flung up her hand, beating him back with a pulse of power he'd never seen before. Without pausing, she turned and ran, lifting her skirts to fly through the camp, heading for the battlefield. Finnlay had no choice but to go after her. He tried calling out, but nothing was going to stop her.

The armies were already arranged, dominating the fringes of the battlefield, but the fighting had not yet begun. Instead, they seemed equally stunned by the sounds and flashes from the forest. Finnlay's legs began to shudder as he ran, but eventually he caught up with Jenn as she ran past the front ranks of soldiers. There she stopped, gasping. Finnlay stopped beside her, doubling over for a moment.

A ripple of awe flooded through the army and he looked up. Nash had emerged from the forest, backing slowly into the empty field. He stumbled, breathless and injured, his neck and chest exposed but blackened with burns. A heavy sword raised in front of him, glowing with power, he appeared oblivious to his surroundings, focusing only on what followed him.

Nash was in the middle of the empty field before Robert finally emerged from the shadows of a huge oak. One side of his face was streaked with blood. His jacket was missing and his once-white shirt was scarlet from hip to shoulder, torn and shredded. He walked with a limp, as though he could barely put weight on his right leg. His left arm was wrapped around his stomach, but he didn't hesitate. His sword remained steady, vibrating quietly with a power Finnlay could easily feel, even from this distance.

Before Robert even cleared the trees, Nash swung, sending a blast towards him. With a heavy arm, Robert raised his sword and deflected the fire into the grass. Without pausing, he sent one of his own, not aiming for Nash, but the ground beneath his feet. Nash stumbled backwards into a gaping hole, coughing as the dust settled. All around, both armies gasped in horror, involuntarily easing away from the fight.

Robert made his slow way into the centre of the field, fending off one blast after another. He was getting weaker by the minute, and yet his shielding never failed, his blasts never dimmed. He was putting all of his energy – everything he had – into the battle. But he wasn't really fighting back, defending, rather than attacking. What was he doing?

'Forcing Nash to spend himself,' Jenn murmured. 'Robert's weak. He knows he can't last much longer. The odds have to be even, Finn.'

Inexorably they moved closer, even as the armies backed away. For the life of him, Finnlay couldn't believe he was this close and yet, nothing touched them. Now he could hear Nash, calling out jibes, insults, everything he could to make Robert fight.

'Even now, when you're so close to losing,' Nash sneered, his words twisted by his burnt mouth, 'you still won't do it, will you? You still won't use it against me. You have all that power inside you, but you're too afraid of using it. I told you caring made you vulnerable. Go on, Enemy, use the Word of Destruction to kill me. You know you want to. If you don't, you'll die, and the Ally will be mine. Lusara will be mine!'

'Never!'

Finnlay's heart sank at the sound of Robert's voice, hoarse and empty. He was on the edge.

'Go on, Enemy,' Nash taunted once more. 'Do it! You know she stands behind you, ready to join me when you fall. She didn't tell you of our meeting yesterday, did she? Of how she trembled when I kissed her?'

'No!' In that instant, Robert swung his sword wide in a great arc. The ground rumbled beneath their feet and the air crackled as a dozen bolts of lightning all joined the tip of his blade in one almighty blast. The discharge erupted in a blinding flash and Nash was tossed in the air, obscured by smoke and flying rubble. When it cleared, Robert was left standing alone, wavering, his shoulders shuddering with each breath.

Before him, Nash lay on the ground, a dark figure against the green grass. Almost as one, the armies held their breath.

Then, slowly, Nash lifted his head, almost toppled backwards before getting onto his knees.

Finnlay gasped. Skin hung from Nash's face, an eye was missing completely. His right arm was nothing more than a mash of bleeding flesh, the rest of his body, almost burned to a crisp – yet he still lived.

'His powers have gone,' Jenn whispered.

Robert's feet were moving even as he raised his sword again. There were no more than a dozen feet between them when a few last words hissed from the remains of Nash's face.

'I told you – you can't kill me like that.'

Robert stopped and dropped his sword and—

Jenn grabbed Finnlay's sleeve. 'Get back.'

'What?'

'Get back. Now!'

'Why?'

'Can't you feel it? Sweet Mineah,' she cried, 'That's why he was draining Nash's power – so he would have no defences left. By the gods, *Robert's going to use the Word!*'

31

Leaving Finnlay behind, Jenn ran as hard as she could. Every step brought the power closer, harsher, like before at Elita. It was the same. Just the same. She couldn't even see where she was going. The demon dominated everything, spinning through her like a gale through trees, ripping and tearing as it went, driven out of Robert with a force of unbearable magnitude.

But it was flawed. Horribly flawed.

. . . you will destroy that which you love most . . .

The demon twisted him, held him captive. He would use the Word – but he would crush it, feed it back into the demon . . . so it wouldn't kill her, so it would kill the demon – and Nash . . .

But it would also kill *Robert!*

She came to a halt, heaving in air, Nash, dazed and bleeding on her right, Robert, black as night on her left. Even as she watched, he raised his hands and the earth began to moan beneath her feet.

She had to stop him.

Without pausing, she brought her fists together, forcing every ounce of her strength through in one mighty burst. A great clap rang through the valley, sharp and deafening. The ground at her feet split open, rending a crack, deepening with every second. Still she held it, pulling in power from the earth, the air, feeling the strain, pushing sinew against muscle, building the fury to a new depth, dark and blinding white. Pure and undefiled.

She would not let him die.

With a shriek, the ground exploded, throwing both Robert and Nash back before a cloud of rubble and mud.

Jenn stumbled, but kept her balance. Her head spun, her knees felt weak, but she stood, determined not to move. Gradually the rumbling subsided. Slowly, painfully, Robert got to his feet and picked up his sword, but it was an act of defiance driven by sheer force of will.

Nash did not get up. Instead, a weak and bloodied hand moved, waving towards his army. Instantly, a dozen men in royal livery galloped towards him, shielding Nash from Robert, their menacing message all too clear. As they collected Nash and put him on a horse, Kenrick rode to the edge of the chasm, his eyes on Robert, full of hatred.

'You killed my father!'

As though waking from a deep sleep, Robert's head came up. With a roar of rage, he leapt over the gaping chasm and swung his sword before the horse's face. It rose on its legs, but Robert was already reaching up to pull Kenrick to the ground. The boy fell with a thud, Robert's blade inches from his throat.

'You killed my wife. Now you will pay!'

The sword came up as Kenrick screamed for help. He threw his arms up in futile defence even as his soldiers rushed forward.

'Robert, look out!' Finnlay called, already moving to help.

For a moment, Robert froze, his gaze staring down the confused and terrified royal guard. They brandished their swords, crowding towards him.

'Get back!' Robert yelled. 'Back, or he dies!'

The soldiers came to a halt. Without taking his eyes from them, Robert hauled Kenrick to his feet. With one swift jerk, he swung his hand, hitting the boy's face so hard, Kenrick fell back. The boy scrambled clear, running for his horse as his men backed away. He was barely in the saddle before they were all galloping away.

'Go on!' Robert roared after him. 'Bring your army against me, coward!'

But Kenrick was running for his life. His horse splashed across the river, hardly touching the makeshift bridge. Jenn couldn't hear anything, but even so, she knew he was already screaming orders for a retreat. The men before him scrambled back in a wave of confusion. Those mounted were turned and vanishing across the field with shameless haste.

'Coward,' Robert repeated, his voice abruptly hoarse.

Jenn glanced at him, hardly hearing the noise from behind: the clattering of swords upon shields and a growing rumble blossoming into a tumultuous cheer. It rang on and on as their army broke ranks and swarmed across the battlefield towards their hero. Robert turned, swaying, slowly, painfully, his will alone holding him upright. First one step, then another, his face came up and his gaze met Jenn's.

Hollow of everything but betrayal.

Finnlay started forward, but Jenn couldn't look away from Robert and the message his eyes carried. Finnlay was almost at his side when Robert stumbled, his sword dropping to the ground. Then Finnlay reached him and Robert collapsed.

'Luc!'

DeMassey slid from his horse and straight into Valena's arms. He held tight to the wad of cloth stopping the bleeding in his stomach and put an arm around her shoulders, steadying himself. All around, the army ran in panic, horses bolted, tents were dragged down. A few, priests mainly, tried to stem the tide, but it was hopeless. Sairead brought her horse alongside his, her gaze sweeping the chaos. 'Valena, what's happening?'

But DeMassey ignored her, holding onto Valena. 'Where's Nash?'

Valena struggled to get him out of the traffic. 'Kenrick brought him back. He's close to death. Let me get your wound fixed and I'll go to him. I'll have to do it quickly.'

DeMassey grabbed her arm, stifling the pain for a moment. 'You can't do it. Not now.'

'But now is the best time!' Valena glanced around. 'He's wounded, defenceless. He won't know the poison until it's too late. Luc, we've never had a better chance!'

'But,' he bit his lip, 'we still need him. To get the Key. We'll never get it without him.'

'I don't care about the Key any more!' Valena tried to drag him towards her tent, but he fought her. 'I just want him dead. Our child will be born before Nash recovers. If he thinks for one moment the baby is his . . . you know what will happen. If you don't have the courage to do this, Luc, then I'll do it on my own. You'll thank me later.'

DeMassey stopped before the door and watched as Sairead rode off after the others. Then he turned to face Valena. 'You'll be throwing your life away for nothing. Kenrick guards Nash now, and he has enough power in him, for all that he's just a boy, to discover your intent and kill you before you can finish it. No, my love, it's too late. Nash will recover. It will take him years, but he will recover. Then, when he gets the Key, we'll take it from him. Don't worry, I'll make sure he never knows about the child.'

Tears filled her eyes. 'I'm afraid.'

'I know. But come, we have to move. I don't want to be the only ones left here when the Enemy comes to take a look.'

Sairead kicked her horse hard, scrambling to steer between the fleeing soldiers.

The Enemy had to be dead. He just had to be. He couldn't survive or . . . or Micah would never be free.

Turn around. Go back and see.

No. Too late.

Not today.

Godfrey swore and bit back his fear as his hands struggled with the last bandage. The moment he was finished, he stepped back, allowing the cart filled with wounded to move off. He moved across the empty space, helping one man knocked over by a fleeing rider. He glanced up to find Osbert emerging from his tent, a single bag in his hand. The man hurried for a horse held waiting for him.

Godfrey dodged more Guilde soldiers and reached Osbert before he could mount up.

'Proctor, you have to tell me what happened.'

'Nash is still alive, if that's what you're worried about,' he said, barely concealing his urgent need to be gone.

'No, for pity's sake, Osbert!' Godfrey grabbed his arm. 'What of Robert?'

A glaze of buried relief filtered across Osbert's eyes before being swallowed up once more by his fear. 'He was still standing when I left the battlefield. I'm sorry, Godfrey, but I have to go. I'll leave a man behind to guard you, but don't tarry long!'

Still standing? After all that?

Godfrey moved back as Osbert mounted up, his horse joining the fleeing stampede. Torn with indecision, he stood there, unable to take a step either way. Then somebody careened into him and he began to run. Nash was still alive. If Godfrey left this lot now, there would be nobody around to pick up the pieces. He couldn't help Robert by crossing the river now.

No matter how much he wanted to.

Aiden sat at the table with his hands clasped together before him, ignoring the meal waiting to his left. Candles had been lit against the encroaching darkness, but the light did nothing to illuminate his heart. Before him sat or stood the remaining magnates of Robert's rebel army. Some bore wounds, others only scowls. In the far corner, gathered in a tight group, sat the army's priests, none of them looking at him.

Suppressing a sigh, Aiden turned back to the last reports. He gestured to Deverin. 'Go on.'

'It's going to be hard to be sure now night is falling, but their camp is virtually empty. Only a few wounded and dying are left behind. We've sent priests and Healers among them. The rest are on a forced march northeast.'

'And Nash survives?'

'That's what Godfrey says. His last report came in a few minutes ago. We won't get another until he returns to Marsay.'

'What he has given us has been invaluable,' Harold ventured. 'That's one brave priest.'

'What I don't understand,' Daniel murmured into the silence, 'is why Kenrick has gone at all. Surely he knows he has the advantage over us now. With Robert badly wounded and his army three times our numbers, he could make a good showing. Why leave his father's death unavenged?'

When Aiden only shrugged, Daniel continued, 'How did Robert know Kenrick wouldn't fight?'

'You'll have to ask Robert, I'm afraid. I have no idea.'

'Probably more sorcery.'

Aiden glanced up to find Abbot Chester had risen from his seat. His hands were folded beneath his surplice, his face as grey as his habit. 'I'm sorry, my lord Bishop, but what I've seen today only enforces everything I've been taught about sorcery. This is not what Lusara should be fighting for and I, for one, will not support it any longer.' With a formal bow, Chester left, two more priests following behind. The others, quiet amongst themselves, remained.

'Well,' Aiden said firmly, 'we'll camp here two more nights, to give the wounded time to recover a little. It will also give us time to bury our dead with proper ceremony. Deverin will keep scouting parties on watch for Kenrick, but I doubt we'll see much of him for a while.'

Deverin nodded. He tugged at his beard and looked up, keeping his voice low. 'I don't mean to keep asking, but Owen won't leave me alone and he's under orders to keep to his bed. How does Robert fare?'

Aiden swallowed but kept his voice steady. 'The Healers are with him as we speak. He lives. What else can we ask?'

'Aye, what indeed?'

Daniel got out of his seat and took one beside Aiden. 'You've got to tell me: I don't understand anything that's going on here. I mean, I've met Governor Nash – how is it he's suddenly a sorcerer? Why was he fighting Robert? Why did that lady – whoever she is – why did she interfere?'

'That,' Aiden sighed again, 'is a very long story, and I'm not sure I have an answer for you. I would suggest . . . '

'Bishop?'

Finnlay approached and came around the table. Every eye in the room was on him. Every man knew he came from Robert's room.

Finnlay said nothing initially. Instead, he stood behind Aiden and leaned forward to whisper in his ear. 'I think you'd better go in now.'

Finnlay left the tent slowly, his head bowed. The magnates were still gathered in the main chamber, but they didn't see him go. Outside, the air was crisp, a frail wind lifting banners here and there, slapping gently against the tents, making fires flare brightly.

Somehow, night had fallen without him noticing. Again the sky was laden with cloud, leaving only a shadow of moonlight visible in the east. Soon that, too, would be gone.

Silently he walked along the path between tents and pavilions, pausing outside McCauly's. He lifted the flap, but the room was empty, no candle lit, no brazier alight against the cold.

'How is he?'

Finnlay turned to find Micah standing in the shadows, a saddled horse behind him.

'Where are you going?'

Micah shrugged. 'Away. Please, Finnlay, don't ask why. I just want to wait until I know . . .'

'Then leave now.' The words came out before he thought them through. As Micah turned, he held up his hand. 'Wait, Micah. Where will you go?'

Without turning, Micah gathered up the reins, 'East. There's something I have to do. Something I should have done a long time ago.'

'East? Your family?'

'No.' Micah shook his head slowly.

'Andrew?' Finnlay's voice was little above a whisper.

'Somebody has to . . . watch over him.'

In the darkness, Finnlay heard the tremor in the voice, the hesitation, the anger. Something had happened, but it was too late to ask. Too late. 'Take care of yourself, Micah.'

Micah nodded, his face in shadow. 'And you take care of him. Goodbye, Finnlay.'

Speechless, Finnlay watched him mount up and ride away. Without even turning, he sent his Senses out through the camp, then began walking again, faster this time, a force guiding his footsteps. He finally came to a stop on the edge of the forest, where huge trees dominated the skyline. There was just enough light from the fires to see her face against the darkness.

Jenn sat with her back to a trunk, her knees up, her arms wrapped around them, oblivious to his approach.

'Jenn?'

She didn't move, so he took a step closer. 'Jenn?'

She turned her head, surprised. 'Sorry, I didn't see you.'

'What are you doing out here?'

'Nothing.'

Finnlay took a deep breath, let it out slowly, encouraging calm, reason, anything but what he felt. 'You should come back.'

'Why?'

'To see Robert.'

Abruptly she got up. 'I don't think so. I'm the last person he would want to see right now. Don't lie and say he's asking for me, either. We both know he's never going to forgive me for what I did today.'

'He's not,' Finnlay swallowed, 'asking for anyone.'

Jenn didn't even look at him. 'Then it's best I stay away. I'll leave at dawn. I should think it's quite safe for you to linger as long as you like without me around. I have to get back to the Enclave.'

'And the Key?' Finnlay murmured. He tried, but the will wasn't there. He couldn't keep silent now. Especially now. 'Just tell me one thing. Why can't you just go and tell Robert you love him? Even if it's a lie. Can't you do that much for him?'

Jenn snapped around, her eyes wide, glowing in reflected fire-light. 'A lie?'

Finnlay frowned. 'Well? Do you love Robert or not?'

'How . . . ' Jenn's voice shook, her mouth opened but the words were forced from deep within. 'How . . . can you ask me that? How can you think that I don't . . . '

'Then tell him.'

'Would he want to hear it? After what I did to him?'

'You did what you had to do. Even I understand that.'

'Don't kid yourself, Finn. Robert doesn't look at it that way. He never has. All his life, the battle has had one single focus: him against the prophecy. That's how the demon was born. He tried to kill it, but I got in the way. He'll never forgive me.'

'But you saved him.'

'No, I didn't. His destiny still lies ahead of him. All I did was postpone it.'

Finnlay paused, then placed his hands on her shoulders, forcing her to look at him. 'Please come and see him, Jenn. Do it for me. Do it for him.'

When she didn't move, his heart trembled and his voice broke. 'Jenn, I beg you. Robert's dying.'

Jenn froze, not breathing, not even blinking. Her mouth opened, her eyes grew wide.

Finnlay went on, afraid to stop now, 'You have to go and see him. Tell him about Andrew. Tell him he has a son. Make all this mean something to him, Jenn. Maybe it will give him something to hold onto. Maybe he'll find some way to survive – but even if he doesn't, let him die knowing you had his son. Tell him you love him. Give him some shred of peace.'

Jenn's breathing came in sharp gasps now. She shook her head again, fear filling her eyes. 'No, I can't. Telling him will only make it worse.'

Finnlay gripped her shoulders hard, shaking her. 'It can't get any worse! Damn you, Jenn! You have to!' Unbidden, his eyes filled with tears, but he went on, adamant, 'He's dying, Jenn. You're the only one who could say or do something to help him in any way at all. By the gods, McCauly is in there with him now, saying prayers for Robert's soul! How long do you want to wait? Until Robert's dead? Do you want to go back to the Enclave knowing you could have done something? Is that all your love means to you?'

Jenn twisted out of his grasp, barely controlling tears of her own. She gazed at him for a long time then, slowly, her eyes turned to the camp behind him. She swallowed loudly and lifted her head. 'Very well. I'll go.'

A soft murmur of voices warmed the pavilion as she approached, a song, hesitant and expectant, pervading the entire camp. Through the canvas walls the small round glow of candles flickered and jumped, creating strange shadows, tall and hideous.

Finnlay led her through the side door and into the antechamber, empty and solitary. Then to the threshold of the bedchamber.

McCauly stood at the end of the bed, his book in one hand, a trium in the other. His voice was so soft she could hardly hear it. Would the gods listen to such murmuring, so quiet, so earnest?

Margaret perched on the side of the bed, a cloth in her hand. Arlie and another Healer stood and approached the door, their faces betraying their concern.

'How is he?'

Arlie kept his voice low. 'Bad. He's lost a lot of blood, too much for too long, and I can't stop it. I think his leg is fractured, and some ribs. There are other wounds besides the one in his side. A deep cut in his back from the dagger. I think something heavy must have fallen on him.'

'Why?'

'He's bleeding inside. You can see the bruising on his stomach. He hasn't regained consciousness since the battle.'

Jenn listened, trying to take in the detail, trying to understand it, trying to believe it. Robert had always been so strong. How could a few injuries do so much damage – to him of all people? 'What can you do?'

'Nothing more.' Arlie bowed his head. 'He put too much energy into fighting Nash when he was already weak. He basically broke every combat rule he'd ever learned, all so he could go on fighting longer than Nash. One way or the other, he was determined to be standing at the end to use the Word. I'm sorry, Jenn. He won't last the night.'

Jenn nodded and they stepped aside. She moved towards the bed and came to a halt. Robert lay unmoving, his eyes closed and still. His breathing was so shallow and slow as to be almost invisible. The cuts on his face had been washed, leaving dark scars above his eyes, on his cheek, his lip. Bandages covered almost his whole torso, but even so, blood seeped through. Where there was no bruising, his skin was white and ancient. All ready for death.

Jenn sat on the side of the bed and reached out to his face. Gently she touched his eyelids, his cheek, her fingers running over the injuries as though they weren't there. Even so still, there was an inborn strength to that beautiful face. So easy to place upon it the features in motion, smiling and laughing, frowning, thinking, worrying.

So hard to forget what it had looked like that night on the ship. A moment, so short, so full of everything she had ever wanted. Just a single moment.

He'd never stopped loving her. Not once. No matter what she did, no matter how she hurt him, betrayed him, he still loved her. Even though he no longer wanted to.

Absently, she took his hand and brought it to her cheek. The flesh was cold, but she held on for a moment, brushing her lips over the back. Carefully then, she placed it back on his chest and sat back. She heard McCauly falter in his prayers, saw Margaret's eyes moisten. 'Please, leave me alone for a moment.'

Nobody moved. Then Finnlay came in, ushered them all out. Dear Finnlay, believing he understood what she was going to do. He would hate her for it, but he would thank her nonetheless.

Eventually the room was empty, the door closed behind them. They were all waiting outside, probably listening, but it didn't matter. Then Jenn turned back to Robert, searching this time not on the surface, but for what lay beneath.

Arlie was right; there was bleeding inside. Bad. Enough to kill a normal man. But there was also something else. Something causing more damage than all the wounds put together.

The demon. Rolling, crashing around inside Robert, great and black, swirling hatred, betrayal, frustration and anger. Seething and bubbling, like a pot of inky poison over a raging furnace. As every part of his body tried to heal itself, the demon cannoned into it, blindly striking out at anything in its path. Unfocused, the demon was carving pieces out of Robert, killing him with every stroke. He wouldn't last the night. Perhaps not even the next hour.

No, Finnlay was wrong. Telling Robert the truth wouldn't stop this. There were too many lies, too many secrets. Micah knew about Andrew, so did Finnlay. Robert would hate both of them as well. And how could she tell him how she felt – now she was joined to the Key, they could never be together, not as long as it existed. The Key would never allow it, and she would die if she tried to break the connection to be with him.

She opened her eyes and watched his face. *Robert?*

Nothing. No flicker of the eyes. Nothing at all. Was she too late?

Robert?

Now. And then. Back to the beginning. Crowned King and empty. Living and flying above, wet with drowning and down to the bottom. Falling leaves on the ground. And blood. Yes. Blood. More everywhere. To feed and fill, live and fly. All in the beginning. Always to the beginning.

Robert? Listen to me.

Father? Betrayed. Failed too. Failed again. Never any good. We're drowning in failure. Water flying your eagle. Gold and black, drowning in blood . . .

Robert! Listen to me. Jenn took his hand, forcing a stronger connection.

Listen? Hesitant. Fading then . . . Who are you? Ah yes, the demon.

No, it's me, Jenn.

Jenn?

Yes.

Nothing for a moment. Then, *My dear sweet Jenny. My love. Light against the Angel of Darkness. Fitting you should come and help us to the end. Your place all along. Silly of us to try and leave without you here.*

Who are you talking about?

Why, the demon and I, of course. Close now. Warm, full of everything. Never realised. Should have stopped fighting it years ago. Then I would have seen what I see now.

What do you see?

How warm it is inside the demon. Never knew hate could feel like this. Comfort, yes. The voice fell silent again, but Jenn couldn't say anything for a moment. Then Robert came back, not stronger exactly, but more deliberate. *What are you doing here?*

You're dying. Robert.

No, not dying. Ending. Stopping the madness. The curse. The prophecy. Us. Now we can't kill you. The prophecy dies with us. Have you come to give us Convocation? End us quickly and painlessly? Use your awesome powers to help end?

No.

Would you if we asked?

Don't ask me.

But you'd have to.

No.

Why not?

I don't want you to die.

Laughter. *You think I'm not here, don't you? You think this rambling is my mind gone beyond repair. But you're wrong. This is real freedom. We would ask you for Convocation, make you face the others, knowing it was you who did it. But we don't trust you to give it to us. Why did you stop us?*

I had to.

Of course. More laughter. *Nash was right. This is a game. A game we lost the moment we fell in love with you. Our names are wrong. We are your ally and you are our enemy. Everything we did, we did to save you.*

I had no choice. I knew what you were going to do. I could see it. I had to stop you. Closing her eyes again, Jenn pinpointed the demon, tearing and ripping through Robert, hurting more, cutting deeper with every second, turning the hatred in upon him, as though he were the thing that needed to be destroyed.

Oh, Robert, you dear fool.

She had to stop it. Now. But there was only one way.

She had to give it something to focus on.

Are you still there, my lovely Jenny?

Yes, I'm still here.

You won't leave us, will you? Before we go? You'll stay with us?

You want me to?

Another hesitation then the voice came again, stripped of all layers of the demon. *I want you with me always.*

There. She had him. Isolated from the demon. Only now could she do it. *Because you love me?*

You know I do. More than you could ever imagine.

She gritted her teeth. *Why? What for? That Bonding stuff was meaningless. We both knew that all along. It just happened. In the moment. We both wanted it – at that moment. I've never under-stood why you made it out to be more than it was. You always kept telling me how you loved me but we both know we were never going to stay together. Don't you think it's time we moved on from that?'*

Moved on?

So clearly now, she could see the demon scrambling together, abruptly ignoring everything else. *From that night in the ruined mill, on the eve of my wedding. Surely it was obvious. I was about to marry that loathsome creature, Eachern, having to allow him to be the first to touch me. I know I was young – but really, how could I choose him when you were there, in the mill, wanting me – and infinitely more appealing than him.* One lie after another. Each giving more to the sick well of self-loathing in her stomach.

For a long time, Robert's voice vanished. Even his presence disappeared. Jenn sat there, holding his hand, watching the demon with her eyes open, willing him to believe the lie. Her stomach turned over again and again, hollow, dead. The demon lay inside him, like a viper, poised and ready to strike. Finally, he came back, soft but inexorable.

So he was right . . . it was nothing more than a game.

If you like.

But on the ship . . . you said . . . I believed . . .

I didn't want you distracted by how you felt about me. You had to have a clear head for the war. I did what I had to do, nothing more. Still she couldn't breathe, waiting for the next, inevitable question.

Nothing more? Did you ever love me? Then? Now?

And then she said it. *No. Never.*

The demon struck, lashing out in heedless fury. The blast blinded her for a moment, but he was too weak to do much damage. When it was gone, she looked down at her hand. A single wound sliced her palm, blood seeping onto the sheets. She clenched her fist and looked back at his face. His eyes were open, staring at her.

Her throat ached, but Jenn met his gaze as steadily as she could. 'Finnlay wanted me to give you some peace. I thought it was time to tell you the truth.' Truth? What truth? Where in any of this has there ever been any truth? Turn that word into a lie as well? Why not? Cast everything to the wind, everything she held sacred, even his love for her. Sacrifice it all, even if she was damned for all eternity! He was awake, breathing. Alive! Watching her with open hatred. He would never look at her again any other way. But at least he would be alive to hate her.

He wouldn't be blind any more.

'They think,' he said, his mouth dry, 'I'm dying?'

'Yes.'

'The army knows?'

'They're worried, but they don't know.'

'I can tell.'

'You can Sense it?'

'Yes. Are you leaving now?'

'I won't stay where I'm not wanted.'

'Wise. On your way out, tell the others to come in. I think I need some help.'

He looked away then and Jenn came to her feet. It was extraordinary. Even though Robert knew the demon existed, he had always been ignorant of how it worked, unable to really see it as she did. But it was so clear now, inside him. Tight, wound up, burning and pulsing, giving him strength, firing him on. Physically healing him, stopping the bleeding, closing up wounds. Slowly but surely. He would survive.

The thought was enough to keep her head up as she turned and left. In the antechamber, the others all turned at her appearance. Still holding on, she said, 'He's asking for you all.'

'How is he?' Margaret asked, already moving for the door.

'Awake. He'll live.' She felt Finnlay's eyes on her, but she couldn't look at him. Instead, she turned and ducked outside, letting the cold night air soothe her burning cheeks, freeze the fire inside. Absently she walked to McCauly's tent. Inside, she searched around for the few things she'd brought with her, shoving them into a bag. Where was her horse? She could saddle it herself. No need to bother anybody.

'Jenn?' Finnlay was beside her, forcing her hands to be still on the bag. 'What happened? Did you tell him about Andrew?'

'No.' Jenn shook her head. Waves of exhaustion crashed over her, but she couldn't stop and rest now. She had to leave. Tonight.

'But what did you say? What did you do?'

She stopped, suddenly empty. Unwillingly, she gazed up at him, tears pricking at her eyes. 'He's alive, Finn. It doesn't matter what I said. What matters is that he'll survive and . . . he's finally free of me.'

Finnlay stared at her a moment, horror written all over his face. He could have turned and stormed out, but instead, he pulled her close, wrapping his arms around her, holding her tight. 'By the gods, Jenn, I'm so sorry.'

Only then, did she let it go.

Here ends
BLACK EAGLE RISING
Third Book of Elita

The story continues
in
THE REBEL'S CAGE
Fourth Book of Elita